TESTED

TESTED

DARREN SLOAN

Savage Press

CHAPTER 1

Sweet 16

It was the morning of August seventeenth, and everything looked just as it always did. The birds were singing as usual, the sound of Mr. Peterson's sprinklers echoed from across the street, and the sun was coming through the window over Jenna Holdren's bed.

Her eyes opened and for a few seconds, the world was normal, but once she had time to organize her thoughts, she remembered what day it was. It was exactly one week until her sixteenth birthday. Her heart felt heavy. She sat up in her bed and looked around her room. It had all the trappings of a typical teen girl. Her laptop was on her desk buried under a mountain of school papers and half read books. Her favorite pink hoodie was draped over the chair. Everything common and steady in her life became precious and special.

Jenna had thought she was prepared for the day to come. She had learned about it in school and her parents had explained about the tests since she was ten. She had all the information she needed, but as she looked over at her calendar and stared at the square with the number twenty-four in it, she wasn't sure she was as ready as she thought she was.

"Jenna! Breakfast!"

"Yeah, mom. I'm coming." Jenna slid out of her bed and threw on her robe. She walked over to the door, and she knew once she opened it, there was nothing she could do. There was nothing she could do if she chose to stay in her room either, but somehow she just felt safer sheltered in the walls over her private space. She took a breath and pulled the door open.

Jenna shuffled into the kitchen. Her brothers Bradley and Brian were fighting over the last strip of turkey bacon while their father had his eyes glued to his tablet.

"Jenna! What are you doing? Unless I missed a memo, you still have school today."

"I'll get dressed after breakfast."

"All right, but you're cutting it real close. Here." Jenna's mother slid a plate at the kitchen table in front of her chair, eggs and some fruit. Jenna slid down onto her seat and picked at her food a bit before finally taking a small bite. Brian and Bradley stopped their struggle for the last scrap of breakfast meat as they noticed their sister's odd behavior.

"Mom? You know what day it is today?"

"Trash day, I believe, right James?" Jenna's father looked up and directed his gaze at Bradley and Brian.

"Boys?"

"We took the trash out! I think Jenna means that it's a week before her birthday." A chill came over the room.

"Oh my god. That's right."

"Keep it together, honey." Jenna's father said.

"I will. I will." Jenna's mother looked over at Jenna with a forced smile, but the tears streaming down her cheeks broke the facade.

"I'm okay, mom. Dad. I know about the tests. I've had all this stuff drummed into me since middle school. I think it's just weird to me now because it's actually here. I'm not sure I totally believed this day would ever come. But here it is."

"I know, sweety, but," Her mother tried to complete her thought, but she ran off into the living room and the sound of her sobs could be heard.

"Finish your breakfast." He then ran after her into the living room.

"Hey, Jen," Brian whispered. "You don't have to freak out over this. Gary and I passed easy, and I was reading that in households with two or more kids, if one passes, they all pass. There's nothing you really have to do or know to get through it. Everything you need to pass is already in you."

"What if I fail?"

"You won't."

"But what if I do?" They both looked away. "I need to get dressed." Jenna got up and headed to the stairs. Along the way, she heard her father trying to calm her mother down. She could still hear them as she crept up the stairs.

Once she got to her room and shut the door, she finally was able to shut their voices out. It was times like that she was grateful her bedroom had an attached bathroom. It had proven time and time again to be a much-needed sanctuary in the darkest of times. She went into her bathroom and stood before the mirror. She noticed that her eyes were a little red and puffy. She reached up and noticed that she had been crying since she left the kitchen. She then turned on the water and filled the sink with cold water. She dipped her hands in and then splashed herself. The water was bracing on her skin. A shock ran up her spine and she scooped up some more water and continued to throw it onto her face. She then grabbed a towel and dried herself off.

She looked back in the mirror, and she could still see the redness in her eyes. She looked down at her modest collection and make-up and reached for her usual jar of foundation, but a sudden feeling of pointlessness came over her and she set it back down. She turned to her shower and switched the water on.

She let her robe drop to the floor and slipped out of her sleep clothes. She stepped into the stream of warm water and closed her eyes as it washed over her. The world outside was shut out and all she could hear was the water trickling past her ears. The water was hot, but she could still feel her tears slipping down her cheeks and then she felt the full force of her sobs rip through her. She fell to her knees as the water kept pouring down onto her.

After ten minutes, Jenna returned to the kitchen fully dressed and refreshed. She glanced at herself in the mirror in the hall and she looked normal. She was falling apart inside, but the world couldn't see that.

She saw that Brian and Bradley were still staring at the entrance to the living room and Jenna could hear her mother crying. She looked over at her brothers and without a word, she slipped out quietly.

Jenna walked up to the door of her friend Aggy Newton's home. She and Aggy had been friends since middle school. They endured summer camp, gym class, and countless Girl Scout cookie drives together.

Jenna had always been a very grounded, logical thinker but Aggy generally had her head in the clouds. She studied astrology and believed in the divinity of fortune cookies.

Jenna rang the doorbell and heard many voices inside. The door opened up and saw Aggy standing before her, smiling as brightly as ever, but as she gazed upon her friend's face, she became troubled.

"What's wrong, Jen?" Aggy asked.

"You know what today is, don't you?"

"A week before your birthday. Of course. Why the bummer?" Jenna stared at Aggy astounded by how oblivious to the situation she appeared to be.

"You know," Jenna urged. "The tests."

"The tests? You're upset over that?" Aggy waved her hand past her face as though Jenna's worries were nothing but dust in the air cluttering her vision.

"I don't know why you're so calm. Your neck's on the chopping block same as mine." Jenna added. Aggy grabbed Jenna and pulled her in close.

"You don't have to worry," Aggy began. "I had a dream last night."

"Am I really in the mood to hear this?" Jenna asked as she stepped away.

"It's good! In my dream we were at your seventeenth birthday!"

"So?"

"So? Come on! Think! You're still going to be here when you turn seventeen! You're going to get through this."

"It was a dream, Aggy."

"You remember when I had a dream last year about getting a perfect score on my history final and then I did?"

"I believe an octopus teacher was also part of that dream."

"The point is that dreams hold deeper meaning and this dream is telling me you are going to pass the tests. And so am I."

"You know I would love to believe that, but it was just a dream. The tests are real."

"My dreams are just as real."

"How's your mom doing?" Sobs came echoing from the back of the house and Jenna felt her question had been answered.

"Not so great. I keep telling her I'm going to be fine, but she just won't listen."

Aggy led Jenna into the kitchen where Aggy's mother was curled up under the kitchen table sobbing into her hands.

"Mrs. Newton?" Jenna asked.

"Don't worry about her," Aggy said. "We've gone through this for the past few mornings. She'll pull herself together soon enough."

Jenna imagined that despite how long the tests had been around, it was a fairly common reaction for most parents. Aggy walked over to the table and knelt down to her mother's eye level.

"Mom, Jen and I are leaving for school in a bit. Are you going to be all right?" Aggy's mother took a deep breath and wiped her tears away. She crawled out from under the table, pulled herself up, and set herself straight.

"I'm sorry, dear. This kind of snuck up on me."

"You knew this day was coming, mom. We both did."

"Yes, but it's just one of those days you are never really prepared to face. When I was young, the tests were new, and it was strange and terrifying. Your generation just accepts it as a part of your lives."

"Because it is."

"I know. It's just still new to me."

"I'm going to be fine, mom."

"You better be." The sound of the school bus stopping in front of the house was heard. Aggy gave her mother a quick kiss on her cheek and both girls went running off to school.

Chapter 2

CHAPTER 2

Assembly

When the bus came to a stop, Jenna hoped that some sense of normality would return at school, but she was sorely disappointed. It was just like at home. Everything looked normal, but there was something just under the surface that changed how it all felt. The popular girls were clustered together as they checked each other out and talked about whatever it was popular girls had to talk about.

The jocks were rough housing on the grass and the slackers were huddled near the library as they tried to finish the homework they were supposed to do the night before. The sun was shining. The sky was blue. Everything that had always been in front of Jenna was there but none of it was the same. None of it felt right.

"Come on." Aggy said as she tugged on Jenna's shoulder.

As they stepped off the bus, and that's when Jenna realized there was a sort of hush over everyone. It wasn't just her and Aggy. It was all the kids who were turning sixteen. It was as it always was. The Testers were always treated like some kind of sideshow attraction the week before they went to the camps. They were like the walking dead in the eyes of most. Jenna was aware of it and could even admit to being one of the onlookers more than once, but just in that moment, she realized how vastly different it felt when you were the one being looked at.

She and Aggy held their heads up high as they made their way to the main building of the school. They hadn't spoken on the bus, but Jenna knew that Aggy felt the same as she did. That they weren't going to let their circumstances change how they lived their lives one bit. They didn't want the pity of the teachers. They didn't react to the disgust of the popular kids. Their lives weren't over, and they weren't going to act as if they were. Once they made it inside, Jenna let out her breath and looked to Aggy.

"Did you see how they looked at us?" Jenna asked.

"Don't think about it, Jenna. They're idiots. Besides, most of them are going to be on this side of it next year."

"I've seen it so many times, but I had no idea. They were looking at us as though we were already dead."

"Don't even say that word! That's not going to happen!" Aggy barked. She always acted so tough and strong, but Jenna knew that even Aggy had her moments.

"I didn't say it was. It just felt like some of them were actually pulling for us to fail."

"Maybe some of them are. There are always those kinds. We'll show 'em."

"You think so?"

"Of course. You've got the odds in your favor, and well, let's face it. Someone as fabulous as me simply can't be stopped."

"You got me there."

They walked out the other side of the building and out to the quad where they got more open-mouthed glares. It seemed once someone saw them; they couldn't stop staring. They crossed over to the cafeteria and headed for one of the vending machines where they each got a bottle of chocolate milk and an apple, their daily pre-class routine.

They sat down at one of the tables outside and tried to screen out everyone's eyes as they ate, but it was difficult.

"I can't wait for it to be over," Jenna said. "If only to end this circus." She crumpled up her empty milk bottle and tossed it into a nearby trash can with precision.

"What do you think it'll be like after?" Aggy asked. "I mean, we come back after everyone thought we'd be, you know. Do you think it'll go back to normal?"

"After the tests, does anything go back to normal?"

"Good point. How's your mom?"

"I'm not sure. From what I saw, not well. My dad was talking to her when I left the house, but she was crying, so who knows? I know she's upset. She's trying to hide it, but she's never been a great liar." Jenna added.

"Why are parents like that? They know what the deal is."

"It's like what your mom said. the whole ESA thing was new for them. We've grown up with it. It's been just another part of our lives." Jenna said

"I guess."

"How about your dad?"

"I haven't really talked to him yet. He usually calls or emails me pretty regularly, but it's been a few days since I've heard from him. I think he may be having a problem as well."

"Sometimes I think the week before the camp is actually harder. It's like being at your own funeral for a week. My brothers were nice to me this morning."

"Really? Wow."

"I know. For once I really needed to hear one of their stupid cut downs."

"Maybe they can give you some tips on the tests."

"They say there's nothing that can be done. Everything you've got to pass is already in you." Jenna said.

"I wish you hadn't said that."

"What? You sounded so confident a few minutes ago."

"It comes and goes. I try to be strong, but there's still that little voice of doubt deep inside. The idea that I could fail." Aggy said. The first bell rang, interrupting Aggy, and everyone stopped whatever they were doing and headed for their homerooms.

As Aggy and Jenna reached the door to their classroom, Ms. Hillborn intercepted them and held out two forms.

"What're these?" Jenna asked.

"I'm sorry, girls, but everyone in your group will be reporting to the gym for their first period."

"Our group?"

"Yes. Test candidates." Jenna looked in and saw that nearly all the desks inside were empty. She turned to Aggy. They turned around and headed for the gym as instructed.

When they got there, a crowd had gathered just outside and was waiting for the doors to open. Jenna and Aggy worked their way into the crowd and Jenna could see that there were a lot of different emotions going on. Some of the kids seemed to be pretty high strung and nervous about the assembly while others were trying to put on a brave face and act like it didn't matter to them. She could even hear a few kids crying, which was generally expected. It seemed everyone was so focused on what they were feeling, no one seemed aware of the presence of anyone else.

The gym doors opened and Mr. Billings, the school principal, stepped out. He was a stout man with a belly that hung down over his belt. His head was free of any hair, and he sported a pair of thick black framed glasses.

"Ladies and gentlemen! If you would please come in and have a seat, in an orderly manner." He said. Everyone's attention shifted to him, and they all began to file in. It wasn't like the many other assemblies that energized the kids. There was very little chatting between friends or even smiles. They were getting a free pass from class, but it was an easy bet to think every one of those children would have gladly gone back to their classes if they could have been spared.

Aggy and Jenna stuck close together, as they always did. Aggy was showing signs of fear, but despite that, she still had a spark of fire in her, and it was enough to insist on Jenna to sit in the front row. She dragged Jenna along and they found a couple seats at the end of the front of the center section. Jenna turned in her seat and looked out at the faces of everyone in the gym. It wasn't like she was surprised to see it. It was just something she wasn't prepared to see. She turned back in her seat and then the doors were shut, and the lights went out. A spotlight came on and a man stepped out from the shadows. He was a handsome looking older man with brown hair. He was wearing a sharp looking black suit with a red tie around his neck. He took his place in the center of the light and looked out at his captive audience.

"Good morning. My name is Richard Fremont. I realize no one is happy to be here, me included. I am here today to speak to you about something you may or may not know about; but by the looks on most of your faces, you do. The tests. I realize to you; these tests may seem like some kind of cruel punishment. They may seem evil in their intent, but nothing could be further from the truth. Eighty years ago, it wasn't just this country but the entire globe that realized we all had a very big problem: overpopulation.

For years, experts seemed to focus on the risks of population loss, but all that while there were explosions of people all around the world. More people than most governments could handle. More people than our environment could handle. Food supplies were running low, and we all began to see a terrible light at the end of the tunnel," Richard then turned to the back wall and a picture came on of a gaunt, odd-looking man. "Until Senator Zachary Lazaras came along. He was a brave pioneer who was unafraid to see the problem and do something about it. It was he who brought forth the Environmental Salvation Act. I'm sure you've all studied about the ESA over the years, but how many of you know the full extent of what it does?" He looked out at the crowd as if expecting a response. "No takers. Understandable. The ESA was a comprehensive body of legislation that sought to ease the burden of our growing population on both our governments and the environment. Parenting licenses were implemented, thereby limiting how many children could be born into a family. Tax incentives for voluntary vasectomies, and the reason you are all here today: The tests," Jenna squirmed in her chair. Everything was becoming uncomfortably real. "As some of you know, when you reach the age of sixteen, you must undergo the tests. These tests are designed to evaluate who you are; physically, mentally and emotionally. They were created to only allow the best of who we are to pass. Once you do pass, you return to your family and resume your lives. You go on knowing that you are worthy of this life and that's a gift that is beyond measure. Of course, there is the fate of those of you who don't pass. For this, I am sorry, but as Senator Lazaras once said, 'Those who fall in sacrifice to others, are the greatest heroes of all.' I realize those words provide little comfort to you, but it was decided a long time ago that the needs of the world were too dire and too important. Should any of you fail to pass the tests, you will be taken to a transition camp. While you are there, you will enjoy every comfort of living. World class food. Your every desire attended to. It is nearly Heaven on Earth. You will live as you've never lived before and anything you could ever want will be provided. At the end of this stay, however, you will be put down; humanely and painlessly. Senator Lazaras was hard fought on this part of his legislation, but he knew, as the world came to realize, that hard choices have to be made. It is a matter of survival." A loud cough came from the back. Jenna spun around and saw a hand up in the air. A young girl, who had clearly been crying, stood up and took a deep breath.

"Weren't the tests supposed to be temporary?" She asked.

"As a matter of fact, yes. They were to be halted once the world population was brought under control. Sadly, that has not happened yet. Despite all our steps in controlling the population, there are still some out there who feel there is no problem. They believe that a higher power will provide and while we can appreciate and respect their beliefs, science has been telling us a very different story. Nearly half the countries in the world don't have enough food to feed more than half of their peoples. Third world countries have been decimated into non-existence and too many developed countries, the United States included, are on the verge of falling. I wish this didn't have to be. I really do. If you are fearful of the tests; if you're afraid you will not pass, think on this. Without the tests, you would be doomed to death no matter what. In this instance, however, we can offer you comfort at your time of passing."

"I was told that we can't see our families if we fail."

"That's not true. All transition camps offer visitation. It's just that many attendees feel it's too painful. If you should find yourself in that situation and if you wish to see your family, we would be more than happy to oblige. This is why we are having this assembly. I wish to educate and prepare you for what you are going to experience. Too many of you have been fed lies and heard rumors that are baseless," A large screen then began to descend from the rafters above. "Please try and relax and open your minds to what will undoubtedly be the most profound experience of your lives."

"Or the last." Aggy whispered. In any other moment, her little quip would have gotten a laugh out of me, but it didn't seem as funny at the time.

A movie began to play which outlined the long history of the ESA. It detailed Senator Lazaras' uphill battle to introduce the law and the years it took to find the votes to get it through. There were challenges from religious groups and human rights groups as well. It was due to the growing urgency for action that helped speed the law through and even after eighty years, there were still protests against it, but those voices had fallen silent against the majority acceptance of the ESA. It had also been documented that Senator Lazaras did not allow his position as leverage to spare his own son from being tested. He passed and Senator Lazaras went on record stating no member of his family was immune from the ESA and that he knew that the sacrifice was meant to be shared by all the citizens of the Earth, if the benefits were to be shared as well.

It was a few years after some success that the ESA was expanded to an international program and several other countries adopted Lazaras' legislation as their own.

The movie then outlined some of the logistical challenges of implementing the law. There had been testing and transition camps built all across the globe. Some of them were as large as airports and football fields in order to accommodate the nearly endless flood of candidates. It had been rough in the beginning but after the first ten years, the process had become more streamlined, and the camps were able to process more children faster.

After the film was done, Richard returned and explained in more detail some of the more recent developments with the ESA as well as explaining where the candidates were to go for pick up and what they were to bring with them. Aggy and Jenna listened but Jenna felt as though the more she heard, the worse she felt. Everyone was so positive about her passing, but the little bit of doubt in her mind seemed to be louder than their voices.

The assembly was over, and Jenna checked her watch and saw that it had gone on for nearly three hours. Everyone got up and walked out of the gym and she saw their faces as they marched past. They all seemed more somber than when they had entered in the first place. It looked as though it was break time because most of the students were out and hanging around with nothing to do. Jenna looked around and saw a hand waving at her. It was connected to an arm, which was connected to a striking young Latin boy with wavy, black hair and deep green eyes.

"Mark!" Jenna called out. She and Mark Hernandez had been seeing each other since the beginning of their Sophomore year. They had been on the tennis team together at first and he soon started popping up in many of her classes the previous year which led to them becoming study partners and they grew closer ever since. Mark ran through the crowd and swept Jenna up in his arms.

"There you are! I tried to find you in there, but it was too dark. That guy didn't freak you out, did he?"

"No, Aggy was with me."

"Hi, Mark." Aggy said. Mark shot her a quick smile but then focused back on Jenna.

"You okay?" He asked.

"I'm fine. I should ask if you're okay. How's your mom taking this?"

"She's a basket case, but I've got good blood. My brothers all passed. Yours did too, right?"

"Yes."

"We'll be fine." Mark had always possessed a genuine confidence that Jenna had found a bit annoying at first, but she grew to appreciate it over time.

"I hope so."

"We will. How about we hit a movie tonight? Take our minds off all of this?"

"I guess we might as well."

"Great. I'll pick you up at eight."

"Okay. I'll see you then." Jenna said and then Mark pulled her close and pressed his lips to hers. She looked back at him with surprise.

"Hey, live while you can, right? I'll see you tonight." Mark said with a wink.

"All right." Jenna said. Mark turned and headed toward a group of his friends who were waiting for him.

"Wow. That was some kiss." Aggy said.

"I know." Aggy's smile then slid away.

"You think he might think it could be the last time for you two to do that?"

"No. You know Mark. I think he's just using it as an excuse to get a little action, but I can't really complain about that, can I? Besides, it may be our last chance."

"Don't say that, Jenna."

"Aggy. It's reality. We have no way of knowing which way the tests will go. There's no absolute. I've heard of kids who had siblings who passed but failed anyway."

"You sound so calm about all of this." Aggy said.

"Are you kidding me? Calm? I'm dying inside! I can't believe that this could be the last week I ever live again. These are the last days I'll see this school. The last days I'll see you or Mark or my family. This could be the last week I can still have any dreams that could come true. I've got plans. I want to go to college. Maybe go into art school, or medical school."

"Art school or medical school?"

"I'm still working that out. The point is I am in a state of total fear that this is all the life I'm going to get to live. I've got a lot more to do. It can't be over already." Jenna felt her voice break and she fell back against a nearby wall and the tears came pouring out.

Chapter 3

Social Life

The day carried on as normal, or as normal as it could be. Jenna kept feeling the pitying stares of her classmates at the back of her head. She held back her rage because as dehumanizing as it felt to her, she couldn't forget that it wouldn't be long until they were in her shoes.

When the final bell rang, Jenna felt her heart rise and she couldn't wait to get on that bus and back home, but as she raced to her locker, she stopped and realized what was waiting for her there. More pity, more sadness. It didn't seem that there was anywhere to escape.

She reached her locker and got her things together. She, along with the rest of the kids set to go to the test camp, had been given a pass on all assignments for the week so she didn't need to take any books home with her. She thought of bringing her history book, if only to keep on top of what the class was doing so she wouldn't fall behind when she got back. For a moment, having it and working toward that goal made her feel as though she would be returning. As if it had been promised to her. She held the book in her hand. It was heavy and real. Her grip tightened on it, but finally she let it go and it fell to the bottom of her locker. "I'll return." She said as she shut the small metal door and headed outside.

Jenna found Aggy near where the bus would be arriving. She was hanging her head down and didn't seem as bright as she normally did.

"What's the matter, Aggy?"

"Nothing. It's just been a crappy day. My teachers kept telling me not to think about the tests, but that just made think about the tests!

Everywhere I turned someone had advice or words of wisdom to help me through this difficult time."

"I know. I got the same thing all day too."

"At this point I don't care if I pass or fail. I just want it to be over. One way or the other."

"Don't say that. Don't even kid about that." Jenna said.

"You know what I mean." Aggy assured.

"Yeah." Jenna turned and saw Mark racing toward her with a big smile on his face. He leapt at her and wrapped his arm around her.

"Hey! We still on for the movie tonight?" He asked.

"Yes! So put me down!" Jenna said through a laugh. Mark set her down and kept hopping with excess energy. "Why are you so hyped?"

"I've got football practice and we have to get psyched! You know that!"

"You're still going to practice?" Jenna asked.

"Why not? It beats moping, right?"

"Uh, yeah. I guess so."

"So, I'll message you when I'm done, and we can meet up."

"All right."

"Catch ya, babe!" Mark then darted off toward the football field.

"Wow. I think he's actually in a better mood when his life is in danger." Aggy said.

"Seems like it, right? Have to admit, it beats the alternative."

"You're right. He's right! What am I doing? I'm feeling sorry for myself!"

"We're going to make it through, Aggy. You and me."

"Yes we are." Jenna took Aggy's hand and squeezed it as only a good friend could.

When Jenna finally returned home, everything seemed quiet. Her brothers weren't home, which was normal, and her parents would be at work for a few more hours. For the briefest of moments, Jenna was blissfully alone, and she was finally able to shut out the world. She ran up to her room and grabbed her music player and hunted through it for any songs that she felt could take her thoughts away; Anything to throw up the walls that would keep the bad thoughts away.

She stretched out on her bed, closed her eyes and pressed play. Most of the songs she chose were high energy anthems with very positive lyrics. She never normally listened to the lyrics, but there were times her ears would catch a word or two and she would realize that a song could really lift her spirits, and that was what she needed.

As the songs played on, she felt herself drift off into a light sleep. She had no chores to do and no homework so she felt she could allow herself that one luxury. After a few songs played, she could feel herself actually begin to smile. She had left the world behind and there was nothing in front of or behind her. There was only that one moment and it was infinite. She then felt a light squeeze on her arm and her eyes popped open and she saw her mother standing over her.

"Mom. Hi."

"I didn't wake you, did I?"

"Kind of."

"I'm sorry. I got home and I didn't hear anyone in the house so I just wanted to check on you."

"It's okay. I must have been out for a while." Jenna turned to her clock and saw that it had been nearly two hours since she had gotten home.

"I also thought we could talk." Jenna knew the tone all too well. It was the tone her mother used whenever she wanted to talk about something serious, and since they had already discussed the birds and the bees, there wasn't really much left on the table other than the tests.

"Mom, I really don't want to even think about it."

"I just wanted to apologize for this morning."

"You don't have to."

"Yes, I do. I understand what a terrible time this must be for you, and carrying on like I did just made it worse."

"It's okay, Mom. I get it."

"That's kind of it. You don't really. You don't get how it feels to see your own child go through something like this. You don't understand how deep the pain goes, but I should understand your pain. I should understand what you need from me as your mother. I forgot. For one moment, I forgot and I lost it."

"Aggy's mom was the same."

"I'm sure. That woman has an emotional breakdown if the mail is late. I try to do a little better than that."

"You do, Mom. You really do."

"It's just for my generation, the ESA still feels new and a little weird. Your generation is one of the first to grow up with it as a reality. To you it's just a part of growing up. It shouldn't be, but it is."

"I just wish everyone could stop acting like it's a big deal."

"But it is a big deal, sweety."

"I know that, but I've got a week before it really has to be. I just want a little time to go back to how things were. I don't want you to break into tears everytime I walk into the room. I want the boys to tease and annoy me like they always do. I want to have this last bit of my life, in case," Jenna's mother shot her hand up and clasped it over Jenna's mouth.

"You will pass. Do you hear me? You will pass." Jenna pulled free from her mother's grip.

"But I might not, and I kind of think that's something we all have to make peace with. I might not pass."

"Your brothers passed with flying colors and you have the same stock as them. Your father and I qualified for a three child parenting license after the first gene test. You will pass."

"That's what I'm trying to focus on, but until I'm on that bus for the camp, I just want to be me and I want you to be you. Can we do that?"

"I can't make any promises, but I'll try."

"Good enough for me."

"So, what do you want for dinner?"

"Isn't tonight meatloaf night?"

"Normally, but I thought maybe you could choose."

"Even if I chose fried chicken?"

"Even if."

"Then. Fried chicken."

"I'll get it started."

"And could I go out tonight?"

"On a school night?"

"Mark asked me to the movies. Please?"

"Fine. You're getting good at this emotional blackmail stuff."

"I learned from the best."

"I guess you did." Jenna's mother said as she wrapped her arms around her daughter.

After dinner that night, the boys cleared the dishes and Jenna went off to meet with Mark at the local theater. When she arrived, she was surprised to see that there was actually a lot of activity that night. She saw Mark waiting for her near the box office and she ran over to him.

"There you are." She said as they kissed.

"I already got the tickets."

"Did I keep you waiting that long?"

"No, I just wanted to treat you. You've had a hard day."

"Thanks, but we kind of both had the same hard day."

"Not me. I'm not letting this test stuff get to me."

"How is that possible?"

"You just don't let it. During practice, I just focused on getting the ball and getting it down the field. I wasn't thinking about anything else."

"But how can you not think about what could possibly be your final days on Earth?"

"Because I see past that. I see us at prom next year. I see us going to college together."

"Really? I didn't know you were even thinking that far."

"I've given it some thought. I love you, Jenna." Jenna stood before Mark in a frozen daze. They felt strongly for each other and Jenna had thought of telling Mark how she really felt a few times, but she never dreamed he would have beaten her to the punch.

"What did you say?"

"I love you. I've wanted to tell you for months, but I just couldn't work up the nerve. I love you." Mark had always been a difficult person to read. He was careful to never let his emotional side ever show and he usually skated through sensitive moments with humor. He was a jock and acted the part to perfection, and there was no room for sentimentality in his guise, but he was standing before Jenna with his heart on his sleeve.

"I love you too." She said. Mark took her in his arms and she felt something different in his embrace. He was holding tighter than normal. As she stepped away, she noticed a small drop sliding down Mark's cheek. She was about to point it out, but he wiped it away with his sleeve and she didn't feel the need to go any further than that.

They went on into the theater, got their snacks and sat down in the auditorium. They just sat silently before the movie began, smiling at each other and sharing something between them that not only didn't need to be talked about, but should not have been talked about. They both knew and that was all that they needed.

After the movie let out, Mark and Jenna left the theater and found a small bench nearby and sat down. They began to talk about the film, recounting their favorite parts. Jenna was just so relieved to finally be talking about something new and different and, for a few hours at least, living her life again. The world was a million miles away and they were the only people around. That was the way it usually was with Mark and Jenna, but it was only then that she truly appreciated it.

A familiar voice then broke their bubble and Jenna turned to see Chandra Brown approaching flanked by her usual entourage. Jenna only really knew Chandra by reputation. She was one of the Elites, despite her status as a freshman. She came from money and that was enough to earn her way into the higher social circles ahead of schedule. She enjoyed her privilege and wasn't afraid to flex her power whenever she saw fit. Jenna had seen Chandra at the assembly so it was clear that they were both on equal footing, as far as the tests were concerned.

"Hello, Mark." Chandra said in a casual tone that seemed to indicate that she knew Mark personally, although Jenna had no recollection of them ever meeting.

"Hey, Chandra." Mark said as he turned from her. Chandra shot a glance over to Jenna but only offered the weakest of smiles as a greeting and then returned her attention to Mark. She bent down a bit and placed her hand on Mark's chest and began to slowly massage it.

"I was wondering if you'd be interested in coming over to my place this Friday. I'm throwing kind of a big going away party. My parents have relaxed all the rules so we can all pretty much do whatever we want. I think it'd be a great way for us all to blow off some steam before the tests. Don't you?"

"Uh, yeah. Sounds great."

"So, you'll come?" Mark looked over at Jenna and he could sense the tension growing.

"Yes. We'll be there." Chandra turned her gaze back over to Jenna.

"Oh. Hi."

"Hello, Chandra."

"I guess you can bring her, if you must; as long as you're there. You know where it is. I'll see you Friday." She said and then marched off.

"You know where it is?" Jenna asked.

"I can explain."

"How do you even know her?"

"She hangs out with the cheerleaders and they hang out with the players. We talked at a couple of post-game parties, but there's nothing there."

"Then how do you know where she lives?"

"Maybe the guys and I went to a couple house parties at her place. Her parents look the other way all the time and they have a full on bar!"

"So you just pretend to like her so you can throw back shots?"

"We were just having fun."

"If sucking up to that rich bitch is your idea of fun, maybe you should just go to that party by yourself. I'm sure Chandra would love that!" Jenna said and stormed away. Mark got up and snagged her by the arm.

"I don't give a damn what she thinks! I'm with you, baby. Come on. We were having a great night until just now. I don't want to fight."

Mark slowly backed Jenna against the wall and began to nibble at her neck, which he knew she couldn't resist.

"Stop." She giggled.

"Come to the party?"

"I hate Chandra. I just want that on the record."

"I got that. I hate her too, but she's got an awesome place."

"Fine. I'll go, but if I see you even touch her, you won't even make it to the testing camp."

Chapter 4

Getting to Normal

The next morning Jenna awoke and things began to seem better to her. She had the day to process everything and it felt as though her dark mood had finally passed and she was able to see some brightness amongst the clouds. It felt as though some inexplicable force beyond her comprehension was filling her with optimism and it felt good to her. It was true that since her brothers passed the tests her odds of passing were significantly great. The same was true for Mark. He had five other siblings go through the tests and they all made it. In fact, as she really thought on it, she didn't know anyone who had older brothers or sisters who didn't pass the tests. She began to think it was more or less a formality and at worst it would take a week away from her Summer break, since all those who test and return must make up the week they missed in June.

She then heard the familiar sounds of morning in the house. Everyone was carrying on with their lives, so Jenna saw no reason she shouldn't either. She got out of bed, dressed and ran down the stairs with a real craving for a big bowl of Sugar Loops. When she burst into the kitchen everyone turned to her and froze in place.

"Please, don't," She said. "Just keep going as if it were normal. Really. Yesterday was tense enough. I don't know if I can live with everyone looking at me like I'm about to die."

"You're right, sweetheart." Her father said and everything resumed. Jenna walked over to the pantry and pulled out the box of cereal and then went to get a bowl.

"Oh, honey," Her mother said. "I can make you something if you want."

"No, thanks, mom. I am actually craving these today."

"It's nothing but sugar."

"Then why do you buy them?" Her mother looked back at her with a bewildered look on her face.

"I don't know. I always got them for you kids when you were younger and I guess it became a habit. It's funny how you can get used to doing something for so long and never question it."

"Well, I need my Sugar Loops today, so let's be grateful for bad habits."

Jenna poured herself a bowl of cereal, filled it with milk and sat down to enjoy her meal. She looked over at her brothers who were busy finishing the homework they failed to finish the night before and then over to her father who was, once more, deeply engaged in his daily news feeds. She took a bite of her cereal and that completed the picture. Everything felt normal and right in that one moment. As Jenna ate, she wished that she could just freeze time right there and live forever in that one blissful second. She looked out the window and saw the sky outside as blue as ever. There were no problems. There were no tests.

"How was the movie last night?"

"It was fine, Mom. It was a distraction at least."

"I'm sure. How's Mark doing?"

"You know him. Nothing bothers him. He's ready to pass the tests so he can get back to football."

"Good man." Her father said, proving that he did pay some attention to what was going on around him beyond the screen of his computer.

"And, we actually got invited to a party."

"A party?"

"Yes. Chandra Brown is having a big party at her house this Friday night."

"Oh. That sounds nice." The boys giggled a bit but Jenna shot them a hard stare and they went back to their work.

"It should be."

"What was that? Why did your brothers laugh?"

"No reason." Jenna said but Bradley looked up from his book and smiled.

"Chandra Brown's parties are legendary."

"How do you know about Chandra's party?" Jenna asked.

"Everyone knows about Chandra's parties and this kickoff party is going to be the party to end all parties." Jenna's mother looked back to her.

"Kickoff party?"

"Kids have them all the time before they leave for the tests. It's the last night to do all the things they might not have a chance to do in case they don't come back. I heard her parents are letting her do whatever she wants. They're getting booze and some pot and everything."

"As options!"

"I don't care if the world is ending on Saturday. You are not going to that party."

"I'm not going to drink or smoke or anything." Jenna said.

"Then why go?" Brian muttered.

"I just need to be there for Mark. I trust him fine, but Chandra is another story."

"I doubt Mark's mother will allow him to go either. Especially after I tell her what I now know. Which I will."

"Mom! You can't!"

"Look, I realize what this is all about, but this just sounds like too much. They are too young to drink or take drugs."

"But it's okay for them to die?" Jenna asked. Time seemed to freeze in that moment and her eyes locked with her mother's.

"Besides, I believe everyone at this table has come to the conclusion that you will not be failing the tests. Once you come back, you'll have the rest of your life to experiment and try new things, but only when you're ready to accept the consequences. Not because you've been pressured to."

"I don't see what the issue here is. You and dad trust me, right?"

"We do."

"And you know I would never do anything bad, right?"

"We do."

"So why can't you just be cool this once? Let this one slide off the parental radar."

"Are you really expecting me and your father to sign off on you going to some unsupervised party where there will be many hormone raging boys with access to liquor and drugs?"

"I can handle it."

"I don't think that you can."

"Dad!"

"I'm sorry, sweety, but I'm with your mom on this. It sounds like a good idea to let those guys blow off steam like that, but I don't really think it's a good environment for you."

"How about this? If Mark's mom lets him go, I can go with him. You trust Mark, don't you?"

"Yes." Her mom said.

"Kind of." Jenna's father added.

"I will call his mother today and tell her what you told me. If she lets him go, I guess you can too."

"Thank you!"

"But you are to be back by eleven."

"Are you kidding me? Eleven? My curfew is midnight on weekends!"

"These are the terms. And if I smell a whiff of liquor or weed on you, you will be in serious trouble when you get back from the tests. Do you agree?"

"Fine. You know, I could have just gone and not told you."

"And I could ground you for the rest of the week. Game, set, match."

After Jenna finished her breakfast, she gathered her things and went to meet Aggy at her house. She found Aggy standing outside just waiting.

"What are you doing out here?" Jenna asked.

"I couldn't take it in there anymore. Ever since I got home yesterday my mom's been pulling out all the old photos and forcing me to relive my life. I couldn't take it anymore. I may have to go to the testing camp early."

"It can't be that bad."

"It is, trust me. Right now she's fitting my old baby clothes on a teddy bear with a picture of me pasted to its face."

"Maybe she needs some help."

"I called my dad and he said he'd fly in before the end of the week. He said he'd look after her."

"I'm sorry she's taking it so hard."

"Thanks, but it's no shock. Ever since their divorce, it's just been me and mom and with all this happening now, she's going into a stress panic."

"I guess it can't be easy when you're the only child."

"No," Aggy said. The sound of her mother crying began to carry outside of the house. Aggy took Jenna by her arm and they marched out to the street. "So, how was your date?"

"Last night? It was good, despite the fact that we ran into Chandra Brown."

"The Ice Queen of Kennedy High?"

"Yes. She invited Mark to the kickoff party she's throwing Friday."

"She invited you to her kickoff party?"

"No. She invited Mark. She acted like I wasn't even there."

"What a bitch."

"Mark said he would go only if he could bring me though."

"So you're actually going to Chandra Brown's kickoff party?"

"Maybe."

"What? What maybe?"

"I asked my mom if I could go and it kind of slipped about the drugs and booze."

"She flipped."

"Kind of. She definitely said I couldn't go, but I made a deal with her. If Mark goes, I go."

"Great."

"Except she's going to tell Mark's mom everything she knows about the party."

"Oh, no." Aggy said.

"Well, at least if I can't go, neither can Mark. Chandra would just love to have him all to herself."

"If you do go, any chance you could bring me?"

"Your mom would never let you go to one of Chandra's parties."

"Yes, but my mom isn't exactly a resident of reality right now. I have to take advantage while I can."

"It would totally burn Chandra if I brought you too."

"Yeah."

"Okay."

"Yes! So when do you think you'll know if it's on or not?"

"Soon. My mom's probably already on the phone with Mark's mom."

"What do you think she'll say?"

"It's hard to tell. Some parents really relax the rules before their kids go for testing. They all figure it could be their last hoorah."

"Except for the transition camp," Aggy added. "I've heard they bring hookers in there. A lot of the boys who fail refuse to die virgins."

"I don't doubt it. I think some parents just want to do one last cool thing before they say good bye."

"It's kind of sad."

"Very." The bus then came roaring up and Aggy and Jenna got in. More normal. It seemed the shock of the tests had worn off and everyone was ready to just live their lives. No more stares or glances from the other kids. They took their seats and felt the jerk of the bus as it lurched forward.

The whole day was totally different from the day before. The whole world seemed to forget all about the tests and everyone was allowed to live their normal lives. Jenna went all the way until lunch before she even remembered that they were coming up.

She joined Aggy in the cafeteria but as she entered, Mark came running up behind her.

"Hey!" He barked.

"What?"

"Your mom called my mom!"

"I'm sorry. I asked my mom if I could go to Chandra's party,"

"You asked if you could go? You don't ask for permission to go to a kickoff party. You just go!"

"So your mom said no to you?"

"No. She said it was okay."

"She did?"

"After about twenty minutes of screaming, yes. She said it would be good for me to get it all out of my system."

"Wow. That's great. Then I can go too. My mom said I could if I went with you."

"I know. That is great, except now I have to be back by eleven."

"So do I."

"Girl, I love you, but sometimes you have to think."

"At least we can go."

"Yeah. I guess we can get in enough fun before we have to leave."

Chapter 5

Cold Hard Facts

Jenna woke up the next day and once more she felt a shift in her mood. She had sworn to herself that she would never wake up thinking of the tests, but as the sun shined down into her bedroom, there was little else she could think of. She tried to pass the thoughts away by concentrating on anything else. She thought about the subject of her college application essay. She thought about how Friday night with Mark was going to go. She thought of everything under the sun twice but her mind came to rest on the exact same problem.

She got out of bed, dressed and headed to the kitchen. Her brothers had already left for school and her father was on the phone in the other room. Only her mother was left as she stood before the sink and washed the breakfast dishes.

"Good morning." Jenna said. Her mother spun around and shot her a smile.

"Good morning, honey. You missed the pancakes, but I think you have time for a quick bowl of cereal."

"Great," Jenna said as she headed to the pantry. When she selected her cereal, she turned to see her mother standing right behind her with a carton of milk in one hand and a bowl and spoon with the other. She let out a little yelp of surprise just before she knocked into her. "Thanks, mom."

"Of course, sweety." Jenna took the milk and bowl and sat down at the table and poured some cereal. She turned her head slightly and noticed her mother's gaze was still on her.

"Is something wrong?"

"No, honey. No. Eat your breakfast." Jenna attempted to do so, but it seemed once she started to do anything, her fears and anxieties about the tests would come back. Tuesday she felt secure because the weekend seemed so far, but Wednesday was so much closer. Just two more days and then her last weekend before heading to the tests. It was coming at her all at once as she tried to eat. All the fear she had tried to push away was washing over her in one gigantic wave of panic. She dropped the spoon and pushed herself away from the table. Her chest became tight and she couldn't breathe. Jenna fell to the floor and tried to force air into her lungs, but the more she tried, the more difficult it became. She felt a hand wrap around her arm and drag her up to her feet.

"Just calm down, sweety. Calm down. It's a panic attack. Just listen to my voice and try to relax." Jenna's mother said as she took Jenna back to the table. Jenna felt the tight grip of her mother's hand on hers and it wasn't long until she could breathe again. Her mother was quick with a glass of water and Jenna drank it down.

"I don't know what just happened."

"I do. The same thing happened to me before I went to my tests. And back then they were even more primitive than they are now. You really would have shit your pants back then."

"Mom."

"It's true."

"Every day someone at school is trying to give us some advice on how to cope, but the more they talk about it, the worse it seems to be. It seems everyone is getting ready for us to fail."

"It's hard, but they're just preparing for a possibility. The outside world has to prepare for the worst, but we have to hope for the best, but you will be coming back." Jenna forced a smile, but her eyes gave away her true pain.

"I spend so much time trying to commit every last detail of my life to memory. Every face, every smell and every feeling. I try to press every-thing together in this scrapbook in my head in case I never come back to it again." Jenna's mother took her chin in hand and pointed her face directly toward her.

"You will come back. Your father and I and your brothers are living proof of that. I was going to wait until before you left to give you this, but, I think you could use it now," Jenna's mother got up and went to the hall closet and took out a small box and brought it back to her. It was a plain brown box with no decoration or writing on it. "I was planning on wrapping it better, but just open it." Jenna lifted the lid off the box and saw a journal inside. She picked it up and just by touching it, she could tell the cover was made of very high grade leather. It was smooth and soft to the touch, but felt tough and indestructible. She opened it up and all the pages were blank. Crisp new pages waiting to be filled.

"Thanks, mom, but I don't get it."

"My mother gave me a journal before I left for my tests. She told me to write everything down while I was there, or else I would go crazy. I don't know if she was right about that, but it did make me feel better to have some way to let out all the madness I was seeing. I want you to take this journal and put down all your feelings while you're away. Don't let them overtake you and distract you. You're going to need a clear head to get through this, and you will get through this." Jenna smiled up at her mother and a tear rolled down her cheek.

"Thanks, mom. I'll use it. I promise."

"I know you will."

"Wow," Jenna said as she felt the weight of the journal in her hand. "Now it all feels more real. This is happening."

"It can seem a bit surreal sometimes, can't it?"

"I don't know if I can do this, mom."

"Very rarely in life are we ever in a position to choose to do only the things we can do. It's what we don't think we can accomplish but do that makes us who we are. You'll doubt yourself, but just know that we will never doubt you." Jenna felt more tears coming and as they did, she tried to think of something to say, but when no words would come, she simply threw her arms around her mother and squeezed as tightly as she could, and she found, happily, that was all she needed to say.

When Jenna and Aggy returned to school the next day, the somber feeling that pervaded the air on Monday had returned. It seemed everyone was thinking as Jenna was. Time seemed to be slipping away faster and faster and it was clear to everyone that their time in the testing camps was fast approaching.

As Jenna walked the halls and deflected the looks of pity and fear, she wished for it all to be over. She thought beyond the tests and saw her returning to school. She saw herself back with Aggy and Mark. She saw everything slowly going back to normal and with the horror of the tests behind her she had only to look forward to her future. That was the day she saw and that was what was getting her through.

As Jenna had said everyone who was due to go to the testing camp was relieved of any homework. They were instead transferred to independent study periods in the library to fill the day. The time there was spent mostly just reading and whispering until the next break. The rules of the library were relaxed a bit for the students forced to attend and they were free to walk about and talk to their friends. They were just warned to keep the noise down to a reasonable level.

Jenna and Aggy were in the back of the library, which was the prime location since not much sound traveled from there to the librarian's desk in the front. Jenna was scanning through a copy of 'Little Women' while Aggy was rifling through the pages of a magazine that she had brought from home.

"This is stupid. Why don't they just give us the day off?" Aggy lamented.

"Rules about mandatory attendance," Jenna said. "If they don't get us in here for enough days, the state pulls its funding. And with so many cuts, the schools are desperate to keep whatever money they can get."

"Still, it seems like a total waste. Why couldn't we just stay in class?" Mark came over to the girls and forced a seat next to Jenna.

"We bring down the curve for the others." He said as he swung his arm around Jenna's shoulders.

"It's true. If we bring up the curve and then leave, it drops everyone down."

"How do you know so much about this?" Aggy asked.

"My dad used to study all the rules about the tests and how the schools handle exiting students. That was back when he was working with that group that was trying to get the tests repealed."

"So we're trapped in this prison for the next three days."

"That's pretty much it. I like it actually. This is a great time for us to just stop and collect our thoughts." Mark let out a little laugh.

"Wow. Have you been reading those pamphlets the counselor's office put out about coping before the tests?"

"Look, I get that you're confident about passing, but I still have my doubts."

"How many times do I have to tell you, baby? It's in your genes. Your family has passed so you will too."

"You don't know that. No one knows what's going to happen or who will pass. I know we're all supposed to be real positive and believe that we'll get through it and I get that. I do. I'm just saying there is a chance it could go the other way and once you make peace with that, the happier you'll be." Aggy gave Jenna an odd look.

"We're supposed to be happy because we think we're going to die?"

"No. I just mean once you accept both outcomes as possible, you start to care a little less and relax."

"So," Mark began. "You've accepted it? You don't care if you die?"

"Of course I care. I am choosing not to let myself go crazy over worrying about it. On Monday, I had never felt so pitied in my life. Everywhere I went I got that look from people, but the next day things seemed to go back to normal and now today, we're back to being pitied creatures and I'm sure that it's only going to get worse after this."

"I kind of like the attention." Aggy said.

"Aggy. All of this isn't some way to get popular."

"No, I mean from my mom. Up until now she couldn't have given a shit about me. She was always wrapped up in her latest business or hobby, but lately she's started being more present. It's been nice. I kind of think that when I get back things might start to get better between us."

"That's kind of messed up."

"Mark!" Jenna barked as she nudged him.

"No, Jenna. He's right. It is really messed up that my mom doesn't start to take an interest in me until I could be taken away forever, but I'm just glad that she's finally come around."

"It's weird. I'm starting to think the tests are going to seem like a vacation after all of this crap."

"And we still have Chandra's party on Friday." Mark cooed.

"I can't believe that's your priority."

"I'm sorry, babe, but I can't get all miserable like you two. I know I'm going to pass. All it's going to be for me is time off school."

"Have you ever heard the saying pride comes before the fall?"

"Spare me, okay? All I know is that I got no homework for the rest of the week and I don't care if we can only stay until eleven, I am going to get wasted at that party!"

"Why do I go out with you again?"

"Because, baby, you know I get you." Mark slid his finger under Jenna's chin and tilted her head as he slowly kissed her. She melted into his embrace and Aggy looked away, feeling awkward. As Mark pulled away, Jenna felt her breath return and realized for the few brief seconds they were kissing, she had no thought of the tests. She looked at him and smiled.

Chapter 6

Pep Talk

When Jenna got home that day, she discovered her brothers huddled in front of the television with their father. She set her bag down and took particular note of how engrossed they appeared by whatever it was they were watching. She walked on into the living room and glanced at the television and saw they were watching a breaking news feed of a riot that broke out at one of the terminals for a testing camp in Montana. There were groups with large signs begging for the children to be spared. They were chanting and screaming as they attempted to come between the children who were due on the buses and the police.

There was some yelling but it broke out into violence quickly. The police tossed tear gas bombs and soon it was just chaos. Soon the feed shut down and they returned to the anchorman in the studio. Their father looked up and saw Jenna watching from the doorway. He then switched the set off.

"Sorry, Jenna."

"That was crazy."

"Always a few bad apples. Every year those protesters show up and wind up making things into a three ring circus." Brian got up and turned to Jenna and smiled.

"Yeah, when it was my turn, there was guy dressed like the grim reaper carrying around all these plastic dolls tied to a long rope. It gets nuts."

"Brian? Maybe your sister doesn't want to hear about this."

"No, Dad, it's good. I should be prepared for whatever could happen."

"Well, you know it's just like all those pro-life and anti-death penalty gatherings; mostly a lot of the same people."

"What about the kids? I mean, do any of them ever get hurt?"

"A few times, yes."

"I heard about some kid in Florida who had his arm broken in some riot before he got on the bus, and the break was so bad, they said he didn't have to go." Bradley offered.

"I read that story too, son, and he did have to go, but only after his cast was removed. Don't fill Jenna's head with any crazy ideas."

"Hey, it would give her a little extra time."

"I can't believe I have to say this out loud, but we are not going to break any part of your sister."

"But what if it just happened?"

"Boys? Go to your rooms. Now," Brian and Bradley smirked at each other and raced upstairs as their father turned to Jenna and took her hand. "Don't listen to them. You have nothing to worry about."

"I know. Mom went through all this with me this morning. I appreciate it, but you and everyone I know can go on and on about how I'm going to pass, but none of it means I really will."

"You seem to be rather fixated on the negative."

"I'm just trying to be realistic."

"I understand that, honey, and I respect that. You know I've always been one to trust in logic over faith, but I feel like this is one of those rare times when faith beats out logic. You have to understand that these tests are designed to gauge you on every conceivable level. Even your mental state."

"What are you talking about?"

"My work with the anti-testers offered me access to a lot of information not readily available to the public, and one bit of insight I found interesting was that over eighty percent of those who do pass are deemed to have had positive outlooks."

"So, if I think happy thoughts I'll pass."

"In a sense, yes. As hard as it may be to grasp, but they do look at your emotional disposition. Positive people just happened to do better in the tests over the others and to a significant degree."

"Fine, then I'll put on a sunny face when I get there, but until then, may I please wallow in my misery?"

"I'd just warn you to practice now. Whatever you feel in the tests has to be real. It isn't like you can just put on a mask and get through it. You have to really believe it. They will be able to tell."

"Thanks, Dad. I'll try."

Jenna went on up to her room. She was anxious to confine herself in the one place where she could forget about the tests for at least a little while. She had been daydreaming about them all day at school. All she wanted to do was get under a spray of hot water and drown out everything else.

She walked into her room, shut the door and locked it tight. She was about to head for the shower when she heard a knock at her door.

"Who is it?" She asked.

"It's us." Her brothers said through the door. Jenna weighed her options but finally decided to open the door.

"What is it, guys?"

"We wanted to talk to you for a bit."

"Is this about the tests? Because I've heard it all from everyone all week so far. I think I can recite it from memory at this point."

"No. You've heard what they want to tell you. We've been through it. We know and we want to give you the straight story." Brian said as he and Bradley pushed into Jenna's room. He shut the door behind them and they both had serious looks on their faces. Jenna was starting to feel her stomach shrink. It wasn't too often that either of them, much less both, were ever so serious about anything.

"Okay. Fine. What?"

"First, watch out for any competition."

"Competition? There's not competition in the tests. The tests are just to qualify your individual traits."

"Wrong. These tests work on a curve just like at school. If everyone performs low, then even someone who might fail could pass. There are a lot of kids who will make sure to screw you over if it means they can get by."

"Also, watch out for the Kamikazes." Bradley said.

"Kamikazes?"

"There are a few testers who actually want to fail but are too chicken to off themselves. They'll throw the test and sometimes, more often than not, they'll take down a few others as collateral damage."

"Don't trust any of the test admins either." Brian warned.

"They're the ones administering the test. They aren't a threat."

"Not all of them, but there are quite a few who actually want you to fail. Some just want the thrill of causing another human to die, while most of the time some of them have betting pools over who will pass or fail and some of them are not above stacking the deck." Brian and Bradley's rants began to sound less factual and more like the emotionally charged accounts given by supposed test survivors who would sometimes seek out fame by publishing a book about their experience in the tests, and the claims would usually turn out to be false, but not after they helped sell a few million books.

"Okay. I think you two have been overdosing on the blogs."

"Look, believe us or don't. We're just telling you what we saw to be true when we were testing."

"You saw all of this?"

"I volunteered for the facility a little bit, hoping it would earn me some brownie points," Bradley began. "I saw a lot of this stuff going down behind the scenes."

"Why didn't you tell anyone? This seems like it should be illegal."

"It's too big for a couple whistle blowers to take down. Besides, it really isn't as widespread as we may make it seem, but it is there and you need to know that there are a lot of people over there that are going to want to see you fail. You can't let them."

"I won't."

"If you have any questions, we're here for you, sis." Bradley said. They then turned and walked out of her room, closing the door behind them. Jenna locked the door again and leaned against the wall as all the information they gave her began to spin through her mind. She knew in their own way, they thought they were helping, but the inside information they offered her left her more distressed than she had been all week. Jenna, like most people, was working under a basic understanding that those who administered the tests were people of great integrity and had no personal stake in it. That they were duty bound to be fair and honest with everyone who tested, but they were only human. They were imperfect and prone to temptation and petty emotions. It was a reasonable thing, but tore away what little calm Jenna was holding onto.

Jenna then ran into her bathroom, turned the water on in the shower, peeled off her clothes and got in as fast as she could. The water washed down her body like a waterfall. It was hot on her skin. She waddled around in the water in order to get an even spray, but stopped and when she did, she began to feel the hot water sting at her skin. It grew more intense, but she just stood there. She looked over at her left arm, which was receiving most of the punishment, and the flesh was starting to turn red and the pain was growing more significant. It hurt her, but as long as her arm hurt, she didn't seem to care about the tests. She basked in her short vacation from her worries. She closed her eyes and despite the growing pain, she could still envision the testing camp based on what she had heard and read so far. She was there. There was a sky above and grass below. There were other kids all around but she couldn't see their faces. The heat was growing more intense. A jet of cool air came over her and the hot water stopped. Jenna opened her eyes and discovered she had fallen down and was on the floor of the shower. Her skin was red and hot to the touch. She looked up and saw her mother kneeling down over her.

"Come on, baby." She said as she pulled Jenna to her feet and led her out to the bed.

"What happened?"

"You were in the shower for over an hour. I came to check on you and found you fallen over like that. What were you doing in there?"

"I, I don't know."

"I realize the closer the day comes, the more intense it's all going to feel. Sometimes that pressure can result in odd behavior like this. I just want you to promise me if there is anything you need to talk about, I mean anything; you will do that first. Please."

"I promise."

"Good," Jenna's mother looked down at her arm and saw that it was still very red. She pulled the covers of the bed over Jenna and made sure she was comfortable. "You're not burned too badly. You just rest and I'll bring up your dinner. Okay?"

"Okay. Thanks."

Later that night, Jenna was feeling better and wandered downstairs where she found her family sitting in the kitchen eating out of a carton of rocky road ice cream. She got herself a spoon and sat down to join them.

"Feeling better?" Jenna's mother asked.

"A little light headed, but yes. I don't know what happened up there."

"It happens more often than you think," Her father said.

"You just had a mild nervous breakdown. It's a rather typical response."

"I just wanted to take a hot shower. I just got lost in so many thoughts."

"What were you thinking about?"

"The tests. What else? Then when I felt the pain on my arm, I knew I should have done something about it, but I didn't want to. Or I didn't know what. My mind just blanked. Thanks for finding me, Mom."

"I had to do something. You had just about used up all the hot water in the house." Jenna let out a giggle and it completely took her by surprise. She realized it had been the first time she had laughed all week and it seemed to be infectious because soon Brian and Bradley were laughing. Soon the kitchen was filled with a chorus of laughter and it was difficult to understand why and even more difficult to stop.

When they all did settle down and get back to the business of eating ice cream, Jenna sat back and looked at her mother and father and her two brothers. She felt as though they hadn't been as they just were in too long.

There was no more talk of the tests that night, and it was another hour until the family had completely emptied the carton of rocky road ice cream.

Chapter 7

The Dress

Friday morning came at last and brought a feeling of relief and dread to Jenna. The moment was approaching and it felt as though an entire lifetime had passed since the beginning of the week. The world had skewed in her eyes and would never look the same again, no matter what happened. She got up and then recalled that she didn't need to go to school. Students who were scheduled to be tested were excused from classes the Friday before they left for their tests. It was a small provision that was put in place in order for families to spend more time together before it was too late. The one humanitarian act the ESA offered, in most people's opinion.

Jenna got dressed and headed down to the kitchen, not sure what to expect, and when she turned the corner she saw there was a large paper banner hanging over the threshold between the living room and kitchen that read 'Happy Birthday Jenna!' in large block letters. There were brightly colored garlands strung over the kitchen table and a vase full of flowers sitting at Jenna's seat. She walked over and examined the flowers. It was a colorful mix of roses, daisies and tulips with some Baby's Breath sprayed in for good measure. She then discovered a card stuck amongst the blossoms. She plucked it out and opened it up.

"Dear Jenna. As your birthday isn't until Monday, we thought we'd get a jump on the party. Love, Mom." The silence was broken by the squeal of a plastic horn. Jenna spun around and saw her family running in. They swarmed around her and hugged her tightly and as the chaos settled, she noticed her father holding a nicely wrapped package with a couple of green balloons attached.

"Happy birthday, sweetheart." He said as he offered her the present. It was a perfect cube sized box with red paper, rainbow colored ribbon and an iridescent bow on top.

"You guys! This is great! I can't believe you did this."

"You really thought we would send you off without a party? We were planning on doing this for dinner, but since you just have to go to that party tonight, we had to improvise."

"I thought you were okay about the party, Mom."

"I'm as okay as any mother should be allowed, but don't push it. Now sit down and open your gift while I get the cake."

"Cake? In the morning?"

"Never mind that," Her father said as he pulled out her chair and sat her down. "Open your present." Jenna watched as her father and brothers sat down around her and looked at the present. For a brief second, she felt time stop. There was something in that moment that she didn't want to lose or let fade by and her instinct told her that if she just stopped moving, everything would just freeze- and stay as it was in that single second.

"Come on, Jenna! Open it!" Brian whined and she was pulled back into reality. She slid her nails under the ribbon and pulled it off the box. She then stuck her fingers between the folds of the paper and began to pull at it. She heard as it began to tear and give way under her pressure. As she pulled the scraps of paper away, she could make out that there was a box inside. A white box with a silver trim. She opened the box and discovered a beautiful silver charm in the shape of a heart with small diamonds fitted along the sides resting on a satin pillow inside.

"Oh, my god!" Jenna said as she took the charm in her hand. As she looked more closely at it, she saw that it was actually a locket. She popped it open and saw a picture of her family inside. She looked to her father who was beaming at her.

"Just something to remember us by when you're away. The tests can get pretty tough and at least with this you can remember us and find some of that courage we've spent the past sixteen years putting into you."

"I love it. Thank you." Jenna leapt up and hugged her father and then went onto hug her mother and even her brothers. She held the locket close to her heart as she sat down again.

"Okay. Now for the cake." Jenna sat up and watched her mother with curiosity that as she went over to the stove and not the fridge. She opened up the door and pulled out a large plate that had a tall stack of pancakes resting on top. They were decorated with frosting and whipped cream and candies in an attempt to make it look like a regular birthday cake. She set it down on the table and Brian and Bradley started pushing candles into it and lit them up. They gathered around and sang 'Happy Birthday' to Jenna as she tried to hold back her laughter and once they were done, she blew them out. Brian plucked the candles out of the stack and then Bradley grabbed the maple syrup and began pouring it all over the cake.

"When did you do this?" Jenna asked. Her mother produced a large knife and sliced into the pancakes, cutting them into triangle portions.

"I had the idea last night and I managed to get up early enough to make this in advance."

"You did all of this today?" Jenna asked.

"I'm used to getting up at the crack of dawn. And at least this time I had a good reason."

"This is fantastic." Jenna watched as her mother carefully balanced a stack of the pancake cake on the knife and dropped it neatly on a smaller plate.

"This looks so good." Jenna said as she watched the frosting and syrup mingle together.

Her first thought was that it looked disgusting, but as she gazed at the sight more, she started to think it sounded pretty good. She took a forkful and stuffed it into her mouth. Her eyes widened as her taste buds nearly exploded from the sweet overload.

"What do you think?"

"I love it!" Jenna said as she continued to scarf down the cake. Brian and Bradley got their slices and had the same reaction. Jenna's mother fixed a plate for herself and her husband. They looked at each other with concern.

"Now I'm not sure how good an idea this was." She said as she poked at the pancakes.

"I think I got Diabetes just looking at it," He said. Jenna's mother took a bite and she looked up at her husband as though she had just had a major revelation. She had no words.

She just started gobbling up the treat faster. "You only live once." He said and then dove in.

After the birthday pancakes were gone, the family just sat back and enjoyed the afterglow.

"That was incredible." Jenna said as she gently patted her stomach. The pancakes proved to be incredibly rich and sweet, but worth every inch she may have added to her waistline.

"Yes, but I think we're all have to go on a diet for the rest of the year." Her mom said.

"If it means we can have that once a year, it's worth it." Bradley said as he was licking his plate clean. Jenna looked over to the floor and saw the box with her locket sitting next to her chair. She picked it up and looked at the locket again. It glinted with the morning sun that was pouring in from outside and looked as though it had come from Heaven.

She sat up and managed to clasp it on by herself. She felt the weight of it around her neck.

"You like it?" Her father asked as he took her hand.

"I love it, Dad. Thank you. Thank you all." Jenna said.

"So," Her mother began. "What have you got planned for your day off?"

"Aggy was going to come by, and we were going to head out and shop around for new clothes for the party tonight."

"Is that right? Well, what were you thinking about wearing to this party?"

"I don't know. I was thinking I could wear that red dress of mine and do my hair up. Splash on some make up."

"This party is a big deal to you, isn't it?"

"Not as much as keeping Mark out of Chandra Brown's talons."

"Okay. I get the picture now. This is a turf war," Her mother said.

"All right boys. Girl talk. Let's finish digesting those pancakes in the living room." Her father said and ushered the boys out. Jenna's mother sat down next to her at the table and there was a look of wisdom in her eyes.

"Do you really think Mark's head could be so easily turned?"

"I don't know. I mean, I trust him, but boys our age are kind of stupid."

"My dear, don't wait for that to change any time soon. Believe me."

"I just need to make sure he keeps his eyes on me. Chandra kind of has a reputation."

"I know the type. I was dating a boy named Steven Wilkes when I was in school. I thought he and I were going to be together forever. Then one day, Melinda LeTour came along and over the span of a month Steve and I went from boyfriend and girlfriend to casual acquaintances."

"What happened?"

"Melinda. She had the boobs and the body and for a sixteen-year-old boy, that's about all you need. He always volunteered to help her study, which I thought was innocent until I found out that neither of them were in any of the same classes. She knew all the tricks to get her hooks into him and she didn't hold back for a second. I didn't stand a chance."

"This is supposed to make me feel better?"

"But I got over that loss and eventually I met a cute, awkward, and sweet man and you call him 'Dad'. You're young and you have a lot of experiences ahead of you. If Mark sticks around, great. If he strays, that's nothing on you and one day you will find the right one."

"So your advice would be not to take this so seriously."

"Yes, but if you insist on playing this little game," Jenna's mother then got up and fetched her purse and then pulled out a small, shiny plastic card and offered it to her. "You're going to play to win."

"Seriously? Your National Bank Card?"

"It's your birthday."

"What's my limit?"

"Just a little less than our house payment would be lovely. Other than that, the sky's the limit."

Aggy and Jenna were walking through the Sunset Falls Shopping Center, trying to navigate through the crowd. They had hoped it would have been far less busy, but it seemed they had walked right into the epicenter of all activity.

"This is nuts!" Aggy said.

"I know. I would have sworn everyone would have gone to the water park today."

"That's not what I mean. This is, possibly, the last weekend of these kids' lives and they are choosing to spend their last days at the mall."

"Well, what do you expect them to do? Go on a three-day trip around the world? Fly to the moon?"

"No, but maybe they could do something more meaningful; something important."

"And why are you here? I told you what I wanted to do and you said yes to this."

"Because I'm your best friend and this is what best friends do."

"I would have understood if you had wanted to do something more meaningful instead. I can shop for clothes by myself."

"No, you can't. I've seen what you get when you shop unsupervised. It's my duty as your best friend to prevent a tragedy like that paisley dress you got last year."

"Whatever." Jenna said.

The girls had been shopping for over two hours and had tried on countless dresses and outfits but hadn't been able to find anything to their liking, and worse, the crowds at the mall seemed to be getting bigger and more unruly. They turned and saw a nearby dress shop and ducked inside for some breathing room. The store was stocked with all kinds of dresses and accessories. The racks went all the way to the back, and they were all divided into different sections. There was casual, business, formal, casual business sections clearly marked and a small clearance section pushed off to the side. It also was oddly deserted, but they decided to take advantage and began to snoop around.

They headed over toward where the party dresses were and started their search. As they checked the racks, Jenna noticed the prices on the dresses and they weren't so much that they shocked her, but they weren't any great bargains either. She grabbed a lovely blue dress with sparkling stones running up the side and across the neckline. She held it up to Aggy and she studied it.

"Not bad. How much?" Jenna checked the tag and felt a little tug at her heart.

"Over three hundred." Jenna said with disappointment.

"So? Your Mom said you could spend whatever you wanted."

"Within reason. I don't know how reasonable this is."

"Mark would kill to see you in something like this."

"I don't know. It's pretty, but is it me?"

"Not even close, but isn't that the point?" Jenna looked at the dress again. Her heart began to race and her face was getting hot.

"I'll try it on, but that's it. I should at least see what it would look like." Jenna then turned away and found a salesclerk who directed her to the fitting rooms in the back.

Jenna slipped the dress on and stepped out of the fitting room with her eyes closed, as though expecting to face a firing squad. She opened her eyes and found that she was standing in front of a mirror, and she saw herself in the dress. It felt comfortable, but it looked like it was clinging to her figure. The stones glinted and danced in the light as she moved. She turned and saw Aggy staring at her with her mouth wide open.

"Well?" Jenna asked.

"You have to get it. You look incredible!"

"I don't know. It's a lot of money."

"Your Mom would so approve."

"Maybe I should call her. Hand me my phone."

"No. There's a chance she might say no, and that would be a crime against fashion. You have to get this dress." Jenna spun around and took stock of her appearance once more. The dress felt so good. So right. She let out a frustrated sigh and turned to Aggy.

"Fine." Jenna relented. She went back into the fitting room to change back, but she couldn't help but get another look at herself in the dress. It was stunning, she thought, but she felt something in her throat and before she realized it, she was crying. She felt the tears coming down her cheeks. It was as if some magic lifted the cloak of a normal life away and she felt the weight of the tests upon her again. It seemed there was no way to escape it. Just when she thought she had buried her fear and anxiety away, it would come rolling back like a stampede. It would happen because of a word or a sound or any other random thing in her day that she would see or hear that would remind her of what was coming and pull her back into despair. The fears that lingered just behind her eyes would creep back like stubborn weeds. One day of being a normal person broke away and it felt like the end of the world all over again. She pressed her hand to her mouth to muffle her cries and she heard Aggy calling for her.

"What's that matter? You fall in?" She asked with a laugh. Jenna took a breath and held it all back, just as she always did.

"I'm fine. Thanks. I'll be right out." Jenna said. She gave herself another look in the mirror and wiped away the tears. Her reflection was her fear but there would be no place for that today, she vowed.

Jenna returned home and found the house was quiet. She held the garment bag her dress was in close.

"Mom?"

"In the kitchen, sweety!" Her mother called out.

"Just checking!" Jenna then dashed up the stairs and slammed the door of her room as she raced in. Jenna held the garment bag up as though the answer to her whole life was within. She laid it out on her bed and unzipped it and just stared down at the dress. It looked even more gorgeous now that she owned it. She slid her hand across the smooth fabric. She knew she should not have spent so much money, but she couldn't allow such an opportunity escape either. She was startled by a knock at her door.

"Jenna? Are you in there?" Her mother asked. "How was the mall? Did you find something nice?"

"Uh, yes, Mom."

"Oh! Let me see it," She said as she pushed the door open. Jenna tried to block her, but it was too late. She had seen the dress. She ran over to it and seemed to be in a state of shock. "This is beautiful, honey!" She picked it up and examined the fabric. Jenna's heart was pounding.

"I have your card." She blurted out as she went for her purse and produced the card. She offered it hoping it would distract her mother from the dress, but she simply snagged the card without diverting her eyes for even a moment.

"You were gone for quite a while, but it clearly was worth the wait. This dress is amazing."

"Thanks. It was a real find. I just need to fix a few things with it and put some accessories together." Jenna tried to take the dress back, but her mother turned away, still admiring the garment.

"I love the stones. They really set it off. How much was it?" Jenna felt her heart fall.

"Uh, I forget."

"You forgot? How can you forget how much you paid for a dress? How much was it?" Jenna then saw she had dropped the receipt for the dress on the floor and she snagged it off the floor and stuffed it in her back pocket. Jenna's mother's gaze grew cold. "Jenna. How much did you pay for this dress?" Jenna took a step back and refused to speak. Her mother then turned away with the dress and started searching it for something. She finally found the tag and scanned it. She then turned back to Jenna. "Three hundred dollars? You spent three hundred dollars on this one dress?"

"You said the sky was the limit."

"I know, but three hundred dollars?"

"I'm sorry, but it just called to me. You see how gorgeous it is!" Jenna's mother then stopped for a moment and tried to fight back her initial rage.

"You're right."

"I am?"

"Yes. I signed off on this, and it's all right."

"It is?"

"We may lose the cable for a month, but yes, it's all right."

"Thanks, mom!" Jenna said as she hugged her mother.

"What are you going to do when Dad sees the credit card bill though?"

"He hasn't seen the credit card bill in over ten years. Don't worry about him."

Chapter 8

CHAPTER 8

The Party

Jenna was standing before her mirror with hair done and in her shoes with the dress on, just as she had envisioned it back at the store. She had spent a little extra time on her make-up and given the results, she judged it to be an excellent use of her time. She looked at her reflection and barely recognized the girl she saw. She had thought she would be happy when she saw how good she looked, but instead she just grew nervous. It all looked wonderful, but she wasn't sure it was her. She heard her door squeak gently and she spun around to see her mother peeking in.

"I'm sorry, but I couldn't resist. I had to see," Her words were lost once her eyes adjusted to her daughter's new look. She was speechless for nearly a half minute as she took in the transformation.

"What do you think?" Jenna asked.

"Breathtaking. You look wonderful, honey!" Her mother then walked up and started fussing with her hair a bit. "Just have to keep those hairs out of your face. Sweety. You look amazing. I'm not sure I'm comfortable letting you go to this party anymore."

"Don't even joke." Jenna said as she turned back to the mirror for another inspection.

"Mark's eyes may never go back into their sockets when he gets a look at you."

"Just as long as it's enough to keep his eyes on me and off of Chandra."

"I thought we discussed this."

"Yes, I know, but still."

"I don't know what this Chandra looks like, but it's a fair bet you're going to blow her out of the water."

The doorbell then rang and Jenna felt her heart pick up a little speed.

"That's Mark. Should I answer the door?"

"No! Wait here. I'll get the door. You make an entrance." Jenna's mother said with excitement. She ran out of the bedroom and trampled down the stairs to the door and opened it and saw Mark standing before her wearing a nice black button-up shirt with a red t-shirt underneath.

"Hi, Mrs. Holdren. Is Jenna ready?"

"Hello, Mark. Come on in. You can see for yourself," Mark stepped into the house and Mrs. Holdren positioned him at the foot of the stairs. "Jenna? You have company!" She called out. Moments later, Jenna appeared at the top of the stairs. She nearly glowed as the light hit the stones on her dress just right. Mark's arms fell to his sides as he watched her carefully descend.

"Hi, Mark."

"Jenna?"

"Who else?"

"You look amazing!"

"Thanks. You look nice too."

"Yeah, but you look amazing!" Mark seemed to be having trouble finding anything other than that to say.

"Hold on!" Jenna's father called out from the next room. "I want to see my little girl before she runs out and," He froze as he ran in from the living room and saw Jenna standing before him and then he saw the dazed look on Mark's face. "Jenna? Is that you?"

"Yes, Dad."

"Doesn't she look wonderful?" Her mother asked.

"Uh, yes. Yes, she looks incredible. Were you two leaving now?"

"I think so, yeah." Jenna said as she secured her clutch purse over her shoulder.

"Well, before you run off, why don't I take Mark and have a little conversation about things." Her father said as he took Mark by his shoulder and pulled him back toward the living room.

"Dad! Don't scare him!"

"We're just going to talk." He said as he and Mark disappeared around the corner.

"Don't worry about your father. You know he's all bark. He likes Mark."

"He looked like he was fit to kill."

"Well, that's how fathers are when their little girls look like this. Are we clear on the curfew?"

"Yes. Leave the party by eleven."

"Right. You have everything?" Jenna popped open her purse and checked the contents.

"I've got money, just in case. Tissues. My cell phone and touch up mascara, should I need it."

"Good girl. I hope you have fun tonight."

"Me too. It could be the last fun I have in a long time."

"Stop. Jut for tonight, there are no tests. There's only this party and no tomorrow. Agreed?"

"Right," Mark and Jenna's father returned and there was a look of fear in Mark's eyes as he returned to Jenna. "What did you talk about?"

"Nothing, sweety. I just sat Mark down and ran through some possible outcomes if the night should take an unexpected turn."

"Please tell me you didn't threaten him."

"Nonsense. I gave him helpful behavioral guidelines."

"It looks like you threatened his life."

"I would never! I just told him that if my little girl cries for even a second, it wouldn't be unheard of if someone's arms got broke."

"Dad!"

"He assured me everything will be fine. Won't it, Mark?"

"Uh, yes, sir!"

"See?" Jenna rolled her eyes and took Mark by his hand as they went to the door.

"Have fun, honey!" Her mother said as the door shut.

"I am so sorry about that, Mark." Jenna said as she and Mark got further from the house.

"It's fine. I get it. Parents can be overprotective, but your dad has nothing to worry about. I'm going to take extra good care of you," Mark then snaked his arm around Jenna's waist and pulled her in for a kiss. The door of the house opened and Mark saw Jenna's father standing with his arms crossed. "Maybe we should just get the Hell out of here now." Mark said and then led Jenna to a car parked nearby.

"What's this?"

"Our ride."

"You drove?"

"I've been driving since I was eleven. My dad taught me."

"But you don't have a license."

"No, but my mom said if I was real careful, I could take the car out. As long as I don't get pulled over, I'm good."

"But what if you do get pulled over?"

"Why do you dwell on the negative so much?" Mark then opened the passenger side of the car and beckoned Jenna in. She slid into her seat and he got behind the wheel from the other side. He turned the car on and pulled out like it was nothing.

"You're not afraid of anything, are you?"

"Life's too short," Mark said. "Why are you always so afraid?"

"I'm not afraid. I'm cautious. There's a difference."

"Not much of one."

"I guess my parents taught me the importance of following the rules."

"Boring! This is the time when we really need to cut loose and live! It could be our last chance. Just let go a little bit. Let's have fun tonight." Jenna looked into Mark's eyes and all her anxieties drifted away and she understood his logic.

"You're right. Let's have fun."

As Mark got closer to Chandra's house, he noticed an increase in traffic and Jenna was becoming a bit nervous about going to the party. Mark turned onto Chandra's street and saw that there was not a single place to park. There were cars packed in on either side of the street and there were even cars parked on Chandra's front lawn.

"Wow. I thought we were getting here early." Mark said as he passed by Chandra's house. He turned at the corner and went up to the next street. It was also packed. There was a little bit of Jenna that was beginning to feel relief that they couldn't find a place to park. She was about to suggest they just go on and do something else, but before she could, Mark swung the car around hard and parked in a little spot that had been hidden in the shadows.

"Whew! Lucky." He said. He looked over at Jenna and she forced a smile back at him.

"Yeah. That was close."

They walked back to Chandra's house. The music could be heard from down the block and the lights lit up the whole street. There were kids running in and out of the house screaming and yelling. There were a few running around with water balloons and tossing them randomly.

"Can you believe her parents actually said yes to all this?" Jenna asked as they approached.

"It's nuts." Mark said. Jenna then saw one of the little trolls with water balloons approaching her out the corner of her eye. She grabbed Mark and dashed toward the house before they could strike.

They walked into the house and saw that it was packed. Everyone was bouncing to the pulsating music and drinks were in everyone's hands. Mark and Jenna tried to push their way through the wall of bodies.

"Where do we go?" Jenna asked.

"I don't know! Just head to the kitchen!" Mark said.

"Why?"

"That's where the drinks should be!"

Jenna and Mark fought their way through the crowd and found a little breathing room in the kitchen. It seemed to be the one room where there was any place to stand. Jenna saw that there were beer kegs on the floor and a full array of liquor bottles on the counters.

"Wow. This is a little more than I thought it would be."

"Relax, babe. Everyone's just having fun." Mark said, just as one of the party guests fell over, vomiting everything she had drunk onto the floor. Chandra then appeared from the crowd flanked, as always, by her entourage.

"Get some towels and clean that shit up," Chandra barked and both her flunkies ran off to fulfill their duty. She then turned to Mark and smiled. "Mark! You made it!" She ran up to him and swung her arms over his shoulders and pulled him in, uncomfortably close. Jenna let out a loud cough and did her best to squeeze between them.

"And I'm here."

"Oh. Jenna. So you are," Chandra said with a dead smile. She then pushed Jenna aside and lit up as her eyes found Mark once more. "Mark. The real action is happening out in the backyard. The pool's open and I've got Jell-O shots out there too. You should really come and check it out."

"That's sounds great, but I didn't bring my trunks. Didn't think we'd be swimming."

"Silly. You don't need your trunks to skinny dip."

"Thanks, Chandra, but I think Mark and I will hang back here for a bit. We just got here after all." Jenna said.

"Mark?"

"I'm with my girl, but we'll be out in a bit." Mark said. Chandra shot Jenna an acidic glance and turned away, back into the crowd.

"What a bitch." Jenna said.

"Forget her. You want a drink?"

"Do they have any soda?"

"Come on, Jenna. I mean a drink drink."

"I don't know. I've never had alcohol."

"Okay. I know a good drink. It's sweet. You won't taste a drop of alcohol. Wait here."

Mark then dashed over to the liquor and started fixing whatever drink he knew how to make. Jenna looked around while she waited for Mark and she was growing more uncomfortable. She was becoming unsure if keeping an eye on Mark was worth being at that party. She recognized a lot of the kids from school, but they were all drunk and acting crazy. The music wasn't even very good. Mark returned with the drinks and handed one to Jenna. It was bright red and seemed to be fizzing.

"What is it?"

"Don't worry. Taste it." Jenna tipped the cup against her lip and the drink trickled into her mouth. It was sweet, as promised. There was a bitter under-taste as well, but overall, she liked it.

"It's good." Jenna said as she went for another sip, but Mark held her hand before she could drink.

"You may want to pace yourself with it, though. There's actually a lot of alcohol in it." He warned.

After she finished the first drink, Jenna began to feel light headed, but she was also beginning to feel relaxed. Mark fixed Jenna up with another and they ventured out to the backyard. It seemed that was where the heart of the party was. There were Tiki torches lit up along the back wall and kids were running around screaming. The pool was the main center of activity. Jenna looked over and it looked as though everyone in the pool was completely naked as well.

As they wandered around taking in everything, Chandra emerged from the crowd once more, this time she was soaking wet wearing only a towel around her waist and a very small bra over her breasts.

"Mark! Come on! Swim with me!" She begged as she reached for his pants.

"That's all right, Chandra. I'm good." He said as he leapt back from her grasp.

"Oh come on. It's fun. The water is nice and warm."

"Probably all the heat coming off the bodies," Jenna said. "Are your parents aware you are running a Roman orgy in their backyard?"

"My parents said I could do whatever I wanted tonight. No questions asked. No excuses given. Kind of like how I live my life."

"Interesting. I mean, I'd have questions. Like, how many of these guys have you screwed so far?"

"Excuse me?"

"Don't act surprised. Everyone knows you're a world class slut. Just like everyone knows you prey on other girls' boyfriends."

"May I remind you that you are not an invited guest? You are only here because Mark brought you, and while I'd hate to kick him out, I would if it meant getting rid of you." Mark pulled Jenna aside and snagged her drink from her.

"She's sorry, Chandra. She's just had a little too much to drink," Mark said as he ushered Jenna away. "What the Hell was that?"

"What?"

"You called Chandra a slut."

"And?"

"Jenna!"

"Look, you wanted me to have a drink, I had a drink. Besides, who cares? So I'm a little honest. So I tell it a little more like it is. I'm having fun. You wanted me to have fun, right?"

"Yes, but not by insulting the host of the party. She's right. You weren't exactly invited."

"Let her throw me out. If I go, you go," Mark then shifted his eyes away for a moment.

"Mark? That's right, isn't it? If I go, you go."

"I really like Chandra's parties."

"Oh my God. You'd throw me under the bus, wouldn't you?"

"Let's not talk about this, okay? No one's getting thrown out. We're all just trying to have fun."

"This party is more important to you than me?"

"I never said that!"

"You kind of just did."

"Look, how about we get away from all this? Come on." Mark then took Jenna's hand and led her back into the house.

They went up the stairs and discovered while the party was raging below, there was another party simmering above. Jenna couldn't see too clearly, but she saw several figures in the shadows mingling together. Mark went down the hall and checked every closed door until they got to the end of the hall and he found one that was empty. It appeared to be some kind of guest room. The décor was drab and minimal and there was only a small twin bed stuck in the corner with beige sheets on it. Mark shut the door and locked it as Jenna leapt up onto the bed and spread out on her back.

"Comfy?" Mark asked as he slid up to her.

"My head's spinning."

"That's normal. Just relax." Mark said as he ran his hand down Jenna's body, stopping at her legs.

"What are you doing?"

"Nothing."

"It doesn't feel like nothing. I told you I wasn't ready."

"I know, but that doesn't mean we can't touch a little, does it?"

"I guess not," Jenna said as she slid her arm around Mark. "She wants you, you know that, right?"

"Who? Chandra?"

"Yes."

"She wants everyone she can't have."

"She can have them. It's you she can't have."

"She won't have me. I'm yours."

"You're such a great guy."

"And you're a great girl. I love this dress." Mark then began to finger along the neckline of the dress. Jenna felt his finger probe along her body and at first it felt nice, but she started to feel as though he were getting closer than she wanted. She slid away from him a bit, but he crawled closer as she did.

"No, Mark."

"Come on. How about a kiss? We can kiss, can't we?" Mark leaned in and brushed his lips against Jenna's. They were soft a bit salty. Her heart was beating faster than ever. The sound from outside was beginning to fade away and all she could hear were their heartbeats. Mark pushed his lips in and Jenna felt his tongue slide into her mouth. His warmth overpowered her and he pressed his body to hers. He was so strong, she thought. His hands carefully explored her body and cupped her breasts gently. "You're so beautiful, baby." He whispered. Jenna felt his hands slide further down and then go up under her dress. She was jolted back and pushed him away.

"Mark! No. I told you I'm not ready!"

"Come on! We go in for testing next week. This could be the last time we'll be able to do this."

"I thought you were sure that you and I were going to pass."

"I am."

"So why can't you wait?"

"I can."

"But you don't want to."

"I just don't see what we're waiting for! I think we're there now." Jenna then noticed a shiny object in Mark's hand. She reached over and grabbed it from him and saw that it was a condom.

"You had this all planned out, didn't you?"

"No."

"Then why do you have this?"

"Just in case. I thought maybe if things went good, maybe,"

"I don't believe this. We have talked about this a thousand times, and every time you said you understood how I felt." Jenna said as she slid off the bed.

"I do understand, but I don't get why you can't understand how I feel! I have needs! Do you realize I'm the only guy on the team who hasn't done it with his girlfriend? All the other guys are getting it regularly, but you keep making me jump through all these hoops."

"I'm sorry, but I just thought that what we had was more important than sex! Who cares what the other guys on the team think anyway? It's none of their business."

"It's not that I care, it's just that, well," Mark began to stammer as Jenna waited for his answer.

"Well?"

"Okay! Fine! I care! I care because I'm the one who gets ripped on all the time for dating a virgin. I care because I'm forced to see my buddies get laid whenever they want while I'm getting nothing!"

"Fine. If it's all that important to you, we can change all of that." Mark got up on his knees and hobbled over to her.

"We can?"

"Yes. We're done. Now you're free to find some girl who will put out for you." Jenna then stormed toward the door and walked out. Before she could make it to the stairs, Mark grabbed her arm.

"You don't mean that! It's the liquor!"

"No, Mark. I'm totally clear on this. If you just want to have sex, you should really find another girl. I've made it clear how I feel about you. If that's not enough, then maybe this isn't what I thought it was and there's no reason to drag it out any longer than we have to."

"Jenna. I love you."

"Then love me enough to respect me. Get over the macho bullshit and be a man."

"You're right. I'm sorry."

"What time is it?" Mark looked down at his watch.

"A little after ten thirty."

"We need to go soon."

"How about one more drink?"

"Fine. A quick one."

"Promise. Why don't you go back to the room? At least we can have a little quiet with our drinks."

"Fine." Jenna then went back to the guest room and sat on the bed awaiting Mark's return.

She waited for what seemed like an eternity. She felt the buzz she had gotten from the last two drinks wear off. She looked over to the clock on the nightstand and it was ten to eleven. Her patience had expired and she got up and ventured out to find Mark.

She made her way back down and found the kitchen. He wasn't there. She pushed her way through the whole house, checking every room but there was no sign of Mark. A feeling of dread filled her stomach and she headed out to the backyard. As she pushed her way through the crowd she scanned every face that came by. The music was growing louder. She looked over at the pool. She saw Chandra running around, laughing. She still had the towel on, but she had lost her bra. Jenna headed toward the pool and as she got closer, she could hear voices. Most of them were unfamiliar, but one stood out. Her heart began to race and soon she was running. She made it to the pool area and she looked down into the water. The pool was full and everyone was splashing around and laughing, but Jenna's skin was growing cold. At last she saw Mark. He was in the water, naked with one of Chandra's friends locked in his arms.

"I had my fun a few minutes ago. Figured I'd loan him out to a friend." Chandra said as she slinked up behind Jenna. She then looked back down at Mark. He finally looked up at Jenna and she was expecting a look of fear and shock on his face, but instead he just smiled and laughed like an idiot. She didn't even wait for him to speak. She turned and saw his clothes piled on a chair. She ran over, rifled through his pants and found the keys to the car. She shot him one last look and then stormed away.

As Jenna forced her way back through the party, she was hoping to feel a tug on her arm or to hear Mark call out for her, but she made it all the way to the front door without any such distraction. She turned and saw no one had been following her. It seemed he wasn't even concerned that she had his keys. She caught a glimpse of herself in the mirror. The dress wasn't quite as pretty anymore. She stormed away from the party, walked back to the car and deliberated over what to do next. It wasn't a long drive and she knew enough about driving to get the car back to her house. She got in, started it up and pushed away her anxieties and drove back home.

Chapter 9

CHAPTER 9

After-Party

Jenna snuck into the house and tried to make as little noise as she could manage. She had parked Mark's car a block away and had the keys with her. She didn't do any damage to it, but she kind of wanted to make him sweat when he realized the car wasn't parked outside her house the next morning.

She went into the kitchen and tried to find something to eat. She didn't know what she wanted to eat but she just knew she wanted to eat. She checked every cupboard but nothing really called to her. She then pulled open the freezer and that's when she saw it. Ice cream. She only saw Vanilla, but she could work with it. She grabbed the ice cream, and then got some chocolate sauce and some whipped cream. She set it all on the table and thought of getting a bowl, but when she saw the carton was only half full, she decided to just finish it off. She poured the syrup in and topped it all off with a mountain of whipped cream and started eating. The light came on and Jenna spun around to see her mother standing at the doorway.

"I thought I heard something," She said as she checked her watch. "On time. I thought for sure you were going to stay out later. I only said you had to be out of that party by eleven. I never said you had to be home by then."

"That's actually what we were planning, but I didn't know you had already figured that out."

"Why do you think I said it like that? I know you. You love to exploit the loopholes. I thought I'd just give you a little challenge. So, not that I mind, but why are you back so early? It's barely midnight. Did you have fun at the party?"

"No." Jenna said as she stabbed her spoon into the ice cream.

"What happened?"

"Men are such jerks, mom!"

"Oh. What did Mark do?"

"Nothing, until we were about to leave. I was right. Chandra was trying to get her hooks into him all night long. We tried to get away from her and we found someplace private."

"You didn't?"

"No, Mom. Although he tried, but we had our talk again and he backed off."

"Good. So what happened?"

"We were about to leave, but he wanted one last drink. He left to go get it, but never came back. I went out to find him and that's when I saw it."

"What?"

"Mark. Naked in the pool with Chandra and one of her clone friends."

"I'm sorry, honey."

"He was drunk, but that's no excuse. He knew what was going on. He just gave in. Why are men like that?"

"I don't know and I don't think they do either. It's just the nature of the beast."

"Was Dad ever like that?"

"When he was younger. I think it's a maturity thing. They have to grow up and see things differently. Mark is at the age where a good time beats out everything else. Are you going to forgive Mark? Give him a second chance?"

"I don't know. Maybe not. I mean, why bother? What's the point? I was looking around at that party. It was insane. Kids were acting like adults. Drinking. Having sex. I kind of realized that no matter how the tests go, nothing is ever going to be the same again, is it?"

"No, sweety. It won't. I think that's the hardest lesson of the test. Everything changes starting now and the world will never look or feel the same."

"Why didn't you tell me about this?"

"Because it's something you just have to find out for yourself. I'll tell you what won't change, though. Your family. Your father and I. Your brothers. We're all still going to be here and we're all going to still love you."

"It's scary. I'm not ready for all of this."

"I know how you feel. It's the eleventh hour and you feel like if you just had one more year; One more month; One more week, you'd be happy."

"Everything seems so much bigger now. I'm not ready for things to get so big."

"It's life. You can't say no. You just do the best you can and hold on with all your might. You can do it, Jenna. I know you can. Even if I wasn't sure that you were going to pass the tests, I'd still put all my money on you to win. You have to start believing that."

"I do, Mom. I do."

"Well, since you're up, I'll tell you now. Since you have two more days until you leave, your father and I were thinking we'd all go up to the beach house. We thought it would be a nice way to,"

"Spend my last days on Earth?"

"You know what I mean. A little burst of fun before you go off for those tests."

"That sounds fun, but could we not?"

"You always love the beach house."

"I do, it's just whenever we go up there the days seem to go by so fast. I kind of want them to drag over the next couple days."

"Trust me. No matter where you go or what you do, time is going to race by. You might as well be someplace fun."

The next morning, Jenna woke up to the sound of the whole house alive with activity. Her parents were making last minute checks before they left and Brian and Bradley were finishing up packing. Jenna slid out of bed and pulled out her suitcase and just threw some shirts and shorts in as well as some toiletries that she thought she might need, including toothpaste and sunscreen. She zipped it up and decided that was all she would need. She then dressed and brought her suitcase down to the foyer. As she set it down, there was a knock at the door. She opened the door and she saw Mark standing before her looking like death warmed over.

"Hi." She said.

"Hey."

"What are you doing here?"

"What do you mean? You took my car. Where is it?" Jenna looked past Mark and saw his mother sitting in another car out on the street.

"She mad at you?"

"Beyond."

"How'd you get home?"

"I don't remember. I don't remember a whole lot from last night."

"You remembered that I took your car."

"Yeah."

"Anything before that?"

"Yes. I know. I was stupid. When I went down to get the drinks, Chandra was right there and she shoved one in my face. I just took a sip and everything got weird."

"And you had sex."

"I don't even remember it."

"Just because you don't remember doing it, doesn't mean it didn't happen."

"I get why you're pissed at me. I'm sorry."

"Your car is on the next block."

"Oh, thank God!" Mark said with great relief. He turned from Jenna and waved to his mother who was still waiting in the car. "It's on the next block! She wanted to scare me!"

"Good girl!" His mother shouted back.

"She knows about what happened?" Jenna asked as Mark turned back to her.

"I guess. I don't know if I told her while I was drunk or what."

"I've been thinking about it and I'm not mad."

"You're not?"

"Anymore. We're about to be tested and that means a lot is going to change. A lot has already changed. Whether you want to admit it or not."

"What are you saying?"

"I'm saying that maybe right now isn't the time to fight. I forgive you for what you did. It was still stupid and thoughtless, but I want us to walk away from this with a clean slate."

"Whoa. Walk away? Come on. I made a mistake. I'm human. We can work this out."

"Maybe we can, but if we can or cannot, I think that will have to wait until after the tests."

"I don't really get this. Are we broken up or not?"

"We are two people. The same two people we've always been. What we'll be in the future will have to wait until after the tests."

"Okay. I get it. That's fine. Just gives me incentive. I'm going to pass and we're going to be together. I screwed up, but I'll make it up to you. I swear." Mark had a fire in his eyes that Jenna recognized.

"Here." She said as she handed Mark the keys to his car. He shot her a quick smile and dashed off to his mother who was still waiting and they drove off. Jenna shut the door and the night before she thought when she closed the door on him, she would feel pain, but much to her surprise, she actually felt free.

Chapter 10

The Long Good Bye

Jenna woke up on Monday morning with the sweet memories of the past weekend still alive in her mind. She looked out the window and saw the sun streaming into her room as it normally did. It was a good day, but when she heard the gentle knock on her door, reality came crashing down on her and her soul felt as though it had turned to lead in the blink of an eye. She looked up and her mother peered in. Her eyes were red and puffy and it was clear she was fighting back a torrent of tears.

"It's time." She said. Her voice was shaky, as were her hands. Jenna looked back at her and nodded.

"All right. I'll be down in a minute," Her mother shut the door and then Jenna slid out of bed. She walked over to the mirror on her dresser and gave herself a good look. "All right. What do you wear?" She asked her reflection. "What do you wear to what could be the beginning of the end of your life?" She pulled open one of the drawers and saw her pants. She pulled out her usual pair of jeans and then went over to her closet and grabbed the first shirt she saw. They looked good, or at least good enough for what was awaiting her. She went on into her bathroom and started up the shower. All the anxiety she had been feeling earlier in the week was nothing compared to what was hitting her in that moment. It was just a few hours away. Before lunch, she would be on a bus that would take her to where she could be chosen to die. It was so surreal to her, but at the same time familiar and expected. She felt like she had been living with it for so long, yet the moment of it becoming real felt so unreal to her.

Jenna finished her shower, dressed and prepared herself for her day. She walked out and saw the bag she had packed for the family's weekend getaway. The scent of sea air and sand was still on it. She picked it up, dumped out whatever was inside and threw it on the bed and began packing again. She just threw in some shirts, some pants and then she went to the bathroom and found a small package she had put together earlier that week. It was small box filled with soaps, shampoo and toothpaste and a few other possible essentials she may need while at the testing camp.

Jenna usually found a certain joy in packing for a trip. She was able to dream and imagine of all the amazing things that might happen for her and then decide what she would need should those things actually happen, but packing for the camp was different. There was no joy or sense of wonder for her. As she pressed down on everything she had packed in order to make sure her case would close, she noticed a drop of moisture fall and it was then she realized she had been crying since she began packing the bag.

Jenna came down to the kitchen with her bag in her hand. She could hear the sound of her family having their breakfast, but as soon as she came within view, everything stopped. They all looked up at her and while they had been telling her over and over about how she was going to pass, they finally had to confront the hated scenario if she did not pass. Jenna set her bag down and sat down at the table. Her mother then fixed her a plate and they all watched her as she began to eat. It was as though they were trying to freeze her image into their brains, if that were to be the last time they'd ever see her again.

"What are we doing?" Her father said. "She's going to pass!"

"Of course!" Her mother added. Brian and Bradley nodded in agreement. They all then looked back at Jenna and while they tried to smile, the pain in their faces was hard to disguise.

"Or, I might not," Jenna said. "I hate to think about it too, but while more than half of those tested who had siblings who passed also passed, there is still a group who failed. I don't like to talk about it, I hate to even think about it, but it's something we all have to accept. This might not work out like we want."

"And are you ready for that, Jenna?" Her mother asked.

"No, but when someone tells you that you're about to die, is anyone ready for that? Can you ever be ready for this?"

"No. I guess not. I just wish there was something we could do or say to make all of this better."

"There is one thing you can do." Jenna said.

"What's that, sweety? Anything!"

"Pass the syrup."

After breakfast Jenna was anxious to go. She wasn't looking forward to getting on the bus, but after having lived with the tension and stress of her possible impending death, the sooner it was over the better, as far as she was concerned. She had her bag set by the door and she was sitting in the living room and watched as the clock on the wall ticked away, minute by minute.

"Honey?" Jenna's mother asked as she approached her.

"No, mom. No."

"What?"

"I don't want the long good bye. I don't want the 'this is the last time we'll be together' speeches. I don't want any of that. This won't be the last time I see you all. If I pass, I'll be back home. If I fail, we'll be given time to say good bye later."

"Fine. You're right. You're just going to be gone for the week. You have everything you need?"

"I think so. I assume if I need anything, they can provide it at the camp."

"They can. It's just nice to be prepared."

"Yeah." Just then the alarm on the clock went off and it was time. Jenna looked to her mother and smiled.

"You'll be back home before you know it." She said.

"I love you, mom." Jenna said and threw her arms around her mother.

"I love you too, sweety." Jenna composed herself and then stood up. She turned and saw her father and brothers standing in front of the door. Her father merely held his arms out and she ran to him.

"I love you! I love you all!"

"We love you too, darling." Her father said. She then looked toward her brothers who seemed to be rather uncomfortable with the high running emotions. Bradley then shrugged his shoulders and pulled his sister into a hug.

"You're going to make it. We know you will." He said. She then slipped away and into Brian's arms.

"I know we give you a lot of shit, but we love you."

"I know, and I allow you to give me shit because I love you." Brian stepped back.

"What do you mean 'allow'?"

"Please. I see those lame pranks of yours a mile away. That morning I said you got me with the plastic wrap on my toilet? I lied. I just said you did because I knew how much it meant to you."

"No. We got you."

"You really didn't."

"Fine. We'll really get you when you get back. We've got a week to come up with some new stuff."

"Bring it." Jenna said with a smile and a catch in her voice. Then there was a knock at the door. It was Aggy.

"Morning, guys. I was coming by to see if Jenna wanted to head to the busses with me."

"Oh, thank you, Aggy, but I think we'll be taking Jenna." Jenna's mother said.

"Are you sure? It gets pretty emotional there and from the looks of it here, you guys are already on the brink. A lot of parents get rides for their kids in order to avoid any emotional breakdowns. My mom got me a limo," Aggy then stepped aside and everyone could see a lavish black stretch limousine outside. "Emotional distance makes it less messy. I heard that sometimes those breakdowns can have a negative effect on test performance."

"Uh, I hadn't heard that."

"I think I read an article about that," Jenna's father said. "The emotional trauma was said to set the tester's natural rhythms off slightly, and in some cases enough to alter performance."

"You know? I think I'll just go with Aggy."

"What?"

"Yeah. I think it's for the best. We've had our little display here. I need to be clear for this. I need to focus on the tests."

"You're right. You're absolutely right," Her father said. "But we will be there to pick you up."

"Deal," Jenna said. She then picked up her bag and turned to Aggy. "Let's go." Aggy took Jenna's hand and they marched out toward the luxury car.

As they piled into the limo, Jenna began to wave at her family but soon the car door shut and that was it. The limo pulled away and there was no going back. The limo was nice. It had leather seats and some festive lighting on the ceiling that shifted from one color to another very slowly.

"I've never been in a limo." Jenna said.

"Me neither. My mom said I deserved to go in style."

"This would be my choice for making a big entrance. How are you feeling?"

"Scared shitless. I threw up like six times last night. I'm really nervous, Jenna."

"Don't be. You're going to make it."

"How about Mark? Should we pick him up too?" Aggy asked. Jenna then realized that they hadn't talked over the past few days and she never had the chance to tell Aggy what had occurred between her and Mark.

"Uh, no. He'll be fine on his own."

"No? Why not? What's happening? Did something happen at that party?"

"I don't want to talk about it."

"Something did happen! Oh my god! Did you and he do it?"

"No!"

"Then what happened?" Jenna let out a deep breath and realized it was either talk about her failed romance or talk about the tests. She chose to take her mind off the bigger worry and as they road to where the busses for the camp were to pick them up, Jenna accounted the whole night of the party to Aggy. When she was done, Aggy was left, for probably the first time in her life, speechless.

"That dog!" Aggy barked.

"I forgave him the next morning, but I don't think we're going to be an item anymore."

"Unbelievable. It's also kind of on Chandra too. You know she got him drunk."

"Probably, but it's fine. I think I have bigger things to worry about now."

Just then the limo stopped. Jenna and Aggy locked eyes and it was as though time held still for them. Then the door opened and they were there. Jenna climbed out of the limo and she saw the busses lined up along the street. They were large gray vehicles that had no exterior marking or words on them. The glass on them was blacked out. They just looked like death to her.

"Wow. This is it," Aggy said. They then both turned and saw the registration area and there was a long line of kids already waiting. There were some kids whose parents brought them and they were having their good bye moments, which were clearly very dramatic and painful to watch. Beyond that, there were picketers chanting about how the ESA was federally sanctioned murder of innocent children.

"Those pro-lifers never miss a beat," Aggy said as she and Jenna found their places in line. From the back it was hard to tune out the screaming and crying of the children and parents alike. Jenna began to turn her head to see who was making the noise. "Don't! Whatever you do, don't turn around. I've heard stories about those things. It's way too upsetting."

"How can you not look? It sounds like they're being chopped into bits."

"Emotionally, they are," A girl ahead of them said. She had a purple Mohawk and a ring through her upper lip. She turned and shot them a quick smile. "I'm Violet Barker."

"Jenna. This is my friend Aggy."

"Nice to meet you."

"You seem pretty calm."

"Because I have prepared for this day since my third birthday. I'm not like all these other pussies. My parents told me about the tests before I could walk. I'm actually looking forward to it."

"You are?"

"Sure. In fact, I've been thinking about throwing 'em."

"What? You mean, fail on purpose?"

"Yes. Look at the world today. Is it such a prize to keep on living? Things are bad now and they are just going to get worse. I'd rather get out now."

"Can you even fail on purpose?" Aggy asked.

"Sure you can," Violet said. A girl in another line began to scream and soon she fell to the ground, heaving and sobbing. A security guard rushed over and helped her up and took her to a medical tent nearby. "That's the seventh freak out this morning. Some people just can't handle it." Violet said.

Jenna finally made it to the front of the line. They took her name and with that, they were able to call up all of her information. They then gave her a number, a bus assignment and she was instructed to wait beyond the red line until her bus was ready to board. She took her bag and went past the red line and sat down on a small bench near the busses. Violet was already there, but she was standing and looked almost anxious to get on board. Aggy soon joined Jenna and they sat together and waited.

There was little talking. There was nothing to be said. They just sat there and watched as the buses would load up and drive away. Most of the kids getting on the buses were white as ghosts. A bus pulled up to them and Jenna's stomach fell. The bus driver got out and instructed everyone to stack their luggage by the side of the street and he would load it all in. Jenna unzipped her bag and pulled out the journal that her mother had given her. She then put her bag with the others and got in line to board the bus. As she got on, she saw Aggy at a seat waving Jenna over, but as she got closer, another girl came along and sat beside Aggy.

"Uh, excuse me, but I was saving that seat for my friend." Aggy said.

"No saving!" The girl barked. Aggy looked up at Jenna.

"Then, I guess I'll just get up and go." Aggy said as she slinked past the girl. They then went further back and found a couple of vacant seats. As they sat down and settled, Violet appeared and sat down with them as well, squeezing tightly against them.

"Here we go." She said.

"You sound like you have some experience with this." Aggy said.

"A little. I've got three brothers and six sisters. They all took the tests and about half passed."

"Only half?"

"Yeah. It happens." Aggy looked to Jenna and they both began to feel worse.

The bus started up and headed out to the highway.

As the bus drove along, there were more freak outs. Some kids would just burst out in tears or they would start screaming. Some even threw up. It was like being in an insane asylum. There were two security guards on board who were trained to help in those cases, but after a while, it was almost too much for the two guards to handle. Jenna opened up her journal and started scribbling down some thoughts. She figured it might help.

Jenna fell asleep at one point and when she awoke, they had arrived at the camp. She looked up and more than half the bus had gotten off. She, Aggy and Violet all got up and started to file out of the bus. When Jenna stepped out she saw a woman who looked rather official standing nearby. She was clad in a government issued uniform and her hair was dark and short.

"Hello." Jenna said.

"Hello, young lady. May I help you?"

"I hope so. I'm not sure where to go."

"Simply follow the line to the reception center."

"Great. Thanks. Also, do you know when the tests begin tomorrow?"

"Tomorrow? My dear, the tests began the minute you stepped off that bus."

Part 2

Chapter 11
Testing Camp

I arrived at the ESA camp with Aggy. The ride over was difficult for us, at least emotionally. I could tell Aggy was on the brink of a total meltdown. She just stared out the window, mumbling to herself. It sounded like she was praying. The rest of the kids on the bus weren't doing much better. There were some freak outs and a few fights. Everyone was on the edge, not that anyone could blame them.

The only one on the bus who was fine, other than the security guards posted at the front of the bus, was a girl named Violet. Aggy and I met her in line at registration and to say she is unique is a gross understatement. She's got purple hair, piercings and most weird of all, she's not afraid of the tests. In fact she mentioned that she was thinking of failing them on purpose. She said that the world is already on the brink of destruction and it's just going to get worse from here on out. I guess I could see her point. The ESA has been trying to bring the human population under control for eighty years already and it doesn't seem like they are any closer. Food supplies are dwindling and there just doesn't seem to be enough of anything to go around. Maybe death would be preferable.

I was standing with a large group of kids waiting to be assigned to a group. They assign everyone to a specific group, and that group will be our testing group. From there, we'll be given room assignments and test schedules for the week. This all seems so big and so overwhelming. The camp's a lot bigger than I had thought it would be. It seemed to go on forever. There were large buildings along the perimeter that were nicely landscaped and almost looked good enough to live in. I assumed that those were the dorms. There were other, larger buildings and they looked to be where some of the tests would be conducted.

The whole facility looked like one giant sports arena with tracks and swimming pools and lots of open fields. It was unlike anything I had imagined. I thought it was going to be smaller, but as I finally saw it, I began to think we had been taken to another country entirely.

As we waited for a counselor to greet us, I saw Aggy growing even more anxious. I was worried about her. She's normally the one who brings me back to the ground. I wasn't sure if I could do the same for her. She kept pacing around nervously; still mumbling just as she was on the bus.

"Aggy!"

"What?"

"Calm down."

"How? How can you be so calm? It's happening. It's all really happening. We're here!"

"Yes, but you knew this was going to happen."

"I did, but there's a difference between knowing something is going to happen and when it actually happens. I'm scared, Jenna. I know I was brave before, but I'm not so sure I can do this anymore." She was falling apart at the seams. I had never seen her so worked up before and it was starting to scare me; although, she was doing better than a lot of the other kids. There was a boy in our group who got down on the ground and curled up into a ball, and I noticed that he was still in that position, gently sobbing into his chest. Everyone else was a lot like Aggy. They were pacing around chattering incoherently or crying or both. It looked like some kind of insane asylum. I wondered if there was something wrong with me that I am was calm.

I heard a commotion coming from one of the other groups. I turned and I saw one group nearby and all of them seemed to be focused on one of their own members. They were booing and yelling at him for some reason.

"What's that all about?" I asked.

"That's Ethan Lazarus."

"Lazarus?"

"Yup. Another one of Senator Lazarus' grandsons. It's his turn to be tested this year."

"Wow. Sucks to be him."

"Doesn't it? I hate the little shit myself, but I kind of feel for him. What is it like to know the whole world hopes you fail? It's not his fault his grandfather was the architect of this legalized holocaust." Violet said.

"I thought you were up for all this."

"I am, don't get me wrong, but I call it like I see it."

"Well, even if everyone is hoping he'll die, I'm sure the odds are in his favor. As far as I've heard, every member of Senator Lazarus' family that's been tested has passed."

"Which makes the world hate them all the more; whenever a Lazarus is put up for the tests, people make up death pools betting whether or not they'll make it."

"You mean if he fails or not."

"Yeah, that too. You never know. It hasn't been unheard of for some testers to have 'accidents' before the end of the tests." I turned to get a better look at Ethan. He was goodlooking. He definitely looked like he grew up with all the advantages and privileges one would expect to grow up with in a political family.

He looked very out of place. His hair was well cared for and he just looked so well put together all the way round. I'd hoped his family would have been wiser than to make him look so perfect before throwing him in with the poor souls his grandfather had all but condemned to death.

As I saw him absorb the hostilities of his group, I began to feel sorry for him. It was a stressful time for everyone, and he was there to be tested just like everyone else. No matter his circumstances outside, he deserved the same respect as anyone else. The shriek of a whistle broke the air and we all turned and saw a counselor standing before us. We were then instructed to join him in the reception lobby for our room assignments.

I got my room and it included a bed with probably the hardest mattress I've ever felt in my life. I was right about the apartment looking bungalows. That's where they were putting us and it actually wasn't too bad. The carpets looked new, as did all the furniture and paint on the walls. My only complaint was my dorm mate. I had hoped to be paired with Aggy, of course, but they have some kind of policy not to put friends together in the same dorm, so I got stuck with Violet. She was actually not too bad a roommate, but when she got on one of her rants, she became a real bummer. I don't think she's ever had a moment of happiness in her entire life.

The building has three floors. The first and third floors were all dorm rooms while the common room was located in the middle of the second floor. That's where the television, snack machines and pay phones were located. I checked it out earlier and it looked clean. The couch was rather nice and it was a good TV. Fifty inches.

Our dorm was on the third floor and had a large front window which gave us a great view of most of the campus. If it weren't for the tests, I would have thought I was having the time of my life.

I loved how the administrators tried to make it all seem like summer camp or something. Some of the kids had actually gotten into it and seemed to have forgotten that their lives were at stake, but I figured whatever they needed to get through this.

Another good thing about this arrangement was that Violet and I had our own bathroom. I wasn't thrilled to have to share it with her, but at least she was the only one I had to share it with. We were also told that cleaning services were daily, but only while we were testing. I was still nervous and scared, but for some reason a little less so. It all did feel like some kind of sleep-away camp thing. Thinking of it in those terms made it all seem a little less serious than it really was. I believed that I'd actually be able to sleep. I wish I could have said the same for Aggy. She was so freaked when she found out we couldn't room together. She never was good with being away from home. I remember the first time she and I went to a sleep over party; she wet her sleeping bag in the middle of the night and spent the rest of the time in the bath tub crying. I could only imagine what she was going through. I finished packing and began to mentally prepare for the orientation meeting that we were to have after dinner. I wasn't sure if it would calm everyone down or make them all freak out.

I got back from our first dinner and orientation and it wasn't as scary as I thought it would be. First off, dinner was actually really good. They must have brought in real cooks for this place. It wasn't the standard public school crap we're used to. There was fresh pasta, fruit and quite a few Vegan options. I guess when it's possible you may die, they do what they can to make you as comfortable as possible.

I saw Ethan Lazarus in the dining hall. He was sitting alone, but that's not to say once or twice a roll or salt shaker didn't come flying at him. As I ate, I kept looking back at him. He looked miserable. It wasn't like he waltzed in acting like he knew he was going to pass the tests. He was just like us. He had no idea what was ahead of him and for all he, or anyone else, knew he could be the first Lazarus to fail.

When I was done eating, I told Aggy I'd catch up with her later and I got up to put my tray back where I had found it. I turned and saw that most everyone left were more focused on their own conversations and all attention to Ethan was gone, so I took the chance and went over to him.

"Hi." I said. He looked up at me with a curious look.

"Hi."

"My name's Jenna Holdren. You're Ethan Lazarus, right?"

"Yeah. You want to hit me in the face or the stomach?"

"What?"

"The face is a popular choice, but I'd really prefer the stomach. I mean, I've got a nice face. I really would like to keep it like this."

"Thanks for the offer, but I don't want to hit you. I just came over to talk to you."

"Why?"

"Because you've been sitting alone all through dinner and I guess I feel kind of bad for you."

"You pity me?"

"I wouldn't put it like that, but yes."

"Look, I don't need your pity. I know I'm just about the most hated person here just like my family is the most hated family in America, but what my grandfather did was the right thing to do. This planet is dangerously overpopulated and unless you and all your friends want to spend the rest of your lives fighting over scraps of food in the street, we're all going to have to make some hard choices. This may seem harsh, but it's for the greater good." Ethan said. It sounded as though he had been giving that speech his entire life.

"So, do you have that whole speech memorized by heart now?"

"Pretty much, yes."

"I just came over here to be nice. I don't care who you are or who your family is. I saw someone who could use a friend."

"Oh. Well, thanks. Although, if you go around saying we're friends, you may end up with just as many enemies as I've got now."

"I'll take my chances." I then sat down and he smiled. It wasn't a forced, polite smile. It was genuine. I could tell he was grateful for the company, and it wasn't hard to figure out why. It was important to have people to back you up, especially when we were all facing the possible end of our lives. No one deserved to be left alone at such a time.

"So, where are you staying?"

"I'm in building C. On the first floor."

"I'm in building C too. Third floor."

"So you have the nice view."

"It's not bad. Who are you rooming with?"

"No one. I was given a single room."

"So, you do get a little privilege around here."

"It's not so much privilege as it's just to protect me. When my older brother Chad tested a couple years ago, there was an incident and he wound up in the hospital."

"I think I remember hearing about that."

"Due to the fact he was so badly injured, he was given an automatic pass out of the tests. That didn't set right with a lot of folks and there were some riots. From that point on, the administrators decided that we were to be given single rooms in order to prevent a repeat of that."

"Makes sense. Must be nice to have your own room."

"I'm pretty much entombed there all day. I only open the door if the staff here gives me the special knock, so I know that it's them."

"Well, I'd still take that over being roommates with Suicide Sally."

"What?"

"The girl I've been stuck with, Violet, she's kind of all about death. She tells me about how many acres of rainforest we're losing per second, and how the atmosphere is slowly deteriorating because of it. She makes me feel guilty for just breathing."

"Sounds fun."

"I was hoping to get my friend Aggy as my roommate, but they have that policy."

"Oh, right. That sucks. I don't know why they do that. I'd think it would help to have a friend nearby."

"Me too. I asked them why they did it like that, but they just gave me some federal run around answer."

"That's what they're trained to do. Answer without answering. I've been around it long enough."

"So I guess you have some kind of inside track on all this government stuff."

"Not as much as you'd think, but I've seen some stuff. I can tell you that when they tell you to do something just do it; even if it makes no sense."

"Noted."

"We better get going. Orientation is in ten minutes. "We continued to chat as we made our way to the common room in our dorm building. When we got there, I was shocked to see how full up it was. Every single person staying there was present. We pushed our way through the crowd and finally found a small space against the back wall. Once we were settled, two counselors came in. They were clad in dark blue jumpsuits with badges on their chests and they both held clipboards in their hands.

"Good evening, testers," the male counselor said. "My name is Trip and this is Venda. We will be your main points of contact for the week. That means if you have any issues, problems or questions, you come to us first. Understood?" The room agreed. "Great. Now, we all know why we're here and the reality of it, but I'd advise you to not think about that. Try to relax and, as hard as it may be, have fun. Stress levels can affect test results and we want you all to pass. I mean that. No one here wants anyone to fail. We are here to support you and help you do the best you can."

"That's right, Trip," Venda said. She was bubbly and had a lot of energy. "Now, I'm sure you all have become familiar with the dorms so for now we want to go over the test schedules. You all here will be group C. We'll be posting the testing schedules on all dorm levels each day. These schedules are made for everyone, but you all should just pay attention to group C. Easy, right? Right. I'll just break it down for you all now real fast. Tomorrow will begin your physical training. You will be meeting in gym C on the north side of campus. Boys will be outdoors while the girls will be in the training facility and that reverses after lunch. The physical training continues on Wednesday in the south field with everyone, boys and girls. After that, you will be assigned to your classes." There was a sudden roar from the crowd.

"Calm down, everyone," Trip said. "These aren't real classes. They're just study sessions to help prepare you for the other tests. There is some book studying to be done if you want to pass the written portion of the tests."

"Right," Venda added. "And those exams are the final leg of the tests. Once they are complete, you will receive your results and that will conclude the testing period."

I pulled up my mental calendar and counted the days of testing and studying that they were describing, and I felt a bit of relief and doubt. Just a few days of preparing and then the tests would be over. It seemed so fast and so simple. It was like I could see the finish line already, but I knew it couldn't be that simple. There was still such dread in my soul. The path may have looked short but it wasn't going to be easy.

"We do want to take a moment to discuss a new addition to the tests this year," Venda continued. I looked around and it seemed her announcement brought back all the worry and stress that seemed to have disappeared so briefly. "Each year we try to improve the results the tests can yield and this year we are introducing the survival challenge," Everyone was taken by surprise with revelation of a new test and I couldn't blame them. I felt like my stomach was falling to the floor.

"First of all, be assured your families will be notified about these changes. Don't worry. Your only job here is to pass the tests," Venda assured us all. "Here is how the Survival Challenge works. We will take all the groups and break them up into separate teams within that group, which factors out to three teams for each group. The teams will then be taken to a remote location and after that it's easy. Just get back here. You will have to rely on your survival instincts and teamwork skills to make it back here. The first team to make it back to base; passes the tests. They get an automatic pass. That's it. You're done." Venda said. The news was greeted with applause and cheers. I could see, even from as far as I was, that Venda's face switched from happy to serious in a brief flash. "The next team to return will simply move on to the next portion of the tests," She said. My stomach lurched because I felt something very bad was about to happen.

"And, finally," Trip chimed in. "The last team to return will automatically fail the tests," He said. The room grew quiet and I just wanted to run away and throw up somewhere. "We realize how hard that is to hear, but we all know and understand what the tests are all about. We need to accept the reality that some among you won't pass."

They proceeded to talk us through the details of the survival challenge. They said it was designed to be a perfect way to fully test and measure our physical and mental abilities. Venda and Trip tried to put a smiley face on the whole situation and tried to keep the tone of the evening upbeat, but it wasn't really working.

After another half hour of questions, they had no choice but to send us to our rooms and we went to our beds and lied in our beds with no hope for sleep.

Chapter 13

Testing Begins

It was the first day of official testing and we were woken up by what had to have been the loudest siren I had ever heard in my life. It was like everyone woke up at the exact same second. Violet and I had already worked out a bathroom schedule, and since she preferred to shower in the evening that left morning open for me. While I was showering, she was dressing and when I was done, she would move in and do whatever she did to get ready in the morning while I'd get dressed. It worked out pretty good, although she's a fast dresser so she cuts my shower time in half easily. I wasn't able to wash my hair as completely as I usually do and it was starting to feel weird and icky once it was dry.

We were instructed to first report for breakfast. We walked into the cafeteria and everything was different. There weren't countless choices of things to eat. We were pretty much limited to oatmeal, eggs, cereal, and fruit. The line was long, but it moved fast as all the food was pro-portioned and premade. The fruit was fresh and the scent of cinnamon was thick in the air thanks to the oatmeal.

As I got my tray of food, I found Violet who had already staked out a table and I sat down with her. I then saw Aggy walk in and I waved her over. Once she got her breakfast she sat down with us.

"Nervous?" She asked.

"Unbelievably." I answered.

"I barely got any sleep last night."

"Really?" Violet said. "I slept like a corpse. With any luck, I'll be one by the end of the week."

"How can you talk like that?"

"Because my eyes are open. Believe me, this all may seem scary to you now, but how scared are you going to be when all the cities collapse and you're forced to hunt for food?"

"You don't know that's going to happen."

"That's what it's all leading up to. The food supply is going to dry up and we'll be eating our pets just to stay alive. Those crazy cat ladies won't seem so crazy then." I looked over at Aggy and I could tell that Violet's theories weren't doing any good to calm her down.

"Don't listen to her, Aggy," I then turned to Violet.

"Don't talk about stuff like that. You don't even know that it's going to happen. The ESA is in place to prevent anything like that from happening."

"You're really going to trust the government to prevent any kind of disaster? You think they have that good a track record? This is the one. This is the one they finally stop. After all the others: Nine eleven, the Washington quake, the bombing in Chicago. Innocent lives lost each time, but this time they'll get it right."

"Look, it's not perfect, but this is different. This isn't some natural disaster or terrorist plot. We can see this coming down the line. If we can get the global population under control, things will improve."

"And how long is that going to take? They were only supposed to have this testing thing for a few years. This is now the eightieth and they're still no closer to their goal."

"Like I said, it's not perfect, but it's better than just letting people run wild in the streets."

"Or is it? Maybe we should just do it. Break down all the walls and let everyone fend for themselves. Repeal all laws. Let people be free to live and survive on their wits." Violet suggested. Aggy and I just listened to what she was saying. We were both too nervous to say anything in opposition.

After breakfast, we split up into boys and girls. The boys went on to the southern field as they had been instructed while the girls were taken to the training facility.

When we entered, I was impressed by how large it was. There was enough room for a full basketball court, a gymnastics set up, and several other training displays, which I was sure we'd learn all about before long. Venda then appeared out from seemingly nowhere and approached us.

"Ladies!" She barked. "Good morning. Today is the day. I hope you got a good night's sleep and your fill at breakfast. You're going to need every advantage you can get here. A lot of instructors here run the tests very methodically, but I prefer to treat them with a bit of fun. I feel it can relax the testee and may result in a better test score, so I want you all to just clear your heads. Banish everything out of there," Her tone was pleasant and easy. I was actually feeling better. "So, to begin, I suggest a little game of basketball," Venda then walked toward us and split our group in half. She pointed to the side I was on. "Team one," She then turned to the other group and that's when I realized Aggy had slipped away and was on the opposite team as me. "Team two. We play to ten points. Go!" Venda yelled and we all raced toward the basketball court. There was already a ball laying in the middle of the hardwood. Both teams scrambled toward it and lined up on either side. Venda came up between us, picked up the ball and held it out in front of her. We were all just staring at the ball, almost like we were trying to will it into our hands. Venda then tossed it high up in the air and two girls leapt up at it. The girl from my team snagged it and it flew back and right into my arms. I bolted forward with it and my mind was a blur. I heard yelling and screaming on both sides of me as I dribbled past the other team and toward the basket. I hadn't played basketball in years, but I was rather good when I did play. I couldn't get those three point long distance shots, but I was great with lay ups. The high pitched squeaks of our sneakers on the floor rang in my ears as I fought my way to the free throw line with hands and arms waving in my face. I finally stopped and leapt up with all my might. I had gotten closer to the basket than I had thought. I saw some of my teammates urging for me to throw them the ball, but I was so close. I raised the ball up and threw it at the basket. I threw it high and much to my astonishment, it went in, barely touching the net. Everyone on my team leapt up and shouted in glee and we went back toward our basket as the other team checked the ball. This went on for another hour.

The other team scored off of us, but we managed to maintain a good lead. We hadn't even had a chance to strategize, but we all started working together as well as any team I'd ever been on. Better in some cases. Some of the girls on my team were playing at a level that was almost ferocious. Like they were playing for their lives, and then I realized, they probably were.

We were tied at nine and the ball was snapped and I caught it. I passed it as soon as it dropped in my hands. The defense was tight so we weren't able to get the ball very far. I got the ball again and was about to pass, but I was surrounded. I didn't have an opening and the basket was nearly a half court away.

There were calls and yells coming at me from every direction. Sweat was running down my face and my hands were getting slippery. I took a breath and pushed off the ground with all my might. I shot the ball up and it arched high up into the air. The trajectory looked good and everyone on the court stopped. Time seemed to go into slow motion as the ball got closer to the basket and as it slipped past the rim, I nearly fell to the ground. All the girls on my team leapt up and cheered as the ball hit the floor and bounced back toward me. I was swept up by my teammates as they paraded me around the court. Once the cheering died down, Venda joined us. She was clapping and had a big smile on her face.

"Very good game, ladies. Congrats to team one. Excellent moves out there. Team two, good hustle. It was a close game and you all played well. If you go past the bleachers there, you'll find the locker rooms. Go and shower off and report back here." She said.

We all marched back toward the bleachers. We walked just so it would take longer and we'd have more time to recover. I felt as though we already ran a thousand laps. If that game wasn't enough for us to pass the tests, I didn't know what else they'd need.

When we got to the locker room, it was neat and well kept. On one side there were some lockers and on the other were the showers which were, thankfully, outfitted with privacy screens. There were just enough showers for each girl, so there wasn't any conflict over that. The sound of all the showers going off at once was almost deafening. I got undressed and stepped into the warm stream of water and rinsed off the sweat and grime I had accumulated while playing. Then, one by one, the showers went off and I realized we were done freshening up. I shut off the water and dressed again, but when we all got out of our showers, we saw that the lockers had all been opened and they had names on them. Our names. We all began to inspect them. When I found my locker, I discovered a red jumpsuit inside of it. The other girls had jumpsuits in their lockers as well. Some were red others were blue.

"What are these?" Aggy asked as she came up behind me. I saw that she was also holding a red jumpsuit.

"I guess we wear these from now on," I said as I slipped my jumpsuit on. The other girls followed suit and we all filed out back into the training facility. Venda was waiting for us on the basketball court and when she saw we had all changed, she smiled.

"Very good! You'd be surprised how many times we have to instruct people specifically to change into their uniform. What you are wearing now is what you will be required to wear to all training and tests throughout the testing period. No exception. You may have noticed that some of you are red while others of you are blue. This is an indication of nothing. There have been rumors spread over the years about one color group favored over the other, but if you look at the previous records you'll see that is not the case. It's only a way of managing each group. Understood?" We all nodded.

We then split off into our different color groups and we began the first battery of physical training. The Reds started off with some high-intensity calisthenics while the blues were sent to the area with the weight machines. Venda stayed with them while a recorded program led us through our paces. At first, I thought I was going to do okay. It didn't seem any more intense than gym class, but before long, things got a lot harder and soon I was drenched with sweat and my back began to hurt. I looked around and it seemed that everyone was having the same problem. A lot of the girls were either limping along through the exercises or have given up completely and were sprawled out on the floor. I did the best I could to keep up, but the pain in my back was growing more intense. We started a move that required us to be half way bent forward and as I leaned into position, the base of my spine felt as though it were on fire. I did the best I could to maintain, but after the sixth rep, I gave up and I just stopped. I was the last one to give up, which I hoped would look good for me. Once I stopped moving, the recorded program finished and a recorded voice announced that the results of that phase had been recorded and we were to move to the next phase. As the day went on, it appeared that the Reds and the blues were being put through the same course, but in reverse. At one point, I realized we were doing something they had already done, while they were doing what we had done. The Reds at that point were climbing the rope. There were six long ropes hung from the ceiling and we went up six at a time.

When I slid down, I saw Violet and Aggy approaching their ropes and I saw them begin their struggle upward. I wanted to stay to cheer them on, or at least be entertained, but I was overheating and I needed air. Venda had told us we were permitted to step outside of the gym at any time for air or water. I walked over to the large door and pushed it open. The air hit me like a blast of ice water. I just leaned up against the wall, enjoying the sensation. I looked across the field and a saw a swarm of boys in blue jumpsuits at the far end running. I figured that would be us tomorrow.

"Hi." I turned and saw a boy in a red jumpsuit approach me. He was tall with dark blonde hair and a pair of the most dazzling blue eyes I had ever seen.

"Hi."

"Shouldn't you be in there? Testing?"

"Taking a break. What are you doing here? Shouldn't you be with your fellow Reds?" He looked down and seemed to just notice what he was wearing.

"I've got some down time. I'm Curtis."

"Jenna. Not that I don't appreciate it, but why are you even talking to me? We're not in the same group or anything."

"Sure we are. We're both Reds."

"Yes, but you're in the boy's program. I'm not."

"I know, I just think it's important that we all kind of reach out to each other. This is really stressful and it helps to have friends. It sure helps me."

"And you just picked me?"

"You are the only one out here. Besides, you look like you could use a friend."

"I've got my best friend here. She's inside climbing the rope."

"We've got to climb ropes? Damn it."

"What's the matter? Can't climb?"

"No. I can't."

"I'm sure you'll do fine."

"Interesting." Curtis said as he looked at me thoughtfully.

"What?" I asked.

"You try so hard to act like none of this is bothering you."

"You base this on what?"

"I saw you yesterday before we got on the bus. With everyone freaking out and breaking down, it's easy to spot the one person keeping it together."

"I just don't think worrying about something you can't control is helpful. I know I'll pass. Both of my brothers passed."

"Ah. A Legacy. That does stack in your favor, I admit, but I've heard about some Legacies who still failed. Recessive genes or something."

"And you're telling me that to make me feel better?"

"No, I'm just impressed how cool you are about everything."

"You seem fairly cool yourself, Curtis."

"Thanks, but in my case, it is a total act. I puked three times on the bus ride up here and three more times last night."

"Sorry."

"Don't feel bad for me. Feel bad for the sap in the bottom bunk." The shrill sound of a whistle pierced the air. Trip and I turned our heads and one of the male counselors was approaching.

"McEntire! Get back to your group. We're choosing sides for the football game."

"All right. I'll be right there." Curtis said and then the counselor walked away, leaving us alone.

"You'd better go. Being late to a test could cost you your life." Curtis gave me a weak smile.

"That'd be funnier if it weren't true," He said. "I'll see you around, Jenna."

"Sure." He then turned from me and ran off, disappearing around the corner.

Chapter 14

Day One

We got back from our first day well after sunset and completely trashed. I don't think I had ever run so much in my life. It was so bad I started to wish I was back in Ms. Benson's gym class. I would have taken six laps around the school over the endless marches we had just endured. The meal break was pretty good though. The one good thing about this whole experience has been the food. They do treat us right in that respect.

Violet went straight to her bed and passed out. I forced myself to stay up long enough to take a shower. I could barely hold the soap, but I couldn't sleep with this gross, gunky feeling all over my body. I can already feel my legs getting sore.

I saw Ethan at dinner tonight. He was eating alone again, but since I was with Aggy and the others, I couldn't really find a way to get over to him. I could see the dirty looks he was getting from everyone else, but he just seemed to ignore it all. I guess he's just used to it, which I think is kind of sad. No should get used to that kind of treatment, no matter who you are.

The second day at camp started off a lot different from the first. We all woke up in pain. I could hear Violet groaning as she slid out of bed and when I made the attempt, all my joints felt like they were on fire. We managed to get dressed and when we joined the others at the dining hall, it looked like everyone was feeling the pain. Every movement and step brought a chorus of cries of pain and we were given a couple aspirins along with our breakfast.

Violet and I sat with Aggy, but she was quiet as we ate. Everyone was. It looked like everyone was too weak to even lift their forks to eat much less engage in meaningless small talk. I looked across the room and there was Ethan again. Alone. It seemed no one was really paying him any mind anymore. They all had bigger things to worry about than him.

Without talking, the meal went by quickly. Aggy and Violet finished first and excused themselves to get ready for the next round of testing. I looked over at Ethan again and he was still there and still alone. I took a deep breath and braced for the pain as I stood up. I picked up my tray and went over to him. His eyes shot up at me as I approached. I felt myself smiling, but I wasn't sure if I had managed it. I went ahead and sat down with him. He didn't seem to object. I asked him how his tests went and his answer was short. He didn't seem to want to get into it and I took that as a sign not to push. I started to tell him about my day. I was hoping hearing about someone else's suffering would help him, but as I began, the sound of a fight outside caught the attention of the room. I turned and I saw a couple of boys through the window wrestling around on the ground and it was clear it wasn't for play. Even from my distance I could see the rage on their faces as they thrashed at each other. Two security guards came running up and pulled them apart. The moment of excitement died down as quickly as it started. I turned back to Ethan, but he was just starting to get up to leave. He smiled and apologized. He said he had to go and get ready for the day and soon I saw I was nearly alone in the entire dining hall and I began to think I should be getting ready as well.

I made it to the field and I saw my group in their red jumpsuits gathered together. I went over and just as I reached them, Venda came running out from the main gym. She looked fresh and relaxed with a big smile on her face. Why shouldn't she look good? It's not like her life is on the line.

She gave us another one of her pep talks and then we got into it hard. More running and jumping and endless cardio. The time just started to blur. Most of it was calisthenics and sometimes it was a game of football or baseball. It didn't seem to matter as long as they kept us moving. The only difference from the previous day was that everyone was already in incredible pain.

The time had finally come for us to return to the classrooms for our practical studies, and I was so grateful for that.

As Aggy and I made our way to our designated room, she leaned against me and I totally understood why.

"I can't feel my legs." She said.

"You're walking."

"It's all a mechanical response."

"Just think about this, it's the last day of this we're going to have."

"Yeah because tomorrow we go on that stupid survival challenge, which is basically make it or break it. Do you realize it could mean automatic failure? Why would they do that to us?"

"Or it could mean automatic success."

"Why must you always look on the bright side?"

"Because if I don't, who will?"

We got to class and a good portion of it was straight out of a wilderness survival guide. I guess since it was the first year for the survival challenge, they wanted to make sure everyone was prepared. We went over basic survival skills such as building fires, catching and cleaning food and identifying poisonous plants. We then spent a good amount of time on first aid techniques, but I didn't see the point to that. If it meant I could take an instant pass on the tests, I would cross that finish line with one leg.

We got out of class two hours before the evening meal. We had a shorter curfew than normal because they were going to be sending people off for the challenge an hour before sunrise.

I only had time for a quick shower before going down to the dining hall with Aggy and Violet. As we walked in my eye caught sight of something I thought I'd never see again; or actually someone. It was Mark. He saw me and ran right over. I noticed he was sporting a green jumpsuit, but I hadn't seen anyone else around in green before. We said our hellos and he told me all about how he missed me and had been searching for me. He seemed surprised to see me in my red suit. I thought for a moment that it was a big campus and there had to be other colors besides blue and red. Aggy gave me a pass so that I could eat with Mark. We found a table in the corner and he told me all about what he had been doing and it was a lot like what I had been doing. No surprise there. As I watched him speak, I started to realize how much I missed him. All that nonsense with Chandra at the party seemed to fade from my memory. The fight felt so petty with us both at the edge of whatever was to come. I then felt Mark take my hand and it felt nice. His skin was soft and warm. Then he smiled. He always got me with that smile. We just talked and talked and before I knew it, we were alone. I checked my watch and it was just a few minutes until lights out. I didn't want to say good bye so quickly. It felt like we had just seen each other after much too long already, but I knew we had to go. The security detail would be sweeping the campus and I was afraid of what would happen if we were caught. It seemed like any infraction could affect the results of the tests and while I consider myself willing to take a risk, my life isn't something I prefer to gamble with.

We said our good byes again and raced off to our respective dorms. I stopped for only a moment and turned around and saw him disappear into the shadows. My heart tugged a bit and then I continued to my dorm.

Chapter 15

CHAPTER 14

Adjustments

I got back a few minutes past curfew but no one saw me. I managed to get in a few hours of sleep. I woke up and noticed it was still dark outside. I hated that. Violet actually got up before me and was already packed and ready to go by the time I was going in for my shower. I tried to move quickly but my body felt like it was filled with lead. I kept hearing Violet shouting at me from outside the bathroom. She was adamant about getting to breakfast as soon as possible.

Once we were done eating, we had to report to the parking lot where we first arrived. I wasn't sure what was supposed to happen after that and my stomach was in knots whenever I thought about what was ahead of us. I felt like I couldn't wait for it to begin but I also didn't want it begin either. I wished I had a device that could rewind time back to when I was twelve and all of this was just a bad dream lurking on the horizon, or if I could blast forward past the tests and on to my life.

No one was talking and I mean no one. The dining hall was dead silent except for the sound of people eating. Even Aggy was quiet. I didn't see Ethan. His usual table was empty. There was no point in putting it off any longer. We were done with breakfast. It was time to go.

When we got to the parking lot, there was a whole fleet of buses waiting and already what looked to be thousands of kids in line to get on them. I saw our group waiting together. There were also groups of kids in other colors of jumpsuits. There were the Blues near the Reds, but past them I saw the yellows and the greens. I knew it was a long shot but I kept my eyes on the green group hoping to see if Mark was with them. He had to be but there were too many and I was too far away.

When Aggy, Violet and I joined our group, I felt like I did when our class would gather before leaving for a field trip in school, but the giddy excitement wasn't there. I looked at the bus and I felt a cold chill run up my spine. Everyone out there was as dispirited as they were during breakfast. There was barely any chatter. In fact, the only sound I could hear were the soft sobs rising up from each group. I looked up and I saw Venda approaching. She was clad in black and there was no smile on her face. She looked more sympathetic than pumped. She came to our group first and folded her arms in front of her. She went through the standard greeting and explained how it was going to work. She said we were in for a three hour ride before we made it to Alpha Camp. We were given room assignments as well. We were going to have at least one night to rest before the test was to begin.

We all got on the bus and I sat down by the window at a seat near the rear. I just sat there watching the kids getting on their buses. It was a sad, slow processional. I saw Aggy coming up the aisle toward my seat. Her eyes were dark and sad. As she sat down, I tried to smile at her but she either didn't see or it didn't mean anything to her. I hated seeing her like that, but I could hardly blame her. More kids were coming onto the bus and when all the seats were nearly taken the doors closed and my heart tightened a bit. The engine roared to life and the bus began to roll away, but it stopped abruptly and Venda came on board. She hurried down the aisle toward me and Aggy. Her face was sad and she reached out to Aggy.

"I'm sorry to tell you this, but your roommate didn't arrive for pick up this morning and when security went to check on her, they found her in the closet of your room. She hanged herself." Aggy clapped her hand to her mouth and I saw tears come down from her eyes almost instantly. She was starting to shake. I wasn't even aware she liked her roommate very much. She never mentioned her.

"When?" Aggy asked.

"Some time after breakfast. It happens sometimes. The pressure can be too much for some. It is policy in these situations to pass the surviving roommate."

"What?"

"It has been a long held policy in these cases. We find discovering the death can have an adverse impact on your performance and we can't get accurate results because of that. If you could please collect your things, we have some paperwork for you to sign before we release you."

"All right." Venda then got off the bus and Aggy started to get her things together.

"You pass? Just like that?"

"I guess so! Oh my God! I can barely breathe."

"I'm so happy for you!"

"Thanks. I wish I could bring you with me."

"It's okay. I'm just glad you made it."

"It's a miracle. I mean, I'm sorry she's dead, but I can go home now. I can go home. I'm going to pray for you Jenna. I know you're going to pass." Aggy then turned away and hurried off the bus. I watched Venda escort Aggy back to the testing center and as we got onto the road, everything was gone.

I nodded off after we got on the highway and after checking my watch it looked like we had only been on the road for an hour. I don't know where we were. It looked like they were taking us up into the mountains. There's nothing but dirt and trees all around and I could barely see the sky past the branches of the trees. It looked so quiet and lonely out there. There was nothing but trees in front and behind us and we still were going deeper in. I thought about the challenge and I began to wonder if I would be able to do it.

The bus turned off the highway and we headed down a dirt path through the woods. I could see what looked to be cabins ahead of us. The bus finally came to a stop and everyone was getting rather anxious to finally stand up.

The camp didn't seem so bad. If the circumstances were just a little different, I might say I could have fun there. The cabins were cleaner than I thought they'd be and the mattresses were softer than I was led to believe. It reminded me of the year I went to summer camp at Lake Kanasu.

I was rooming in one cabin with five other girls, including Violet. I was glad she was there but I really missed Aggy. She'd be able to help me keep my sanity. Everyone was chatting and talking happy as if they were on some fun sleep over or something. They either didn't understand how serious the situation was, or they did and were just choosing to make it fun in some attempt to keep their fear from taking over. I get that.

We were sleeping in bunk beds and Violet took the one under me. I could hear her breathing. She was choosing to aggressively ignore the other girls. I'm not sure what goes through her mind. She's either trying to make a plan on how to survive, or she's just thinking about how she's going to lose the challenge on purpose. I couldn't read her like I can read Aggy.

We were all summoned to the main dining hall on the other side of the camp. I guessed that was where we were going to get our last meal and all the information we needed for the challenge. I couldn't believe it was happening. I was surrounded by it all but I still couldn't believe it. Sometimes I didn't even think about the prospect of me losing so much as I thought that some of these kids would lose. They wouldn't make it and everytime I thought that, a cold wave passed through me. I just wished I could fast forward past all of this and just get right to the part where Mom and Dad came to pick me up and take me home. I wanted it to be all over.

I was right. We had our last big dinner and it was big and it was good. It was a buffet and they had everything you could ever hope for. Chinese food, Italian, steaks and burgers and don't even get me started on the dessert bar. They had things there I had never heard of but now that I've had them, I just want more! The food was so good, I think I even saw Violet smile while she was eating. If the food could make that girl enjoy life, it had to be good.

Once we were done eating and sitting in the afterglow, some counselors came in and they started a presentation about the survival challenge. They outlined all of the rules and passed out survival packs for us. They were just backpacks loaded up with survival gear. There's a backpack, a solar blanket, some canned food with a Swiss Army knife, some matches and a few bottles of water. The rules were rather simple. After Breakfast we would be dispatched after our groups are divided into teams of seven. Four teams, one team per color, would be taken to one of many predesignated camp sites and from there it's basically a race, but it's more than that. It isn't just about getting back to the testing facility first, but getting there the right way, whatever that means. They explained that any team of seven arriving first would officially pass the tests. The second team would move on to the next phase of testing, and the final group of seven would be failed. Everybody was aware of that but hearing the words again pretty much killed the vibe for everyone.

The whole room was quiet and everyone just looked awkwardly at each other. Everyone was wondering who would pass and who would fail. The tension was thick and the counselors tried to bring the room back, but it was too late. They adjourned the meeting and we came back to our dorms.

Everyone was pretty somber. Usually there would be some music playing from one of the dorms down the hall and there would be screaming and laughing and giggling. The sounds of life, but as soon as we got back to our dorms, it was quiet as a tomb. Violet even seemed troubled. I honestly thought she would have cheered up after everything we had been told. She's just lying in her bed staring into space. It was time to go to bed. Tomorrow was going to be Hell, to put it lightly.

We had breakfast and it was the most depressing meal I've ever endured. Still no one was talking and every few minutes someone would break out into tears; not that I don't blame them, of course. Now we're waiting to be put into our teams. There are so many kids here. I have no idea who they're going to break us all up into teams of seven. However they're doing it is taking a good long time. We were given numbers and I heard they were to designate which camp site we were going to be taken to. I drew number one hundred twenty three. I then began to wonder how many camp sites there were out there and I started to get real nervous. I crumpled the paper up and tossed it away, being careful to recall the numbers on it, just in case. I then saw a familiar face smiling at me. It was Curtis. He was with his group and he waved at me. I wanted to go over and say hi, but we were forbidden for leaving our groups. That was when he got up and walked over to me.

"Curtis!" I said. "You can't do that!"

"If they want to fail me for wanting to talk to a pretty girl, I welcome it. At least I'll die happy."

"Wow."

"Too corny?"

"No. It's the first time I've heard anyone actually speak in the last twelve hours."

"I know. I guess the looming prospect of death kind of has every-one's tongue."

"So, why are you so not depressed?"

"Confidence. Total and completely unwarranted confidence."

"I wish I had some of that."

"You look pretty together to me. I think you're going to do great."

"Thanks. I hope so."

"Tell you what; when we start, come find me. I can make a spot for you on my team."

"How?"

"Kick someone off."

"I know you're kidding, but if you're not, I couldn't do that."

"Why not? Check out who I have on my team." Curtis said and then pointed back to his group and then I saw him.

"You have Ethan Lazarus?"

"We drew the short straw. We could 'lose' him and you could take his spot."

"Thanks, but I think I'll just do it on my own. Good luck to you out there though." Curtis just smiled at me and jogged back to his team. I noticed Ethan and he looked even more lonely than usual. He didn't even dare make eye contact with anyone. I didn't know how I managed it, but I felt sorry for the guy. I was with people I had come to consider friends and despite being new connections; they brought me a sense of safety. I couldn't imagine attempting this with no one in your corner.

More teams were selected and processed but Violet and I were still with our team, waiting for something to happen. I noticed that some yellow and green teams were nearby. I tried to see if I could see Mark among them, but they were too far away.

"Team Red. Unit one twenty three!" Venda called out. We all stood up and faced her. Her expression was stern but it soon relaxed into a smile. "Good morning, everyone. It's time. I want you all the separate into groups of seven." She said. Everyone scrambled around but soon we began to form into the appropriate teams. I was standing near one group and figured I'd join them, but then I felt Violet reach over and pull me toward her group in the middle. I looked up at her ready to ask why, but the mask of fear on her face answered my question. I then realized she was still holding my hand. Tight.

"This is happening." She whispered.

"I thought you wanted this."

"I did too, but now it's here and I have to admit I wasn't expecting it to feel like this. This is really happening."

"Of course it is. It's what we've been stressing over since we all turned sixteen."

"I just didn't expect it to feel this real. Please don't leave me."

"Okay. Fine. It doesn't matter. We'll get through this. We just have to shoot for making it in second and we'll be good."

"No! We have to come in first! I can't take this testing anymore! I have to get out of here!"

"Calm down, Violet. Just breathe. You've been doing great so far. Even if you have to continue on to the next phase of testing, I'm sure you'll pass."

"But this is the only way to make sure. Jenna. Promise me we'll come in first!"

"I promise."

Once out teams were chosen up, Venda had us all gather around her. She explained in more detail about the rules, which seemed to put a lot of kids to ease. She said that there were over two hundred groups and each group would have a first, second and third place. So there were over fourteen hundred kids who could make it and it just felt like the odds improved. After one last equipment check the teams were released and we all headed out into the wilds. I noticed the teams stayed close for the first few yards but eventually began to break apart and go on their own. Our team began to widen but I noticed Violet still had her hand tightly clasped to mine. I looked up at her and smiled.

"Just for a few minutes more," She begged. "I just need a little more time."

"Fine. Just try and walk a little faster."

Chapter 16
Survival Challenge 1

We had been hiking for several hours and finally stopped to take a break. We lost visual contact with the other teams soon after we left the camp. They're out there though. Everyone seems very anxious about staying ahead but no one is completely certain how far we are from the testing facility and we can't risk burning through our supplies too quickly. From the distance we drove, it felt like to me that it could take two days to get back to the facility. Maybe three.

I fished around my backpack and found a can of fruit cocktail. I was hungry enough to eat everything I had, but I knew we needed to conserve. Just in case.

Violet had been very quiet. She was sitting against a tree with her knees tucked into her chest and muttering under her breath to herself. It's been disturbing watching her lose her cool, but I understand. I guess it was to be expected. The brave front she put up before is just crashing down on her. Maybe she was hoping for some last minute miracle to save her from this. I think we all were, but there was no miracle and here we are in the forest with our survival on the line.

The others on my team seemed to be okay with the situation and were adjusting to the situation. I heard them chatting about fishing and hunting for food, if the need arose. I hadn't really thought about that myself, but hearing them talk about it made sense. We weren't sure how long we'd be out there and the food that was given would barely last a day much less two. I wondered where the other teams were. I hadn't heard anyone for some time yet. They had to be out there. We all started from the same place. Maybe there were some teams so determined to reach the goal first, they were sprinting back. Maybe they would make it, or maybe they'd tire out and fall behind. There's no way to tell. I'm just trying to focus on my journey and my team.

I wish I had seen Mark before we left. I wanted to know how he was doing. We only spoke that one time and I wasn't sure if he was doing so well then. Why was I focusing on other people when I should have been focusing on me? I couldn't help it. I heard the others finishing up their snacks.

We journeyed even deeper into the forest and it's even less clear where we're headed. I'd been checking my compass and it appeared we were on track, but again, we hadn't seen anyone else out there. Not even any sign of anyone else. What if we're closer than I realized and everyone had made it back to the facility already? What if we're last? Thoughts like that sent chills through my spine. Maybe we could just stay out there. We managed to catch some fish and we got a fire going. It's clear this team had the survival skills. We could just stay out there in the forest and live off the land for the rest of our lives. Seems kind of screwed up when that appears to be a more appealing idea than returning to society. I was kind of optimistic until the challenge began. If only we had seen someone else out there I think I would have felt better.

I went for a walk to clear my mind and much to my relief I finally discovered another team nearby. It was Curtis's team. I saw them through the brush and it looked as though they were doing as well as my team was. They had a fire going and they were cooking what looked to have been a raccoon over the open flame. I stepped out and they were on guard at first but when Curtis noticed me, he calmed them down. It was just so great to see anyone, but to see Curtis was even better. I didn't know him well, but I could tell if he wanted to be first to the facility, he would be. To know he was no further along than our team was a great relief.

"How's your team going?" He asked as we sat by the fire.

"They're good. We caught some fish for dinner. We'll be getting an early start tomorrow."

"Shouldn't you be sleeping then?"

"Yes, but who can sleep."

"Right?"

"How about you? Shouldn't you and your guys be sleeping?"

"Perhaps, but me team and I have been talking and we think we have a better plan to win this thing."

"Really?"

"We can't take any chances with this."

"So what's your big plan?"

"I don't really think I should tell you. I'm not even a hundred percent about it."

"Now you're just getting me more curious," I then remembered that Ethan was on his team and I looked around but couldn't see him anywhere. "Where's Ethan?"

"Lazarus? He's not allowed this close to the fire. He's over there." Curtis pointed toward the darkness beyond the glow of their camp and as my eyes adjusted I could make out a lone figure slumped against the trunk of a tree.

"Is that really called for?"

"Mr. Privilege over there is going to get a free ticket out of this and you know it."

"Probably, but why torture him now?"

"Just to let him know a little misery. Give him a little taste of what it's like to be one of the little people his family tramples over on a daily basis."

"Isn't that a little petty?"

"Yes. It is, but we voted on it."

"Fine. I guess I should be getting back to my camp. I'll see you around?"

"I hope so."

"Okay. Good night." I then got up and headed back to my camp.

As I walked into the darkness and I felt only the memory of the warm fire, I heard a voice whisper to me. I turned and saw Ethan skulking toward me.

"Jenna?"

"Ethan. Are you all right?"

"Cold and hungry, but otherwise fine."

"Hungry? You haven't eaten?"

"They looted my bag and took all the food that was in it and as far as dinner, they just toss me the bones of whatever they've been eating."

"Are you going to be all right?"

"I'll survive. I figure I can hunt for something while they sleep."

"Are you sure that's wise?"

"No, but you do what you gotta do, right?"

"I suppose."

"I'm just glad to see you. You're doing okay?"

"Yeah. My team has gotten a strong start. I think it'll be good."

"Great. I really hope you make it."

"Thanks. I hope you do too." Ethan then let out a nervous laugh. "Doubtful."

"Why do you say that?"

"You know what Curtis's big plan is?"

"He told you?"

"I overheard. He's going to hunt."

"Hunt what?"

"People. He figures if they're the only team left, they have to win."

"What are you saying?"

"He's going to kill to win! They've been talking about it since we left the camp. They had this all figured out days ago and do you think they're going to spare me? I'm dead. I am a dead man."

"I think you may have misunderstood."

"You think so? You don't think the pressure to win this wouldn't be enough to drive anyone to kill if they thought that was the only way they could survive?"

"I don't know."

"I'm just telling you so that you know. Keep your eyes open and be on guard. Curtis likes you, but I don't think he would think twice about killing you if it meant saving his own hide. I have to go." Ethan then bolted back toward his camp, trying to be as quiet as possible. I then saw the fire from Curtis's camp go out.

I found my way back to my team and I slid into my sleeping bag. I tried to get some sleep, but what Ethan told me was keeping me up. I knew the tests can push people to do things they would never normally do, but it's hard to believe anyone could be driven that far. At least, I would hope it would be.

Chapter 17

Survival Challenge 2

Our first morning in the woods and it was not pleasant. Terry Nelson appointed himself the time keeper for our team and went around waking everyone up just a few minutes before dawn. We made our way down to the nearby stream and attempted to catch some fish for breakfast. I have never been a good fisher and it didn't help me any that I was only half awake. It was quite a sight to see.

A few kids put together some rather hasty fishing poles while others fashioned some small spears and they just stood over the water throwing their ridiculous sticks into the water. They caught a few fish but after they were cleaned and cooked, they weren't much to fill an ant's stomach. We then began to forge around the forest and we managed to find a bunch of fruit bearing bushes. After determining that they weren't poisonous, we gorged ourselves. I squirreled a bagful away for later and as soon as the sun was fully up over the horizon, we were on our way again.

More marching through this endless forest and not a single clue to the presence of anyone else. I guess the teams spread out pretty far from each other. There weren't even any signs of anyone's old camps. I was getting nervous again. Since the tests began I've tried to act like failing wasn't possible, but there in the forest with so many against me, that idea seemed a little naive.

Violet calmed down a bit. She's accepted her reality and she's doing everything she can to be an asset to our journey. We never stopped to designate responsibilities but everyone just seemed to choose their roles.

Terry was our time keeper. Abigail Mckenna was our food gatherer. She scouted around and found anything that could be used as food. Jerry Price found himself in charge of our water supply and Violet had become quite skilled at setting up camp. She was the only one of us who knew how to start a fire with only two sticks or stones. I asked her how she found out about how to do that and she told me she had been a Girl Scout for six years. I couldn't really see it. I had been a scout for only a few months before I realized it wasn't for me. All the girls were a little too cheerful and energetic for me. It got annoying fast, but I could hardly believe a girl like Violet would be able to put up with it for six years.

"I didn't mind it at first. It was only after I left the scouts that I came to embrace the 'dark side'.

"We tried to hold to a schedule of walking for three hours and then stopping to rest. Someone had suggested it because they said it looked better if we returned in better health than the others, even if we only came in second. No one talked about coming in third. No one dared.

We were about to pack up our second camp and continue on our way. By the looks of how far we had come and how much further we had to go, I didn't see us getting back to the testing facility in any less than three days, even if we walked all night. I wasn't happy about being stuck in the wild for so long, but it made me feel a little more secure that everyone else was going to be trapped out here for that long as well.

Break number two for the day. It was time for lunch and supplies were slim. I only had the last bit of food in my back pack and the others were cooking up what was left of our fish from the morning. I was not thrilled with fish for lunch, but I was so hungry I couldn't think of saying no. I could smell the fish cooking. It reminded me of one year when we went fishing over summer vacation. Dad and the boys caught so many fish; it's all we had to eat for a whole week. It took a month to get the stink out of our clothes when we got back home. One night, Brian bet Bradley ten bucks if he would eat a fish head and much to all of our horror, he did it. Eyes and all. It was so much simpler back then.

Time is funny. It goes by so fast but when we look back, it seems so long and far away. Like a distant star you see in the sky every night.

After lunch, we tried to rest but I was too anxious to sit still; so once more, I opted to go exploring and I'm so glad I did. Not only did I see another team nearby, but Mark was with them! They were just packing up to resume their travels but I had enough time to catch Mark's attention and we finally talked. It was good to see him again. It felt like I hadn't seen him in weeks. He looked a little thinner than usual, but that was typical of the tests. They usually cost you about five or ten pounds. He seemed rather confident about the challenge. I guess one of his teammates was acting as a scout and they knew that among their group, they were in the lead. My heart eased at that news. I had been so worried about him, but it looked like he was doing okay. He kissed me before they left and promised he would see me at the finish line. I wished him luck and saw him disappear into the trees ahead.

I made my way back to camp just as everyone was getting ready to leave. I saw Violet packing my things for me.

"About time. Where'd you go running off to?"

"Just a little walk. I found another team nearby."

"Another team?" Violet asked with urgency.

"Relax. Not part of our group. It was Mark."

"Oh. The boyfriend."

"It was just good to see him again. I didn't get a chance to wish him luck before we started this."

"You should be worrying less about him and more about us. Jerry was checking things up the trail and he found the remains of a camp."

"Whose group?"

"We don't know but we just have to assume they're in our group and they are ahead of us. We're now going for five hours and we rest for a half hour."

"Five hours? We're not machines!"

"We have a lot of ground to cover. Come on!" Violet said as she slid my pack back to me.

We'd been walking for five hours and the sun had gone down and we made our way by only the faint light of a small torch Violet made. We finally stopped when we came to what looked to be an old summer camp that seemed to have been forgotten. Much of the grounds were grown over, but there were a couple of cabins still standing and they even had beds in them.

It was a fight, but it was finally decided that we were going to stop for the night. Not soon enough for me. My legs were on fire and I had to walk another mile, I was sure my feet would explode. We all got ourselves settled and then Abigail went out looking for food. For as dark as it was, I wasn't too optimistic, which was too bad because my stomach was giving me almost as much pain as my legs were.

I walked into one of the cabins and it was dark but I could see by the light of the moon and I could see enough to get around. There was a small bed near one of the windows so I dropped my pack onto it, claiming it as my own. I sat down and it felt so good. It was so good I didn't even care I was alone in an old wooden shack that was probably full of spiders and other little creepy crawlers. I just stretched out on the mattress and smiled. I was so happy I wasn't going to have to sleep on the ground.

I tried to stay awake long enough for Abigail to return with food, but my fatigue beat out my hunger and I fell asleep without dinner. It felt so good to sleep on a mattress again, even if it was a hard, lumpy thing. I tried to enjoy as much of it as I could and I savored every moment.

The morning came too early for my taste. I woke up and I saw the sky outside the window. It was turning a light purple as the sun began to slowly rise. I got up and tried to get my bearings. It seemed I was the first one up. I packed my bag and checked on everyone else. They were all where they were supposed to be, except Abigail. It looked like she didn't come back from her hunting expedition. Everyone was still asleep and I thought maybe it would be good if I could find something for them to eat when they woke up. I headed out into the forest and since I had no weapons to hunt with, I started looking for anything that was growing on the trees. I found a few berries and fruits but then I saw the

Holy Grail. Down a slight hill there were the remains of what appeared to have been an orchard. Most of the trees were dead, but there was one that was alive and well and bearing the finest looking apples I had ever seen. They were big and round and red as blood. I bolted for the tree and I came barreling at it with all my force. I lunged forward and hit the tree trunk like a freight train. The tree shook and thankfully almost every apple on the tree fell down to the ground. I fell to my knees and grabbed up as many as I could. My hands were trembling and my stomach lurched. I couldn't wait. I took one of the apples and took a big bite out of it. It was so sweet and juicy, I nearly blacked out. I gobbled up the rest of it down to its core and tossed it away. I grabbed another apple and took a few more bites until I felt I was properly fed. My arms stopped shaking and I gathered up the rest of the apples, excited to share them with the others. As I was leaving the secret spot, I noticed something in the tall grass. I thought it was another apple by its red color but when I got closer I saw that it wasn't an apple, but an arm. It was Abigail's and it was covered in blood.

I ran back to camp and woke everyone up. After I told them what I had found, they insisted on proof so I took them back to where I had found Abigail. It looked like she had her skull cracked open with a nearby rock and left to rot. I looked around for footprints but there were none to be found. As everyone looked around for more clues, I stopped and remembered what Ethan had told me. I tried to push it away as too crazy to be true, but I turned back to Abigail and I saw the fear that had been present in her dead eyes. It wasn't a four legged animal that killed her.

"We have to go!" I said.

"We can't just leave. Abigail was killed." Jerry said.

"Whoever did this could still be around. We have to keep moving."

"She needs to be put to rest."

"You want to bury her? Out here?"

"We can mark the grave and tell them where her body is when we get back. I just don't think we should just leave her out here to rot."

I looked back at her corpse. I'll never forget the look on her face; in a mask of shock and fear.

"Violet? Help me dig the grave. The rest of you bring her body over here." I said. Violet and I got on our knees and started digging in the dirt as quickly as we could. There was no talking. There was nothing to say. Jerry and the others dragged Abigail's body to the makeshift hole we had dug up and we gently laid her to rest. We covered up the grave and stood over it as we all whispered our prayers. We stayed there with our hands clasped together for another twenty minutes until time could no longer be ignored. We broke away, gathered up our things and soon we were back on the trails.

Part 3

Chapter 18

Chain of Command

As they pushed through the woods, Jenna kept her eyes peeled for any odd sounds. She had only been afraid of mosquitoes or roaming animals, but after burying Abigail she realized there was a greater threat.

As they marched through the woods, all she could think about was what Ethan had told her. She couldn't believe it at first. Curtis didn't seem like the kind of person to do anything so horrific, but the more she thought about it, the more it made sense. In fact, for a moment she was almost jealous she hadn't thought of it first. She started to slow down when she noticed the rest of her team stop and begin to set up camp.

"What are you doing?"

"Setting up camp. What does it look like?" Jerry said as he began clearing the area of loose leaves.

"What are we going to do about food?" Violet asked.

"That was Abigail's job."

"We all saw what she did. We can fish as well as she could." Jenna stood still as they all just went about their chores as if nothing had happened.

"Are you people insane? Abigail was murdered!"

"What do you expect us to do about that, Jenna?" Jerry asked.

"We have to keep moving. I think if we can make the main highway, we'll be okay."

"Maybe it was just an accident. Who would kill just to win this?"

"Are you kidding me? Who wouldn't? I didn't say anything before because I barely believed it myself, but I spoke to Ethan Lazarus and he told me that his team was planning on killing everyone else to make sure they're first. They're out here with us and anyone could be a target."

"That's insane. You really think they could take out all the other teams?"

"They got Abigail. Who's to say they can't get us? I think the safest thing to do is to get out of these woods. We're sitting ducks here."

"I haven't seen anyone out here for hours. I think we're pretty much alone out here."

"I can't believe you are ignoring this like it's nothing."

"I'm not going to panic. If it'll make you feel better, we can get back on the road after we've eaten. I think I saw a stream a few yards back. I'll see what I can find." Jerry then pushed forward through the brush surrounding the campsite, but as he stepped over a large log, a cord leap up out of the dirt around his leg and it pulled at his leg so hard, it broke. Jenna heard his bone snap and he crumpled to the ground, howling in pain. She then heard another snap behind her and the other members of her team were being taken down before her eyes. Violet let out a shrill scream and ran off into the woods. Jenna tried to stop her, but she felt something under her feet. She leapt up just before the trap caught her and she fell to the ground hard. Everything grew quiet and then she heard a footstep nearby. Jenna rolled away under some bushes and as quietly as she could, she buried herself with leaves and dirt. She saw a boot come into view. It was Curtis. Soon others emerged from the surrounding woods. Jenna's heart began to pound. She could hear Curtis whispering to his friends and once he was done, they broke off and went to Jenna's teammates who were still incapacitated. Curtis circled around the area as if in search of something. She then heard Jerry whimpering to someone. It sounded like a conversation but she couldn't hear the other side of it and then a shot rang out and the conversation was over. Jenna was trembling.

A few more shots rang out. Tears were running down Jenna's cheeks. She tried to choke back her breath but it was difficult. She pulled the dead leaves covering her closer and started to pray for a miracle. Curtis and his friends converged in the middle of the camp. There were only six sets of legs. Someone was missing and Jenna was pretty sure she knew who it was. She wondered what they had done with Ethan.

Jenna watched intently, waiting for them to leave but they just stood together in the middle of the area. They began to break apart, but they still weren't leaving. Curtis walked right up to where Jenna was hiding and her pulse leapt. She could hear her heart pounding in her ears. She carefully looked up and through the thin branches of the bush; she saw Curtis's eyes staring down at her. She wanted to scream but there was nothing in her. Curtis knelt down and looked around as if he didn't want anyone to know he had found something.

"I know Ethan told you what we were planning and I know it seems scary, but I told you there's a place for you with us, Jenna. Just come out and join us. I can only control these guys so much. If they find you they might kill you and if you aren't with us that's the only way this is going to end," Jenna wrapped her arms around herself to keep from shaking any more than she already was. "Please, Jenna. I like you. I don't want to hurt you." He looked down and her eyes met his through the dark brambles. Her pulse began to slow. His eyes were so deep and gentle. It almost made her forget how he and his friends had just killed her entire team. He slowly slid his hand along the ground toward Jenna and turned it over, as if offering it to her; offering her a chance to live. Jenna didn't know what to do. Her survival instincts urged her to take his hand and offer. It wasn't how she wanted to win, but they would win and be able to live. It would only take the sacrifice of everyone else trying to live. She was ashamed of the part of her that wanted to take his hand. She curled up under the bush in resistance. Curtis looked annoyed, but understanding. A shot rang out and took all the attention. The other members of Curtis's team went running. Curtis looked back over at Jenna.

"There'll always be a place for you on my team. Just come find me before it's too late." Curtis then leapt to his feet and raced into the words with the rest of his team.

Jenna waited, trembling under that bush for almost two hours until she finally slid out. She looked around and everything was quiet again as if nothing had ever occurred. She took a few steps and she saw Jerry's body on the ground. The dirt beneath him was growing dark red with his blood. Panic took control and she gathered up all the supplies she could and was about to leave, but she didn't know where to go. She walked back slowly and leaned up against a tree. She pressed her back to it and slid down to the ground and she broke down, at last, sobbing into her arms.

Chapter 19

On Your Own

Jenna managed to pull herself together and got back on her way. She was at a disadvantage without her team, but she was determined to get back to the testing facility. She found the trail they had been following originally and continued on. She was determined to get to the main highway. She just felt she would be safer there. In the woods, there were a million places for someone to hide and the traps that Curtis and his team had set were surprisingly complex.

As Jenna made her way through the woods, she wondered how Curtis was able to get his hands on any guns. She remembered that the testing facility monitored any firearms that were brought into it and she just assumed they would have taken them away before sending Curtis away for the survival challenge, but it would seem that assumption had been wrong.

Jenna would stop if she heard even the slightest noise. Whenever a branch shook or the leaves blew, she would jump out of her skin. She tried to be aware of anyone near her, but it seemed Curtis and his team were too good to be detected.

As Jenna turned around a slight bend, she heard soft sobbing from the bottom of a nearby ravine. She looked down and while it was difficult to see, Jenna could make out some dark hair.

"Violet?" Jenna asked. The sobbing stopped and Violet stepped out to the open, looking up at Jenna.

"You're not dead!" She exclaimed with excitement.

"How did you get all the way out here?" Jenna asked.

"I don't know. I just ran and I didn't stop. What was all that?"

"It's what I was saying! Curtis's team is taking out all the other teams."

"What are we going to do?"

"We're going to get to the testing facility and finish this. He has weapons and quite a bit of experience by the looks of it, but that doesn't change the fact that we can still win."

Jenna helped Violet climb back up to the trail above and they continued on together. Jenna divided up the supplies she had with Violet and after a few hours of hiking, Violet seemed to calm down.

Jenna still couldn't help but wonder what Curtis had done to Ethan. Had they killed him already? Was it too late for him? It nagged at her but when a column of black smoke rose up through the trees, Jenna's focus was stolen.

"What's that?" Jenna asked.

"Nothing good. We better just stay on the trail." Violet said.

"What if someone needs help?"

"I'm sure whoever it is can handle it themselves."

"Just go on ahead. I'll catch up." Jenna said as she headed toward the smoke. Violet grabbed Jenna's arm and pulled her back.

"Are you insane? It could be a trap or maybe it's too late to help! We're so close to the highway. Like you said, once we get there, it'll be a straight shot back to the testing facility and we're safe and alive."

"Just go. I'll catch up. I promise."

"Fine, but I'm not coming back if you go missing."

"That's okay. I get it. Just go." Violet turned away and continued down along the trail while Jenna walked off the path toward the smoke.

Jenna pushed through a thick bank of trees and came out the other side to find a camp that had been trashed. Bodies were strewn along the ground and there was blood in the dirt and splashed against the surrounding trees.

Jenna saw the small fire in the middle of the camp and that was where the smoke was coming from. She found a bottle of water on the ground and used it to put out the flames. She looked down into the fire pit and saw what was burning. It was a shirt, but she recognized it. It looked like something that Mark owned. Her thoughts finally came to Mark and she could hardly believe he hadn't come up for her before. She wondered if he was all right as well. He was so close to her team, it wasn't a far cry to believe that Curtis had found them as well. Jenna looked around once more and it was clear she was too late to be of any help. She gathered up anything useful and left.

As Jenna made her way back to the trail, she began to feel as though someone was watching her. She stopped and looked around but it was quiet. A breeze blew by and the limbs of the trees above swayed easily at its force. She returned to her pace and for a while felt safe but then the feeling returned. She spun around and she heard footsteps running. Her pulse rose. There was someone near. She tried to pretend she didn't know. She continued walking. When she heard the footsteps again, she quickened her pace and whoever was following kept up with her. Before she knew it, Jenna was in a full run, praying she'd make it back to the trail, but then something hit her from behind and she fell to the ground. She turned over onto her back and her attacker leapt up quickly.

"Mark?" She asked.

"Jenna!" Mark said.

"What are you doing?"

"I was hiding! I don't know what's going on. Some guys with guns came out of nowhere and they killed my team! Just like that!"

"They didn't find you?"

"No. I was getting fire wood. Oh my God. They're dead! They're all dead!"

"Calm down! They got my team too."

"You? They attacked you?" Mark said with a bit of anger in his voice.

"It's fine. I got away. Violet and I are trying to get to the main highway. I think we'll be safer there."

"No place is safe. You saw what they did to my team! They're animals!"

"Think of it like this; while they're out here killing, we can make it to the testing facility first and pass." Mark looked at Jenna intently as he thought about what she had said. He looked back at what remained of his camp and then turned back to Jenna.

"Fine. At least if we die, we die together." He said. Jenna let out a gentle laugh and smirked at Mark as he approached.

"That's the spirit."

Chapter 20

CHAPTER 19

Split

Jenna and Mark were trudging through the brush as they tried to catch up with Violet. Mark took the lead while Jenna held back. The weight of the past few hours began to push down on her. When the challenge began she thought it was going to be bad enough, but she had no idea how to process what was happening. She had never seen a dead body before and while the blood was horrific, the one thing she couldn't get out of her mind was their eyes. The frozen fear in their eyes. It was like they were staring back at her very soul and they haunted her. She tried to push the images from her mind, but they wouldn't leave and they only became more vivid. Her hands were beginning to tremble and she was having trouble staying on the path. She felt a warm breeze passing over her and then there was a sound and she leapt and dove for cover with lightning speed. Her whole body was shaking and Mark ran to her.

"What? What is it?"

"I heard something!" She said. Mark peered out for anything unusual, but there was nothing.

"It was just the wind." Jenna looked around and he was right. There was nothing. She got back up and a feeling of embarrassment came over her. It just seemed that every strange sound or unexpected movement in the corner of her eye could be a threat. She turned away from Mark just as she felt a tear slip from her eye.

"I'm sorry." She said, forcing her voice from breaking.

"It's okay. I'm jumping at shadows too. They could be anywhere out there."

"Is that seriously supposed to calm me down?"

"Let's just keep moving. The sooner we get out of here, the better."

They continued on their way and after some time Jenna was able to relax and push away the fear and focus on the goal at hand. She forced herself to see what was happening as no change to her expectations of herself. She intended to survive from the beginning and there was no reason for that to change. Whatever Curtis and his team were doing was not going to keep Jenna from seeing her family again.

They soon found themselves back on the trail and that helped put Jenna to ease. The only thing that did trouble her was the fact that they had not seen any sign of Violet and she didn't think it was possible that she could have gotten so far from them in such a short amount of time. There were no fresh footprints and there didn't seem to be any sign that anyone had been through the area recently. Jenna felt a cold spark in the pit of her stomach.

"Are you all right?" Mark asked.

"I don't know. We should have caught up with Violet by now."

"She probably just hauled ass out of here like we should be doing."

"I just don't think she could have gotten so far ahead of us."

"Who is she anyway?"

"Me and Aggy met her on the bus to the testing facility. She was difficult but she won us over."

"Are really that invested in her?" Jenna looked back at Mark. She knew what he meant and it horrified her that he could have even seriously considered such a terrible thought.

"I don't leave my friends behind; whether I've known them for days or years. Besides, she isn't equipped to handle this. She's probably curled up in a ball somewhere."

"I don't think we have the time to search right now. We are at risk every second we're out here."

"I get that. Just give me a little time. We can't just abandon her. We can just set up camp here for tonight."

"Camp? You want to stay in this spot?"

"We have to keep rested. Besides, it doesn't look like anyone has been here in a long time. Just go and find something to eat. I'll meet you back at this tree in fifteen minutes." Jenna said. Mark fought back the urge to argue with her, but he knew it was pointless. He checked his watch and with a warning glare he turned away and disappeared into the brush.

Jenna walked off the path and tried to find any sign of a human presence but there was nothing. She started up an incline toward a cluster of dead trees and then she heard something. It was faint but distinct. She kept pushing forward until she could accurately identify the sound. It was crying. Someone was lightly sobbing and it was getting closer and closer. Jenna reached the cluster of old trees. They were hard and gray as fog. The dirt was dry and dead. The sobbing was loud enough to hear constantly. Jenna followed the sound to a broken stump jutting out of the dead soil. She noticed the old trunk was hollow and she peered inside and saw Violet curled up, holding her legs to her body tightly.

"Violet?" Jenna asked. Violet looked up and the glimmer of recognition lit up her face.

"Jenna!" Violet cried as she crawled forward. Jenna noticed a trail of blood on the ground and then she saw Violet's leg was bleeding.

"What happened?"

"I don't know. I was making my way and then they came out of nowhere."

"Who?"

"I don't know! Curtis' team I guess. They were fast and I panicked. I just ran as fast as I could." Violet crawled out of the tree trunk and attempted to stand up, but she fell to her knee instantly. Jenna then could see the wound on Violet's leg was deeper than it looked.

"What happened to your leg?"

"I hardly noticed when it happened. One of them tried to stab me. I thought I got away but after I caught my breath I saw that I was bleeding." Jenna forced Violet down and pulled up her pant leg. The wound was much deeper than she thought. She touched the skin around the wound and Violet let out a sharp yelp.

"Infection is already setting in." Jenna put down her bag and pulled out the small first aid kit inside. There wasn't much to use but she made the best of the little she had. Jenna instructed Violet to keep pressure on the wound. It had been bleeding for too long as it was. Jenna cleaned it as best she could and applied some anti-bacterial gel before wrapping it. Fortunately, there was just enough gauze to cover it tightly. Jenna looked around and found some reeds and was able to string them together so that she could apply a rough tourniquet.

"That'll stop the bleeding for now, but we have to get you some real medical treatment fast."

"It hurts."

"It'll get better in a few minutes, but we have to get you to a doctor soon."

"I don't want to die out here, Jenna. I know what I've been saying but now that this is happening,"

"I know, Violet. I get it. We're just going to rest and eat here for the night and tomorrow we start again."

"No! Jenna, we have to keep moving. Curtis is out here! He is out here now!"

"Marching any further without rest or food is just going to make us easier targets. The brush is heavy here. We can keep our cover for a few hours."

"It won't be enough!"

"It's going to have to be. Now come on." Jenna then helped Violet back up on her feet and led her back down the hill.

Chapter 21

Crawling Through the Night

Jenna and Mark were hunched in the dark. They had found an area especially thick with brush to establish camp. They had neglected to build a fire as they were worried it would attract some unwanted attention. Jenna looked over and saw that Violet was resting. She seemed fine, but Jenna could see the dressing of the wound was already drenched with more blood.

"We're going to need more supplies." Jenna whispered.

"How are we going to find any?"

"The camps Curtis has already hit. Maybe he left their supplies behind."

"Or we could just get up and get back on the road. This isn't about winning the challenge anymore, Jenna. It's about surviving."

"That is what this challenge has been all about from the start, Mark. The dynamics have changed a bit, but we're still in this to live."

"You really think Curtis is out here? Maybe he and his team are already back at the facility. Maybe we've already lost."

"He wants to make sure he wins this thing. He won't leave until everyone else is dead. I know it."

"How can you be so sure?"

"I don't really care if I'm right or not, Mark. I'm just trying to get through this and I don't want to lose any more friends. Just promise me you're in this with me. Please." Jenna said. Mark could barely see her face in the darkness, but he could see her eyes. He could see the strength in them as easily as he could see the fear. He thought if he could push a little more, she would come around to his thinking, but he thought about what she had been saying and he wasn't sure if he was ready to take the chance. Death was waiting for them. It was unavoidable and it didn't matter if it happened in the woods or at the facility. There was really no reason to have any hope, but he preferred to be without hope with Jenna.

"Fine. We'll do this your way."

"Thank you." Mark smiled and leaned back against the brush. Jenna reached for him and pulled him back. He then realized the noise he was making and they were trying to remain as quiet as possible. He mouthed 'sorry' to her and they settled back, still on guard.

"How are we going to sleep?"

"Violet seems to be doing all right. As for us, I'm not sure I can sleep even if I tried."

"You need to rest."

"I'll be fine. The stress will keep me strong."

"I'm not moving on this, Jen. You need to sleep. I'll keep watch first."

"Fine. If you anything happens,"

"Just sleep." Jenna gave him a weak smile and got down on the ground and made something of a nest out of the dirt and twigs. She moved slowly and made as little noise as she could manage. Once she was done, she curled up, closed her eyes and sleep came faster than she thought it would.

It felt as though she had only been out for a few seconds before she was awoken by the sound of footsteps. She looked around. Violet was still resting but Mark was missing. The footsteps were close but sounded like they were heading away from the camp. Jenna wanted to see who it was, but it was too risky to give away her position. She crawled over to Violet and gently jostled her awake.

"What?" Violet asked. Her voice was weak and broken.

"Someone is near the camp," Jenna whispered. Violet's eyes widened but Jenna clapped her hand to her mouth to prevent her from saying anything. "I'm going to go around and see who it is. Don't move from this spot. Understand?" Violet gently nodded her head. Jenna then got up on her knees and carefully stalked away through a small trail that they had cleared earlier. It weaved around the area and when she was far enough away, she looked up through the tall grass. She saw figures wandering around. It was too dark to tell who they were, but it was clear that Mark was not among them. Jenna started to get anxious. It had to be Curtis and his team. Had they come here by accident? It seemed their location was too far and particular for it to be a coincidence. They were there for a purpose. Jenna was becoming increasingly worried. She hadn't heard anything, but she had been sleeping so deeply. She had to find Mark. She felt her foot hit a rock in the dirt. It was large. She picked it up and flung it with all her strength. Not only did she hear it land, the intruders did as well. They reacted quickly and soon were headed to where the rock had landed. She waited a few moments and when she thought they were far enough away, she raced back to camp in hopes of finding something that would inform on what had happened to Mark.

Jenna returned and indicated to Violet to remain quiet. She started to search around, but there wasn't much to find. It was too dark. Jenna kept searching around with her hands until she felt something that made her heart sink. She had found a spot on the ground that was warm and wet. It felt like just a small spot at first but there was a bigger spot nearby. She looked at her hand and as she feared, it was blood. Tears began to form in her eyes. She looked down further and as her eyes adjusted, she could see a trail of blood leading away.

Jenna followed the blood trail and it led her into the brush. She pushed on as carefully as she could until she finally came to a clear spot and there, in the dirt, was Mark in a puddle of his own blood. Jenna couldn't control herself as she let out a painful cry. She ran to him. His body was still warm, but there was no life left. His body was limp. Jenna knelt over him, quietly weeping.

"It didn't have to be like this." Curtis said. Jenna spun around and saw him standing before her with a bloody knife in his hand.

"Why are you doing this?"

"That's a fairly stupid question, don't you think? I'm doing this to win. To live."

"You killed Mark!"

"Was that his name? Okay. I'm sorry, but I try to keep a certain distance from my victims. Getting to know them can make it difficult."

"So now what? You're going to kill me?"

"No! No, Jenna! When I told you there was a place for you on my team, I meant it. I don't want to hurt you. I didn't want to hurt anyone."

"Yet here we are."

"What I have done, I did out of necessity. I mean, come on! Our lives are at stake here! I don't know about you, but I want to make sure I make it through these tests."

"You didn't have to kill anyone. We can all get out of this alive!"

"Not everyone. By my calculations, at the end of this survival challenge, roughly thirty-six percent of these kids are going to get a one-way ticket to the death camp. Not counting the others who would move onto the rest of the tests and still fail. I'm doing most of these kids a favor. No anxious waiting. No painful farewells to their families. A quick, clean honorable death."

"And who are you to decide who should die? How do you believe you get to make that choice?"

"Law of the jungle, babe. Survival of the fittest."

"You think you're any better than the people who put us through these tests?"

"I don't care about being better than them or anyone else. All I care about is getting out of here alive so I can live my life. I thought that was what you wanted too."

"Mark was a part of my life! You killed him!"

"I'm sorry for that, but there's really only one place free on my team, and as I have said, it's yours. Join us. You can be free of all of this!"

"You've killed. You've killed so many innocent people."

"But I won't get charged. My dad is an attorney and he did some research into this and it turns out, we are immune from the law, for the most part. If I would be charged, a case could be made that I was driven to these actions by extraordinary stress. He could have the case thrown out just like that; the perfect crime. I'm offering you a way out of this Jenna. All you have to do is say yes."

"Is that all?"

"Well, and take care of your friend." Curtis said as he tossed the knife to Jenna.

"Violet?"

"She's dead weight anyway. Just put her out of her misery and we can get back to our lives tomorrow." Jenna stood up and picked up the knife. Mark's blood was dripping off the blade.

"What's to keep me from gutting you right here and now?"

"The fact that you're surrounded by the rest of my team and one wrong move and you join Mark over there."

"What a friend."

"I'm sorry, but I can only be so generous. Just do it, Jenna. It'll be much easier for you. Trust me." Jenna looked at the knife in her hand and then over to Mark's lifeless body. The tears were forcing their way out, but the anger in her soul boiled away whatever sadness she had been feeling. It was like a tornado in her mind. She looked back to Curtis.

"No." Jenna threw the blade back down to the ground at Curtis' feet.

"Think about what you're doing, Jenna. If you're not with us, you're against us and I can't help you when that happens." Jenna turned away from Curtis and went back to Mark. She looked down at his face. The color was leaving his skin, but he looked so peaceful.

"I'm sorry." She whispered.

"Sorry for what?" Curtis asked. Jenna then reached into her pocket and pulled out a lighter that had also been packed in with her supplies. She quickly several small fires in the dry grass which soon grew out of control. There were screams in the darkness as Curtis' team tried to escape the flames. Jenna leapt up and raced past Curtis, knocking him down as she did. She looked back and the fire was growing larger by the second. The screams and panicked cries of Curtis and his team echoed in the night.

Jenna returned to the camp and pulled Violet up to her feet.

"Jenna! What's going on? Where's Mark? Is that a fire!?"

"Just run!" Jenna barked as she pulled Violet along.

"I can't! My leg!" Violet cried. Jenna took her arm.

"I'm sorry, but you have to. Now run!"

Jenna and Violet ran as fast and as far as they could. Violet's wound started bleeding again and they stopped for a moment so Jenna could look at it.

"Does it hurt?" Jenna asked.

"Yes!" Violet said through a storm of pain. Jenna grabbed some nearby plant leaves and made a makeshift bandage out of them. She wrapped them over Violet's wound and hoped at least they wouldn't make anything worse.

"That should hold until you get back to the facility."

"I can't tell. Is the light I'm seeing the sun rising or the fire getting out of control?" Violet asked. Jenna turned and saw that it was actually both. She could see the sun rising up over the horizon, but the bright aura of the raging fire was lighting up the area almost just as well.

"Don't worry about it. We have some breathing room now."

"What are you talking about? What's going on? Where's Mark?" Violet asked. Jenna looked up at her and tried to say the words, but her throat closed up and she just looked away. "Oh," Violet said. There were no details but it was clear what had happened. "What do we do now?" Jenna stood up, wiped the tears from her eyes and took a deep breath.

"We win this thing."

Chapter 22

Morning Rises

The sun was up and while Jenna couldn't see the light of the fire she had set. She could only see the smoke rising up into the sky. She felt a pang of guilt about causing the fire, but there was no other way. If she hadn't done anything they would have killed her just as they had killed Mark.

Jenna allowed Violet to rest for a few minutes more than she wanted. Her wound was still bleeding, but it had slowed. Jenna kept a look out for Curtis and his team, but it seemed they had lost them. The fire turned out to be a better cover than Jenna had expected it to be.

"How far are we from the road?" Violet asked. Jenna hadn't even thought about that in all the excitement. "I mean, going by the smoke, it looks like we're actually getting further from it."

"Maybe. We had to get out of there."

"But we have to get back on the path. If we don't,"

"Look! I know! I wasn't exactly thinking straight at the moment, okay?" Jenna snapped. Violet slid back into the brush.

"I'm sorry."

"No. I'm sorry. It's just been stressful."

"I'm sorry about Mark."

"Thanks, but we both knew this was a possibility. I guess for all our preparing, we're never really ready when it happens."

"Are you sure we weren't followed?"

"I don't think we were. I haven't heard anyone nearby."

"Maybe they decided to forget about us and went on back to the facility. I mean, if they took out the other groups, they don't need to kill us to win."

"No, but it looked to me like they've acquired a taste for killing. We have to assume they will be willing to take us out just because they want to."

"This is so messed up."

"That is the understatement of the year."

"I just want to get back to the road and back to the facility. I don't even care if we come in second place. I will gladly face another phase of tests if I can survive this."

"Don't worry. We're going to make it. Can you walk?" Jenna asked. Violet took a deep breath and attempted to get to her feet. She stood up to her full height and seemed to be carrying her weight on both legs. She took a step and with a wince of pain, she fell to her knee. Jenna hurried to her, but she waved her off.

"I'm fine. I can make it." Violet said as she got back up. Jenna looked down at the makeshift dressing on Violet's wound and it was clear it was not doing the job. Blood was dripping down into her shoe and it looked more infected than before.

"It looks bad, Violet. I'm not going to lie."

"I don't care. We get to the facility, they can fix it. Let's just go."

Jenna and Violet found their path again and using the smoke from the fire as a guide, they found their way back to the main road. Jenna knew they were headed in the right direction because she could hear the crackle of the fire getting louder. They passed a thicket of dead grass and she could see the fire. It had burned off a lot of dead land and there was more to go. Thankfully there was no sign of Curtis or his henchmen. When she realized Mark's body might still be in the middle of the blaze, her heart seized up a bit in her chest. It had been so long, if his body were there, it was probably burned and charred beyond recognition. She thought of Mark's mother. She was going to be destroyed and it will only make it worse that she wouldn't have anything of Mark's to hold on to.

"Wait here." Jenna said as she found a dark space to hide Violet.

"Where are you going?"

"Wait here." Jenna then headed toward the fire. She could hear the snapping and crackle of the dead weeds and wood burning. The heat was getting intense and she felt sweat all over her body. She stopped short of the flames and tried to see if Mark's body was still there. Through the amber waves, she could see a dark figure laying on the ground. It was Mark. It didn't look like him, but it was him. Jenna closed her eyes, said a prayer and bolted forward with all her strength. She held her arms over her head in an attempt to protect her from the flames. She got past the wall of fire and she ran to Mark's corpse and saw that his skin was charred and burned away. The fire had passed by the area and seemed to stay in the surrounding brush. There was blood dried on his flesh and it stunk unlike anything she had ever seen. She reached for his head and miraculously, the necklace Mark wore around his neck every day had not been damaged. There was no time for final good byes or last words. There was no time to remember and wish him peace. She snapped the necklace off of him and bolted back out of the flames.

When she came out of the inferno, she tumbled across the dirt. She got up and dead leaves and dirt clung to her sweaty flesh. She returned to Violet who got up as she approached.

"What the Hell was that? Are you insane?"

"I just had to get something." Jenna said as she held the necklace close to her heart.

"You're crazy, you know that?"

"Only the sane are crazy anymore."

Jenna and Violet continued on their way. It was clear they had fallen far behind and there was no way to tell how many other teams in their group were in the race. Jenna was assuming Curtis had killed everyone else, but she was hoping that wasn't the case. She looked over to Violet and it seemed that she had gotten used to the pain as she was keeping a fair pace.

They came up over a large hill and when they reached the peak, they say what looked to have once been some kind of farm. There was a barn and a farmhouse which were both barely standing anymore. Jenna saw a torn piece of fabric on the ground and she assumed that it was a part of a tent.

"It looks like someone set up camp here." Jenna said.

"And it looks like Curtis got here and took care of that." Violet added.

"Let's just check to see if they left any supplies behind. We need everything we can get."

Jenna and Violet headed down and searched around. Jenna took the farm house while Violet explored around the barn. As she got close to the main door, she could hear breathing. She pulled the door open and peeked in. It was dark, but the breathing was louder. It was close. Violet walked in and even with the light streaming in through the broken roof, it was nearly impossible to see. She followed the sound of the breathing and when she checked inside a makeshift stall, she saw Ethan Lazarus tied up. It looked like he had been there for some time. He looked up at her and let out a faint cry.

"Please! Help me!"

"What happened?"

"Curtis. He and the rest of my team tied me up in here. Please let me go!"

"You're Ethan Lazarus. The son of the Senator."

"Yes." He said with a guilty tone.

"Why wouldn't Curtis just kill you like all the others?"

"He said it would be too easy. He wants me to fail the test. He wants me coming in last. Said he'd have them send a search party for me after it was too late. He's setting me up to die! Please! Let me go!" Violet looked down at the broken boy before her and she was torn. She was one of the many outraged and suspicious that every member of the Lazarus family managed to pass the tests with no problem. She believed they were using their influence to subvert the tests to protect their own while millions of innocents were left to die. It was one point that she could agree with Curtis. She thought quickly and realized that if Jenna knew he was here, she would want to free him. Violet noticed a white piece of fabric nearby. It looked like it had been keeping him quiet for a while until he had managed to get it off. Violet picked it up and her calm, cool demeanor began to fill Ethan with dread. He tried to beg her to stop, but his voice was weak and he was so tired. He felt tears coming down his cheek and he was shaking his head, protesting what Violet was about to do. She knelt down and tied his gag back on, tight. She looked him in the eye.

"I'm sorry, I am, but your family has to learn that they are not above the law. Particularly the ones they are responsible for." She then stood up, walked out of the barn and shut the door. Ethan could hear Violet outside talking to someone else. He recognized Jenna's voice. He tried to cry out, but it was no use. He tried to make some kind of noise, but he was just too weak. He could barely move. The voices then faded away and he fell silent, accepting his fate.

"Did you find anything?" Jenna asked.

"No. Just some rats in the barn."

Chapter 23

The Highway

Jenna and Violet were pushing forward as best they could. They stayed close to heavily wooded areas in order to preserve as much cover as possible. There had been no sign of Curtis but Jenna wasn't ready to accept that he was gone. Violet was still struggling to keep up, but Jenna had found some fresh medical supplies at the previous camps and was able to make a more secure dressing for her wound. It still hurt and it was clearly infected, but she could stand on it.

As they emerged from a cluster of bushes, they could see the highway a few yards ahead. Violet grabbed Jenna and hopped up and down in celebration, holding back the pain the action brought her.

"We made it." Jenna said with great relief. The highway was a direct route back to the testing facility. It was still a lengthy hike, but the goal was within sight. Jenna could hardly believe they were finally so close. Her joy was dampened a bit as she realized all that was lost. So many innocent lives were taken and even though his reasons were understandable, Curtis was nothing more than a murderer and as long as they didn't know where he was, they were at risk. Violet hurried toward the road, but Jenna grabbed her.

"What? There's the road home! Well, sort of."

"I know, but Curtis could still be out here."

"Maybe he's not going to kill us. I mean, it looks like he got everyone else. He doesn't need to kill us."

"We don't know for sure. Even with all the killings, he may still only be coming in second. If he gets to the facility before us,"

"Stop." Violet said sharply.

"We see the road. That's enough. Keep to the brush for now and stay quiet."

They continued on parallel to the road and for about an hour it was deathly quiet. There wasn't even any breeze or birds singing. It was like a death field.

"Did you see Ethan?" Jenna asked.

"What? Why would you ask that?"

"Because when Curtis and his team surrounded us, I didn't see Ethan."

"Oh. I don't know. Maybe Curtis killed him first."

"Maybe."

"Why do you even care?"

"I know he's the guy everyone wants to see lose, but I guess I felt bad for him. It's hard enough going through this, but going through it with everyone wanting you to fail must be a nightmare."

"It would serve his family right. They pass the tests every damn year. This is the first time someone from their family could actually fail. Maybe if that happens, they'll repeal this whole thing. His death could save millions."

"I don't know if I feel right forcing that much responsibility on anyone."

"It might as well be him. It was his family that started this."

"I know that, but it wasn't his idea."

"Are you actually defending Ethan Lazarus?"

"I've talked to him. I think I'm just about the only one who has since he came here. He's not a terrible person."

"It's not about him being terrible or not. It's about what his family has done to everyone."

"So he has to pay the price for what his family did years ago?"

"It's not fair, but yes." Jenna shook her head to what Violet had said. She recalled Ethan's face. It was always so sad and lonely. She figured he at least had the courage to come. There had been a few years when the subject from the Lazarus family would go 'missing' just before the tests would begin. That caused such an uproar; a law was passed soon after that banned all international travel within three months of someone's sixteenth birthday. The Lazarus' tried to get it thrown out, but there was too much demand from the public and it became law. After that, they were forced to participate. It was hard to see why they were so resistant since they proved to be invincible since they were offered up for the tests.

Jenna and Violet continued on in silence. Violet looked over and it felt like they had been walking for ages but they had only progressed a few miles. Her leg was starting to hurt again and she could feel blood seeping from her bandages. She stopped for a moment and saw a crimson splotch forming over the bandage. Jenna turned to her and noticed the same thing.

"I've got more first-aid stuff. I can redress that."

"No."

"It's bleeding."

"We are too close now. I'm not going to slow down just for a new band aid."

"If you don't, you might just lose that leg and amputees aren't known to pass the tests." Jenna said. Violet thought for a second and realized she was right.

"Fine." Violet said and she walked over to a nearby rock and began to unravel the dressing. Jenna knelt down and took out some gauze, tape and a small tube of anti-bacterial gel. There wasn't much left, but it would be enough.

Jenna had Violet's wound cleaned and covered up and it looked like she would be good until they got to the testing facility. It all felt like it was coming to a long desired end. Jenna didn't care if they came in second and had to endure a final phase of testing. She just wanted it over.

"What's that?" Violet asked. Jenna twisted her head around and her heart dropped. There was something on the ground behind a large growth of reeds. She couldn't tell what it was exactly, but it looked like it had a distinctly human looking arm.

"Wait here." Jenna said as she crept toward whatever it was. She thought she knew what was waiting for her and it was making her sick, but she was getting used to the feeling she got just before she found a dead body.

As she approached, she discovered that it was indeed a corpse, but as she turned it over, she clapped her hand to her mouth. It was Curtis. Her mind short circuited as she looked down on his body. It looked like he had been stabbed many repeatedly in his chest. Blood was trickling down from his mouth. She stepped back and ran to Violet.

"Come on." Jenna said with urgency.

"What is it? What's going on?" Violet asked. Jenna took her hand and pulled her along.

"Just come on! Run if you can!" Jenna and Violet picked up their pace, but just like that, someone leapt out of nowhere. Jenna and Violet stumbled back.

"Not another step." It was a boy Jenna recognized from Curtis' team. He was tall and had an athletic build. He was smiling, but it was a sick kind of smile.

"Who are you?" Jenna asked.

"I'm Barrett."

"You were on Curtis' team."

"I was."

"You killed him?"

"Had to be done."

"Why?"

"It turns out when he was talking about how his dad would get us off, he really only meant himself. We didn't have any promise of protection and we all decided he had to go."

"Now his murder will just be added to the others."

"No. We all thought it out. He killed all those other testers and we killed him out of self-defense."

"And you think they'll believe you?"

"No one to say otherwise. No one but you two." Barrett then produced a knife from behind his back. There was still blood on the blade dripping down to his hand. She then heard rustling coming from all around and it was clear they were once more surrounded.

"What if we promise not to say anything?" Violet asked. Barrett smiled at her with a curious look in his eyes.

"And you really expect us to believe you?"

"Please! We can all still make it and pass the test! It doesn't have to be like this!" Barrett relaxed his posture and paced around slowly. His other team mates appeared at last and they seemed to be waiting for him to signal them. Jenna only assumed they were all armed as well. Barrett finally stopped and his eyes found Violet. He held the knife to her and then flipped it over in his hand, offering the bloody handle to her. She looked at it and then back at him, confused.

"You want to live? Prove you won't tell. Kill her," He said, indicating to Jenna. "If you want to run with us, you need to take a share of the guilt." Violet took the knife and she was trembling. Jenna looked at her, unsure of what was happening. Violet then turned to Jenna with tears streaming down her face.

"I'm sorry." She said and then lunged forward. Jenna leapt away, half expecting her move. The others started to yell, urging Violet to kill Jenna. Violet wasn't quick enough and Jenna was able to break away from the others and she bolted away into the brush.

As Jenna ran away, she could hear Barrett barking orders and the others acknowledging them. Jenna hadn't been totally sure Violet was going to turn on her, but after everything that had happened, it wasn't a total surprise. Violet wanted an end to it all and as she was already badly injured, she probably didn't see any choice.

Jenna back tracked as far as she could manage until she couldn't hear the others searching for her anymore. She finally returned to the dilapidated farm they had found the day before. She realized it was only a matter of time before Violet would lead them there, so Jenna went about searching for anything that could be used as a weapon or a good hiding place. She approached the old barn and pushed the door open and then she saw someone sprawled out on the ground. She ran over and saw that it was Ethan, tied up rather well. She knelt down and pressed her hand to his face. He woke up and his eyes expanded and he began to laugh hysterically under the gag that was wrapped over his mouth. She pulled it free.

"You came back! Oh, thank God! She sent you back!"

"She?" Jenna asked.

"That dark haired girl; She did send you back here to save me, didn't she?"

"No, I'm sorry. I was actually here looking for a place to hide."

"Why? I thought you were on your way to the facility."

"We were, but they ambushed us."

"Curtis." Ethan said with contempt.

"No. He's dead."

"What?"

"Barrett killed him and is planning to claim self-defense after getting rid of any witnesses."

"That's not good. Curtis was a little unhinged but Barrett is flat out nuts. You have to untie me! Please!" Ethan begged. Jenna loosened his ties and he leapt up with his regained freedom.

"Oh God! Thank you! Thank you so much!" He sang.

"Thank me after we get out of this alive."

Chapter 24

Rescue

Ethan and Jenna were hiding in the darkest corner of the old barn. Jenna offered up what few provisions she had left and Ethan gobbled them up in record time. Ethan was in a terrible state. His face was sallow and scarred and he couldn't stop trembling. There were deep and dark lines under his eyes which were both terribly bloodshot. He just looked as though he had been put through some stuff. Jenna could see she hadn't been the only one fighting for their life.

"How'd they treat you?" Jenna asked.

"Like a prince. How do you think?"

"I was just asking."

"Sorry. I'm just not used to being treated nicely."

"It was that bad?"

"It wasn't easy. After they got bored of just insulting me, they started to get physical. It was just light torment at first until they dog piled on me one night and just beat on me."

"You don't look that bad."

"I curled up into a ball. I think they were pissed I protected myself because it just got worse from there. They took my supplies and wouldn't let me eat. When Curtis got his bright idea to take out the other teams, they talked about killing me first, but then he thought it would be worse for me if they just tied me up somewhere so that I would fail the tests. Send a message."

"You don't seem affected by this."

"I knew everyone wanted me dead from day one. None of any of this has been a surprise; except for you saving me. Why'd you do that?"

"While I understand why they did what they did, I can't say that I agree. The test isn't your fault and you're at risk the same as us. You deserve as much a chance to survive as anyone else." Jenna said. Ethan looked back at her with his mouth wide open and a tear forming in the corner of his eye.

"Wow," He said with a catch in his throat. "I don't know if you mean all of that, but it sure is good to hear."

The sound of something stalking through the tall grass outside broke the moment. Jenna pulled Ethan toward her and the slid further into the darkness. She knew any hiding place was going to be discovered inevitably. It was only a matter of time. She could hear someone talking outside. She didn't recognize a couple of voices, but then she heard Violet. She couldn't make out what they were saying, but she knew it was Violet. Their footsteps got closer to the barn and Jenna could feel her heart pounding in her chest. The only way out was the front gate and there was no way of leaving through there without catching hunters' attention. Jenna then noticed Ethan's short, panicked breaths. She looked in his eyes and there was nothing but pure fear.

"Stay here." Jenna whispered. Ethan nodded as she got up and skulked over toward an old workbench nearby. There was a shovel leaning up against the all. She took it and held it tight in both hands. She slipped toward the front of the barn. Ethan tried to beg her to return, but he didn't know how to communicate the message non-verbally.

As Jenna reached the front, the doors began to move and one of Barrett's teammates crept in. Before he could see a thing, Jenna was on top of him as she drove the shovel down onto his head. The sound it made was dull and hard and he fell to the ground in a heap. Ethan ran over to Jenna instantly.

"Is he dead?" Ethan asked. Jenna saw that the intruder was still breathing, but it was clear he was going to be out for a long time.

"Just stunned." She said.

"Now what? They're going to come looking for him!"

"Then we won't be here when they come. I'm going to open the door and when I do, I want you to run like Hell. Just go straight as far and as fast as you can."

"But,"

"You heard me!"

"Yes." Ethan said. Jenna walked over and took a look outside. The coast seemed to be clear. She pulled the door open a bit more and looked at Ethan.

"Now!" She barked. Ethan broke forward and charged through into the tall grass and Jenna was close behind.

Jenna and Ethan put as much distance between them and the barn as they could. They wandered through the woods until Ethan finally collapsed in a heap behind a pile of rocks. The sky was growing dim but Jenna kept an eye out for any activity.

"Where are we?" Ethan asked between breaths.

"I don't know."

"Is there anyone out there?"

"I don't know."

"We're going to die, aren't we?"

"I don't know, but I'm losing confidence." Ethan finally sat up. His face was shiny from the sweat that coated his skin. His eyes looked even darker.

"What exactly is your plan?"

"Go for as long as possible without being killed. How does that work for you?"

"I mean, what are we doing? While I don't know where we are, I do know we are a lot further from the testing facility than ever! If we don't get back soon, we are going to fail."

"I don't know! Okay? I wasn't really prepared to deal with someone going nuts and killing everyone."

"For all we know, Barrett and his followers are back at the testing facility filling out their release forms."

"Fine. You're right. We need to get back but we also need to be sure it's safe."

"How do we do that?"

"We just do it. I haven't seen any activity out there for the last two hours. I'm willing to risk it if you are." Ethan then tried to get up, but his legs gave out and he fell back down onto his back.

"Maybe in another hour."

Jenna sat down next to Ethan and leaned against one of the nearby rocks. As she rested, she began to realize how tired she really was. It was as though every muscle in her body ignited at once. She looked down at Ethan and his eyes were shut and his breathing looked like it was slowing down. She nudged his head with her foot and his eyes popped open.

"Don't fall asleep."

"I haven't slept in almost three days. Please!"

"I'm sorry, but we only have time to rest for a little bit because when we get back up, we're making one last push to the testing facility. We are going to get back there and face whatever waiting for us there."

"If we get there alive."

"I'm starting to think if Barrett is even slightly smart, he and his grunts gave up on us and went back."

"So we get back and then what?"

"With any luck, we'll at least come in second in our group."

"You think that's lucky? We could have won and gotten out of the tests!"

"We could come in last and fail. Coming in second at least gives us a shot at passing."

"This isn't fair!" Ethan barked. "I should have been with the first group. It wasn't supposed to happen like this. No Lazarus in history has ever failed."

"And you haven't failed yet!" Jenna said as she took Ethan by the collar of his shirt. Their eyes locked and while she saw his raw, unfiltered fear in his eyes, he could see the fiery determination in hers. She released him and he fell back down to the ground.

"You really believe all that?"

"I really have no choice. When you're at the end of the universe, you either believe you can be saved, or you die and I haven't gone through everything I've gone through just to die. Have you?" She asked. Ethan leaned up onto his elbows and for the first time since she had met him, he smiled.

"Not a chance."

Chapter 25

Life and Death

Jenna and Ethan said a quiet prayer before setting out to return to the testing facility. She tried to sound confident for Ethan's benefit, but she knew as well as he did that the threat of Barrett was all too real. She took comfort that she still had not seen or heard any activity in the area and the further they traveled the more confident she was that he and his followers had left. She then began to worry what they would be returning to.

Everything was a blur and she wasn't even sure how much time had passed since the survival challenge began. It felt to her like it had been weeks. She couldn't remember the last time she was able to stop for even a second and allow her brain to stop. She was becoming convinced even if she survived the tests, the stress would end up killing her.

The sky was growing black above them but what little of the terrain she could see was looking familiar to her. Her heart was pounding in her chest. She thought back to the first time she had ever ridden a roller coaster. She remembered waiting in that line feeling her stomach hop and her heart skip as she saw the coaster roar across the track. She knew in her brain there was no real danger, but in her heart the danger was real. She recalled her father taking her hand and squeezing. She looked up at him and he smiled at her.

"It only looks worse than it really is," He said as he knelt down to meet her eyes. "Our minds play tricks and when we're scared, they make everything scarier to us."

"Why?"

"Because there's a part of everyone that wants to run away when things get hard, but you have the power to be brave and get past the fear. It's like a test your brain puts to you to see how worthy you are. If you can pass, there's no limit to what you can do." His words echoed in her mind for years after that moment and whenever Jenna felt any kind of fear, she remembered that day and his words.

They began to break through new territory and Jenna was pleased with their progress. She glanced over and saw Ethan keeping pace with her quite well. While he was keeping up, he did look as though if he stopped for even a brief moment, he would collapse. She was thinking it was the first time he ever had to really work for anything.

"How much further?" He asked.

"Just keep going! Harder to hit a moving target!" Jenna's heart started to race. She felt they were close. She knew it couldn't be much longer and as they came upon the rise, she saw the lights of the testing facility glowing in the distance. She could see the gates and most importantly, she could see people walking the perimeter. She let out a loud cry and she began to push herself even harder. Her legs were on fire and it felt as though the muscles in her thighs were going to burst through her flesh. She heard Ethan close behind. Her vision started to grow dark. Her brain was on fire. She felt her feet finally hit the asphalt. She tried to pump her legs harder, trying to go faster. Her legs were shooting with pain. She saw the entrance of the testing facility. It was so close she thought for a moment it was an illusion, but as she heard the voices of other people growing louder, she knew it was real. She had made it and when she realized that, she stopped and her legs gave out almost instantly. She tried to keep her eyes open, but they shut against her will and the sound of panicked voices surrounding her filled her ears. She couldn't pick up what they were saying as she finally gave in to her fatigue.

It felt like it has been days until the light returned to her eyes. Her vision was blurry and she could only see shapeless blobs in white. Her vision began to return and she saw that she was in a hospital room. There were tubes stuck in her arms and her legs were bandaged up.

Panic took her over but as she attempted to get out of the bed, she discovered that her legs weren't as cooperative as she thought they would be. She could feel, but they just weren't strong enough to move.

"Help!" She called out. The door flew open and three nurses came running in and started tending to the machines that she was hooked up to. She was absolutely confused. She tried to ask what was going on, but no one seemed to even notice she was in the room.

"Enough!" An authoritative voice called out. Jenna saw an older woman walk through the door into the room. She had short, dark red hair and was wearing a neatly pressed white lab coat over a rather drab gray suit. The nurses finished what they were doing and filed out as quickly as they could. The older woman looked over at Jenna and smiled.

"Look who's finally up."

"Who are you? Where am I?"

"I'm Dr. Miller. As for where you are, this is the medical ward of this testing facility. You were found collapsed outside the main entrance. We've been very concerned about you and Mr. Lazarus."

"Things got a little out of control out there."

"You don't have to tell me. We know all about Barrett and everything he did to pass this survival challenge."

"You do? Did he confess?"

"No. We reviewed the footage."

"What footage? What are you talking about?"

"The test was monitored at all times."

"Wait. They saw everything that was happening? They saw it all and did nothing?" Jenna's head was becoming warm which was normal when she was on the verge of losing her temper.

"It is not the place of the Testing Committee to interfere with the tests in any way. There was nothing that could be done."

"Innocent people were killed! I don't see how nothing could be done!"

"I don't know what to tell you. It is a harsh reality, but it's just the way it is. I'm sorry." Jenna felt too weak to argue anymore. The weight of the previous days was falling down upon her so quickly.

"What about Barrett? What's going to happen to him?"

"I know you don't want to hear this, but he and his group have been passed. While the actions of Barrett and his group cannot be condoned, the rules of the test have enabled them to evade charges."

"They killed those kids! They killed Mark! Just because it was in the name of the tests they walk?"

"I'm sorry, but yes."

"What about me? Did I fail?"

"No. You and Mr. Lazarus made it, just barely, into the second tier. While you did not earn an automatic pass, you both will go on to the next phase of the test."

"After everything we went through?"

"I'm sorry, but the point of these tests is to weed out the weak from the strong and the rules must be adhered to."

"So why am I here?"

"Because when you came back to us, you were in pretty bad shape. Nothing serious, but we just need to keep you rested for a couple days. After that, you may resume the tests."

"Yay." Jenna said with little enthusiasm. Dr. Miller then walked up to Jenna and smiled.

"It was impressive how you survived. I'm not really at liberty to say officially, but coming in the way you did pretty much assures that you will pass these tests."

"Really?"

"I know it may seem hard to believe now, but I had to face my tests as well. As you can see, I made it, but only barely. There was one girl in my group who just amazed everyone. Skilled and smart. I've seen your results up until now. She didn't do half as well as you."

"Thanks."

"Just get some rest. The sooner you finish these tests, the sooner you can get to the rest of your life."

Jenna finally settled into her rest. There was so much on her troubled mind, but rest was all she could handle. She drifted blissfully into her slumber and swam in the deepest depths of her dreams. She saw a world past the tests. She saw her family and her friends. She could even see college and all the amazing things she would be able to do. She felt her life blooming before her and all she had to do was pass one more test.

She was pulled from her fantasies by a sharp finger poking at her arm. She opened her eyes and saw Ethan standing over her bed.

"Did I wake you?" He asked. He was wearing a robe over his hospital gown and was holding himself up on a pair of crutches.

"Yes, but it's okay. What's going on?"

"I couldn't sleep until I knew you were okay. These doctors don't tell you much."

"Where did they put you?"

"In the room next door actually."

"They let you out of your bed?"

"No, but it's late and the nursing staff at night don't really care what we do. I just wanted a chance to thank you."

"For what?"

"What do you mean 'for what'? You saved my life. If it weren't for you, I'd still be out there. I don't know how you did it."

"Sometimes you just have to push past the fear."

"I mean, why did you save me? I'm the grandson of the man who started these tests. I don't think there's a single person here who wouldn't have gladly hung me out to dry. You could have just left me to rot."

"That's not how I do it. You're not to blame for what your family has done. Besides, honestly? If I let you die and I passed, I'm sure your family would do everything in their power to ruin my life."

"You're probably right. My father can be very vindictive."

"I also did it because it was the right thing to do." Jenna said with a smile.

"I won't forget it. Thank you."

"You're welcome. Now get back to your room and let me sleep. These tests aren't over yet."

Chapter 26

Road to Recovery

After the first night in the medical ward, Jenna felt her strength returning to her. She was adequately hydrated and the pain in her legs was easing away. She was able to stand under her own power and the headaches she had been experiencing were gone. She felt as though she could conquer the world, but the doctors insisted she take one more day before resuming the test.

As the physical tests had concluded and all information about the strength and ability of all subjects had been recorded. The next phase of the test was to gauge mental ability and intelligence. The following tests were to take the form of a series of standardized tests. Jenna felt a bit of relief in that. She wasn't ready to get back into any intense physical training again. She was glad that all she had to do to prepare for the next tests was simply open books.

Several textbooks were sent to her room so that she could get a jump on her studies. The subjects of all the books varied and ranged from simple arithmetic to advanced world history and everything in between. A letter came with the books and advised that the upcoming tests would encompass each and every subject. It was daunting, but Jenna dove in.

She was in deep concentration as she read through her books. Much of the material was familiar. It seemed the tests would be at the level she was at in school, which made her a bit more confident. A familiar voice broke her concentration.

"Hi." Violet said. Jenna looked up and as her eyes fell upon Violet, her anger rose up.

"Violet? What are you doing here? I thought you passed. Along with Barrett."

"He sold me out. He said that the whole thing was my idea and cut a deal for him and the rest of his group."

"Wow. Who would think a psychopath couldn't be trusted?"

"I'm sorry, Jenna," Violet began, but as she took a step forward, Jenna threw her hand up, halting her.

"Not another step. You turned on me out there. You were actually going to kill me."

"I was desperate. You don't understand."

"The Hell I don't!" Jenna barked. "We are all under the gun here! All of us! You were on my team! I trusted you!"

"I didn't think I was going to make it. I was scared."

"Again. So is everyone else. I think that's the one great thing about the tests. It's the equalizer. We all have the same amount of risk on the table, which means there's no reason to turn on each other. We all risk the same thing. Our lives."

"I know there's really nothing I can say to make this better, but I am sorry."

"Fine," Jenna said as she returned to her books. "You're sorry. Got it. Good bye." Jenna could feel Violet's eyes on her; waiting for something to be said, but Jenna had nothing more to say. She realized they hadn't known each other for long and they hadn't really been such good friends, but her betrayal was stinging all the same. It wasn't as though she had told someone something about her behind her back or had done any other thing anyone in the world would consider a direct betrayal. She had directly threatened her life and that was something not many could forgive, and Jenna would not be ashamed to say she was among those. The sound of footsteps walking away down the hall caught Jenna's ear and she looked up. Violet was gone and while she felt smiling would be an appropriate reaction, she only felt sad in her heart. She had never liked turning cold on anyone, but after what Violet had done, she saw no other option.

The day drew on and Jenna had worked her way through nearly half of her text books. Her eyes began to ache and she leaned back against her pillow, thinking the time for a break had come. She stared up at the ceiling and closed her eyes and envisioned her corneas relaxing at long last. All the facts and figures danced in her brain. Then smoky shadows of the past ordeal began to crop up. She saw Mark's body on the ground. It was so clear in her imagination. Every detail was there and it was like she was staring down at his lifeless body all over again. Her eyes popped open and she bolted up from her all too brief rest. Her thoughts were a dizzying swirl and she wasn't sure how she could keep any facts straight in her head while she was still reeling from her moment of survival.

"You okay?" Ethan asked. Jenna looked up and saw Ethan stroll in.

"No crutches?"

"Don't need them. How are you feeling?"

"Physically, better."

"What about non-physically?"

"I'm not sure. I've been studying for the test tomorrow, but all I can think about is the past few days."

"I know. I'm having the same problem. How do they expect us to just get over all of that?"

"I don't know, but we're going to have to. They aren't going to change the rules for us. Not even you." Jenna said with a smirk.

"Don't think I haven't thought about it, but you're right. Maybe if we could study together that would help."

"Together?"

"Sure. I think it might help me if there was someone who could kind of keep me focused. I crack those books open and five minutes later I'm face down on my pillow."

"I don't know how much help I can be."

"It would mostly be moral support. Please?"

"Fine," Jenna said with a hesitant smile. "I guess it would be nice to have someone else in the room."

"I'll get the books."

Chapter 27

The Returning Hero

The next morning, Jenna and Ethan were released from their medical care and deemed fit to continue their test. Jenna was actually relieved to be up and walking again. When she returned to her dorm building, she noticed there were a lot fewer girls and it was a lot quieter. She opened the door to her room and there was a sense of comfort as she looked upon her bed, untouched and waiting for her. She then looked to the other side of the room and as she expected, all of Violet's things were gone. They had told her Violet had been moved to another room on another level. While there wasn't much that could be done, the people in charge at least agreed sharing a room with someone who tried to kill her was unacceptable.

Jenna flopped down on to her bed and she welcomed the expected creaking of the springs of the mattress. She could hear the sink dripping in the bathroom and the unmistakable aroma of cheap perfume and cheap weed still haunted the air. It felt to her like almost a lifetime since she had seen those walls and she was surprised by how much she missed it.

After a few more minutes of reacquainting herself with her room, she sat down at her desk and returned to her studying. She was told the first series of tests were to begin after noon that day so she only had a few hours left to prepare. She opened up the last book she was studying from and tried to pick up where she had left off. It was difficult to concentrate. Her mind was still a swirl of thoughts and emotions. She tried to push away the nightmares she had lived through if only long enough to get through the test. She was so close and she couldn't bear failing after enduring so much. She blocked away all her stray thoughts, but then she thought once more about Mark. The image of him on the ground, lifeless, kept flashing across her mind. The concept of him being gone was still so hard for her to grasp. She was planning on forgiving him after the tests were complete. She knew, in her heart, what happened at the party was just a stupid mistake. She and Mark had something deeper and she didn't want to throw it away and she was sure he didn't want to either. She could see it all.

After their test results came in, they would meet and share the good news that they both passed and that was when Jenna would tell him that she forgave him and they could be together again. She had even thought of finally giving him what he's been wanting for so long because she had come to want it too. She felt the time to take the relationship to the next level had come and she was ready to be with him physically. It wasn't as though she hadn't thought about it before, but lately, the urge to be with him like that was growing stronger and more urgent. It wasn't that she was afraid she would lose him. She just felt she wanted to be that close.

The end of the test was going to be the beginning of a new life for them both. She wanted to share that with him, but it seemed everything had changed and she wasn't sure what she was going to do. She looked down at her book and noticed tiny drops on the page and she reached up to her face and realized she was crying. She shut the book and leaned back in her chair and took a deep breath. Everyone had been telling her how important it was to get past the pain, but she couldn't do that anymore. He was gone and it felt like it was finally really hitting her.

The tears didn't stop and soon she felt her stomach seize up. She finally allowed herself the grief and she cried for almost a solid hour. She screamed and prayed and did anything and everything she could to express her pain. She leapt up onto her mattress and started punching it. She thought of the tests and Barrett and Curtis and everything and with all of that rage, she punched away. She hit her mattress over and over with growing force. Eventually, she managed to break through the sheets and through the mattress itself. Her hand slid through and she could feel the springs scratching against her flesh. After a few moments, she stopped and she noticed the deep scratches that covered her hands.

Jenna ran to the bathroom and ran her hands under the water in the sink. She wiped away the blood and tended to the scratches with the first aid kit that was still in the medicine cabinet.

Once she was done and her hands were well bandaged, she returned to her desk and sat down. She resolved to pass the test because she knew that was what Mark would want. He wanted her to survive and she would; for herself and for him.

Chapter 28

Finals

Jenna emerged from her room and saw that she had fifteen minutes until the final test was to begin. She let out a deep breath and started down the hall. She saw others stepping out from their dorms. They funneled through quietly and it felt like a death march. No glances or passing smiles. Jenna looked around and saw only dead faces with tear stained eyes. Some of the girls were trembling as they prodded themselves on.

When Jenna finally stepped outside, she was somewhat relieved to see the sky and it was even more reassuring to see so many other kids bustling around the campus. It almost felt normal. For just the briefest of moments, she actually was able to forget about the test. It was just a normal day, but that relief was gone all too quickly and her stress fell back upon her shoulders like a lead weight.

As she walked across the campus to the building her group was supposed to meet in, her stomach started to jump. A sharp pain grew deep inside of her guts and she wanted to turn and run back to her dorm room. She just wanted it to be over. She looked around hoping to find Ethan's face among the crowd, but there was no sign of him. She was even hoping to see Violet. Any familiar face would be a blessing. She thought about Aggy and how if she were there she'd be able to make it better, but she was alone; more alone than she had ever been in her life.

She was directed upon entry to a large meeting room off of the lobby. It looked like a classroom from a college movie. There were long rows of seats that were stacked over each other like a stadium and they all seemed to curve so as to force everyone's eyes to the front of the room where there was a lone desk.

Many of the seats were already taken but Jenna spotted a free seat at the end of one of the rows. She sat down at it as quickly as she could. She kept thinking to herself that the sooner it began, the sooner it would be over. She sat quietly as more people filed in and soon every seat was taken and the room went quiet. The doors shut and it was like everyone could feel everyone else's pulses shoot through the roof.

There was a door near the desk at the front of the room and it opened up. A man stepped out. He didn't look familiar to Jenna. He was dressed in a nicely fitted black suit and held a briefcase in his hand. He walked over to his desk and set the case down on it. He looked up and scanned the room carefully.

"Good afternoon," He said. There was no response. "I understand what you all must be feeling right now, believe it or not, and I am sorry how troubled you all must be. I wish I could assure you all that this will be easy and you will pass, but the reality is there will be a number of you who will fail. The sooner you accept that reality, the easier it will be for you in the future."

He opened the briefcase and took out a thick stack of papers. As he set them upon the desk, he looked back up at the kids. He smiled and when Jenna saw it, a chill ran down her back.

"This isn't the test. These are just some forms you need to fill out before you take the test," He then began to distribute the forms. Jenna took hers and she scanned it quickly. It looked like some kind of con-tract. "This is a consent form that states you agree to accept the results of the test, no matter the outcome. I will admit that in the past it was not unheard of for families to sue when the results of their test were not what they hoped for. I'm sure it's been said before, but once more, these tests are designed to test your strength on every level. They are not biased or stacked against anyone. The results are verified three times and are genuine. Please keep that in mind as you continue on from this point."

After reading through the forms carefully, Jenna signed them and soon she saw others signing as well. It took some time for them all to be collected, but once they were, the man stacked them neatly and put them back into his briefcase.

Everyone was then instructed to separate into their groups. Jenna was told her group would be convening on the third floor. She passed on the elevators and decided rather to take the stairs. It would give her some few precious moments of peace, she thought. She trudged up the stairs as slowly as she could manage but as she reached the landing on level two, she accepted that there was no point in putting off the inevitable.

Jenna made it to the third floor and she saw the room where she was intended to go. She walked in and it looked like a classroom proper. There were six rows of desks, seven desks per row. There was no one else there yet, so Jenna thought she was the first. She took a seat in the middle of one of the rows. She wasn't sure what difference it would make if she sat in the front or in the back.

"Oh!" A voice called from behind. Jenna turned and saw a woman racing in. She was also in a conservative suit with her red hair done up in a tight bun. "You're early. I think the rest of your group is outside in the hall. I guess they're enjoying these last few moments before the shit hits the fan." She was carrying two large cases in her hands. She set them upon the desk at the front of the room. Jenna's heart skipped.

"Are those the tests?" Jenna asked.

"Yes," The woman said as she slapped her hand on one of the cases. "I'm Rita Harrison and I will administer your test today." She said as she walked over to Jenna; offering her hand.

"Jenna Holdren." Jenna said with a forced smile.

"Good to meet you," Rita looked back at Jenna with a look of fascination. "I can only imagine what's going through your mind right now. I remember when I was taking my test. My stomach was in a knot three days before. How are you holding up?"

"Still standing."

"That you are. You look like you'll do well."

"How can you tell?"

"I've been doing this a long time. I can't qualify this with anything scientific, but I've just developed a kind sense about who will pass and who will fail. For what it's worth, you've got 'pass' written all over you."

"Thanks." Jenna said. The remaining kids in Jenna's group began to come in and they took their seats quickly and quietly. Jenna turned for a moment and she saw Violet sitting down at one of the desks at the very back. Their eyes locked for a second but then Jenna turned away.

Once everyone was seated, Rita shut the door and took her place in the front of the room. She clapped her hands together and smiled.

"Good afternoon, everyone. My name is Rita Harrison and I will be administering your test today. This portion of the examination will take about four hours to complete. You will be permitted two bathroom breaks. After this test you will have a one hour break and then return for the second portion; which you will have another four hours to complete. When the test is complete, you may return to your dorm rooms. Test results will be posted on Friday morning. Good luck to you all." Rita then turned to her desk and opened one of her cases. There was a large stack of thick booklets inside and she grabbed an armful. She began to pass them out. She set a booklet on Jenna's desk and Jenna looked back at her.

"Is this the test?" She asked.

"All forty pages. My advice would be not to rush. Use the four hours."

After the test books were distributed, Rita then passed out pencils and informed them if they needed more, they had only to ask. Jenna looked down at her test book and laid her hand upon it. It was much larger than she thought it would be. She slid her fingers along the spine of the book. After so long of picturing the moment, to have the actual test sitting in front of her was almost beyond comprehension. Her entire life, or death, sat before her. There were a few spouts of crying coming from all around the room. The boy sitting next to Jenna seemed to be keeping it inside, but he was shaking as he clutched his desk and tears were pouring down his cheek.

"All right," Rita said as she sat at her desk. "You may begin." Everyone opened up their books at the same time and they buried their heads down. Jenna flipped through the pages to the first question. She stared at the page and for a moment, it looked like all the words were blurring in her vision. She tried to read the first question, but as she read it to herself, the meaning became tangled. She then slammed her fists against her forehead. She looked around, afraid her tantrum was being noticed, but everyone was focused on their own tests. Jenna looked back down at the page and it was normal and she could read the words clearly. She set her pencil to the paper and filled in the first question.

The questions started out easy, she felt. She almost felt foolish for having spent so much time studying. She was able to get through twenty pages of the test with confidence in her answers, but she noticed they did begin to become more difficult. She looked up and was shocked to have seen over two hours had passed. She pushed through the remainder of the test and toward the end; the questions were challenging her beyond what she thought she could do. She could feel sweat forming along her forehead. At one point, she found herself reading the same question over and over again without realizing it.

When Jenna finally got to the last question, she almost came to tears. Her hand was trembling. She answered it and with a heave of relief, she closed the book. She leaned back in her chair and saw she had finished only ten minutes early. She looked back down at the book and doubt began to creep through her mind. Certain questions came back to her mind and she was starting to doubt her answers. All the possibilities were rushing back to her. She reopened the book and scanned through as many pages as she could manage. It was blur of words and answer bubbles.

"Time." Rita announced. Everyone set their pencils down and shut their books. Everyone got up and hurried out of the room. Jenna just kept staring at the book on her desk. Rita came up to her and took it away.

"I answered them all." Jenna said.

"Most kids do. I think four hours is a little more than is needed. How do you think you did?"

"I don't know. I thought I was doing okay at first, but it got so hard. I can't even remember most of my answers."

"Don't worry. I'm sure you did fine. Go and relax. Get something to eat. This isn't over yet."

Chapter 29

Accounts Due

As Jenna looked down at the lunch on her tray, she wondered if anyone in charge cared that a cheese sandwich with tomato soup was hardly a fitting final meal. She was curious who came up with that day's menu and what the other options were available. She felt since it was the day of the final test they would have served something a little more impressive. She thought they would have at least had a sundae bar or something fun. She obsessed over the food, hoping to keep any thoughts about the test away from her conscious mind.

She sat down and noted how quiet it was. Everyone was shambling around like zombies. She saw a few kids trying to eat, but before they could take a bite, they broke out in tears. Jenna set down her sandwich and chose to eat her soup first. She wasn't totally sure if she'd be able to keep anything solid down anyway.

As Jenna slid the spoon into her mouth, she saw Violet approaching. Her upset stomach no longer bothered her as rage began to replace any anxiety she had been feeling. By her trajectory, Jenna knew where Violet was going.

"Hi," Violet said in a small voice as she stood before Jenna. "I know you hate me and I don't blame you, but I was just wondering if I could just sit here. You don't have to talk. I just don't think I could stand to sit alone."

"There are other tables. Ask someone else."

"I would except everyone knows what happened out there and they don't like me very much anymore either."

"Yet you come to the person you actually tried to kill. Interesting logic."

"Look, I'm sorry. I know saying that is nothing in light of what I did, but I don't know what else I can say. I was scared."

"You were the one saying you actually wanted to fail the test. You said you didn't care."

"That was before it was so real. I got scared and I made a desperate and stupid choice."

"Especially since you got sold out."

"And I'm paying for it."

"You're paying for it? We could have gotten through the survival challenge and maybe even placed first. We would have passed and been back home by now!"

"I know!" Violet whined. "I'm,"

"No!" Jenna barked as she cut Violet off. "I don't think I could stand to hear you say that word again."

"You're the closest thing to a friend I have here anymore. May I just sit with you?" Jenna leaned back in her chair and thought about the request. She looked around the room and everyone was staring at them. She looked back up at Violet and saw the tears streaking down her cheeks. She was alone; as alone as anyone could ever be and there were so many times that Jenna felt the same way when she first arrived. Even with Aggy along, she felt alone and vulnerable and it was the worst feeling she had ever felt.

"You don't speak a word."

"Yes! Thank you." Violet said as she took her seat. Jenna glared at her for a moment longer and then went back to eating her lunch.

After lunch, everyone went back to their testing rooms. It was a quiet and solemn march for everyone. Jenna and her group filed back into their room and took their seats with no ceremony or noise. Rita was sitting at her desk and was smiling, which kind of annoyed Jenna. There was no malice behind it; it just felt like it was inappropriate. There was no joy to be had in that room and to act as if there were, was a crime.

Rita stood and came around to the front of her desk. Her smile glared over the room and Jenna could sense she wasn't the only one annoyed with it.

"Before I distribute the second half of this test, I just wanted to let you know, on behalf of myself and the United States Government, how proud of you we all are. This isn't an easy thing to do and it is gratifying to see so many of you showing such strength and courage. I remember the day of my final tests. I don't think I have ever been so scared in my life. I realize the reality is that some of you will not pass. I'm sure that's a reality you've come to accept as well, which makes you all the more brave in my opinion. As we move into this final stage of the test, I would like to advise you all to not give up. It may seem ridiculous to you now, but it has been known to happen that some people break under the pressure and actually forfeit the test; which at this point would lead to an automatic fail. I know it seems hard and hopeless to you, but it is far better to see this through to the end than to just quit. Keep strong." Rita then proceeded to hand out the test booklets.

The new booklets were a little thinner than the first ones, which Jenna thought was good. She opened it up and scanned the first page. The questions seemed normal. She then flipped through the rest of the booklet, hoping to spot any trouble ahead. There were much fewer math sections than in the first one, but there were many more essay questions. Jenna hated those the most because it was hard to concentrate enough to string a coherent thought together in her head much less write it down. She flipped back to the front of the booklet and then Rita signaled for them to begin.

Jenna leaned over her test and focused everything on it. The questions didn't seem to get any harder, but they were still exceptionally challenging. They depth of knowledge dipped a little further than her textbooks had equipped her for. She found herself guessing more than she was comfortable with.

The room was quiet as they took the test. It seemed the maddening terror had finally settled into a simple, persistent fear. All that could be heard was the sound of pencils rubbing against paper. Jenna kept answering the questions and flipping over page after page. She wasn't even paying attention to how far she was getting. She just focused what she was doing at that moment. Time blurred in her head. It wasn't even a consideration. She just wanted to answer the questions and get out.

When Jenna flipped over to the last page, she was startled. She looked up and saw that she had only ten minutes left until the test was over. She scanned the page and thankfully she found the final questions to be rather easy. She answered them all and just as she shut the booklet, the time ticked over and it was over. Some kids who had not finished threw their pencils to the floor in frustration. Rita stood up once more and harnessed the room's attention.

"The time is up. Please pass the booklets forward, whether they are completed or not. I would assure you all though, that a finished test does not mean you have passed any more than an incomplete test means you have failed. Whatever answers you have left will be taken into account in the final tally. The results will be processed and you will be notified no later than Friday morning. Your families will be notified to come pick you up after the test results are final, but they will not reveal the exact results until they arrive here. Until then, try and relax and enjoy your time. There will be special events throughout the campus to entertain you and the library will be open all day and night for your convenience."

Jenna raised her hand as a nagging question troubled her.

"How will we get our results?" A light went on in Rita's eyes and she went into her desk and pulled out a small box.

"I'm glad you reminded me," She said. She opened the box and took out a small black device. It looked like a small phone. She held it up for everyone to see. "This little device is wired to the main data banks and your test results will be sent directly to it. Keep it with you at all times." She said. She then proceeded to hand out the devices to everyone and as they took it, they were dismissed."

Jenna walked with the crowd out of the building. All the while, she heard murmurs from all around lamenting answers they should have given or crying over how they were sure that they had failed. Jenna just wanted to get to her room and be alone. She saw a few new flyers being put up advertising some of the special functions that were supposed to distract everyone from the fact they may not have long to live. She doubted some pointless concert by a local band would alleviate anyone's stress.

Jenna finally got to her dorm and rushed in, slamming the door behind her. She dove onto the bed and as soon as she pushed her face against the pillow, she began to cry. It felt like years of sorrow was pouring out of her in one terrible torrent. Her stomach was seizing up but she didn't want to move. She didn't want to eat or drink. She didn't even want to listen to any music. Her only solace was lying on her bed, curled up and sobbing like a newborn babe. Waiting for the rest of her life to be decided.

Chapter 30
Waiting is the Hardest Part

Jenna had fallen asleep and as she woke, she saw light pour in from the window. It was morning but that brought her no comfort. All she had to look forward to was a day of waiting to find out if she had passed or failed. Just the thought of waiting for that news all day made her stomach ache all over again.

She got up and realized she was still in her clothes. She thought that she should shower and change, but as she took her first step to the bathroom, she wondered why to even bother. While the test results were not in, it still felt like the end of the world to her. She was staring at a wall of fire and all there was to do was wait for it to come and swallow her up whole. She fell back onto the bed, feeling hopeless once more. She thought of going out to get something to eat, but she knew everyone out there would just tell her how she had to be positive and to be strong and have faith in your strength and those words, she knew, would feel like sandpaper along an open wound. She didn't want any encouragement and she didn't want any inspirational quotes. She wanted things to be normal, as they were before the tests. She wanted to be home and secure that there was a future ahead of her. She knew there was no promise of that and therefore, there was no reason to go out.

Jenna fell stretched out on her bed and stared up at the ceiling as she forced herself to sleep. She closed her eyes and let her mind wander in hopes she could just fall asleep again; but the more she tried to do it, the more anxious her thoughts became. After an hour of trying, she sat up in frustration, threw her pillow across the room and then stormed into the bathroom and had a shower.

Jenna walked out to the quad outside of her dorm building and it seemed everyone shared her concern. There was no laughter or high spirits. Everyone was shambling along like zombies. It appeared the staff was doing everything they could to help, but it wasn't enough. There were fliers and signs for all kinds of shows and events throughout the day, but it didn't seem anyone cared. Jenna went on to the cafeteria. As upset as she was, her stomach was beginning to require attention.

She walked into the cafeteria and there were more dispirited kids inside. The aroma of waffles and cinnamon permeated the air. Jenna saw that they were offering an honest to God brunch buffet with everything from eggs to sushi. However upset she was, she couldn't take her eyes off the spread. She then decided the only thing worse than being depressed was being depressed and hungry, so she went on to fix that problem.

After she ate, Jenna went back to her room and hoped to be able to sleep some more, but it wasn't working. She then went down to the library. She reasoned that it would be quiet and reading always helped her in times of stress. When she got there, it was empty except for the librarian. She nodded hello and went on to find something to read. She scanned the shelves and just grabbed books. She didn't even look at them; she just needed something to distract her.

Jenna took a seat at one of the tables and set the books beside her. She had gathered a collection of novels and research books and even a few magazines. She set the first book in front of her and started to read. She read the first page nearly twenty times in a row until she realized her brain wasn't letting the information in. Once she got to the bottom of the page, her fears would creep in and everything she had read blurred in her mind. The words became nonsense and it was like she was reading something in another language. After two hours of this, she began to develop a headache and went back to her room to lie down.

Jenna spent the rest of the day desperately trying to occupy her mind but everything resulted in a headache. By about five in the evening, she relegated herself to her room. The day was nearly over and she still hadn't gotten her results. She wasn't sure if it was a good sign or a bad one. She was trying once more to sleep, hoping she would wake up beyond the test and past all the worry, but he was disturbed by a knock on her door.

"What?" She barked as she opened her door.

"Hi." Ethan said.

"Ethan. Hi. What are you doing here?"

"I came by because I wanted to thank you."

"For what?"

"What do you think? You saved my life."

"I thought you already thanked me for that."

"Only with words, but I've been trying to find a way to really say it, and I think I've found it. I need you to come with me."

"What?"

"Come with me. Please." Jenna did not want to leave, but her curiosity was pleasantly taking up most of her thoughts. She hoped whatever he was going to show her would help her to avoid worrying for a little bit more.

Ethan took Jenna back to the medical building. She tried to ask where he was taking her, but he was insistent that it be a surprise. They walked through the doors and none of the staff stopped them as they proceeded into the restricted areas.

"Uh," Jenna began.

"Don't worry," Ethan said. "I've cleared us both. We can go anywhere. Come on."

They took the elevator up to the fourth level, which required the use of a key. Jenna's curiosity was growing. She wasn't sure if she should be excited or scared. Maybe Ethan was going to take her to have her brain swapped out or to be part of some insane experiment that would have her dismissed from the test.

They came upon a hall that looked like a real hospital and at the end of the hall was a closed door. Next to the door was a window with blinds which were shut. Ethan took Jenna to the door and then stopped as he turned to face her.

"I need you to stand right here." He said as he positioned her in front of the window.

"What is this?"

"You'll see. Just wait here." He said as he went into the room and shut the door behind him. After a few minutes, the blinds began to move. They opened and then she saw a bed inside the room. There was someone in the bed. It was hard to tell who it was. They were asleep with tubes coming out all over the place. They also had casts on their arms and legs. Jenna stepped closer and she could see the person's face. Her legs began to shake.

"Mark?" She uttered. She ran into the room and Ethan caught her.

"Easy. Easy."

"It's Mark! He's alive!"

"Yes. I know he doesn't look so great now, but he's alive."

"Can I talk to him?"

"He's in a medically induced coma, for his own good; but the doctors are assured that he will make it through."

"I don't understand this. How? I saw him dead out there!"

"It was close, but they managed to get to him just in time. I know it's horrible that they allowed it to happen, but at least they saved him."

"Please don't expect me to be grateful to them for that. They only did it because if he did die, they would be facing legal action."

"You're probably right, but the important thing is he's going to live."

"They're letting you show this to me?"

"I managed to talk to my dad and he was able to arrange this for you. Right now only family members are allowed access to Mark, but I made your case and after some friendly pressure from the family, the ESA agreed."

"Blackmail?"

"Whatever works. I don't ask questions. The point is Mark's alive." Jenna walked over to the bed and took Mark's one good hand. She looked upon his broken and damaged body.

"He looks so peaceful." She said.

"Again, it's just a coma. He will wake up in a few days." Jenna then realized something and she was panicked again.

"But the test! He won't,"

"Automatic pass. After what he's been through, it was the least that could be done. Now after you pass, you two can be together again."

"How do you even know that's what I wanted?"

"I saw the two of you together. I'm not blind. I've instructed the doctors to notify you as well as his mother when he wakes up," A loud signal went off and Jenna and Ethan were surprised by it. They soon realized it was coming from Ethan's pocket. He produced the small device he had been given after his test. "Results are in." He said as he clicked on the small black machine. The screen lit up and he stared down at it. His eyes grew wide as he studied whatever it was he was seeing. He shut it off and held it to his chest. His face looked pained at first. He then looked Jenna in her eye and smiled. "I passed!" He exclaimed. Jenna leapt up and hugged him. She was happy for his good news, but all the while she was still worried about what she would hear. "Oh my God," Ethan said breathlessly. "I passed. I really passed."

"It's great, Ethan."

"Check yours. Maybe you got your results." Jenna took her device out, but there was no news.

"Nothing yet."

"I'm sorry."

"It's fine. It will come."

"I should go tell my dad the good news. I guess you and Mark can hang out for a bit, right?"

"Thanks." Ethan then ran out of the room. Jenna turned to Mark. She leaned over him and kissed him gently on his forehead. She just stared at him as she carefully traced her fingers through his hair.

Ethan brought Jenna back to her dorm room and as they came to her door, she was actually smiling.

"Thank you, Ethan. I know it couldn't have been easy to wrangle that favor."

"Don't worry about it. Seeing you smile is worth it."

"Good night. I guess I'll see you tomorrow."

"On the bus home, yes. I'm you'll pass."

"Thanks."

"Good night." Ethan said as he walked back down the hall. Jenna went into her room and went straight to her bed. She rested her head on the pillow and rejoiced that all her plans she had for her and Mark had not been destroyed after all. He would be fine and they could be together again. Her eyes were growing heavy the more she thought about it. Her peace was disturbed by the sound of her device signaling her results were in. She bolted up right and grabbed the device. She flipped it on and the words were on the screen. She had prepared herself for so long to see them, but it was a totally different thing to see them as a reality. She set the device down and simply fell back down on the pillow. It seemed all the worrying and waiting had exhausted her. At least, she thought, she knew at last.

Chapter 31

The Results Are In

The day had come at last: The final day. The main facility had been closed and all the dorms were empty. The kids were being instructed to go to the parking lot where their families would be waiting to either take them home or tell them good-bye. The buses were lined up and ready to take the failing groups on to the next phase. There was a reception area opposite that where families would come to claim their children. As Jenna approached, it looked like Heaven and Hell in the same place.

It wasn't hard to tell who was going where. The failing kids were gathered together and most of them were crying, as were their families who had just heard the news. Jenna's hands were getting sweaty as she waited for her family to come. She sat down on a small bench and waited. She jumped whenever she heard one of the buses rev up. They sounded like monsters roaring with rage.

Jenna saw Violet appear out of the crowd. Their eyes locked and she approached.

"Hi." Violet said.

"Hi." Jenna responded. Her voice was empty and soulless.

"I passed," Violet said with a little bounce.

"Great."

"I know you don't care and I'm probably wasting my breath, but once more, I'm sorry."

"I know. You're sorry and that's fine. You will have to live with what you did for the rest of your life. That's as much punishment as I can give you."

"If I could do it again,"

"Don't! Don't play that game with me. I don't care what you would do if you had another chance. I only care about what you DID do. That's what matters. That's what lasts. Good intentions aren't worth a whole lot if you don't live up to them."

"Good bye." Violet said sheepishly.

"Good bye."

It felt like hours were going by. The crowds were dwindling. There were only two buses left. Jenna checked her watch and was growing anxious. She saw one of the counselors walking by.

"Excuse me?" Jenna asked.

"Yes?"

"Do you know where I can find Ethan Lazarus is? I haven't seen him all day."

"Lazarus? He was picked up by his father last night."

"Last night?"

"Yes. I hate it when the government plays favorites too, but what can you do?"

Jenna sat back down, a bit disappointed. She had wanted to see him one last time before they departed. Despite everything, he had become rather endearing to her. She also wanted to thank him again for letting her know about Mark. She was happy to know that Mark would wake up and have the rest of his life to look forward to.

At last, Jenna saw her parents' car drive up. Her parents got out and her Brian and Bradley leapt out of the back seat. They all were running to her and they slammed into her with one great big hug. Her mother was crying and laughing at the same time.

"My baby! My baby!" She cried as she held Jenna close. Everyone was talking at once, patting her on the back and telling her how proud they all are. They were swarming in around her. She finally pulled back and stepped away.

"Stop!" She barked. Tears were starting to form in the corner of her eyes. They all looked at her in disbelief.

"Jenna? Baby? What is it? Wait. Don't. Whatever it is, you can tell us on the ride home." Her mother said.

"I'm not going home, Mom."

"What?" Her father asked. Jenna took out her test results and held them up for her family to see.

"I failed!" She said. "I failed the test."

"No," Her mother said. "No. No. NO! You passed! You had to! No! You passed!"

"I failed. I'm not here to be taken home. I'm here to say good-bye. That bus over there is for me."

"There has to be some mistake, Jenna." Her father offered.

"The results were verified, Dad. I failed and before I go, I want you all to know how much I love you," She turned to her brothers and narrowed her eyes. "You two have been pains in my ass for all my life, pretty much, but you have also been a couple of the best friends I've ever had. You watched over me when you could and I want you to know that I noticed. We've fought, but I never doubted that we loved each other." She said. Their only response was to start crying as they grabbed her into a tight hug.

"We can smuggle you out. No one will notice." Brian whispered. Jenna stepped back and smiled.

"If only it were that easy. I'm sorry," Jenna then turned to her mother, who was still crying uncontrollably. She reached out to her and as her hand got close; her mother snatched it and held it tightly in hers. "I'm sorry, Mom."

"No. Don't apologize. This isn't your fault. It's theirs. This has to be a mistake. They screwed up the scores or something. We're going to fight this," She said. "We'll take this to the highest court in the land. We'll get you a make-up test. We'll,"

"Mom! Stop," Jenna said, interrupting her mother. "You know as well as I do that no one has ever successfully challenged the results of the test. There's nothing that can be done."

"I don't care! We'll sell the house! We'll,"

"No, Mom. I don't want this to ruin your lives too. I've had months to prepare myself for this outcome and I am prepared. I was upset, to say the least, when I saw the results but I think I've accepted it. These are the rules and this is how it works. I love you and I want to know that you will all go on to live your lives after this. You remember what you told me when Gramma died? You told me she would always be with me as long as I remembered her."

"You're too young, baby. You're too young."

"It's not about being too young or old enough. Life can make sense and it can be random in equal parts. There's no way to know. I couldn't have asked for a better mother. You were always there when I needed you and sometimes when I didn't know I needed you. You made all the little pains go away and helped to ease the big ones. I love you." Jenna's mother couldn't speak through her tears, but threw her arms around her, holding her so tight she had to struggle to breathe.

Jenna then looked to her father who was clearly struggling to keep the tears back. He had his hand over his mouth as if he were holding it shut to keep from screaming. Jenna leaned in close to him and nudged his arm.

"Dad, what can I say? You always had to play bad cop, but even when you did I knew you loved us. I think it's because of you I'm so hard on myself. You wouldn't let us get away with anything and that has made me tougher on myself and I need to thank you for that. It isn't easy, but I know it's the better path. I love you and I am so sorry." Jenna said as she hugged him.

"Stop saying that," He whispered to her. "Your mother is right. This is not your fault. Don't think for a second that you didn't do everything you could. You gave it your best and for whatever reason, it didn't work out, but not because you didn't give it your all."

"I guess my all wasn't enough."

"It's not unheard of for mistakes to be made. I read an article that said nearly five percent of all test results have turned out to be wrong. We can fight this."

"Dad,"

"Look, you don't have any say in this. I have friends. I'm going to make some calls and we're going to figure this out. We have time. There have been a few cases in which test results were overturned."

"Too few to think it could happen now. Please, Dad, just don't waste your time."

"Nothing I can do to save the life of one of my children could ever be a waste of time. We're going to get you out of this. I promise you." Jenna just smiled at her father's pledge. They were scared and so was she. If there was a way they could rescue her, she would be all for it, but the odds of that happening were too great to even seriously consider.

With one last round of hugs and kisses, Jenna bid a final farewell to her family and gathered her things. She headed over toward the buses and she saw there was only one left. She walked over to it and the counselor standing by the door looked at her with tired, yet sympathetic eyes.

"Your results?" She asked. Jenna handed over the device and the counselor inspected it. "All right. You're clear. Take a seat on the bus. We should arrive to the camp before sundown. I am sorry."

"Thank you." Jenna said. She walked up onto the bus and she looked upon the other passengers. It was somber and heartbreaking as she looked upon their faces and saw their tear stained cheeks. Jenna found an empty seat at the back of the bus and she nestled in and shut her eyes. After a few more minutes, the door was closed and the bus revved to life. It shook slightly as it started up, but soon it became steady as it made it to the main road leading out of the facility. Jenna looked out the window and she saw her family still standing in the middle of the parking lot, waving at the bus as it left. She tried to smile, but it was too much of an effort. She pressed her head against the window and closed her eyes and just felt the steady vibration of the bus as it drove away.

END PHASE I

Thanks for reading this first installment of my new 'Tested' series. I am humbled and grateful for the time we have shared and I hope you enjoyed this book. Please read on for a preview of Phase II of Tested.

Chapter 1

The motion of the bus was smooth and almost comforting after a while. Jenna had fallen asleep at last, despite the many outbursts of crying from the other kids. It wasn't as though she really blamed them. They were being taken to the place where they would live until the day they'd be killed. There was no other reaction to have.

Their crying had eased back and Jenna came to the conclusion that everyone had gone past the point of tears. Crying was a function of fear and there was no more reason to be afraid. They knew what was waiting for them and there was no point in resisting or fighting it. Acceptance seemed to have settled in among them all, but that didn't mean they weren't still sad.

There was no one on the bus that Jenna recognized. There were a few she might have seen on the campus of the testing facility, but no one she had ever spoken to. She knew that none of them were from her group. She was among strangers, but that seemed to be a fact that brought her some comfort. There was no one there to coach her about looking on the bright side or explaining how they knew how she felt. During her time at the testing facility she had come to realize that sympathy could sometimes be a bad thing.

The sky was growing dark and Jenna was wondering when they were finally going to stop. The bus then came to a halt, as if in answer to her curiosity. No one made any moves to get off the bus. The longer they stayed on it, the further they were from death. The bus door opened and a man in a well-tailored suit came on board.

"Good evening, everyone," He said. "My name is Brad Dennison. I'm the director of this facility and I'd like to welcome you here to this resort. I am aware of the circumstances, and for that I am sorry, but I want to assure you all that my staff and I will be tireless in our efforts to make this time of your life the most comfortable and enjoyable you've ever experienced," His words did not rouse anyone and he knew that would be the case. "Your bags will be taken to your rooms for you. Take your time in adjusting. You can register at the front desk just beyond those doors," Brad said. Jenna glanced out the window and as dark as it was, she could tell they were parked in front of what looked like a rather high end hotel. "Whenever you are ready. There's no rush." He said and then got off the bus. Slowly some of the kids got up and went on into the hotel. Jenna took a breath and decided there was no point in putting off the inevitable. She got up and walked off the bus and proceeded into the hotel.

It was warm when she walked in and if felt as though she had walked onto a movie set. The light was dim and the floor was made of a smooth, white marble. Soft music was playing over the loudspeakers. Jenna walked up to the front desk where she was greeted by a bright young man with dark hair and sparkling green eyes.

"Welcome to The Hollow. What is the name?"

"Jenna. Jenna Holdren."

"Right," He said as he typed her name into the computer. He looked back at her and flashed that smile again.

"Right here. I understand why you are here and I am,"

"Please don't say you're sorry. I've been hearing that enough."

"Right. Then you in room two fifty three. Here's the key," He said as he slid a card key to her. "There is a full itinerary of activities for you to enjoy. All amenities will be free of charge, including room service and our spa services."

"Spa?"

"Yes." He said as he pointed toward a large sign that indicated there was a spa adjacent to the lobby.

"Well, it sounds great. If you don't mind me asking, is this a real hotel?"

"Of course. The management of The Hollow volunteers the services to the ESA every year. It's their way of doing what they can to ease your burden. They appreciate the sacrifice you're making. That is why all services are free. You aren't even expected to tip. There are even some services we provide that are 'off book'."

"Oh, okay. Well, I guess I'll just settle into my room."

"Wonderful idea. My name is Andrew, by the way. If you need anything, just ask for me."

"Thanks. I will." Jenna then headed for the elevators. Jenna approached the door to her room and with a trembling hand she jammed the key card into the door slot. It opened easily and she walked in and was hit by the unmistakable aroma of a hotel room. The air was so fresh and cool. The bed was made and the remote to the TV was sitting on the night table. She then went to the bathroom and it was sparkling clean. It was a far cry from her bathroom at her dorm and she realized she didn't have to share it with anyone. There was a full complement of luxurious soaps and lotions sitting next to the sink. She smiled a bit. It may have been the place she would die, she thought, but she was definitely going in style.

Dear Reader

CHAPTER 32

I want to thank you for reading the first part of my new series, 'Tested'. I hope you enjoyed it so far. I really enjoyed writing the character of Jenna Holdren. She's strong and knows her mind but still has a little vulnerability. She may have failed but she's not taking it lying down. Let me know if you want to know more. Find me on Facebook at WWW.Facebook.com/darrensloanwriter and let your voice be heard.

Sincerely,

D.S.

Tested
By
Darren Sloan

Also From Darren Sloan

<u>Jason of The Valley</u>
Jason of The Valley
Something's Always Wrong
No Good Without You
This Is Your Past
Beautiful Days
<u>Demon Hunters</u>
Demon Hunters
Second Coming
Love & Fire
Beginner Demon
Fable
Until The End of Time
<u>The Dark Books</u>
The Book of Morgan: Blood Is the New Black
The Book of Jackal: Bad Seed Rising
The Book of Jericho: Hell On Earth
<u>Miscellaneous</u>
Machine
House of Stolen Light
Copyright© 2017 Darren Sloan
All Rights Reserved
Chapter 1

CHAPTER 35

Sweet 16

It was the morning of August seventeenth, and everything looked just as it always did. The birds were singing as usual, the sound of Mr. Peterson's sprinklers echoed from across the street, and the sun was coming through the window over Jenna Holdren's bed.

Her eyes opened and for a few seconds, the world was normal, but once she had time to organize her thoughts, she remembered what day it was. It was exactly one week until her sixteenth birthday. Her heart felt heavy. She sat up in her bed and looked around her room. It had all the trappings of a typical teen girl. Her laptop was on her desk buried under a mountain of school papers and half read books. Her favorite pink hoodie was draped over the chair. Everything common and steady in her life became precious and special.

Jenna had thought she was prepared for the day to come. She had learned about it in school and her parents had explained about the tests since she was ten. She had all the information she needed, but as she looked over at her calendar and stared at the square with the number twenty-four in it, she wasn't sure she was as ready as she thought she was.

"Jenna! Breakfast!"

"Yeah, mom. I'm coming." Jenna slid out of her bed and threw on her robe. She walked over to the door, and she knew once she opened it, there was nothing she could do. There was nothing she could do if she chose to stay in her room either, but somehow she just felt safer sheltered in the walls over her private space. She took a breath and pulled the door open.

Jenna shuffled into the kitchen. Her brothers Bradley and Brian were fighting over the last strip of turkey bacon while their father had his eyes glued to his tablet.

"Jenna! What are you doing? Unless I missed a memo, you still have school today."

"I'll get dressed after breakfast."

"All right, but you're cutting it real close. Here." Jenna's mother slid a plate at the kitchen table in front of her chair, eggs and some fruit. Jenna slid down onto her seat and picked at her food a bit before finally taking a small bite. Brian and Bradley stopped their struggle for the last scrap of breakfast meat as they noticed their sister's odd behavior.

"Mom? You know what day it is today?"

"Trash day, I believe, right James?" Jenna's father looked up and directed his gaze at Bradley and Brian.

"Boys?"

"We took the trash out! I think Jenna means that it's a week before her birthday." A chill came over the room.

"Oh my god. That's right."

"Keep it together, honey." Jenna's father said.

"I will. I will." Jenna's mother looked over at Jenna with a forced smile, but the tears streaming down her cheeks broke the facade.

"I'm okay, mom. Dad. I know about the tests. I've had all this stuff drummed into me since middle school. I think it's just weird to me now because it's actually here. I'm not sure I totally believed this day would ever come. But here it is."

"I know, sweety, but," Her mother tried to complete her thought, but she ran off into the living room and the sound of her sobs could be heard.

"Finish your breakfast." He then ran after her into the living room.

"Hey, Jen," Brian whispered. "You don't have to freak out over this. Gary and I passed easy, and I was reading that in households with two or more kids, if one passes, they all pass. There's nothing you really have to do or know to get through it. Everything you need to pass is already in you."

"What if I fail?"

"You won't."

"But what if I do?" They both looked away. "I need to get dressed." Jenna got up and headed to the stairs. Along the way, she heard her father trying to calm her mother down. She could still hear them as she crept up the stairs.

Once she got to her room and shut the door, she finally was able to shut their voices out. It was times like that she was grateful her bedroom had an attached bathroom. It had proven time and time again to be a much-needed sanctuary in the darkest of times. She went into her bathroom and stood before the mirror. She noticed that her eyes were a little red and puffy. She reached up and noticed that she had been crying since she left the kitchen. She then turned on the water and filled the sink with cold water. She dipped her hands in and then splashed herself. The water was bracing on her skin. A shock ran up her spine and she scooped up some more water and continued to throw it onto her face. She then grabbed a towel and dried herself off.

She looked back in the mirror, and she could still see the redness in her eyes. She looked down at her modest collection and make-up and reached for her usual jar of foundation, but a sudden feeling of pointlessness came over her and she set it back down. She turned to her shower and switched the water on.

She let her robe drop to the floor and slipped out of her sleep clothes. She stepped into the stream of warm water and closed her eyes as it washed over her. The world outside was shut out and all she could hear was the water trickling past her ears. The water was hot, but she could still feel her tears slipping down her cheeks and then she felt the full force of her sobs rip through her. She fell to her knees as the water kept pouring down onto her.

After ten minutes, Jenna returned to the kitchen fully dressed and refreshed. She glanced at herself in the mirror in the hall and she looked normal. She was falling apart inside, but the world couldn't see that.

She saw that Brian and Bradley were still staring at the entrance to the living room and Jenna could hear her mother crying. She looked over at her brothers and without a word, she slipped out quietly.

Jenna walked up to the door of her friend Aggy Newton's home. She and Aggy had been friends since middle school. They endured summer camp, gym class, and countless Girl Scout cookie drives together.

Jenna had always been a very grounded, logical thinker but Aggy generally had her head in the clouds. She studied astrology and believed in the divinity of fortune cookies.

Jenna rang the doorbell and heard many voices inside. The door opened up and saw Aggy standing before her, smiling as brightly as ever, but as she gazed upon her friend's face, she became troubled.

"What's wrong, Jen?" Aggy asked.

"You know what today is, don't you?"

"A week before your birthday. Of course. Why the bummer?" Jenna stared at Aggy astounded by how oblivious to the situation she appeared to be.

"You know," Jenna urged. "The tests."

"The tests? You're upset over that?" Aggy waved her hand past her face as though Jenna's worries were nothing but dust in the air cluttering her vision.

"I don't know why you're so calm. Your neck's on the chopping block same as mine." Jenna added. Aggy grabbed Jenna and pulled her in close.

"You don't have to worry," Aggy began. "I had a dream last night."

"Am I really in the mood to hear this?" Jenna asked as she stepped away.

"It's good! In my dream we were at your seventeenth birthday!"

"So?"

"So? Come on! Think! You're still going to be here when you turn seventeen! You're going to get through this."

"It was a dream, Aggy."

"You remember when I had a dream last year about getting a perfect score on my history final and then I did?"

"I believe an octopus teacher was also part of that dream."

"The point is that dreams hold deeper meaning and this dream is telling me you are going to pass the tests. And so am I."

"You know I would love to believe that, but it was just a dream. The tests are real."

"My dreams are just as real."

"How's your mom doing?" Sobs came echoing from the back of the house and Jenna felt her question had been answered.

"Not so great. I keep telling her I'm going to be fine, but she just won't listen."

Aggy led Jenna into the kitchen where Aggy's mother was curled up under the kitchen table sobbing into her hands.

"Mrs. Newton?" Jenna asked.

"Don't worry about her," Aggy said. "We've gone through this for the past few mornings. She'll pull herself together soon enough."

Jenna imagined that despite how long the tests had been around, it was a fairly common reaction for most parents. Aggy walked over to the table and knelt down to her mother's eye level.

"Mom, Jen and I are leaving for school in a bit. Are you going to be all right?" Aggy's mother took a deep breath and wiped her tears away. She crawled out from under the table, pulled herself up, and set herself straight.

"I'm sorry, dear. This kind of snuck up on me."

"You knew this day was coming, mom. We both did."

"Yes, but it's just one of those days you are never really prepared to face. When I was young, the tests were new, and it was strange and terrifying. Your generation just accepts it as a part of your lives."

"Because it is."

"I know. It's just still new to me."

"I'm going to be fine, mom."

"You better be." The sound of the school bus stopping in front of the house was heard. Aggy gave her mother a quick kiss on her cheek and both girls went running off to school.

Chapter 2

CHAPTER 36

Assembly

When the bus came to a stop, Jenna hoped that some sense of normality would return at school, but she was sorely disappointed. It was just like at home. Everything looked normal, but there was something just under the surface that changed how it all felt. The popular girls were clustered together as they checked each other out and talked about whatever it was popular girls had to talk about.

The jocks were rough housing on the grass and the slackers were huddled near the library as they tried to finish the homework they were supposed to do the night before. The sun was shining. The sky was blue. Everything that had always been in front of Jenna was there but none of it was the same. None of it felt right.

"Come on." Aggy said as she tugged on Jenna's shoulder.

As they stepped off the bus, and that's when Jenna realized there was a sort of hush over everyone. It wasn't just her and Aggy. It was all the kids who were turning sixteen. It was as it always was. The Testers were always treated like some kind of sideshow attraction the week before they went to the camps. They were like the walking dead in the eyes of most. Jenna was aware of it and could even admit to being one of the onlookers more than once, but just in that moment, she realized how vastly different it felt when you were the one being looked at.

She and Aggy held their heads up high as they made their way to the main building of the school. They hadn't spoken on the bus, but Jenna knew that Aggy felt the same as she did. That they weren't going to let their circumstances change how they lived their lives one bit. They didn't want the pity of the teachers. They didn't react to the disgust of the popular kids. Their lives weren't over, and they weren't going to act as if they were. Once they made it inside, Jenna let out her breath and looked to Aggy.

"Did you see how they looked at us?" Jenna asked.

"Don't think about it, Jenna. They're idiots. Besides, most of them are going to be on this side of it next year."

"I've seen it so many times, but I had no idea. They were looking at us as though we were already dead."

"Don't even say that word! That's not going to happen!" Aggy barked. She always acted so tough and strong, but Jenna knew that even Aggy had her moments.

"I didn't say it was. It just felt like some of them were actually pulling for us to fail."

"Maybe some of them are. There are always those kinds. We'll show 'em."

"You think so?"

"Of course. You've got the odds in your favor, and well, let's face it. Someone as fabulous as me simply can't be stopped."

"You got me there."

They walked out the other side of the building and out to the quad where they got more open-mouthed glares. It seemed once someone saw them; they couldn't stop staring. They crossed over to the cafeteria and headed for one of the vending machines where they each got a bottle of chocolate milk and an apple, their daily pre-class routine.

They sat down at one of the tables outside and tried to screen out everyone's eyes as they ate, but it was difficult.

"I can't wait for it to be over," Jenna said. "If only to end this circus." She crumpled up her empty milk bottle and tossed it into a nearby trash can with precision.

"What do you think it'll be like after?" Aggy asked. "I mean, we come back after everyone thought we'd be, you know. Do you think it'll go back to normal?"

"After the tests, does anything go back to normal?"

"Good point. How's your mom?"

"I'm not sure. From what I saw, not well. My dad was talking to her when I left the house, but she was crying, so who knows? I know she's upset. She's trying to hide it, but she's never been a great liar." Jenna added.

"Why are parents like that? They know what the deal is."

"It's like what your mom said. the whole ESA thing was new for them. We've grown up with it. It's been just another part of our lives." Jenna said

"I guess."

"How about your dad?"

"I haven't really talked to him yet. He usually calls or emails me pretty regularly, but it's been a few days since I've heard from him. I think he may be having a problem as well."

"Sometimes I think the week before the camp is actually harder. It's like being at your own funeral for a week. My brothers were nice to me this morning."

"Really? Wow."

"I know. For once I really needed to hear one of their stupid cut downs."

"Maybe they can give you some tips on the tests."

"They say there's nothing that can be done. Everything you've got to pass is already in you." Jenna said.

"I wish you hadn't said that."

"What? You sounded so confident a few minutes ago."

"It comes and goes. I try to be strong, but there's still that little voice of doubt deep inside. The idea that I could fail." Aggy said. The first bell rang, interrupting Aggy, and everyone stopped whatever they were doing and headed for their homerooms.

As Aggy and Jenna reached the door to their classroom, Ms. Hillborn intercepted them and held out two forms.

"What're these?" Jenna asked.

"I'm sorry, girls, but everyone in your group will be reporting to the gym for their first period."

"Our group?"

"Yes. Test candidates." Jenna looked in and saw that nearly all the desks inside were empty. She turned to Aggy. They turned around and headed for the gym as instructed.

When they got there, a crowd had gathered just outside and was waiting for the doors to open. Jenna and Aggy worked their way into the crowd and Jenna could see that there were a lot of different emotions going on. Some of the kids seemed to be pretty high strung and nervous about the assembly while others were trying to put on a brave face and act like it didn't matter to them. She could even hear a few kids crying, which was generally expected. It seemed everyone was so focused on what they were feeling, no one seemed aware of the presence of anyone else.

The gym doors opened and Mr. Billings, the school principal, stepped out. He was a stout man with a belly that hung down over his belt. His head was free of any hair, and he sported a pair of thick black framed glasses.

"Ladies and gentlemen! If you would please come in and have a seat, in an orderly manner." He said. Everyone's attention shifted to him, and they all began to file in. It wasn't like the many other assemblies that energized the kids. There was very little chatting between friends or even smiles. They were getting a free pass from class, but it was an easy bet to think every one of those children would have gladly gone back to their classes if they could have been spared.

Aggy and Jenna stuck close together, as they always did. Aggy was showing signs of fear, but despite that, she still had a spark of fire in her, and it was enough to insist on Jenna to sit in the front row. She dragged Jenna along and they found a couple seats at the end of the front of the center section. Jenna turned in her seat and looked out at the faces of everyone in the gym. It wasn't like she was surprised to see it. It was just something she wasn't prepared to see. She turned back in her seat and then the doors were shut, and the lights went out. A spotlight came on and a man stepped out from the shadows. He was a handsome looking older man with brown hair. He was wearing a sharp looking black suit with a red tie around his neck. He took his place in the center of the light and looked out at his captive audience.

"Good morning. My name is Richard Fremont. I realize no one is happy to be here, me included. I am here today to speak to you about something you may or may not know about; but by the looks on most of your faces, you do. The tests. I realize to you; these tests may seem like some kind of cruel punishment. They may seem evil in their intent, but nothing could be further from the truth. Eighty years ago, it wasn't just this country but the entire globe that realized we all had a very big problem: overpopulation.

For years, experts seemed to focus on the risks of population loss, but all that while there were explosions of people all around the world. More people than most governments could handle. More people than our environment could handle. Food supplies were running low, and we all began to see a terrible light at the end of the tunnel," Richard then turned to the back wall and a picture came on of a gaunt, odd-looking man. "Until Senator Zachary Lazaras came along. He was a brave pioneer who was unafraid to see the problem and do something about it. It was he who brought forth the Environmental Salvation Act. I'm sure you've all studied about the ESA over the years, but how many of you know the full extent of what it does?" He looked out at the crowd as if expecting a response. "No takers. Understandable. The ESA was a comprehensive body of legislation that sought to ease the burden of our growing population on both our governments and the environment. Parenting licenses were implemented, thereby limiting how many children could be born into a family. Tax incentives for voluntary vasectomies, and the reason you are all here today: The tests," Jenna squirmed in her chair. Everything was becoming uncomfortably real. "As some of you know, when you reach the age of sixteen, you must undergo the tests. These tests are designed to evaluate who you are; physically, mentally and emotionally. They were created to only allow the best of who we are to pass. Once you do pass, you return to your family and resume your lives. You go on knowing that you are worthy of this life and that's a gift that is beyond measure. Of course, there is the fate of those of you who don't pass. For this, I am sorry, but as Senator Lazaras once said, 'Those who fall in sacrifice to others, are the greatest heroes of all.' I realize those words provide little comfort to you, but it was decided a long time ago that the needs of the world were too dire and too important. Should any of you fail to pass the tests, you will be taken to a transition camp. While you are there, you will enjoy every comfort of living. World class food. Your every desire attended to. It is nearly Heaven on Earth. You will live as you've never lived before and anything you could ever want will be provided. At the end of this stay, however, you will be put down; humanely and painlessly. Senator Lazaras was hard fought on this part of his legislation, but he knew, as the world came to realize, that hard choices have to be made. It is a matter of survival." A loud cough came from the back. Jenna spun around and saw a hand up in the air. A young girl, who had clearly been crying, stood up and took a deep breath.

"Weren't the tests supposed to be temporary?" She asked.

"As a matter of fact, yes. They were to be halted once the world population was brought under control. Sadly, that has not happened yet. Despite all our steps in controlling the population, there are still some out there who feel there is no problem. They believe that a higher power will provide and while we can appreciate and respect their beliefs, science has been telling us a very different story. Nearly half the countries in the world don't have enough food to feed more than half of their peoples. Third world countries have been decimated into non-existence and too many developed countries, the United States included, are on the verge of falling. I wish this didn't have to be. I really do. If you are fearful of the tests; if you're afraid you will not pass, think on this. Without the tests, you would be doomed to death no matter what. In this instance, however, we can offer you comfort at your time of passing."

"I was told that we can't see our families if we fail."

"That's not true. All transition camps offer visitation. It's just that many attendees feel it's too painful. If you should find yourself in that situation and if you wish to see your family, we would be more than happy to oblige. This is why we are having this assembly. I wish to educate and prepare you for what you are going to experience. Too many of you have been fed lies and heard rumors that are baseless," A large screen then began to descend from the rafters above. "Please try and relax and open your minds to what will undoubtedly be the most profound experience of your lives."

"Or the last." Aggy whispered. In any other moment, her little quip would have gotten a laugh out of me, but it didn't seem as funny at the time.

A movie began to play which outlined the long history of the ESA. It detailed Senator Lazaras' uphill battle to introduce the law and the years it took to find the votes to get it through. There were challenges from religious groups and human rights groups as well. It was due to the growing urgency for action that helped speed the law through and even after eighty years, there were still protests against it, but those voices had fallen silent against the majority acceptance of the ESA. It had also been documented that Senator Lazaras did not allow his position as leverage to spare his own son from being tested. He passed and Senator Lazaras went on record stating no member of his family was immune from the ESA and that he knew that the sacrifice was meant to be shared by all the citizens of the Earth, if the benefits were to be shared as well.

It was a few years after some success that the ESA was expanded to an international program and several other countries adopted Lazaras' legislation as their own.

The movie then outlined some of the logistical challenges of implementing the law. There had been testing and transition camps built all across the globe. Some of them were as large as airports and football fields in order to accommodate the nearly endless flood of candidates. It had been rough in the beginning but after the first ten years, the process had become more streamlined, and the camps were able to process more children faster.

After the film was done, Richard returned and explained in more detail some of the more recent developments with the ESA as well as explaining where the candidates were to go for pick up and what they were to bring with them. Aggy and Jenna listened but Jenna felt as though the more she heard, the worse she felt. Everyone was so positive about her passing, but the little bit of doubt in her mind seemed to be louder than their voices.

The assembly was over, and Jenna checked her watch and saw that it had gone on for nearly three hours. Everyone got up and walked out of the gym and she saw their faces as they marched past. They all seemed more somber than when they had entered in the first place. It looked as though it was break time because most of the students were out and hanging around with nothing to do. Jenna looked around and saw a hand waving at her. It was connected to an arm, which was connected to a striking young Latin boy with wavy, black hair and deep green eyes.

"Mark!" Jenna called out. She and Mark Hernandez had been seeing each other since the beginning of their Sophomore year. They had been on the tennis team together at first and he soon started popping up in many of her classes the previous year which led to them becoming study partners and they grew closer ever since. Mark ran through the crowd and swept Jenna up in his arms.

"There you are! I tried to find you in there, but it was too dark. That guy didn't freak you out, did he?"

"No, Aggy was with me."

"Hi, Mark." Aggy said. Mark shot her a quick smile but then focused back on Jenna.

"You okay?" He asked.

"I'm fine. I should ask if you're okay. How's your mom taking this?"

"She's a basket case, but I've got good blood. My brothers all passed. Yours did too, right?"

"Yes."

"We'll be fine." Mark had always possessed a genuine confidence that Jenna had found a bit annoying at first, but she grew to appreciate it over time.

"I hope so."

"We will. How about we hit a movie tonight? Take our minds off all of this?"

"I guess we might as well."

"Great. I'll pick you up at eight."

"Okay. I'll see you then." Jenna said and then Mark pulled her close and pressed his lips to hers. She looked back at him with surprise.

"Hey, live while you can, right? I'll see you tonight." Mark said with a wink.

"All right." Jenna said. Mark turned and headed toward a group of his friends who were waiting for him.

"Wow. That was some kiss." Aggy said.

"I know." Aggy's smile then slid away.

"You think he might think it could be the last time for you two to do that?"

"No. You know Mark. I think he's just using it as an excuse to get a little action, but I can't really complain about that, can I? Besides, it may be our last chance."

"Don't say that, Jenna."

"Aggy. It's reality. We have no way of knowing which way the tests will go. There's no absolute. I've heard of kids who had siblings who passed but failed anyway."

"You sound so calm about all of this." Aggy said.

"Are you kidding me? Calm? I'm dying inside! I can't believe that this could be the last week I ever live again. These are the last days I'll see this school. The last days I'll see you or Mark or my family. This could be the last week I can still have any dreams that could come true. I've got plans. I want to go to college. Maybe go into art school, or medical school."

"Art school or medical school?"

"I'm still working that out. The point is I am in a state of total fear that this is all the life I'm going to get to live. I've got a lot more to do. It can't be over already." Jenna felt her voice break and she fell back against a nearby wall and the tears came pouring out.

Chapter 3

Social Life

The day carried on as normal, or as normal as it could be. Jenna kept feeling the pitying stares of her classmates at the back of her head. She held back her rage because as dehumanizing as it felt to her, she couldn't forget that it wouldn't be long until they were in her shoes.

When the final bell rang, Jenna felt her heart rise and she couldn't wait to get on that bus and back home, but as she raced to her locker, she stopped and realized what was waiting for her there. More pity, more sadness. It didn't seem that there was anywhere to escape.

She reached her locker and got her things together. She, along with the rest of the kids set to go to the test camp, had been given a pass on all assignments for the week so she didn't need to take any books home with her. She thought of bringing her history book, if only to keep on top of what the class was doing so she wouldn't fall behind when she got back. For a moment, having it and working toward that goal made her feel as though she would be returning. As if it had been promised to her. She held the book in her hand. It was heavy and real. Her grip tightened on it, but finally she let it go and it fell to the bottom of her locker. "I'll return." She said as she shut the small metal door and headed outside.

Jenna found Aggy near where the bus would be arriving. She was hanging her head down and didn't seem as bright as she normally did.

"What's the matter, Aggy?"

"Nothing. It's just been a crappy day. My teachers kept telling me not to think about the tests, but that just made think about the tests!

Everywhere I turned someone had advice or words of wisdom to help me through this difficult time."

"I know. I got the same thing all day too."

"At this point I don't care if I pass or fail. I just want it to be over. One way or the other."

"Don't say that. Don't even kid about that." Jenna said.

"You know what I mean." Aggy assured.

"Yeah." Jenna turned and saw Mark racing toward her with a big smile on his face. He leapt at her and wrapped his arm around her.

"Hey! We still on for the movie tonight?" He asked.

"Yes! So put me down!" Jenna said through a laugh. Mark set her down and kept hopping with excess energy. "Why are you so hyped?"

"I've got football practice and we have to get psyched! You know that!"

"You're still going to practice?" Jenna asked.

"Why not? It beats moping, right?"

"Uh, yeah. I guess so."

"So, I'll message you when I'm done, and we can meet up."

"All right."

"Catch ya, babe!" Mark then darted off toward the football field.

"Wow. I think he's actually in a better mood when his life is in danger." Aggy said.

"Seems like it, right? Have to admit, it beats the alternative."

"You're right. He's right! What am I doing? I'm feeling sorry for myself!"

"We're going to make it through, Aggy. You and me."

"Yes we are." Jenna took Aggy's hand and squeezed it as only a good friend could.

When Jenna finally returned home, everything seemed quiet. Her brothers weren't home, which was normal, and her parents would be at work for a few more hours. For the briefest of moments, Jenna was blissfully alone, and she was finally able to shut out the world. She ran up to her room and grabbed her music player and hunted through it for any songs that she felt could take her thoughts away; Anything to throw up the walls that would keep the bad thoughts away.

She stretched out on her bed, closed her eyes and pressed play. Most of the songs she chose were high energy anthems with very positive lyrics. She never normally listened to the lyrics, but there were times her ears would catch a word or two and she would realize that a song could really lift her spirits, and that was what she needed.

As the songs played on, she felt herself drift off into a light sleep. She had no chores to do and no homework so she felt she could allow herself that one luxury. After a few songs played, she could feel herself actually begin to smile. She had left the world behind and there was nothing in front of or behind her. There was only that one moment and it was infinite. She then felt a light squeeze on her arm and her eyes popped open and she saw her mother standing over her.

"Mom. Hi."

"I didn't wake you, did I?"

"Kind of."

"I'm sorry. I got home and I didn't hear anyone in the house so I just wanted to check on you."

"It's okay. I must have been out for a while." Jenna turned to her clock and saw that it had been nearly two hours since she had gotten home.

"I also thought we could talk." Jenna knew the tone all too well. It was the tone her mother used whenever she wanted to talk about something serious, and since they had already discussed the birds and the bees, there wasn't really much left on the table other than the tests.

"Mom, I really don't want to even think about it."

"I just wanted to apologize for this morning."

"You don't have to."

"Yes, I do. I understand what a terrible time this must be for you, and carrying on like I did just made it worse."

"It's okay, Mom. I get it."

"That's kind of it. You don't really. You don't get how it feels to see your own child go through something like this. You don't understand how deep the pain goes, but I should understand your pain. I should understand what you need from me as your mother. I forgot. For one moment, I forgot and I lost it."

"Aggy's mom was the same."

"I'm sure. That woman has an emotional breakdown if the mail is late. I try to do a little better than that."

"You do, Mom. You really do."

"It's just for my generation, the ESA still feels new and a little weird. Your generation is one of the first to grow up with it as a reality. To you it's just a part of growing up. It shouldn't be, but it is."

"I just wish everyone could stop acting like it's a big deal."

"But it is a big deal, sweety."

"I know that, but I've got a week before it really has to be. I just want a little time to go back to how things were. I don't want you to break into tears everytime I walk into the room. I want the boys to tease and annoy me like they always do. I want to have this last bit of my life, in case," Jenna's mother shot her hand up and clasped it over Jenna's mouth.

"You will pass. Do you hear me? You will pass." Jenna pulled free from her mother's grip.

"But I might not, and I kind of think that's something we all have to make peace with. I might not pass."

"Your brothers passed with flying colors and you have the same stock as them. Your father and I qualified for a three child parenting license after the first gene test. You will pass."

"That's what I'm trying to focus on, but until I'm on that bus for the camp, I just want to be me and I want you to be you. Can we do that?"

"I can't make any promises, but I'll try."

"Good enough for me."

"So, what do you want for dinner?"

"Isn't tonight meatloaf night?"

"Normally, but I thought maybe you could choose."

"Even if I chose fried chicken?"

"Even if."

"Then. Fried chicken."

"I'll get it started."

"And could I go out tonight?"

"On a school night?"

"Mark asked me to the movies. Please?"

"Fine. You're getting good at this emotional blackmail stuff."

"I learned from the best."

"I guess you did." Jenna's mother said as she wrapped her arms around her daughter.

After dinner that night, the boys cleared the dishes and Jenna went off to meet with Mark at the local theater. When she arrived, she was surprised to see that there was actually a lot of activity that night. She saw Mark waiting for her near the box office and she ran over to him.

"There you are." She said as they kissed.

"I already got the tickets."

"Did I keep you waiting that long?"

"No, I just wanted to treat you. You've had a hard day."

"Thanks, but we kind of both had the same hard day."

"Not me. I'm not letting this test stuff get to me."

"How is that possible?"

"You just don't let it. During practice, I just focused on getting the ball and getting it down the field. I wasn't thinking about anything else."

"But how can you not think about what could possibly be your final days on Earth?"

"Because I see past that. I see us at prom next year. I see us going to college together."

"Really? I didn't know you were even thinking that far."

"I've given it some thought. I love you, Jenna." Jenna stood before Mark in a frozen daze. They felt strongly for each other and Jenna had thought of telling Mark how she really felt a few times, but she never dreamed he would have beaten her to the punch.

"What did you say?"

"I love you. I've wanted to tell you for months, but I just couldn't work up the nerve. I love you." Mark had always been a difficult person to read. He was careful to never let his emotional side ever show and he usually skated through sensitive moments with humor. He was a jock and acted the part to perfection, and there was no room for sentimentality in his guise, but he was standing before Jenna with his heart on his sleeve.

"I love you too." She said. Mark took her in his arms and she felt something different in his embrace. He was holding tighter than normal. As she stepped away, she noticed a small drop sliding down Mark's cheek. She was about to point it out, but he wiped it away with his sleeve and she didn't feel the need to go any further than that.

They went on into the theater, got their snacks and sat down in the auditorium. They just sat silently before the movie began, smiling at each other and sharing something between them that not only didn't need to be talked about, but should not have been talked about. They both knew and that was all that they needed.

After the movie let out, Mark and Jenna left the theater and found a small bench nearby and sat down. They began to talk about the film, recounting their favorite parts. Jenna was just so relieved to finally be talking about something new and different and, for a few hours at least, living her life again. The world was a million miles away and they were the only people around. That was the way it usually was with Mark and Jenna, but it was only then that she truly appreciated it.

A familiar voice then broke their bubble and Jenna turned to see Chandra Brown approaching flanked by her usual entourage. Jenna only really knew Chandra by reputation. She was one of the Elites, despite her status as a freshman. She came from money and that was enough to earn her way into the higher social circles ahead of schedule. She enjoyed her privilege and wasn't afraid to flex her power whenever she saw fit. Jenna had seen Chandra at the assembly so it was clear that they were both on equal footing, as far as the tests were concerned.

"Hello, Mark." Chandra said in a casual tone that seemed to indicate that she knew Mark personally, although Jenna had no recollection of them ever meeting.

"Hey, Chandra." Mark said as he turned from her. Chandra shot a glance over to Jenna but only offered the weakest of smiles as a greeting and then returned her attention to Mark. She bent down a bit and placed her hand on Mark's chest and began to slowly massage it.

"I was wondering if you'd be interested in coming over to my place this Friday. I'm throwing kind of a big going away party. My parents have relaxed all the rules so we can all pretty much do whatever we want. I think it'd be a great way for us all to blow off some steam before the tests. Don't you?"

"Uh, yeah. Sounds great."

"So, you'll come?" Mark looked over at Jenna and he could sense the tension growing.

"Yes. We'll be there." Chandra turned her gaze back over to Jenna.

"Oh. Hi."

"Hello, Chandra."

"I guess you can bring her, if you must; as long as you're there. You know where it is. I'll see you Friday." She said and then marched off.

"You know where it is?" Jenna asked.

"I can explain."

"How do you even know her?"

"She hangs out with the cheerleaders and they hang out with the players. We talked at a couple of post-game parties, but there's nothing there."

"Then how do you know where she lives?"

"Maybe the guys and I went to a couple house parties at her place. Her parents look the other way all the time and they have a full on bar!"

"So you just pretend to like her so you can throw back shots?"

"We were just having fun."

"If sucking up to that rich bitch is your idea of fun, maybe you should just go to that party by yourself. I'm sure Chandra would love that!" Jenna said and stormed away. Mark got up and snagged her by the arm.

"I don't give a damn what she thinks! I'm with you, baby. Come on. We were having a great night until just now. I don't want to fight."

Mark slowly backed Jenna against the wall and began to nibble at her neck, which he knew she couldn't resist.

"Stop." She giggled.

"Come to the party?"

"I hate Chandra. I just want that on the record."

"I got that. I hate her too, but she's got an awesome place."

"Fine. I'll go, but if I see you even touch her, you won't even make it to the testing camp."

Chapter 4

Getting to Normal

The next morning Jenna awoke and things began to seem better to her. She had the day to process everything and it felt as though her dark mood had finally passed and she was able to see some brightness amongst the clouds. It felt as though some inexplicable force beyond her comprehension was filling her with optimism and it felt good to her. It was true that since her brothers passed the tests her odds of passing were significantly great. The same was true for Mark. He had five other siblings go through the tests and they all made it. In fact, as she really thought on it, she didn't know anyone who had older brothers or sisters who didn't pass the tests. She began to think it was more or less a formality and at worst it would take a week away from her Summer break, since all those who test and return must make up the week they missed in June.

She then heard the familiar sounds of morning in the house. Everyone was carrying on with their lives, so Jenna saw no reason she shouldn't either. She got out of bed, dressed and ran down the stairs with a real craving for a big bowl of Sugar Loops. When she burst into the kitchen everyone turned to her and froze in place.

"Please, don't," She said. "Just keep going as if it were normal. Really. Yesterday was tense enough. I don't know if I can live with everyone looking at me like I'm about to die."

"You're right, sweetheart." Her father said and everything resumed. Jenna walked over to the pantry and pulled out the box of cereal and then went to get a bowl.

"Oh, honey," Her mother said. "I can make you something if you want."

"No, thanks, mom. I am actually craving these today."

"It's nothing but sugar."

"Then why do you buy them?" Her mother looked back at her with a bewildered look on her face.

"I don't know. I always got them for you kids when you were younger and I guess it became a habit. It's funny how you can get used to doing something for so long and never question it."

"Well, I need my Sugar Loops today, so let's be grateful for bad habits."

Jenna poured herself a bowl of cereal, filled it with milk and sat down to enjoy her meal. She looked over at her brothers who were busy finishing the homework they failed to finish the night before and then over to her father who was, once more, deeply engaged in his daily news feeds. She took a bite of her cereal and that completed the picture. Everything felt normal and right in that one moment. As Jenna ate, she wished that she could just freeze time right there and live forever in that one blissful second. She looked out the window and saw the sky outside as blue as ever. There were no problems. There were no tests.

"How was the movie last night?"

"It was fine, Mom. It was a distraction at least."

"I'm sure. How's Mark doing?"

"You know him. Nothing bothers him. He's ready to pass the tests so he can get back to football."

"Good man." Her father said, proving that he did pay some attention to what was going on around him beyond the screen of his computer.

"And, we actually got invited to a party."

"A party?"

"Yes. Chandra Brown is having a big party at her house this Friday night."

"Oh. That sounds nice." The boys giggled a bit but Jenna shot them a hard stare and they went back to their work.

"It should be."

"What was that? Why did your brothers laugh?"

"No reason." Jenna said but Bradley looked up from his book and smiled.

"Chandra Brown's parties are legendary."

"How do you know about Chandra's party?" Jenna asked.

"Everyone knows about Chandra's parties and this kickoff party is going to be the party to end all parties." Jenna's mother looked back to her.

"Kickoff party?"

"Kids have them all the time before they leave for the tests. It's the last night to do all the things they might not have a chance to do in case they don't come back. I heard her parents are letting her do whatever she wants. They're getting booze and some pot and everything."

"As options!"

"I don't care if the world is ending on Saturday. You are not going to that party."

"I'm not going to drink or smoke or anything." Jenna said.

"Then why go?" Brian muttered.

"I just need to be there for Mark. I trust him fine, but Chandra is another story."

"I doubt Mark's mother will allow him to go either. Especially after I tell her what I now know. Which I will."

"Mom! You can't!"

"Look, I realize what this is all about, but this just sounds like too much. They are too young to drink or take drugs."

"But it's okay for them to die?" Jenna asked. Time seemed to freeze in that moment and her eyes locked with her mother's.

"Besides, I believe everyone at this table has come to the conclusion that you will not be failing the tests. Once you come back, you'll have the rest of your life to experiment and try new things, but only when you're ready to accept the consequences. Not because you've been pressured to."

"I don't see what the issue here is. You and dad trust me, right?"

"We do."

"And you know I would never do anything bad, right?"

"We do."

"So why can't you just be cool this once? Let this one slide off the parental radar."

"Are you really expecting me and your father to sign off on you going to some unsupervised party where there will be many hormone raging boys with access to liquor and drugs?"

"I can handle it."

"I don't think that you can."

"Dad!"

"I'm sorry, sweety, but I'm with your mom on this. It sounds like a good idea to let those guys blow off steam like that, but I don't really think it's a good environment for you."

"How about this? If Mark's mom lets him go, I can go with him. You trust Mark, don't you?"

"Yes." Her mom said.

"Kind of." Jenna's father added.

"I will call his mother today and tell her what you told me. If she lets him go, I guess you can too."

"Thank you!"

"But you are to be back by eleven."

"Are you kidding me? Eleven? My curfew is midnight on weekends!"

"These are the terms. And if I smell a whiff of liquor or weed on you, you will be in serious trouble when you get back from the tests. Do you agree?"

"Fine. You know, I could have just gone and not told you."

"And I could ground you for the rest of the week. Game, set, match."

After Jenna finished her breakfast, she gathered her things and went to meet Aggy at her house. She found Aggy standing outside just waiting.

"What are you doing out here?" Jenna asked.

"I couldn't take it in there anymore. Ever since I got home yester-day my mom's been pulling out all the old photos and forcing me to relive my life. I couldn't take it anymore. I may have to go to the testing camp early."

"It can't be that bad."

"It is, trust me. Right now she's fitting my old baby clothes on a teddy bear with a picture of me pasted to its face."

"Maybe she needs some help."

"I called my dad and he said he'd fly in before the end of the week. He said he'd look after her."

"I'm sorry she's taking it so hard."

"Thanks, but it's no shock. Ever since their divorce, it's just been me and mom and with all this happening now, she's going into a stress panic."

"I guess it can't be easy when you're the only child."

"No," Aggy said. The sound of her mother crying began to carry outside of the house. Aggy took Jenna by her arm and they marched out to the street. "So, how was your date?"

"Last night? It was good, despite the fact that we ran into Chandra Brown."

"The Ice Queen of Kennedy High?"

"Yes. She invited Mark to the kickoff party she's throwing Friday."

"She invited you to her kickoff party?"

"No. She invited Mark. She acted like I wasn't even there."

"What a bitch."

"Mark said he would go only if he could bring me though."

"So you're actually going to Chandra Brown's kickoff party?"

"Maybe."

"What? What maybe?"

"I asked my mom if I could go and it kind of slipped about the drugs and booze."

"She flipped."

"Kind of. She definitely said I couldn't go, but I made a deal with her. If Mark goes, I go."

"Great."

"Except she's going to tell Mark's mom everything she knows about the party."

"Oh, no." Aggy said.

"Well, at least if I can't go, neither can Mark. Chandra would just love to have him all to herself."

"If you do go, any chance you could bring me?"

"Your mom would never let you go to one of Chandra's parties."

"Yes, but my mom isn't exactly a resident of reality right now. I have to take advantage while I can."

"It would totally burn Chandra if I brought you too."

"Yeah."

"Okay."

"Yes! So when do you think you'll know if it's on or not?"

"Soon. My mom's probably already on the phone with Mark's mom."

"What do you think she'll say?"

"It's hard to tell. Some parents really relax the rules before their kids go for testing. They all figure it could be their last hoorah."

"Except for the transition camp," Aggy added. "I've heard they bring hookers in there. A lot of the boys who fail refuse to die virgins."

"I don't doubt it. I think some parents just want to do one last cool thing before they say good bye."

"It's kind of sad."

"Very." The bus then came roaring up and Aggy and Jenna got in. More normal. It seemed the shock of the tests had worn off and everyone was ready to just live their lives. No more stares or glances from the other kids. They took their seats and felt the jerk of the bus as it lurched forward.

The whole day was totally different from the day before. The whole world seemed to forget all about the tests and everyone was allowed to live their normal lives. Jenna went all the way until lunch before she even remembered that they were coming up.

She joined Aggy in the cafeteria but as she entered, Mark came running up behind her.

"Hey!" He barked.

"What?"

"Your mom called my mom!"

"I'm sorry. I asked my mom if I could go to Chandra's party,"

"You asked if you could go? You don't ask for permission to go to a kickoff party. You just go!"

"So your mom said no to you?"

"No. She said it was okay."

"She did?"

"After about twenty minutes of screaming, yes. She said it would be good for me to get it all out of my system."

"Wow. That's great. Then I can go too. My mom said I could if I went with you."

"I know. That is great, except now I have to be back by eleven."

"So do I."

"Girl, I love you, but sometimes you have to think."

"At least we can go."

"Yeah. I guess we can get in enough fun before we have to leave."

Chapter 5

Cold Hard Facts

Jenna woke up the next day and once more she felt a shift in her mood. She had sworn to herself that she would never wake up thinking of the tests, but as the sun shined down into her bedroom, there was little else she could think of. She tried to pass the thoughts away by concentrating on anything else. She thought about the subject of her college application essay. She thought about how Friday night with Mark was going to go. She thought of everything under the sun twice but her mind came to rest on the exact same problem.

She got out of bed, dressed and headed to the kitchen. Her brothers had already left for school and her father was on the phone in the other room. Only her mother was left as she stood before the sink and washed the breakfast dishes.

"Good morning." Jenna said. Her mother spun around and shot her a smile.

"Good morning, honey. You missed the pancakes, but I think you have time for a quick bowl of cereal."

"Great," Jenna said as she headed to the pantry. When she selected her cereal, she turned to see her mother standing right behind her with a carton of milk in one hand and a bowl and spoon with the other. She let out a little yelp of surprise just before she knocked into her. "Thanks, mom."

"Of course, sweety." Jenna took the milk and bowl and sat down at the table and poured some cereal. She turned her head slightly and noticed her mother's gaze was still on her.

"Is something wrong?"

"No, honey. No. Eat your breakfast." Jenna attempted to do so, but it seemed once she started to do anything, her fears and anxieties about the tests would come back. Tuesday she felt secure because the weekend seemed so far, but Wednesday was so much closer. Just two more days and then her last weekend before heading to the tests. It was coming at her all at once as she tried to eat. All the fear she had tried to push away was washing over her in one gigantic wave of panic. She dropped the spoon and pushed herself away from the table. Her chest became tight and she couldn't breathe. Jenna fell to the floor and tried to force air into her lungs, but the more she tried, the more difficult it became. She felt a hand wrap around her arm and drag her up to her feet.

"Just calm down, sweety. Calm down. It's a panic attack. Just listen to my voice and try to relax." Jenna's mother said as she took Jenna back to the table. Jenna felt the tight grip of her mother's hand on hers and it wasn't long until she could breathe again. Her mother was quick with a glass of water and Jenna drank it down.

"I don't know what just happened."

"I do. The same thing happened to me before I went to my tests. And back then they were even more primitive than they are now. You really would have shit your pants back then."

"Mom."

"It's true."

"Every day someone at school is trying to give us some advice on how to cope, but the more they talk about it, the worse it seems to be. It seems everyone is getting ready for us to fail."

"It's hard, but they're just preparing for a possibility. The outside world has to prepare for the worst, but we have to hope for the best, but you will be coming back." Jenna forced a smile, but her eyes gave away her true pain.

"I spend so much time trying to commit every last detail of my life to memory. Every face, every smell and every feeling. I try to press everything together in this scrapbook in my head in case I never come back to it again." Jenna's mother took her chin in hand and pointed her face directly toward her.

"You will come back. Your father and I and your brothers are living proof of that. I was going to wait until before you left to give you this, but, I think you could use it now," Jenna's mother got up and went to the hall closet and took out a small box and brought it back to her. It was a plain brown box with no decoration or writing on it. "I was planning on wrapping it better, but just open it." Jenna lifted the lid off the box and saw a journal inside. She picked it up and just by touching it, she could tell the cover was made of very high grade leather. It was smooth and soft to the touch, but felt tough and indestructible. She opened it up and all the pages were blank. Crisp new pages waiting to be filled.

"Thanks, mom, but I don't get it."

"My mother gave me a journal before I left for my tests. She told me to write everything down while I was there, or else I would go crazy. I don't know if she was right about that, but it did make me feel better to have some way to let out all the madness I was seeing. I want you to take this journal and put down all your feelings while you're away. Don't let them overtake you and distract you. You're going to need a clear head to get through this, and you will get through this." Jenna smiled up at her mother and a tear rolled down her cheek.

"Thanks, mom. I'll use it. I promise."

"I know you will."

"Wow," Jenna said as she felt the weight of the journal in her hand. "Now it all feels more real. This is happening."

"It can seem a bit surreal sometimes, can't it?"

"I don't know if I can do this, mom."

"Very rarely in life are we ever in a position to choose to do only the things we can do. It's what we don't think we can accomplish but do that makes us who we are. You'll doubt yourself, but just know that we will never doubt you." Jenna felt more tears coming and as they did, she tried to think of something to say, but when no words would come, she simply threw her arms around her mother and squeezed as tightly as she could, and she found, happily, that was all she needed to say.

When Jenna and Aggy returned to school the next day, the somber feeling that pervaded the air on Monday had returned. It seemed everyone was thinking as Jenna was. Time seemed to be slipping away faster and faster and it was clear to everyone that their time in the testing camps was fast approaching.

As Jenna walked the halls and deflected the looks of pity and fear, she wished for it all to be over. She thought beyond the tests and saw her returning to school. She saw herself back with Aggy and Mark. She saw everything slowly going back to normal and with the horror of the tests behind her she had only to look forward to her future. That was the day she saw and that was what was getting her through.

As Jenna had said everyone who was due to go to the testing camp was relieved of any homework. They were instead transferred to independent study periods in the library to fill the day. The time there was spent mostly just reading and whispering until the next break. The rules of the library were relaxed a bit for the students forced to attend and they were free to walk about and talk to their friends. They were just warned to keep the noise down to a reasonable level.

Jenna and Aggy were in the back of the library, which was the prime location since not much sound traveled from there to the librarian's desk in the front. Jenna was scanning through a copy of 'Little Women' while Aggy was rifling through the pages of a magazine that she had brought from home.

"This is stupid. Why don't they just give us the day off?" Aggy lamented.

"Rules about mandatory attendance," Jenna said. "If they don't get us in here for enough days, the state pulls its funding. And with so many cuts, the schools are desperate to keep whatever money they can get."

"Still, it seems like a total waste. Why couldn't we just stay in class?" Mark came over to the girls and forced a seat next to Jenna.

"We bring down the curve for the others." He said as he swung his arm around Jenna's shoulders.

"It's true. If we bring up the curve and then leave, it drops everyone down."

"How do you know so much about this?" Aggy asked.

"My dad used to study all the rules about the tests and how the schools handle exiting students. That was back when he was working with that group that was trying to get the tests repealed."

"So we're trapped in this prison for the next three days."

"That's pretty much it. I like it actually. This is a great time for us to just stop and collect our thoughts." Mark let out a little laugh.

"Wow. Have you been reading those pamphlets the counselor's office put out about coping before the tests?"

"Look, I get that you're confident about passing, but I still have my doubts."

"How many times do I have to tell you, baby? It's in your genes. Your family has passed so you will too."

"You don't know that. No one knows what's going to happen or who will pass. I know we're all supposed to be real positive and believe that we'll get through it and I get that. I do. I'm just saying there is a chance it could go the other way and once you make peace with that, the happier you'll be." Aggy gave Jenna an odd look.

"We're supposed to be happy because we think we're going to die?"

"No. I just mean once you accept both outcomes as possible, you start to care a little less and relax."

"So," Mark began. "You've accepted it? You don't care if you die?"

"Of course I care. I am choosing not to let myself go crazy over worrying about it. On Monday, I had never felt so pitied in my life. Everywhere I went I got that look from people, but the next day things seemed to go back to normal and now today, we're back to being pitied creatures and I'm sure that it's only going to get worse after this."

"I kind of like the attention." Aggy said.

"Aggy. All of this isn't some way to get popular."

"No, I mean from my mom. Up until now she couldn't have given a shit about me. She was always wrapped up in her latest business or hobby, but lately she's started being more present. It's been nice. I kind of think that when I get back things might start to get better between us."

"That's kind of messed up."

"Mark!" Jenna barked as she nudged him.

"No, Jenna. He's right. It is really messed up that my mom doesn't start to take an interest in me until I could be taken away forever, but I'm just glad that she's finally come around."

"It's weird. I'm starting to think the tests are going to seem like a vacation after all of this crap."

"And we still have Chandra's party on Friday." Mark cooed.

"I can't believe that's your priority."

"I'm sorry, babe, but I can't get all miserable like you two. I know I'm going to pass. All it's going to be for me is time off school."

"Have you ever heard the saying pride comes before the fall?"

"Spare me, okay? All I know is that I got no homework for the rest of the week and I don't care if we can only stay until eleven, I am going to get wasted at that party!"

"Why do I go out with you again?"

"Because, baby, you know I get you." Mark slid his finger under Jenna's chin and tilted her head as he slowly kissed her. She melted into his embrace and Aggy looked away, feeling awkward. As Mark pulled away, Jenna felt her breath return and realized for the few brief seconds they were kissing, she had no thought of the tests. She looked at him and smiled.

Chapter 6

Pep Talk

When Jenna got home that day, she discovered her brothers huddled in front of the television with their father. She set her bag down and took particular note of how engrossed they appeared by whatever it was they were watching. She walked on into the living room and glanced at the television and saw they were watching a breaking news feed of a riot that broke out at one of the terminals for a testing camp in Montana. There were groups with large signs begging for the children to be spared. They were chanting and screaming as they attempted to come between the children who were due on the buses and the police.

There was some yelling but it broke out into violence quickly. The police tossed tear gas bombs and soon it was just chaos. Soon the feed shut down and they returned to the anchorman in the studio. Their father looked up and saw Jenna watching from the doorway. He then switched the set off.

"Sorry, Jenna."

"That was crazy."

"Always a few bad apples. Every year those protesters show up and wind up making things into a three ring circus." Brian got up and turned to Jenna and smiled.

"Yeah, when it was my turn, there was guy dressed like the grim reaper carrying around all these plastic dolls tied to a long rope. It gets nuts."

"Brian? Maybe your sister doesn't want to hear about this."

"No, Dad, it's good. I should be prepared for whatever could happen."

"Well, you know it's just like all those pro-life and anti-death penalty gatherings; mostly a lot of the same people."

"What about the kids? I mean, do any of them ever get hurt?"

"A few times, yes."

"I heard about some kid in Florida who had his arm broken in some riot before he got on the bus, and the break was so bad, they said he didn't have to go." Bradley offered.

"I read that story too, son, and he did have to go, but only after his cast was removed. Don't fill Jenna's head with any crazy ideas."

"Hey, it would give her a little extra time."

"I can't believe I have to say this out loud, but we are not going to break any part of your sister."

"But what if it just happened?"

"Boys? Go to your rooms. Now," Brian and Bradley smirked at each other and raced upstairs as their father turned to Jenna and took her hand. "Don't listen to them. You have nothing to worry about."

"I know. Mom went through all this with me this morning. I appreciate it, but you and everyone I know can go on and on about how I'm going to pass, but none of it means I really will."

"You seem to be rather fixated on the negative."

"I'm just trying to be realistic."

"I understand that, honey, and I respect that. You know I've always been one to trust in logic over faith, but I feel like this is one of those rare times when faith beats out logic. You have to understand that these tests are designed to gauge you on every conceivable level. Even your mental state."

"What are you talking about?"

"My work with the anti-testers offered me access to a lot of information not readily available to the public, and one bit of insight I found interesting was that over eighty percent of those who do pass are deemed to have had positive outlooks."

"So, if I think happy thoughts I'll pass."

"In a sense, yes. As hard as it may be to grasp, but they do look at your emotional disposition. Positive people just happened to do better in the tests over the others and to a significant degree."

"Fine, then I'll put on a sunny face when I get there, but until then, may I please wallow in my misery?"

"I'd just warn you to practice now. Whatever you feel in the tests has to be real. It isn't like you can just put on a mask and get through it. You have to really believe it. They will be able to tell."

"Thanks, Dad. I'll try."

Jenna went on up to her room. She was anxious to confine herself in the one place where she could forget about the tests for at least a little while. She had been daydreaming about them all day at school. All she wanted to do was get under a spray of hot water and drown out everything else.

She walked into her room, shut the door and locked it tight. She was about to head for the shower when she heard a knock at her door.

"Who is it?" She asked.

"It's us." Her brothers said through the door. Jenna weighed her options but finally decided to open the door.

"What is it, guys?"

"We wanted to talk to you for a bit."

"Is this about the tests? Because I've heard it all from everyone all week so far. I think I can recite it from memory at this point."

"No. You've heard what they want to tell you. We've been through it. We know and we want to give you the straight story." Brian said as he and Bradley pushed into Jenna's room. He shut the door behind them and they both had serious looks on their faces. Jenna was starting to feel her stomach shrink. It wasn't too often that either of them, much less both, were ever so serious about anything.

"Okay. Fine. What?"

"First, watch out for any competition."

"Competition? There's not competition in the tests. The tests are just to qualify your individual traits."

"Wrong. These tests work on a curve just like at school. If everyone performs low, then even someone who might fail could pass. There are a lot of kids who will make sure to screw you over if it means they can get by."

"Also, watch out for the Kamikazes." Bradley said.

"Kamikazes?"

"There are a few testers who actually want to fail but are too chicken to off themselves. They'll throw the test and sometimes, more often than not, they'll take down a few others as collateral damage."

"Don't trust any of the test admins either." Brian warned.

"They're the ones administering the test. They aren't a threat."

"Not all of them, but there are quite a few who actually want you to fail. Some just want the thrill of causing another human to die, while most of the time some of them have betting pools over who will pass or fail and some of them are not above stacking the deck." Brian and Bradley's rants began to sound less factual and more like the emotionally charged accounts given by supposed test survivors who would sometimes seek out fame by publishing a book about their experience in the tests, and the claims would usually turn out to be false, but not after they helped sell a few million books.

"Okay. I think you two have been overdosing on the blogs."

"Look, believe us or don't. We're just telling you what we saw to be true when we were testing."

"You saw all of this?"

"I volunteered for the facility a little bit, hoping it would earn me some brownie points," Bradley began. "I saw a lot of this stuff going down behind the scenes."

"Why didn't you tell anyone? This seems like it should be illegal."

"It's too big for a couple whistle blowers to take down. Besides, it really isn't as widespread as we may make it seem, but it is there and you need to know that there are a lot of people over there that are going to want to see you fail. You can't let them."

"I won't."

"If you have any questions, we're here for you, sis." Bradley said. They then turned and walked out of her room, closing the door behind them. Jenna locked the door again and leaned against the wall as all the information they gave her began to spin through her mind. She knew in their own way, they thought they were helping, but the inside information they offered her left her more distressed than she had been all week. Jenna, like most people, was working under a basic understanding that those who administered the tests were people of great integrity and had no personal stake in it. That they were duty bound to be fair and honest with everyone who tested, but they were only human. They were imperfect and prone to temptation and petty emotions. It was a reasonable thing, but tore away what little calm Jenna was holding onto.

Jenna then ran into her bathroom, turned the water on in the shower, peeled off her clothes and got in as fast as she could. The water washed down her body like a waterfall. It was hot on her skin. She waddled around in the water in order to get an even spray, but stopped and when she did, she began to feel the hot water sting at her skin. It grew more intense, but she just stood there. She looked over at her left arm, which was receiving most of the punishment, and the flesh was starting to turn red and the pain was growing more significant. It hurt her, but as long as her arm hurt, she didn't seem to care about the tests. She basked in her short vacation from her worries. She closed her eyes and despite the growing pain, she could still envision the testing camp based on what she had heard and read so far. She was there. There was a sky above and grass below. There were other kids all around but she couldn't see their faces. The heat was growing more intense. A jet of cool air came over her and the hot water stopped. Jenna opened her eyes and discovered she had fallen down and was on the floor of the shower. Her skin was red and hot to the touch. She looked up and saw her mother kneeling down over her.

"Come on, baby." She said as she pulled Jenna to her feet and led her out to the bed.

"What happened?"

"You were in the shower for over an hour. I came to check on you and found you fallen over like that. What were you doing in there?"

"I, I don't know."

"I realize the closer the day comes, the more intense it's all going to feel. Sometimes that pressure can result in odd behavior like this. I just want you to promise me if there is anything you need to talk about, I mean anything; you will do that first. Please."

"I promise."

"Good," Jenna's mother looked down at her arm and saw that it was still very red. She pulled the covers of the bed over Jenna and made sure she was comfortable. "You're not burned too badly. You just rest and I'll bring up your dinner. Okay?"

"Okay. Thanks."

Later that night, Jenna was feeling better and wandered downstairs where she found her family sitting in the kitchen eating out of a carton of rocky road ice cream. She got herself a spoon and sat down to join them.

"Feeling better?" Jenna's mother asked.

"A little light headed, but yes. I don't know what happened up there."

"It happens more often than you think," Her father said.

"You just had a mild nervous breakdown. It's a rather typical response."

"I just wanted to take a hot shower. I just got lost in so many thoughts."

"What were you thinking about?"

"The tests. What else? Then when I felt the pain on my arm, I knew I should have done something about it, but I didn't want to. Or I didn't know what. My mind just blanked. Thanks for finding me, Mom."

"I had to do something. You had just about used up all the hot water in the house." Jenna let out a giggle and it completely took her by surprise. She realized it had been the first time she had laughed all week and it seemed to be infectious because soon Brian and Bradley were laughing. Soon the kitchen was filled with a chorus of laughter and it was difficult to understand why and even more difficult to stop.

When they all did settle down and get back to the business of eating ice cream, Jenna sat back and looked at her mother and father and her two brothers. She felt as though they hadn't been as they just were in too long.

There was no more talk of the tests that night, and it was another hour until the family had completely emptied the carton of rocky road ice cream.

Chapter 7

The Dress

Friday morning came at last and brought a feeling of relief and dread to Jenna. The moment was approaching and it felt as though an entire lifetime had passed since the beginning of the week. The world had skewed in her eyes and would never look the same again, no matter what happened. She got up and then recalled that she didn't need to go to school. Students who were scheduled to be tested were excused from classes the Friday before they left for their tests. It was a small provision that was put in place in order for families to spend more time together before it was too late. The one humanitarian act the ESA offered, in most people's opinion.

Jenna got dressed and headed down to the kitchen, not sure what to expect, and when she turned the corner she saw there was a large paper banner hanging over the threshold between the living room and kitchen that read 'Happy Birthday Jenna!' in large block letters. There were brightly colored garlands strung over the kitchen table and a vase full of flowers sitting at Jenna's seat. She walked over and examined the flowers. It was a colorful mix of roses, daisies and tulips with some Baby's Breath sprayed in for good measure. She then discovered a card stuck amongst the blossoms. She plucked it out and opened it up.

"Dear Jenna. As your birthday isn't until Monday, we thought we'd get a jump on the party. Love, Mom." The silence was broken by the squeal of a plastic horn. Jenna spun around and saw her family running in. They swarmed around her and hugged her tightly and as the chaos settled, she noticed her father holding a nicely wrapped package with a couple of green balloons attached.

"Happy birthday, sweetheart." He said as he offered her the present. It was a perfect cube sized box with red paper, rainbow colored ribbon and an iridescent bow on top.

"You guys! This is great! I can't believe you did this."

"You really thought we would send you off without a party? We were planning on doing this for dinner, but since you just have to go to that party tonight, we had to improvise."

"I thought you were okay about the party, Mom."

"I'm as okay as any mother should be allowed, but don't push it. Now sit down and open your gift while I get the cake."

"Cake? In the morning?"

"Never mind that," Her father said as he pulled out her chair and sat her down. "Open your present." Jenna watched as her father and brothers sat down around her and looked at the present. For a brief second, she felt time stop. There was something in that moment that she didn't want to lose or let fade by and her instinct told her that if she just stopped moving, everything would just freeze- and stay as it was in that single second.

"Come on, Jenna! Open it!" Brian whined and she was pulled back into reality. She slid her nails under the ribbon and pulled it off the box. She then stuck her fingers between the folds of the paper and began to pull at it. She heard as it began to tear and give way under her pressure. As she pulled the scraps of paper away, she could make out that there was a box inside. A white box with a silver trim. She opened the box and discovered a beautiful silver charm in the shape of a heart with small diamonds fitted along the sides resting on a satin pillow inside.

"Oh, my god!" Jenna said as she took the charm in her hand. As she looked more closely at it, she saw that it was actually a locket. She popped it open and saw a picture of her family inside. She looked to her father who was beaming at her.

"Just something to remember us by when you're away. The tests can get pretty tough and at least with this you can remember us and find some of that courage we've spent the past sixteen years putting into you."

"I love it. Thank you." Jenna leapt up and hugged her father and then went onto hug her mother and even her brothers. She held the locket close to her heart as she sat down again.

"Okay. Now for the cake." Jenna sat up and watched her mother with curiosity that as she went over to the stove and not the fridge. She opened up the door and pulled out a large plate that had a tall stack of pancakes resting on top. They were decorated with frosting and whipped cream and candies in an attempt to make it look like a regular birthday cake. She set it down on the table and Brian and Bradley started pushing candles into it and lit them up. They gathered around and sang 'Happy Birthday' to Jenna as she tried to hold back her laughter and once they were done, she blew them out. Brian plucked the candles out of the stack and then Bradley grabbed the maple syrup and began pouring it all over the cake.

"When did you do this?" Jenna asked. Her mother produced a large knife and sliced into the pancakes, cutting them into triangle portions.

"I had the idea last night and I managed to get up early enough to make this in advance."

"You did all of this today?" Jenna asked.

"I'm used to getting up at the crack of dawn. And at least this time I had a good reason."

"This is fantastic." Jenna watched as her mother carefully balanced a stack of the pancake cake on the knife and dropped it neatly on a smaller plate.

"This looks so good." Jenna said as she watched the frosting and syrup mingle together.

Her first thought was that it looked disgusting, but as she gazed at the sight more, she started to think it sounded pretty good. She took a forkful and stuffed it into her mouth. Her eyes widened as her taste buds nearly exploded from the sweet overload.

"What do you think?"

"I love it!" Jenna said as she continued to scarf down the cake. Brian and Bradley got their slices and had the same reaction. Jenna's mother fixed a plate for herself and her husband. They looked at each other with concern.

"Now I'm not sure how good an idea this was." She said as she poked at the pancakes.

"I think I got Diabetes just looking at it," He said. Jenna's mother took a bite and she looked up at her husband as though she had just had a major revelation. She had no words.

She just started gobbling up the treat faster. "You only live once." He said and then dove in.

After the birthday pancakes were gone, the family just sat back and enjoyed the afterglow.

"That was incredible." Jenna said as she gently patted her stomach. The pancakes proved to be incredibly rich and sweet, but worth every inch she may have added to her waistline.

"Yes, but I think we're all have to go on a diet for the rest of the year." Her mom said.

"If it means we can have that once a year, it's worth it." Bradley said as he was licking his plate clean. Jenna looked over to the floor and saw the box with her locket sitting next to her chair. She picked it up and looked at the locket again. It glinted with the morning sun that was pouring in from outside and looked as though it had come from Heaven.

She sat up and managed to clasp it on by herself. She felt the weight of it around her neck.

"You like it?" Her father asked as he took her hand.

"I love it, Dad. Thank you. Thank you all." Jenna said.

"So," Her mother began. "What have you got planned for your day off?"

"Aggy was going to come by, and we were going to head out and shop around for new clothes for the party tonight."

"Is that right? Well, what were you thinking about wearing to this party?"

"I don't know. I was thinking I could wear that red dress of mine and do my hair up. Splash on some make up."

"This party is a big deal to you, isn't it?"

"Not as much as keeping Mark out of Chandra Brown's talons."

"Okay. I get the picture now. This is a turf war," Her mother said.

"All right boys. Girl talk. Let's finish digesting those pancakes in the living room." Her father said and ushered the boys out. Jenna's mother sat down next to her at the table and there was a look of wisdom in her eyes.

"Do you really think Mark's head could be so easily turned?"

"I don't know. I mean, I trust him, but boys our age are kind of stupid."

"My dear, don't wait for that to change any time soon. Believe me."

"I just need to make sure he keeps his eyes on me. Chandra kind of has a reputation."

"I know the type. I was dating a boy named Steven Wilkes when I was in school. I thought he and I were going to be together forever. Then one day, Melinda LeTour came along and over the span of a month Steve and I went from boyfriend and girlfriend to casual acquaintances."

"What happened?"

"Melinda. She had the boobs and the body and for a sixteen-year-old boy, that's about all you need. He always volunteered to help her study, which I thought was innocent until I found out that neither of them were in any of the same classes. She knew all the tricks to get her hooks into him and she didn't hold back for a second. I didn't stand a chance."

"This is supposed to make me feel better?"

"But I got over that loss and eventually I met a cute, awkward, and sweet man and you call him 'Dad'. You're young and you have a lot of experiences ahead of you. If Mark sticks around, great. If he strays, that's nothing on you and one day you will find the right one."

"So your advice would be not to take this so seriously."

"Yes, but if you insist on playing this little game," Jenna's mother then got up and fetched her purse and then pulled out a small, shiny plastic card and offered it to her. "You're going to play to win."

"Seriously? Your National Bank Card?"

"It's your birthday."

"What's my limit?"

"Just a little less than our house payment would be lovely. Other than that, the sky's the limit."

Aggy and Jenna were walking through the Sunset Falls Shopping Center, trying to navigate through the crowd. They had hoped it would have been far less busy, but it seemed they had walked right into the epicenter of all activity.

"This is nuts!" Aggy said.

"I know. I would have sworn everyone would have gone to the water park today."

"That's not what I mean. This is, possibly, the last weekend of these kids' lives and they are choosing to spend their last days at the mall."

"Well, what do you expect them to do? Go on a three-day trip around the world? Fly to the moon?"

"No, but maybe they could do something more meaningful; something important."

"And why are you here? I told you what I wanted to do and you said yes to this."

"Because I'm your best friend and this is what best friends do."

"I would have understood if you had wanted to do something more meaningful instead. I can shop for clothes by myself."

"No, you can't. I've seen what you get when you shop unsupervised. It's my duty as your best friend to prevent a tragedy like that paisley dress you got last year."

"Whatever." Jenna said.

The girls had been shopping for over two hours and had tried on countless dresses and outfits but hadn't been able to find anything to their liking, and worse, the crowds at the mall seemed to be getting bigger and more unruly. They turned and saw a nearby dress shop and ducked inside for some breathing room. The store was stocked with all kinds of dresses and accessories. The racks went all the way to the back, and they were all divided into different sections. There was casual, business, formal, casual business sections clearly marked and a small clearance section pushed off to the side. It also was oddly deserted, but they decided to take advantage and began to snoop around.

They headed over toward where the party dresses were and started their search. As they checked the racks, Jenna noticed the prices on the dresses and they weren't so much that they shocked her, but they weren't any great bargains either. She grabbed a lovely blue dress with sparkling stones running up the side and across the neckline. She held it up to Aggy and she studied it.

"Not bad. How much?" Jenna checked the tag and felt a little tug at her heart.

"Over three hundred." Jenna said with disappointment.

"So? Your Mom said you could spend whatever you wanted."

"Within reason. I don't know how reasonable this is."

"Mark would kill to see you in something like this."

"I don't know. It's pretty, but is it me?"

"Not even close, but isn't that the point?" Jenna looked at the dress again. Her heart began to race and her face was getting hot.

"I'll try it on, but that's it. I should at least see what it would look like." Jenna then turned away and found a salesclerk who directed her to the fitting rooms in the back.

Jenna slipped the dress on and stepped out of the fitting room with her eyes closed, as though expecting to face a firing squad. She opened her eyes and found that she was standing in front of a mirror, and she saw herself in the dress. It felt comfortable, but it looked like it was clinging to her figure. The stones glinted and danced in the light as she moved. She turned and saw Aggy staring at her with her mouth wide open.

"Well?" Jenna asked.

"You have to get it. You look incredible!"

"I don't know. It's a lot of money."

"Your Mom would so approve."

"Maybe I should call her. Hand me my phone."

"No. There's a chance she might say no, and that would be a crime against fashion. You have to get this dress." Jenna spun around and took stock of her appearance once more. The dress felt so good. So right. She let out a frustrated sigh and turned to Aggy.

"Fine." Jenna relented. She went back into the fitting room to change back, but she couldn't help but get another look at herself in the dress. It was stunning, she thought, but she felt something in her throat and before she realized it, she was crying. She felt the tears coming down her cheeks. It was as if some magic lifted the cloak of a normal life away and she felt the weight of the tests upon her again. It seemed there was no way to escape it. Just when she thought she had buried her fear and anxiety away, it would come rolling back like a stampede. It would happen because of a word or a sound or any other random thing in her day that she would see or hear that would remind her of what was coming and pull her back into despair. The fears that lingered just behind her eyes would creep back like stubborn weeds. One day of being a normal person broke away and it felt like the end of the world all over again. She pressed her hand to her mouth to muffle her cries and she heard Aggy calling for her.

"What's that matter? You fall in?" She asked with a laugh. Jenna took a breath and held it all back, just as she always did.

"I'm fine. Thanks. I'll be right out." Jenna said. She gave herself another look in the mirror and wiped away the tears. Her reflection was her fear but there would be no place for that today, she vowed.

Jenna returned home and found the house was quiet. She held the garment bag her dress was in close.

"Mom?"

"In the kitchen, sweety!" Her mother called out.

"Just checking!" Jenna then dashed up the stairs and slammed the door of her room as she raced in. Jenna held the garment bag up as though the answer to her whole life was within. She laid it out on her bed and unzipped it and just stared down at the dress. It looked even more gorgeous now that she owned it. She slid her hand across the smooth fabric. She knew she should not have spent so much money, but she couldn't allow such an opportunity escape either. She was startled by a knock at her door.

"Jenna? Are you in there?" Her mother asked. "How was the mall? Did you find something nice?"

"Uh, yes, Mom."

"Oh! Let me see it," She said as she pushed the door open. Jenna tried to block her, but it was too late. She had seen the dress. She ran over to it and seemed to be in a state of shock. "This is beautiful, honey!" She picked it up and examined the fabric. Jenna's heart was pounding.

"I have your card." She blurted out as she went for her purse and produced the card. She offered it hoping it would distract her mother from the dress, but she simply snagged the card without diverting her eyes for even a moment.

"You were gone for quite a while, but it clearly was worth the wait. This dress is amazing."

"Thanks. It was a real find. I just need to fix a few things with it and put some accessories together." Jenna tried to take the dress back, but her mother turned away, still admiring the garment.

"I love the stones. They really set it off. How much was it?" Jenna felt her heart fall.

"Uh, I forget."

"You forgot? How can you forget how much you paid for a dress? How much was it?" Jenna then saw she had dropped the receipt for the dress on the floor and she snagged it off the floor and stuffed it in her back pocket. Jenna's mother's gaze grew cold. "Jenna. How much did you pay for this dress?" Jenna took a step back and refused to speak. Her mother then turned away with the dress and started searching it for something. She finally found the tag and scanned it. She then turned back to Jenna. "Three hundred dollars? You spent three hundred dollars on this one dress?"

"You said the sky was the limit."

"I know, but three hundred dollars?"

"I'm sorry, but it just called to me. You see how gorgeous it is!" Jenna's mother then stopped for a moment and tried to fight back her initial rage.

"You're right."

"I am?"

"Yes. I signed off on this, and it's all right."

"It is?"

"We may lose the cable for a month, but yes, it's all right."

"Thanks, mom!" Jenna said as she hugged her mother.

"What are you going to do when Dad sees the credit card bill though?"

"He hasn't seen the credit card bill in over ten years. Don't worry about him."

Chapter 8

CHAPTER 42

The Party

Jenna was standing before her mirror with hair done and in her shoes with the dress on, just as she had envisioned it back at the store. She had spent a little extra time on her make-up and given the results, she judged it to be an excellent use of her time. She looked at her reflection and barely recognized the girl she saw. She had thought she would be happy when she saw how good she looked, but instead she just grew nervous. It all looked wonderful, but she wasn't sure it was her. She heard her door squeak gently and she spun around to see her mother peeking in.

"I'm sorry, but I couldn't resist. I had to see," Her words were lost once her eyes adjusted to her daughter's new look. She was speechless for nearly a half minute as she took in the transformation.

"What do you think?" Jenna asked.

"Breathtaking. You look wonderful, honey!" Her mother then walked up and started fussing with her hair a bit. "Just have to keep those hairs out of your face. Sweety. You look amazing. I'm not sure I'm comfortable letting you go to this party anymore."

"Don't even joke." Jenna said as she turned back to the mirror for another inspection.

"Mark's eyes may never go back into their sockets when he gets a look at you."

"Just as long as it's enough to keep his eyes on me and off of Chandra."

"I thought we discussed this."

"Yes, I know, but still."

"I don't know what this Chandra looks like, but it's a fair bet you're going to blow her out of the water."

The doorbell then rang and Jenna felt her heart pick up a little speed.

"That's Mark. Should I answer the door?"

"No! Wait here. I'll get the door. You make an entrance." Jenna's mother said with excitement. She ran out of the bedroom and trampled down the stairs to the door and opened it and saw Mark standing before her wearing a nice black button-up shirt with a red t-shirt underneath.

"Hi, Mrs. Holdren. Is Jenna ready?"

"Hello, Mark. Come on in. You can see for yourself," Mark stepped into the house and Mrs. Holdren positioned him at the foot of the stairs. "Jenna? You have company!" She called out. Moments later, Jenna appeared at the top of the stairs. She nearly glowed as the light hit the stones on her dress just right. Mark's arms fell to his sides as he watched her carefully descend.

"Hi, Mark."

"Jenna?"

"Who else?"

"You look amazing!"

"Thanks. You look nice too."

"Yeah, but you look amazing!" Mark seemed to be having trouble finding anything other than that to say.

"Hold on!" Jenna's father called out from the next room. "I want to see my little girl before she runs out and," He froze as he ran in from the living room and saw Jenna standing before him and then he saw the dazed look on Mark's face. "Jenna? Is that you?"

"Yes, Dad."

"Doesn't she look wonderful?" Her mother asked.

"Uh, yes. Yes, she looks incredible. Were you two leaving now?"

"I think so, yeah." Jenna said as she secured her clutch purse over her shoulder.

"Well, before you run off, why don't I take Mark and have a little conversation about things." Her father said as he took Mark by his shoulder and pulled him back toward the living room.

"Dad! Don't scare him!"

"We're just going to talk." He said as he and Mark disappeared around the corner.

"Don't worry about your father. You know he's all bark. He likes Mark."

"He looked like he was fit to kill."

"Well, that's how fathers are when their little girls look like this. Are we clear on the curfew?"

"Yes. Leave the party by eleven."

"Right. You have everything?" Jenna popped open her purse and checked the contents.

"I've got money, just in case. Tissues. My cell phone and touch up mascara, should I need it."

"Good girl. I hope you have fun tonight."

"Me too. It could be the last fun I have in a long time."

"Stop. Jut for tonight, there are no tests. There's only this party and no tomorrow. Agreed?"

"Right," Mark and Jenna's father returned and there was a look of fear in Mark's eyes as he returned to Jenna. "What did you talk about?"

"Nothing, sweety. I just sat Mark down and ran through some possible outcomes if the night should take an unexpected turn."

"Please tell me you didn't threaten him."

"Nonsense. I gave him helpful behavioral guidelines."

"It looks like you threatened his life."

"I would never! I just told him that if my little girl cries for even a second, it wouldn't be unheard of if someone's arms got broke."

"Dad!"

"He assured me everything will be fine. Won't it, Mark?"

"Uh, yes, sir!"

"See?" Jenna rolled her eyes and took Mark by his hand as they went to the door.

"Have fun, honey!" Her mother said as the door shut.

"I am so sorry about that, Mark." Jenna said as she and Mark got further from the house.

"It's fine. I get it. Parents can be overprotective, but your dad has nothing to worry about. I'm going to take extra good care of you," Mark then snaked his arm around Jenna's waist and pulled her in for a kiss. The door of the house opened and Mark saw Jenna's father standing with his arms crossed. "Maybe we should just get the Hell out of here now." Mark said and then led Jenna to a car parked nearby.

"What's this?"

"Our ride."

"You drove?"

"I've been driving since I was eleven. My dad taught me."

"But you don't have a license."

"No, but my mom said if I was real careful, I could take the car out. As long as I don't get pulled over, I'm good."

"But what if you do get pulled over?"

"Why do you dwell on the negative so much?" Mark then opened the passenger side of the car and beckoned Jenna in. She slid into her seat and he got behind the wheel from the other side. He turned the car on and pulled out like it was nothing.

"You're not afraid of anything, are you?"

"Life's too short," Mark said. "Why are you always so afraid?"

"I'm not afraid. I'm cautious. There's a difference."

"Not much of one."

"I guess my parents taught me the importance of following the rules."

"Boring! This is the time when we really need to cut loose and live! It could be our last chance. Just let go a little bit. Let's have fun tonight." Jenna looked into Mark's eyes and all her anxieties drifted away and she understood his logic.

"You're right. Let's have fun."

As Mark got closer to Chandra's house, he noticed an increase in traffic and Jenna was becoming a bit nervous about going to the party. Mark turned onto Chandra's street and saw that there was not a single place to park. There were cars packed in on either side of the street and there were even cars parked on Chandra's front lawn.

"Wow. I thought we were getting here early." Mark said as he passed by Chandra's house. He turned at the corner and went up to the next street. It was also packed. There was a little bit of Jenna that was beginning to feel relief that they couldn't find a place to park. She was about to suggest they just go on and do something else, but before she could, Mark swung the car around hard and parked in a little spot that had been hidden in the shadows.

"Whew! Lucky." He said. He looked over at Jenna and she forced a smile back at him.

"Yeah. That was close."

They walked back to Chandra's house. The music could be heard from down the block and the lights lit up the whole street. There were kids running in and out of the house screaming and yelling. There were a few running around with water balloons and tossing them randomly.

"Can you believe her parents actually said yes to all this?" Jenna asked as they approached.

"It's nuts." Mark said. Jenna then saw one of the little trolls with water balloons approaching her out the corner of her eye. She grabbed Mark and dashed toward the house before they could strike.

They walked into the house and saw that it was packed. Everyone was bouncing to the pulsating music and drinks were in everyone's hands. Mark and Jenna tried to push their way through the wall of bodies.

"Where do we go?" Jenna asked.

"I don't know! Just head to the kitchen!" Mark said.

"Why?"

"That's where the drinks should be!"

Jenna and Mark fought their way through the crowd and found a little breathing room in the kitchen. It seemed to be the one room where there was any place to stand. Jenna saw that there were beer kegs on the floor and a full array of liquor bottles on the counters.

"Wow. This is a little more than I thought it would be."

"Relax, babe. Everyone's just having fun." Mark said, just as one of the party guests fell over, vomiting everything she had drunk onto the floor. Chandra then appeared from the crowd flanked, as always, by her entourage.

"Get some towels and clean that shit up," Chandra barked and both her flunkies ran off to fulfill their duty. She then turned to Mark and smiled. "Mark! You made it!" She ran up to him and swung her arms over his shoulders and pulled him in, uncomfortably close. Jenna let out a loud cough and did her best to squeeze between them.

"And I'm here."

"Oh. Jenna. So you are," Chandra said with a dead smile. She then pushed Jenna aside and lit up as her eyes found Mark once more. "Mark. The real action is happening out in the backyard. The pool's open and I've got Jell-O shots out there too. You should really come and check it out."

"That's sounds great, but I didn't bring my trunks. Didn't think we'd be swimming."

"Silly. You don't need your trunks to skinny dip."

"Thanks, Chandra, but I think Mark and I will hang back here for a bit. We just got here after all." Jenna said.

"Mark?"

"I'm with my girl, but we'll be out in a bit." Mark said. Chandra shot Jenna an acidic glance and turned away, back into the crowd.

"What a bitch." Jenna said.

"Forget her. You want a drink?"

"Do they have any soda?"

"Come on, Jenna. I mean a drink drink."

"I don't know. I've never had alcohol."

"Okay. I know a good drink. It's sweet. You won't taste a drop of alcohol. Wait here."

Mark then dashed over to the liquor and started fixing whatever drink he knew how to make. Jenna looked around while she waited for Mark and she was growing more uncomfortable. She was becoming unsure if keeping an eye on Mark was worth being at that party. She recognized a lot of the kids from school, but they were all drunk and acting crazy. The music wasn't even very good. Mark returned with the drinks and handed one to Jenna. It was bright red and seemed to be fizzing.

"What is it?"

"Don't worry. Taste it." Jenna tipped the cup against her lip and the drink trickled into her mouth. It was sweet, as promised. There was a bitter under-taste as well, but overall, she liked it.

"It's good." Jenna said as she went for another sip, but Mark held her hand before she could drink.

"You may want to pace yourself with it, though. There's actually a lot of alcohol in it." He warned.

After she finished the first drink, Jenna began to feel light headed, but she was also beginning to feel relaxed. Mark fixed Jenna up with another and they ventured out to the backyard. It seemed that was where the heart of the party was. There were Tiki torches lit up along the back wall and kids were running around screaming. The pool was the main center of activity. Jenna looked over and it looked as though everyone in the pool was completely naked as well.

As they wandered around taking in everything, Chandra emerged from the crowd once more, this time she was soaking wet wearing only a towel around her waist and a very small bra over her breasts.

"Mark! Come on! Swim with me!" She begged as she reached for his pants.

"That's all right, Chandra. I'm good." He said as he leapt back from her grasp.

"Oh come on. It's fun. The water is nice and warm."

"Probably all the heat coming off the bodies," Jenna said. "Are your parents aware you are running a Roman orgy in their backyard?"

"My parents said I could do whatever I wanted tonight. No questions asked. No excuses given. Kind of like how I live my life."

"Interesting. I mean, I'd have questions. Like, how many of these guys have you screwed so far?"

"Excuse me?"

"Don't act surprised. Everyone knows you're a world class slut. Just like everyone knows you prey on other girls' boyfriends."

"May I remind you that you are not an invited guest? You are only here because Mark brought you, and while I'd hate to kick him out, I would if it meant getting rid of you." Mark pulled Jenna aside and snagged her drink from her.

"She's sorry, Chandra. She's just had a little too much to drink," Mark said as he ushered Jenna away. "What the Hell was that?"

"What?"

"You called Chandra a slut."

"And?"

"Jenna!"

"Look, you wanted me to have a drink, I had a drink. Besides, who cares? So I'm a little honest. So I tell it a little more like it is. I'm having fun. You wanted me to have fun, right?"

"Yes, but not by insulting the host of the party. She's right. You weren't exactly invited."

"Let her throw me out. If I go, you go," Mark then shifted his eyes away for a moment.

"Mark? That's right, isn't it? If I go, you go."

"I really like Chandra's parties."

"Oh my God. You'd throw me under the bus, wouldn't you?"

"Let's not talk about this, okay? No one's getting thrown out. We're all just trying to have fun."

"This party is more important to you than me?"

"I never said that!"

"You kind of just did."

"Look, how about we get away from all this? Come on." Mark then took Jenna's hand and led her back into the house.

They went up the stairs and discovered while the party was raging below, there was another party simmering above. Jenna couldn't see too clearly, but she saw several figures in the shadows mingling together. Mark went down the hall and checked every closed door until they got to the end of the hall and he found one that was empty. It appeared to be some kind of guest room. The décor was drab and minimal and there was only a small twin bed stuck in the corner with beige sheets on it. Mark shut the door and locked it as Jenna leapt up onto the bed and spread out on her back.

"Comfy?" Mark asked as he slid up to her.

"My head's spinning."

"That's normal. Just relax." Mark said as he ran his hand down Jenna's body, stopping at her legs.

"What are you doing?"

"Nothing."

"It doesn't feel like nothing. I told you I wasn't ready."

"I know, but that doesn't mean we can't touch a little, does it?"

"I guess not," Jenna said as she slid her arm around Mark. "She wants you, you know that, right?"

"Who? Chandra?"

"Yes."

"She wants everyone she can't have."

"She can have them. It's you she can't have."

"She won't have me. I'm yours."

"You're such a great guy."

"And you're a great girl. I love this dress." Mark then began to finger along the neckline of the dress. Jenna felt his finger probe along her body and at first it felt nice, but she started to feel as though he were getting closer than she wanted. She slid away from him a bit, but he crawled closer as she did.

"No, Mark."

"Come on. How about a kiss? We can kiss, can't we?" Mark leaned in and brushed his lips against Jenna's. They were soft a bit salty. Her heart was beating faster than ever. The sound from outside was beginning to fade away and all she could hear were their heartbeats. Mark pushed his lips in and Jenna felt his tongue slide into her mouth. His warmth overpowered her and he pressed his body to hers. He was so strong, she thought. His hands carefully explored her body and cupped her breasts gently. "You're so beautiful, baby." He whispered. Jenna felt his hands slide further down and then go up under her dress. She was jolted back and pushed him away.

"Mark! No. I told you I'm not ready!"

"Come on! We go in for testing next week. This could be the last time we'll be able to do this."

"I thought you were sure that you and I were going to pass."

"I am."

"So why can't you wait?"

"I can."

"But you don't want to."

"I just don't see what we're waiting for! I think we're there now." Jenna then noticed a shiny object in Mark's hand. She reached over and grabbed it from him and saw that it was a condom.

"You had this all planned out, didn't you?"

"No."

"Then why do you have this?"

"Just in case. I thought maybe if things went good, maybe,"

"I don't believe this. We have talked about this a thousand times, and every time you said you understood how I felt." Jenna said as she slid off the bed.

"I do understand, but I don't get why you can't understand how I feel! I have needs! Do you realize I'm the only guy on the team who hasn't done it with his girlfriend? All the other guys are getting it regularly, but you keep making me jump through all these hoops."

"I'm sorry, but I just thought that what we had was more important than sex! Who cares what the other guys on the team think anyway? It's none of their business."

"It's not that I care, it's just that, well," Mark began to stammer as Jenna waited for his answer.

"Well?"

"Okay! Fine! I care! I care because I'm the one who gets ripped on all the time for dating a virgin. I care because I'm forced to see my buddies get laid whenever they want while I'm getting nothing!"

"Fine. If it's all that important to you, we can change all of that." Mark got up on his knees and hobbled over to her.

"We can?"

"Yes. We're done. Now you're free to find some girl who will put out for you." Jenna then stormed toward the door and walked out. Before she could make it to the stairs, Mark grabbed her arm.

"You don't mean that! It's the liquor!"

"No, Mark. I'm totally clear on this. If you just want to have sex, you should really find another girl. I've made it clear how I feel about you. If that's not enough, then maybe this isn't what I thought it was and there's no reason to drag it out any longer than we have to."

"Jenna. I love you."

"Then love me enough to respect me. Get over the macho bullshit and be a man."

"You're right. I'm sorry."

"What time is it?" Mark looked down at his watch.

"A little after ten thirty."

"We need to go soon."

"How about one more drink?"

"Fine. A quick one."

"Promise. Why don't you go back to the room? At least we can have a little quiet with our drinks."

"Fine." Jenna then went back to the guest room and sat on the bed awaiting Mark's return.

She waited for what seemed like an eternity. She felt the buzz she had gotten from the last two drinks wear off. She looked over to the clock on the nightstand and it was ten to eleven. Her patience had expired and she got up and ventured out to find Mark.

She made her way back down and found the kitchen. He wasn't there. She pushed her way through the whole house, checking every room but there was no sign of Mark. A feeling of dread filled her stomach and she headed out to the backyard. As she pushed her way through the crowd she scanned every face that came by. The music was growing louder. She looked over at the pool. She saw Chandra running around, laughing. She still had the towel on, but she had lost her bra. Jenna headed toward the pool and as she got closer, she could hear voices. Most of them were unfamiliar, but one stood out. Her heart began to race and soon she was running. She made it to the pool area and she looked down into the water. The pool was full and everyone was splashing around and laughing, but Jenna's skin was growing cold. At last she saw Mark. He was in the water, naked with one of Chandra's friends locked in his arms.

"I had my fun a few minutes ago. Figured I'd loan him out to a friend." Chandra said as she slinked up behind Jenna. She then looked back down at Mark. He finally looked up at Jenna and she was expecting a look of fear and shock on his face, but instead he just smiled and laughed like an idiot. She didn't even wait for him to speak. She turned and saw his clothes piled on a chair. She ran over, rifled through his pants and found the keys to the car. She shot him one last look and then stormed away.

As Jenna forced her way back through the party, she was hoping to feel a tug on her arm or to hear Mark call out for her, but she made it all the way to the front door without any such distraction. She turned and saw no one had been following her. It seemed he wasn't even concerned that she had his keys. She caught a glimpse of herself in the mirror. The dress wasn't quite as pretty anymore. She stormed away from the party, walked back to the car and deliberated over what to do next. It wasn't a long drive and she knew enough about driving to get the car back to her house. She got in, started it up and pushed away her anxieties and drove back home.

Chapter 9

CHAPTER 43

After-Party

Jenna snuck into the house and tried to make as little noise as she could manage. She had parked Mark's car a block away and had the keys with her. She didn't do any damage to it, but she kind of wanted to make him sweat when he realized the car wasn't parked outside her house the next morning.

She went into the kitchen and tried to find something to eat. She didn't know what she wanted to eat but she just knew she wanted to eat. She checked every cupboard but nothing really called to her. She then pulled open the freezer and that's when she saw it. Ice cream. She only saw Vanilla, but she could work with it. She grabbed the ice cream, and then got some chocolate sauce and some whipped cream. She set it all on the table and thought of getting a bowl, but when she saw the carton was only half full, she decided to just finish it off. She poured the syrup in and topped it all off with a mountain of whipped cream and started eating. The light came on and Jenna spun around to see her mother standing at the doorway.

"I thought I heard something," She said as she checked her watch. "On time. I thought for sure you were going to stay out later. I only said you had to be out of that party by eleven. I never said you had to be home by then."

"That's actually what we were planning, but I didn't know you had already figured that out."

"Why do you think I said it like that? I know you. You love to exploit the loopholes. I thought I'd just give you a little challenge. So, not that I mind, but why are you back so early? It's barely midnight. Did you have fun at the party?"

"No." Jenna said as she stabbed her spoon into the ice cream.

"What happened?"

"Men are such jerks, mom!"

"Oh. What did Mark do?"

"Nothing, until we were about to leave. I was right. Chandra was trying to get her hooks into him all night long. We tried to get away from her and we found someplace private."

"You didn't?"

"No, Mom. Although he tried, but we had our talk again and he backed off."

"Good. So what happened?"

"We were about to leave, but he wanted one last drink. He left to go get it, but never came back. I went out to find him and that's when I saw it."

"What?"

"Mark. Naked in the pool with Chandra and one of her clone friends."

"I'm sorry, honey."

"He was drunk, but that's no excuse. He knew what was going on. He just gave in. Why are men like that?"

"I don't know and I don't think they do either. It's just the nature of the beast."

"Was Dad ever like that?"

"When he was younger. I think it's a maturity thing. They have to grow up and see things differently. Mark is at the age where a good time beats out everything else. Are you going to forgive Mark? Give him a second chance?"

"I don't know. Maybe not. I mean, why bother? What's the point? I was looking around at that party. It was insane. Kids were acting like adults. Drinking. Having sex. I kind of realized that no matter how the tests go, nothing is ever going to be the same again, is it?"

"No, sweety. It won't. I think that's the hardest lesson of the test. Everything changes starting now and the world will never look or feel the same."

"Why didn't you tell me about this?"

"Because it's something you just have to find out for yourself. I'll tell you what won't change, though. Your family. Your father and I. Your brothers. We're all still going to be here and we're all going to still love you."

"It's scary. I'm not ready for all of this."

"I know how you feel. It's the eleventh hour and you feel like if you just had one more year; One more month; One more week, you'd be happy."

"Everything seems so much bigger now. I'm not ready for things to get so big."

"It's life. You can't say no. You just do the best you can and hold on with all your might. You can do it, Jenna. I know you can. Even if I wasn't sure that you were going to pass the tests, I'd still put all my money on you to win. You have to start believing that."

"I do, Mom. I do."

"Well, since you're up, I'll tell you now. Since you have two more days until you leave, your father and I were thinking we'd all go up to the beach house. We thought it would be a nice way to,"

"Spend my last days on Earth?"

"You know what I mean. A little burst of fun before you go off for those tests."

"That sounds fun, but could we not?"

"You always love the beach house."

"I do, it's just whenever we go up there the days seem to go by so fast. I kind of want them to drag over the next couple days."

"Trust me. No matter where you go or what you do, time is going to race by. You might as well be someplace fun."

The next morning, Jenna woke up to the sound of the whole house alive with activity. Her parents were making last minute checks before they left and Brian and Bradley were finishing up packing. Jenna slid out of bed and pulled out her suitcase and just threw some shirts and shorts in as well as some toiletries that she thought she might need, including toothpaste and sunscreen. She zipped it up and decided that was all she would need. She then dressed and brought her suitcase down to the foyer. As she set it down, there was a knock at the door. She opened the door and she saw Mark standing before her looking like death warmed over.

"Hi." She said.

"Hey."

"What are you doing here?"

"What do you mean? You took my car. Where is it?" Jenna looked past Mark and saw his mother sitting in another car out on the street.

"She mad at you?"

"Beyond."

"How'd you get home?"

"I don't remember. I don't remember a whole lot from last night."

"You remembered that I took your car."

"Yeah."

"Anything before that?"

"Yes. I know. I was stupid. When I went down to get the drinks, Chandra was right there and she shoved one in my face. I just took a sip and everything got weird."

"And you had sex."

"I don't even remember it."

"Just because you don't remember doing it, doesn't mean it didn't happen."

"I get why you're pissed at me. I'm sorry."

"Your car is on the next block."

"Oh, thank God!" Mark said with great relief. He turned from Jenna and waved to his mother who was still waiting in the car. "It's on the next block! She wanted to scare me!"

"Good girl!" His mother shouted back.

"She knows about what happened?" Jenna asked as Mark turned back to her.

"I guess. I don't know if I told her while I was drunk or what."

"I've been thinking about it and I'm not mad."

"You're not?"

"Anymore. We're about to be tested and that means a lot is going to change. A lot has already changed. Whether you want to admit it or not."

"What are you saying?"

"I'm saying that maybe right now isn't the time to fight. I forgive you for what you did. It was still stupid and thoughtless, but I want us to walk away from this with a clean slate."

"Whoa. Walk away? Come on. I made a mistake. I'm human. We can work this out."

"Maybe we can, but if we can or cannot, I think that will have to wait until after the tests."

"I don't really get this. Are we broken up or not?"

"We are two people. The same two people we've always been. What we'll be in the future will have to wait until after the tests."

"Okay. I get it. That's fine. Just gives me incentive. I'm going to pass and we're going to be together. I screwed up, but I'll make it up to you. I swear." Mark had a fire in his eyes that Jenna recognized.

"Here." She said as she handed Mark the keys to his car. He shot her a quick smile and dashed off to his mother who was still waiting and they drove off. Jenna shut the door and the night before she thought when she closed the door on him, she would feel pain, but much to her surprise, she actually felt free.

Chapter 10

The Long Good Bye

Jenna woke up on Monday morning with the sweet memories of the past weekend still alive in her mind. She looked out the window and saw the sun streaming into her room as it normally did. It was a good day, but when she heard the gentle knock on her door, reality came crashing down on her and her soul felt as though it had turned to lead in the blink of an eye. She looked up and her mother peered in. Her eyes were red and puffy and it was clear she was fighting back a torrent of tears.

"It's time." She said. Her voice was shaky, as were her hands. Jenna looked back at her and nodded.

"All right. I'll be down in a minute," Her mother shut the door and then Jenna slid out of bed. She walked over to the mirror on her dresser and gave herself a good look. "All right. What do you wear?" She asked her reflection. "What do you wear to what could be the beginning of the end of your life?" She pulled open one of the drawers and saw her pants. She pulled out her usual pair of jeans and then went over to her closet and grabbed the first shirt she saw. They looked good, or at least good enough for what was awaiting her. She went on into her bathroom and started up the shower. All the anxiety she had been feeling earlier in the week was nothing compared to what was hitting her in that moment. It was just a few hours away. Before lunch, she would be on a bus that would take her to where she could be chosen to die. It was so surreal to her, but at the same time familiar and expected. She felt like she had been living with it for so long, yet the moment of it becoming real felt so unreal to her.

Jenna finished her shower, dressed and prepared herself for her day. She walked out and saw the bag she had packed for the family's weekend getaway. The scent of sea air and sand was still on it. She picked it up, dumped out whatever was inside and threw it on the bed and began packing again. She just threw in some shirts, some pants and then she went to the bathroom and found a small package she had put together earlier that week. It was small box filled with soaps, shampoo and toothpaste and a few other possible essentials she may need while at the testing camp.

Jenna usually found a certain joy in packing for a trip. She was able to dream and imagine of all the amazing things that might happen for her and then decide what she would need should those things actually happen, but packing for the camp was different. There was no joy or sense of wonder for her. As she pressed down on everything she had packed in order to make sure her case would close, she noticed a drop of moisture fall and it was then she realized she had been crying since she began packing the bag.

Jenna came down to the kitchen with her bag in her hand. She could hear the sound of her family having their breakfast, but as soon as she came within view, everything stopped. They all looked up at her and while they had been telling her over and over about how she was going to pass, they finally had to confront the hated scenario if she did not pass. Jenna set her bag down and sat down at the table. Her mother then fixed her a plate and they all watched her as she began to eat. It was as though they were trying to freeze her image into their brains, if that were to be the last time they'd ever see her again.

"What are we doing?" Her father said. "She's going to pass!"

"Of course!" Her mother added. Brian and Bradley nodded in agreement. They all then looked back at Jenna and while they tried to smile, the pain in their faces was hard to disguise.

"Or, I might not," Jenna said. "I hate to think about it too, but while more than half of those tested who had siblings who passed also passed, there is still a group who failed. I don't like to talk about it, I hate to even think about it, but it's something we all have to accept. This might not work out like we want."

"And are you ready for that, Jenna?" Her mother asked.

"No, but when someone tells you that you're about to die, is anyone ready for that? Can you ever be ready for this?"

"No. I guess not. I just wish there was something we could do or say to make all of this better."

"There is one thing you can do." Jenna said.

"What's that, sweety? Anything!"

"Pass the syrup."

After breakfast Jenna was anxious to go. She wasn't looking forward to getting on the bus, but after having lived with the tension and stress of her possible impending death, the sooner it was over the better, as far as she was concerned. She had her bag set by the door and she was sitting in the living room and watched as the clock on the wall ticked away, minute by minute.

"Honey?" Jenna's mother asked as she approached her.

"No, mom. No."

"What?"

"I don't want the long good bye. I don't want the 'this is the last time we'll be together' speeches. I don't want any of that. This won't be the last time I see you all. If I pass, I'll be back home. If I fail, we'll be given time to say good bye later."

"Fine. You're right. You're just going to be gone for the week. You have everything you need?"

"I think so. I assume if I need anything, they can provide it at the camp."

"They can. It's just nice to be prepared."

"Yeah." Just then the alarm on the clock went off and it was time. Jenna looked to her mother and smiled.

"You'll be back home before you know it." She said.

"I love you, mom." Jenna said and threw her arms around her mother.

"I love you too, sweety." Jenna composed herself and then stood up. She turned and saw her father and brothers standing in front of the door. Her father merely held his arms out and she ran to him.

"I love you! I love you all!"

"We love you too, darling." Her father said. She then looked toward her brothers who seemed to be rather uncomfortable with the high running emotions. Bradley then shrugged his shoulders and pulled his sister into a hug.

"You're going to make it. We know you will." He said. She then slipped away and into Brian's arms.

"I know we give you a lot of shit, but we love you."

"I know, and I allow you to give me shit because I love you." Brian stepped back.

"What do you mean 'allow'?"

"Please. I see those lame pranks of yours a mile away. That morning I said you got me with the plastic wrap on my toilet? I lied. I just said you did because I knew how much it meant to you."

"No. We got you."

"You really didn't."

"Fine. We'll really get you when you get back. We've got a week to come up with some new stuff."

"Bring it." Jenna said with a smile and a catch in her voice. Then there was a knock at the door. It was Aggy.

"Morning, guys. I was coming by to see if Jenna wanted to head to the busses with me."

"Oh, thank you, Aggy, but I think we'll be taking Jenna." Jenna's mother said.

"Are you sure? It gets pretty emotional there and from the looks of it here, you guys are already on the brink. A lot of parents get rides for their kids in order to avoid any emotional breakdowns. My mom got me a limo," Aggy then stepped aside and everyone could see a lavish black stretch limousine outside. "Emotional distance makes it less messy. I heard that sometimes those breakdowns can have a negative effect on test performance."

"Uh, I hadn't heard that."

"I think I read an article about that," Jenna's father said. "The emotional trauma was said to set the tester's natural rhythms off slightly, and in some cases enough to alter performance."

"You know? I think I'll just go with Aggy."

"What?"

"Yeah. I think it's for the best. We've had our little display here. I need to be clear for this. I need to focus on the tests."

"You're right. You're absolutely right," Her father said. "But we will be there to pick you up."

"Deal," Jenna said. She then picked up her bag and turned to Aggy. "Let's go." Aggy took Jenna's hand and they marched out toward the luxury car.

As they piled into the limo, Jenna began to wave at her family but soon the car door shut and that was it. The limo pulled away and there was no going back. The limo was nice. It had leather seats and some festive lighting on the ceiling that shifted from one color to another very slowly.

"I've never been in a limo." Jenna said.

"Me neither. My mom said I deserved to go in style."

"This would be my choice for making a big entrance. How are you feeling?"

"Scared shitless. I threw up like six times last night. I'm really nervous, Jenna."

"Don't be. You're going to make it."

"How about Mark? Should we pick him up too?" Aggy asked. Jenna then realized that they hadn't talked over the past few days and she never had the chance to tell Aggy what had occurred between her and Mark.

"Uh, no. He'll be fine on his own."

"No? Why not? What's happening? Did something happen at that party?"

"I don't want to talk about it."

"Something did happen! Oh my god! Did you and he do it?"

"No!"

"Then what happened?" Jenna let out a deep breath and realized it was either talk about her failed romance or talk about the tests. She chose to take her mind off the bigger worry and as they road to where the busses for the camp were to pick them up, Jenna accounted the whole night of the party to Aggy. When she was done, Aggy was left, for probably the first time in her life, speechless.

"That dog!" Aggy barked.

"I forgave him the next morning, but I don't think we're going to be an item anymore."

"Unbelievable. It's also kind of on Chandra too. You know she got him drunk."

"Probably, but it's fine. I think I have bigger things to worry about now."

Just then the limo stopped. Jenna and Aggy locked eyes and it was as though time held still for them. Then the door opened and they were there. Jenna climbed out of the limo and she saw the busses lined up along the street. They were large gray vehicles that had no exterior marking or words on them. The glass on them was blacked out. They just looked like death to her.

"Wow. This is it," Aggy said. They then both turned and saw the registration area and there was a long line of kids already waiting. There were some kids whose parents brought them and they were having their good bye moments, which were clearly very dramatic and painful to watch. Beyond that, there were picketers chanting about how the ESA was federally sanctioned murder of innocent children.

"Those pro-lifers never miss a beat," Aggy said as she and Jenna found their places in line. From the back it was hard to tune out the screaming and crying of the children and parents alike. Jenna began to turn her head to see who was making the noise. "Don't! Whatever you do, don't turn around. I've heard stories about those things. It's way too upsetting."

"How can you not look? It sounds like they're being chopped into bits."

"Emotionally, they are," A girl ahead of them said. She had a purple Mohawk and a ring through her upper lip. She turned and shot them a quick smile. "I'm Violet Barker."

"Jenna. This is my friend Aggy."

"Nice to meet you."

"You seem pretty calm."

"Because I have prepared for this day since my third birthday. I'm not like all these other pussies. My parents told me about the tests before I could walk. I'm actually looking forward to it."

"You are?"

"Sure. In fact, I've been thinking about throwing 'em."

"What? You mean, fail on purpose?"

"Yes. Look at the world today. Is it such a prize to keep on living? Things are bad now and they are just going to get worse. I'd rather get out now."

"Can you even fail on purpose?" Aggy asked.

"Sure you can," Violet said. A girl in another line began to scream and soon she fell to the ground, heaving and sobbing. A security guard rushed over and helped her up and took her to a medical tent nearby. "That's the seventh freak out this morning. Some people just can't handle it." Violet said.

Jenna finally made it to the front of the line. They took her name and with that, they were able to call up all of her information. They then gave her a number, a bus assignment and she was instructed to wait beyond the red line until her bus was ready to board. She took her bag and went past the red line and sat down on a small bench near the busses. Violet was already there, but she was standing and looked almost anxious to get on board. Aggy soon joined Jenna and they sat together and waited.

There was little talking. There was nothing to be said. They just sat there and watched as the buses would load up and drive away. Most of the kids getting on the buses were white as ghosts. A bus pulled up to them and Jenna's stomach fell. The bus driver got out and instructed everyone to stack their luggage by the side of the street and he would load it all in. Jenna unzipped her bag and pulled out the journal that her mother had given her. She then put her bag with the others and got in line to board the bus. As she got on, she saw Aggy at a seat waving Jenna over, but as she got closer, another girl came along and sat beside Aggy.

"Uh, excuse me, but I was saving that seat for my friend." Aggy said.

"No saving!" The girl barked. Aggy looked up at Jenna.

"Then, I guess I'll just get up and go." Aggy said as she slinked past the girl. They then went further back and found a couple of vacant seats. As they sat down and settled, Violet appeared and sat down with them as well, squeezing tightly against them.

"Here we go." She said.

"You sound like you have some experience with this." Aggy said.

"A little. I've got three brothers and six sisters. They all took the tests and about half passed."

"Only half?"

"Yeah. It happens." Aggy looked to Jenna and they both began to feel worse.

The bus started up and headed out to the highway.

As the bus drove along, there were more freak outs. Some kids would just burst out in tears or they would start screaming. Some even threw up. It was like being in an insane asylum. There were two security guards on board who were trained to help in those cases, but after a while, it was almost too much for the two guards to handle. Jenna opened up her journal and started scribbling down some thoughts. She figured it might help.

Jenna fell asleep at one point and when she awoke, they had arrived at the camp. She looked up and more than half the bus had gotten off. She, Aggy and Violet all got up and started to file out of the bus. When Jenna stepped out she saw a woman who looked rather official standing nearby. She was clad in a government issued uniform and her hair was dark and short.

"Hello." Jenna said.

"Hello, young lady. May I help you?"

"I hope so. I'm not sure where to go."

"Simply follow the line to the reception center."

"Great. Thanks. Also, do you know when the tests begin tomorrow?"

"Tomorrow? My dear, the tests began the minute you stepped off that bus."

Part 2

Chapter 11

Testing Camp

I arrived at the ESA camp with Aggy. The ride over was difficult for us, at least emotionally. I could tell Aggy was on the brink of a total meltdown. She just stared out the window, mumbling to herself. It sounded like she was praying. The rest of the kids on the bus weren't doing much better. There were some freak outs and a few fights. Everyone was on the edge, not that anyone could blame them.

The only one on the bus who was fine, other than the security guards posted at the front of the bus, was a girl named Violet. Aggy and I met her in line at registration and to say she is unique is a gross understatement. She's got purple hair, piercings and most weird of all, she's not afraid of the tests. In fact she mentioned that she was thinking of failing them on purpose. She said that the world is already on the brink of destruction and it's just going to get worse from here on out. I guess I could see her point. The ESA has been trying to bring the human population under control for eighty years already and it doesn't seem like they are any closer. Food supplies are dwindling and there just doesn't seem to be enough of anything to go around. Maybe death would be preferable.

I was standing with a large group of kids waiting to be assigned to a group. They assign everyone to a specific group, and that group will be our testing group. From there, we'll be given room assignments and test schedules for the week. This all seems so big and so overwhelming. The camp's a lot bigger than I had thought it would be. It seemed to go on forever. There were large buildings along the perimeter that were nicely landscaped and almost looked good enough to live in. I assumed that those were the dorms. There were other, larger buildings and they looked to be where some of the tests would be conducted.

The whole facility looked like one giant sports arena with tracks and swimming pools and lots of open fields. It was unlike anything I had imagined. I thought it was going to be smaller, but as I finally saw it, I began to think we had been taken to another country entirely.

As we waited for a counselor to greet us, I saw Aggy growing even more anxious. I was worried about her. She's normally the one who brings me back to the ground. I wasn't sure if I could do the same for her. She kept pacing around nervously; still mumbling just as she was on the bus.

"Aggy!"

"What?"

"Calm down."

"How? How can you be so calm? It's happening. It's all really happening. We're here!"

"Yes, but you knew this was going to happen."

"I did, but there's a difference between knowing something is going to happen and when it actually happens. I'm scared, Jenna. I know I was brave before, but I'm not so sure I can do this anymore." She was falling apart at the seams. I had never seen her so worked up before and it was starting to scare me; although, she was doing better than a lot of the other kids. There was a boy in our group who got down on the ground and curled up into a ball, and I noticed that he was still in that position, gently sobbing into his chest. Everyone else was a lot like Aggy. They were pacing around chattering incoherently or crying or both. It looked like some kind of insane asylum. I wondered if there was something wrong with me that I am was calm.

I heard a commotion coming from one of the other groups. I turned and I saw one group nearby and all of them seemed to be focused on one of their own members. They were booing and yelling at him for some reason.

"What's that all about?" I asked.

"That's Ethan Lazarus."

"Lazarus?"

"Yup. Another one of Senator Lazarus' grandsons. It's his turn to be tested this year."

"Wow. Sucks to be him."

"Doesn't it? I hate the little shit myself, but I kind of feel for him. What is it like to know the whole world hopes you fail? It's not his fault his grandfather was the architect of this legalized holocaust." Violet said.

"I thought you were up for all this."

"I am, don't get me wrong, but I call it like I see it."

"Well, even if everyone is hoping he'll die, I'm sure the odds are in his favor. As far as I've heard, every member of Senator Lazarus' family that's been tested has passed."

"Which makes the world hate them all the more; whenever a Lazarus is put up for the tests, people make up death pools betting whether or not they'll make it."

"You mean if he fails or not."

"Yeah, that too. You never know. It hasn't been unheard of for some testers to have 'accidents' before the end of the tests." I turned to get a better look at Ethan. He was goodlooking. He definitely looked like he grew up with all the advantages and privileges one would expect to grow up with in a political family.

He looked very out of place. His hair was well cared for and he just looked so well put together all the way round. I'd hoped his family would have been wiser than to make him look so perfect before throwing him in with the poor souls his grandfather had all but condemned to death.

As I saw him absorb the hostilities of his group, I began to feel sorry for him. It was a stressful time for everyone, and he was there to be tested just like everyone else. No matter his circumstances outside, he deserved the same respect as anyone else. The shriek of a whistle broke the air and we all turned and saw a counselor standing before us. We were then instructed to join him in the reception lobby for our room assignments.

I got my room and it included a bed with probably the hardest mattress I've ever felt in my life. I was right about the apartment looking bungalows. That's where they were putting us and it actually wasn't too bad. The carpets looked new, as did all the furniture and paint on the walls. My only complaint was my dorm mate. I had hoped to be paired with Aggy, of course, but they have some kind of policy not to put friends together in the same dorm, so I got stuck with Violet. She was actually not too bad a roommate, but when she got on one of her rants, she became a real bummer. I don't think she's ever had a moment of happiness in her entire life.

The building has three floors. The first and third floors were all dorm rooms while the common room was located in the middle of the second floor. That's where the television, snack machines and pay phones were located. I checked it out earlier and it looked clean. The couch was rather nice and it was a good TV. Fifty inches.

Our dorm was on the third floor and had a large front window which gave us a great view of most of the campus. If it weren't for the tests, I would have thought I was having the time of my life.

I loved how the administrators tried to make it all seem like summer camp or something. Some of the kids had actually gotten into it and seemed to have forgotten that their lives were at stake, but I figured whatever they needed to get through this.

Another good thing about this arrangement was that Violet and I had our own bathroom. I wasn't thrilled to have to share it with her, but at least she was the only one I had to share it with. We were also told that cleaning services were daily, but only while we were testing. I was still nervous and scared, but for some reason a little less so. It all did feel like some kind of sleep-away camp thing. Thinking of it in those terms made it all seem a little less serious than it really was. I believed that I'd actually be able to sleep. I wish I could have said the same for Aggy. She was so freaked when she found out we couldn't room together. She never was good with being away from home. I remember the first time she and I went to a sleep over party; she wet her sleeping bag in the middle of the night and spent the rest of the time in the bath tub crying. I could only imagine what she was going through. I finished packing and began to mentally prepare for the orientation meeting that we were to have after dinner. I wasn't sure if it would calm everyone down or make them all freak out.

I got back from our first dinner and orientation and it wasn't as scary as I thought it would be. First off, dinner was actually really good. They must have brought in real cooks for this place. It wasn't the standard public school crap we're used to. There was fresh pasta, fruit and quite a few Vegan options. I guess when it's possible you may die, they do what they can to make you as comfortable as possible.

I saw Ethan Lazarus in the dining hall. He was sitting alone, but that's not to say once or twice a roll or salt shaker didn't come flying at him. As I ate, I kept looking back at him. He looked miserable. It wasn't like he waltzed in acting like he knew he was going to pass the tests. He was just like us. He had no idea what was ahead of him and for all he, or anyone else, knew he could be the first Lazarus to fail.

When I was done eating, I told Aggy I'd catch up with her later and I got up to put my tray back where I had found it. I turned and saw that most everyone left were more focused on their own conversations and all attention to Ethan was gone, so I took the chance and went over to him.

"Hi." I said. He looked up at me with a curious look.

"Hi."

"My name's Jenna Holdren. You're Ethan Lazarus, right?"

"Yeah. You want to hit me in the face or the stomach?"

"What?"

"The face is a popular choice, but I'd really prefer the stomach. I mean, I've got a nice face. I really would like to keep it like this."

"Thanks for the offer, but I don't want to hit you. I just came over to talk to you."

"Why?"

"Because you've been sitting alone all through dinner and I guess I feel kind of bad for you."

"You pity me?"

"I wouldn't put it like that, but yes."

"Look, I don't need your pity. I know I'm just about the most hated person here just like my family is the most hated family in America, but what my grandfather did was the right thing to do. This planet is dangerously overpopulated and unless you and all your friends want to spend the rest of your lives fighting over scraps of food in the street, we're all going to have to make some hard choices. This may seem harsh, but it's for the greater good." Ethan said. It sounded as though he had been giving that speech his entire life.

"So, do you have that whole speech memorized by heart now?"

"Pretty much, yes."

"I just came over here to be nice. I don't care who you are or who your family is. I saw someone who could use a friend."

"Oh. Well, thanks. Although, if you go around saying we're friends, you may end up with just as many enemies as I've got now."

"I'll take my chances." I then sat down and he smiled. It wasn't a forced, polite smile. It was genuine. I could tell he was grateful for the company, and it wasn't hard to figure out why. It was important to have people to back you up, especially when we were all facing the possible end of our lives. No one deserved to be left alone at such a time.

"So, where are you staying?"

"I'm in building C. On the first floor."

"I'm in building C too. Third floor."

"So you have the nice view."

"It's not bad. Who are you rooming with?"

"No one. I was given a single room."

"So, you do get a little privilege around here."

"It's not so much privilege as it's just to protect me. When my older brother Chad tested a couple years ago, there was an incident and he wound up in the hospital."

"I think I remember hearing about that."

"Due to the fact he was so badly injured, he was given an automatic pass out of the tests. That didn't set right with a lot of folks and there were some riots. From that point on, the administrators decided that we were to be given single rooms in order to prevent a repeat of that."

"Makes sense. Must be nice to have your own room."

"I'm pretty much entombed there all day. I only open the door if the staff here gives me the special knock, so I know that it's them."

"Well, I'd still take that over being roommates with Suicide Sally."

"What?"

"The girl I've been stuck with, Violet, she's kind of all about death. She tells me about how many acres of rainforest we're losing per second, and how the atmosphere is slowly deteriorating because of it. She makes me feel guilty for just breathing."

"Sounds fun."

"I was hoping to get my friend Aggy as my roommate, but they have that policy."

"Oh, right. That sucks. I don't know why they do that. I'd think it would help to have a friend nearby."

"Me too. I asked them why they did it like that, but they just gave me some federal run around answer."

"That's what they're trained to do. Answer without answering. I've been around it long enough."

"So I guess you have some kind of inside track on all this government stuff."

"Not as much as you'd think, but I've seen some stuff. I can tell you that when they tell you to do something just do it; even if it makes no sense."

"Noted."

"We better get going. Orientation is in ten minutes. "We continued to chat as we made our way to the common room in our dorm building. When we got there, I was shocked to see how full up it was. Every single person staying there was present. We pushed our way through the crowd and finally found a small space against the back wall. Once we were settled, two counselors came in. They were clad in dark blue jumpsuits with badges on their chests and they both held clipboards in their hands.

"Good evening, testers," the male counselor said. "My name is Trip and this is Venda. We will be your main points of contact for the week. That means if you have any issues, problems or questions, you come to us first. Understood?" The room agreed. "Great. Now, we all know why we're here and the reality of it, but I'd advise you to not think about that. Try to relax and, as hard as it may be, have fun. Stress levels can affect test results and we want you all to pass. I mean that. No one here wants anyone to fail. We are here to support you and help you do the best you can."

"That's right, Trip," Venda said. She was bubbly and had a lot of energy. "Now, I'm sure you all have become familiar with the dorms so for now we want to go over the test schedules. You all here will be group C. We'll be posting the testing schedules on all dorm levels each day. These schedules are made for everyone, but you all should just pay attention to group C. Easy, right? Right. I'll just break it down for you all now real fast. Tomorrow will begin your physical training. You will be meeting in gym C on the north side of campus. Boys will be outdoors while the girls will be in the training facility and that reverses after lunch. The physical training continues on Wednesday in the south field with everyone, boys and girls. After that, you will be assigned to your classes." There was a sudden roar from the crowd.

"Calm down, everyone," Trip said. "These aren't real classes. They're just study sessions to help prepare you for the other tests. There is some book studying to be done if you want to pass the written portion of the tests."

"Right," Venda added. "And those exams are the final leg of the tests. Once they are complete, you will receive your results and that will conclude the testing period."

I pulled up my mental calendar and counted the days of testing and studying that they were describing, and I felt a bit of relief and doubt. Just a few days of preparing and then the tests would be over. It seemed so fast and so simple. It was like I could see the finish line already, but I knew it couldn't be that simple. There was still such dread in my soul. The path may have looked short but it wasn't going to be easy.

"We do want to take a moment to discuss a new addition to the tests this year," Venda continued. I looked around and it seemed her announcement brought back all the worry and stress that seemed to have disappeared so briefly. "Each year we try to improve the results the tests can yield and this year we are introducing the survival challenge," Everyone was taken by surprise with revelation of a new test and I couldn't blame them. I felt like my stomach was falling to the floor.

"First of all, be assured your families will be notified about these changes. Don't worry. Your only job here is to pass the tests," Venda assured us all. "Here is how the Survival Challenge works. We will take all the groups and break them up into separate teams within that group, which factors out to three teams for each group. The teams will then be taken to a remote location and after that it's easy. Just get back here. You will have to rely on your survival instincts and teamwork skills to make it back here. The first team to make it back to base; passes the tests. They get an automatic pass. That's it. You're done." Venda said. The news was greeted with applause and cheers. I could see, even from as far as I was, that Venda's face switched from happy to serious in a brief flash. "The next team to return will simply move on to the next portion of the tests," She said. My stomach lurched because I felt something very bad was about to happen.

"And, finally," Trip chimed in. "The last team to return will automatically fail the tests," He said. The room grew quiet and I just wanted to run away and throw up somewhere. "We realize how hard that is to hear, but we all know and understand what the tests are all about. We need to accept the reality that some among you won't pass."

They proceeded to talk us through the details of the survival challenge. They said it was designed to be a perfect way to fully test and measure our physical and mental abilities. Venda and Trip tried to put a smiley face on the whole situation and tried to keep the tone of the evening upbeat, but it wasn't really working.

After another half hour of questions, they had no choice but to send us to our rooms and we went to our beds and lied in our beds with no hope for sleep.

Chapter 13

Testing Begins

It was the first day of official testing and we were woken up by what had to have been the loudest siren I had ever heard in my life. It was like everyone woke up at the exact same second. Violet and I had already worked out a bathroom schedule, and since she preferred to shower in the evening that left morning open for me. While I was showering, she was dressing and when I was done, she would move in and do whatever she did to get ready in the morning while I'd get dressed. It worked out pretty good, although she's a fast dresser so she cuts my shower time in half easily. I wasn't able to wash my hair as completely as I usually do and it was starting to feel weird and icky once it was dry.

We were instructed to first report for breakfast. We walked into the cafeteria and everything was different. There weren't countless choices of things to eat. We were pretty much limited to oatmeal, eggs, cereal, and fruit. The line was long, but it moved fast as all the food was proportioned and premade. The fruit was fresh and the scent of cinnamon was thick in the air thanks to the oatmeal.

As I got my tray of food, I found Violet who had already staked out a table and I sat down with her. I then saw Aggy walk in and I waved her over. Once she got her breakfast she sat down with us.

"Nervous?" She asked.

"Unbelievably." I answered.

"I barely got any sleep last night."

"Really?" Violet said. "I slept like a corpse. With any luck, I'll be one by the end of the week."

"How can you talk like that?"

"Because my eyes are open. Believe me, this all may seem scary to you now, but how scared are you going to be when all the cities collapse and you're forced to hunt for food?"

"You don't know that's going to happen."

"That's what it's all leading up to. The food supply is going to dry up and we'll be eating our pets just to stay alive. Those crazy cat ladies won't seem so crazy then." I looked over at Aggy and I could tell that Violet's theories weren't doing any good to calm her down.

"Don't listen to her, Aggy," I then turned to Violet.

"Don't talk about stuff like that. You don't even know that it's going to happen. The ESA is in place to prevent anything like that from happening."

"You're really going to trust the government to prevent any kind of disaster? You think they have that good a track record? This is the one. This is the one they finally stop. After all the others: Nine eleven, the Washington quake, the bombing in Chicago. Innocent lives lost each time, but this time they'll get it right."

"Look, it's not perfect, but this is different. This isn't some natural disaster or terrorist plot. We can see this coming down the line. If we can get the global population under control, things will improve."

"And how long is that going to take? They were only supposed to have this testing thing for a few years. This is now the eightieth and they're still no closer to their goal."

"Like I said, it's not perfect, but it's better than just letting people run wild in the streets."

"Or is it? Maybe we should just do it. Break down all the walls and let everyone fend for themselves. Repeal all laws. Let people be free to live and survive on their wits." Violet suggested. Aggy and I just listened to what she was saying. We were both too nervous to say anything in opposition.

After breakfast, we split up into boys and girls. The boys went on to the southern field as they had been instructed while the girls were taken to the training facility.

When we entered, I was impressed by how large it was. There was enough room for a full basketball court, a gymnastics set up, and several other training displays, which I was sure we'd learn all about before long. Venda then appeared out from seemingly nowhere and approached us.

"Ladies!" She barked. "Good morning. Today is the day. I hope you got a good night's sleep and your fill at breakfast. You're going to need every advantage you can get here. A lot of instructors here run the tests very methodically, but I prefer to treat them with a bit of fun. I feel it can relax the testee and may result in a better test score, so I want you all to just clear your heads. Banish everything out of there," Her tone was pleasant and easy. I was actually feeling better. "So, to begin, I suggest a little game of basketball," Venda then walked toward us and split our group in half. She pointed to the side I was on. "Team one," She then turned to the other group and that's when I realized Aggy had slipped away and was on the opposite team as me. "Team two. We play to ten points. Go!" Venda yelled and we all raced toward the basketball court. There was already a ball laying in the middle of the hardwood. Both teams scrambled toward it and lined up on either side. Venda came up between us, picked up the ball and held it out in front of her. We were all just staring at the ball, almost like we were trying to will it into our hands. Venda then tossed it high up in the air and two girls leapt up at it. The girl from my team snagged it and it flew back and right into my arms. I bolted forward with it and my mind was a blur. I heard yelling and screaming on both sides of me as I dribbled past the other team and toward the basket. I hadn't played basketball in years, but I was rather good when I did play. I couldn't get those three point long distance shots, but I was great with lay ups. The high pitched squeaks of our sneakers on the floor rang in my ears as I fought my way to the free throw line with hands and arms waving in my face. I finally stopped and leapt up with all my might. I had gotten closer to the basket than I had thought. I saw some of my teammates urging for me to throw them the ball, but I was so close. I raised the ball up and threw it at the basket. I threw it high and much to my astonishment, it went in, barely touching the net. Everyone on my team leapt up and shouted in glee and we went back toward our basket as the other team checked the ball. This went on for another hour.

The other team scored off of us, but we managed to maintain a good lead. We hadn't even had a chance to strategize, but we all started working together as well as any team I'd ever been on. Better in some cases. Some of the girls on my team were playing at a level that was almost ferocious. Like they were playing for their lives, and then I realized, they probably were.

We were tied at nine and the ball was snapped and I caught it. I passed it as soon as it dropped in my hands. The defense was tight so we weren't able to get the ball very far. I got the ball again and was about to pass, but I was surrounded. I didn't have an opening and the basket was nearly a half court away.

There were calls and yells coming at me from every direction. Sweat was running down my face and my hands were getting slippery. I took a breath and pushed off the ground with all my might. I shot the ball up and it arched high up into the air. The trajectory looked good and everyone on the court stopped. Time seemed to go into slow motion as the ball got closer to the basket and as it slipped past the rim, I nearly fell to the ground. All the girls on my team leapt up and cheered as the ball hit the floor and bounced back toward me. I was swept up by my teammates as they paraded me around the court. Once the cheering died down, Venda joined us. She was clapping and had a big smile on her face.

"Very good game, ladies. Congrats to team one. Excellent moves out there. Team two, good hustle. It was a close game and you all played well. If you go past the bleachers there, you'll find the locker rooms. Go and shower off and report back here." She said.

We all marched back toward the bleachers. We walked just so it would take longer and we'd have more time to recover. I felt as though we already ran a thousand laps. If that game wasn't enough for us to pass the tests, I didn't know what else they'd need.

When we got to the locker room, it was neat and well kept. On one side there were some lockers and on the other were the showers which were, thankfully, outfitted with privacy screens. There were just enough showers for each girl, so there wasn't any conflict over that. The sound of all the showers going off at once was almost deafening. I got undressed and stepped into the warm stream of water and rinsed off the sweat and grime I had accumulated while playing. Then, one by one, the showers went off and I realized we were done freshening up. I shut off the water and dressed again, but when we all got out of our showers, we saw that the lockers had all been opened and they had names on them. Our names. We all began to inspect them. When I found my locker, I discovered a red jumpsuit inside of it. The other girls had jumpsuits in their lockers as well. Some were red others were blue.

"What are these?" Aggy asked as she came up behind me. I saw that she was also holding a red jumpsuit.

"I guess we wear these from now on," I said as I slipped my jumpsuit on. The other girls followed suit and we all filed out back into the training facility. Venda was waiting for us on the basketball court and when she saw we had all changed, she smiled.

"Very good! You'd be surprised how many times we have to instruct people specifically to change into their uniform. What you are wearing now is what you will be required to wear to all training and tests throughout the testing period. No exception. You may have noticed that some of you are red while others of you are blue. This is an indication of nothing. There have been rumors spread over the years about one color group favored over the other, but if you look at the previous records you'll see that is not the case. It's only a way of managing each group. Understood?" We all nodded.

We then split off into our different color groups and we began the first battery of physical training. The Reds started off with some high-intensity calisthenics while the blues were sent to the area with the weight machines. Venda stayed with them while a recorded program led us through our paces. At first, I thought I was going to do okay. It didn't seem any more intense than gym class, but before long, things got a lot harder and soon I was drenched with sweat and my back began to hurt. I looked around and it seemed that everyone was having the same problem. A lot of the girls were either limping along through the exercises or have given up completely and were sprawled out on the floor. I did the best I could to keep up, but the pain in my back was growing more intense. We started a move that required us to be half way bent forward and as I leaned into position, the base of my spine felt as though it were on fire. I did the best I could to maintain, but after the sixth rep, I gave up and I just stopped. I was the last one to give up, which I hoped would look good for me. Once I stopped moving, the recorded program finished and a recorded voice announced that the results of that phase had been recorded and we were to move to the next phase. As the day went on, it appeared that the Reds and the blues were being put through the same course, but in reverse. At one point, I realized we were doing something they had already done, while they were doing what we had done. The Reds at that point were climbing the rope. There were six long ropes hung from the ceiling and we went up six at a time.

When I slid down, I saw Violet and Aggy approaching their ropes and I saw them begin their struggle upward. I wanted to stay to cheer them on, or at least be entertained, but I was overheating and I needed air. Venda had told us we were permitted to step outside of the gym at any time for air or water. I walked over to the large door and pushed it open. The air hit me like a blast of ice water. I just leaned up against the wall, enjoying the sensation. I looked across the field and a saw a swarm of boys in blue jumpsuits at the far end running. I figured that would be us tomorrow.

"Hi." I turned and saw a boy in a red jumpsuit approach me. He was tall with dark blonde hair and a pair of the most dazzling blue eyes I had ever seen.

"Hi."

"Shouldn't you be in there? Testing?"

"Taking a break. What are you doing here? Shouldn't you be with your fellow Reds?" He looked down and seemed to just notice what he was wearing.

"I've got some down time. I'm Curtis."

"Jenna. Not that I don't appreciate it, but why are you even talking to me? We're not in the same group or anything."

"Sure we are. We're both Reds."

"Yes, but you're in the boy's program. I'm not."

"I know, I just think it's important that we all kind of reach out to each other. This is really stressful and it helps to have friends. It sure helps me."

"And you just picked me?"

"You are the only one out here. Besides, you look like you could use a friend."

"I've got my best friend here. She's inside climbing the rope."

"We've got to climb ropes? Damn it."

"What's the matter? Can't climb?"

"No. I can't."

"I'm sure you'll do fine."

"Interesting." Curtis said as he looked at me thoughtfully.

"What?" I asked.

"You try so hard to act like none of this is bothering you."

"You base this on what?"

"I saw you yesterday before we got on the bus. With everyone freaking out and breaking down, it's easy to spot the one person keeping it together."

"I just don't think worrying about something you can't control is helpful. I know I'll pass. Both of my brothers passed."

"Ah. A Legacy. That does stack in your favor, I admit, but I've heard about some Legacies who still failed. Recessive genes or something."

"And you're telling me that to make me feel better?"

"No, I'm just impressed how cool you are about everything."

"You seem fairly cool yourself, Curtis."

"Thanks, but in my case, it is a total act. I puked three times on the bus ride up here and three more times last night."

"Sorry."

"Don't feel bad for me. Feel bad for the sap in the bottom bunk." The shrill sound of a whistle pierced the air. Trip and I turned our heads and one of the male counselors was approaching.

"McEntire! Get back to your group. We're choosing sides for the football game."

"All right. I'll be right there." Curtis said and then the counselor walked away, leaving us alone.

"You'd better go. Being late to a test could cost you your life." Curtis gave me a weak smile.

"That'd be funnier if it weren't true," He said. "I'll see you around, Jenna."

"Sure." He then turned from me and ran off, disappearing around the corner.

Chapter 14

Day One

We got back from our first day well after sunset and completely trashed. I don't think I had ever run so much in my life. It was so bad I started to wish I was back in Ms. Benson's gym class. I would have taken six laps around the school over the endless marches we had just endured. The meal break was pretty good though. The one good thing about this whole experience has been the food. They do treat us right in that respect.

Violet went straight to her bed and passed out. I forced myself to stay up long enough to take a shower. I could barely hold the soap, but I couldn't sleep with this gross, gunky feeling all over my body. I can already feel my legs getting sore.

I saw Ethan at dinner tonight. He was eating alone again, but since I was with Aggy and the others, I couldn't really find a way to get over to him. I could see the dirty looks he was getting from everyone else, but he just seemed to ignore it all. I guess he's just used to it, which I think is kind of sad. No should get used to that kind of treatment, no matter who you are.

The second day at camp started off a lot different from the first. We all woke up in pain. I could hear Violet groaning as she slid out of bed and when I made the attempt, all my joints felt like they were on fire. We managed to get dressed and when we joined the others at the dining hall, it looked like everyone was feeling the pain. Every movement and step brought a chorus of cries of pain and we were given a couple aspirins along with our breakfast.

Violet and I sat with Aggy, but she was quiet as we ate. Everyone was. It looked like everyone was too weak to even lift their forks to eat much less engage in meaningless small talk. I looked across the room and there was Ethan again. Alone. It seemed no one was really paying him any mind anymore. They all had bigger things to worry about than him.

Without talking, the meal went by quickly. Aggy and Violet finished first and excused themselves to get ready for the next round of testing. I looked over at Ethan again and he was still there and still alone. I took a deep breath and braced for the pain as I stood up. I picked up my tray and went over to him. His eyes shot up at me as I approached. I felt myself smiling, but I wasn't sure if I had managed it. I went ahead and sat down with him. He didn't seem to object. I asked him how his tests went and his answer was short. He didn't seem to want to get into it and I took that as a sign not to push. I started to tell him about my day. I was hoping hearing about someone else's suffering would help him, but as I began, the sound of a fight outside caught the attention of the room. I turned and I saw a couple of boys through the window wrestling around on the ground and it was clear it wasn't for play. Even from my distance I could see the rage on their faces as they thrashed at each other. Two security guards came running up and pulled them apart. The moment of excitement died down as quickly as it started. I turned back to Ethan, but he was just starting to get up to leave. He smiled and apologized. He said he had to go and get ready for the day and soon I saw I was nearly alone in the entire dining hall and I began to think I should be getting ready as well.

I made it to the field and I saw my group in their red jumpsuits gathered together. I went over and just as I reached them, Venda came running out from the main gym. She looked fresh and relaxed with a big smile on her face. Why shouldn't she look good? It's not like her life is on the line.

She gave us another one of her pep talks and then we got into it hard. More running and jumping and endless cardio. The time just started to blur. Most of it was calisthenics and sometimes it was a game of football or baseball. It didn't seem to matter as long as they kept us moving. The only difference from the previous day was that everyone was already in incredible pain.

The time had finally come for us to return to the classrooms for our practical studies, and I was so grateful for that.

As Aggy and I made our way to our designated room, she leaned against me and I totally understood why.

"I can't feel my legs." She said.

"You're walking."

"It's all a mechanical response."

"Just think about this, it's the last day of this we're going to have."

"Yeah because tomorrow we go on that stupid survival challenge, which is basically make it or break it. Do you realize it could mean automatic failure? Why would they do that to us?"

"Or it could mean automatic success."

"Why must you always look on the bright side?"

"Because if I don't, who will?"

We got to class and a good portion of it was straight out of a wilderness survival guide. I guess since it was the first year for the survival challenge, they wanted to make sure everyone was prepared. We went over basic survival skills such as building fires, catching and cleaning food and identifying poisonous plants. We then spent a good amount of time on first aid techniques, but I didn't see the point to that. If it meant I could take an instant pass on the tests, I would cross that finish line with one leg.

We got out of class two hours before the evening meal. We had a shorter curfew than normal because they were going to be sending people off for the challenge an hour before sunrise.

I only had time for a quick shower before going down to the dining hall with Aggy and Violet. As we walked in my eye caught sight of something I thought I'd never see again; or actually someone. It was Mark. He saw me and ran right over. I noticed he was sporting a green jumpsuit, but I hadn't seen anyone else around in green before. We said our hellos and he told me all about how he missed me and had been searching for me. He seemed surprised to see me in my red suit. I thought for a moment that it was a big campus and there had to be other colors besides blue and red. Aggy gave me a pass so that I could eat with Mark. We found a table in the corner and he told me all about what he had been doing and it was a lot like what I had been doing. No surprise there. As I watched him speak, I started to realize how much I missed him. All that nonsense with Chandra at the party seemed to fade from my memory. The fight felt so petty with us both at the edge of whatever was to come. I then felt Mark take my hand and it felt nice. His skin was soft and warm. Then he smiled. He always got me with that smile. We just talked and talked and before I knew it, we were alone. I checked my watch and it was just a few minutes until lights out. I didn't want to say good bye so quickly. It felt like we had just seen each other after much too long already, but I knew we had to go. The security detail would be sweeping the campus and I was afraid of what would happen if we were caught. It seemed like any infraction could affect the results of the tests and while I consider myself willing to take a risk, my life isn't something I prefer to gamble with.

We said our good byes again and raced off to our respective dorms. I stopped for only a moment and turned around and saw him disappear into the shadows. My heart tugged a bit and then I continued to my dorm.

Chapter 15

CHAPTER 48

Adjustments

I got back a few minutes past curfew but no one saw me. I managed to get in a few hours of sleep. I woke up and noticed it was still dark outside. I hated that. Violet actually got up before me and was already packed and ready to go by the time I was going in for my shower. I tried to move quickly but my body felt like it was filled with lead. I kept hearing Violet shouting at me from outside the bathroom. She was adamant about getting to breakfast as soon as possible.

Once we were done eating, we had to report to the parking lot where we first arrived. I wasn't sure what was supposed to happen after that and my stomach was in knots whenever I thought about what was ahead of us. I felt like I couldn't wait for it to begin but I also didn't want it begin either. I wished I had a device that could rewind time back to when I was twelve and all of this was just a bad dream lurking on the horizon, or if I could blast forward past the tests and on to my life.

No one was talking and I mean no one. The dining hall was dead silent except for the sound of people eating. Even Aggy was quiet. I didn't see Ethan. His usual table was empty. There was no point in putting it off any longer. We were done with breakfast. It was time to go.

When we got to the parking lot, there was a whole fleet of buses waiting and already what looked to be thousands of kids in line to get on them. I saw our group waiting together. There were also groups of kids in other colors of jumpsuits. There were the Blues near the Reds, but past them I saw the yellows and the greens. I knew it was a long shot but I kept my eyes on the green group hoping to see if Mark was with them. He had to be but there were too many and I was too far away.

When Aggy, Violet and I joined our group, I felt like I did when our class would gather before leaving for a field trip in school, but the giddy excitement wasn't there. I looked at the bus and I felt a cold chill run up my spine. Everyone out there was as dispirited as they were during breakfast. There was barely any chatter. In fact, the only sound I could hear were the soft sobs rising up from each group. I looked up and I saw Venda approaching. She was clad in black and there was no smile on her face. She looked more sympathetic than pumped. She came to our group first and folded her arms in front of her. She went through the standard greeting and explained how it was going to work. She said we were in for a three hour ride before we made it to Alpha Camp. We were given room assignments as well. We were going to have at least one night to rest before the test was to begin.

We all got on the bus and I sat down by the window at a seat near the rear. I just sat there watching the kids getting on their buses. It was a sad, slow processional. I saw Aggy coming up the aisle toward my seat. Her eyes were dark and sad. As she sat down, I tried to smile at her but she either didn't see or it didn't mean anything to her. I hated seeing her like that, but I could hardly blame her. More kids were coming onto the bus and when all the seats were nearly taken the doors closed and my heart tightened a bit. The engine roared to life and the bus began to roll away, but it stopped abruptly and Venda came on board. She hurried down the aisle toward me and Aggy. Her face was sad and she reached out to Aggy.

"I'm sorry to tell you this, but your roommate didn't arrive for pick up this morning and when security went to check on her, they found her in the closet of your room. She hanged herself." Aggy clapped her hand to her mouth and I saw tears come down from her eyes almost instantly. She was starting to shake. I wasn't even aware she liked her roommate very much. She never mentioned her.

"When?" Aggy asked.

"Some time after breakfast. It happens sometimes. The pressure can be too much for some. It is policy in these situations to pass the surviving roommate."

"What?"

"It has been a long held policy in these cases. We find discovering the death can have an adverse impact on your performance and we can't get accurate results because of that. If you could please collect your things, we have some paperwork for you to sign before we release you."

"All right." Venda then got off the bus and Aggy started to get her things together.

"You pass? Just like that?"

"I guess so! Oh my God! I can barely breathe."

"I'm so happy for you!"

"Thanks. I wish I could bring you with me."

"It's okay. I'm just glad you made it."

"It's a miracle. I mean, I'm sorry she's dead, but I can go home now. I can go home. I'm going to pray for you Jenna. I know you're going to pass." Aggy then turned away and hurried off the bus. I watched Venda escort Aggy back to the testing center and as we got onto the road, everything was gone.

I nodded off after we got on the highway and after checking my watch it looked like we had only been on the road for an hour. I don't know where we were. It looked like they were taking us up into the mountains. There's nothing but dirt and trees all around and I could barely see the sky past the branches of the trees. It looked so quiet and lonely out there. There was nothing but trees in front and behind us and we still were going deeper in. I thought about the challenge and I began to wonder if I would be able to do it.

The bus turned off the highway and we headed down a dirt path through the woods. I could see what looked to be cabins ahead of us. The bus finally came to a stop and everyone was getting rather anxious to finally stand up.

The camp didn't seem so bad. If the circumstances were just a little different, I might say I could have fun there. The cabins were cleaner than I thought they'd be and the mattresses were softer than I was led to believe. It reminded me of the year I went to summer camp at Lake Kanasu.

I was rooming in one cabin with five other girls, including Violet. I was glad she was there but I really missed Aggy. She'd be able to help me keep my sanity. Everyone was chatting and talking happy as if they were on some fun sleep over or something. They either didn't understand how serious the situation was, or they did and were just choosing to make it fun in some attempt to keep their fear from taking over. I get that.

We were sleeping in bunk beds and Violet took the one under me. I could hear her breathing. She was choosing to aggressively ignore the other girls. I'm not sure what goes through her mind. She's either trying to make a plan on how to survive, or she's just thinking about how she's going to lose the challenge on purpose. I couldn't read her like I can read Aggy.

We were all summoned to the main dining hall on the other side of the camp. I guessed that was where we were going to get our last meal and all the information we needed for the challenge. I couldn't believe it was happening. I was surrounded by it all but I still couldn't believe it. Sometimes I didn't even think about the prospect of me losing so much as I thought that some of these kids would lose. They wouldn't make it and everytime I thought that, a cold wave passed through me. I just wished I could fast forward past all of this and just get right to the part where Mom and Dad came to pick me up and take me home. I wanted it to be all over.

I was right. We had our last big dinner and it was big and it was good. It was a buffet and they had everything you could ever hope for. Chinese food, Italian, steaks and burgers and don't even get me started on the dessert bar. They had things there I had never heard of but now that I've had them, I just want more! The food was so good, I think I even saw Violet smile while she was eating. If the food could make that girl enjoy life, it had to be good.

Once we were done eating and sitting in the afterglow, some counselors came in and they started a presentation about the survival challenge. They outlined all of the rules and passed out survival packs for us. They were just backpacks loaded up with survival gear. There's a backpack, a solar blanket, some canned food with a Swiss Army knife, some matches and a few bottles of water. The rules were rather simple. After Breakfast we would be dispatched after our groups are divided into teams of seven. Four teams, one team per color, would be taken to one of many predesignated camp sites and from there it's basically a race, but it's more than that. It isn't just about getting back to the testing facility first, but getting there the right way, whatever that means. They explained that any team of seven arriving first would officially pass the tests. The second team would move on to the next phase of testing, and the final group of seven would be failed. Everybody was aware of that but hearing the words again pretty much killed the vibe for everyone.

The whole room was quiet and everyone just looked awkwardly at each other. Everyone was wondering who would pass and who would fail. The tension was thick and the counselors tried to bring the room back, but it was too late. They adjourned the meeting and we came back to our dorms.

Everyone was pretty somber. Usually there would be some music playing from one of the dorms down the hall and there would be screaming and laughing and giggling. The sounds of life, but as soon as we got back to our dorms, it was quiet as a tomb. Violet even seemed troubled. I honestly thought she would have cheered up after everything we had been told. She's just lying in her bed staring into space. It was time to go to bed. Tomorrow was going to be Hell, to put it lightly.

We had breakfast and it was the most depressing meal I've ever endured. Still no one was talking and every few minutes someone would break out into tears; not that I don't blame them, of course. Now we're waiting to be put into our teams. There are so many kids here. I have no idea who they're going to break us all up into teams of seven. However they're doing it is taking a good long time. We were given numbers and I heard they were to designate which camp site we were going to be taken to. I drew number one hundred twenty three. I then began to wonder how many camp sites there were out there and I started to get real nervous. I crumpled the paper up and tossed it away, being careful to recall the numbers on it, just in case. I then saw a familiar face smiling at me. It was Curtis. He was with his group and he waved at me. I wanted to go over and say hi, but we were forbidden for leaving our groups. That was when he got up and walked over to me.

"Curtis!" I said. "You can't do that!"

"If they want to fail me for wanting to talk to a pretty girl, I welcome it. At least I'll die happy."

"Wow."

"Too corny?"

"No. It's the first time I've heard anyone actually speak in the last twelve hours."

"I know. I guess the looming prospect of death kind of has everyone's tongue."

"So, why are you so not depressed?"

"Confidence. Total and completely unwarranted confidence."

"I wish I had some of that."

"You look pretty together to me. I think you're going to do great."

"Thanks. I hope so."

"Tell you what; when we start, come find me. I can make a spot for you on my team."

"How?"

"Kick someone off."

"I know you're kidding, but if you're not, I couldn't do that."

"Why not? Check out who I have on my team." Curtis said and then pointed back to his group and then I saw him.

"You have Ethan Lazarus?"

"We drew the short straw. We could 'lose' him and you could take his spot."

"Thanks, but I think I'll just do it on my own. Good luck to you out there though." Curtis just smiled at me and jogged back to his team. I noticed Ethan and he looked even more lonely than usual. He didn't even dare make eye contact with anyone. I didn't know how I managed it, but I felt sorry for the guy. I was with people I had come to consider friends and despite being new connections; they brought me a sense of safety. I couldn't imagine attempting this with no one in your corner.

More teams were selected and processed but Violet and I were still with our team, waiting for something to happen. I noticed that some yellow and green teams were nearby. I tried to see if I could see Mark among them, but they were too far away.

"Team Red. Unit one twenty three!" Venda called out. We all stood up and faced her. Her expression was stern but it soon relaxed into a smile. "Good morning, everyone. It's time. I want you all the separate into groups of seven." She said. Everyone scrambled around but soon we began to form into the appropriate teams. I was standing near one group and figured I'd join them, but then I felt Violet reach over and pull me toward her group in the middle. I looked up at her ready to ask why, but the mask of fear on her face answered my question. I then realized she was still holding my hand. Tight.

"This is happening." She whispered.

"I thought you wanted this."

"I did too, but now it's here and I have to admit I wasn't expecting it to feel like this. This is really happening."

"Of course it is. It's what we've been stressing over since we all turned sixteen."

"I just didn't expect it to feel this real. Please don't leave me."

"Okay. Fine. It doesn't matter. We'll get through this. We just have to shoot for making it in second and we'll be good."

"No! We have to come in first! I can't take this testing anymore! I have to get out of here!"

"Calm down, Violet. Just breathe. You've been doing great so far. Even if you have to continue on to the next phase of testing, I'm sure you'll pass."

"But this is the only way to make sure. Jenna. Promise me we'll come in first!"

"I promise."

Once out teams were chosen up, Venda had us all gather around her. She explained in more detail about the rules, which seemed to put a lot of kids to ease. She said that there were over two hundred groups and each group would have a first, second and third place. So there were over fourteen hundred kids who could make it and it just felt like the odds improved. After one last equipment check the teams were released and we all headed out into the wilds. I noticed the teams stayed close for the first few yards but eventually began to break apart and go on their own. Our team began to widen but I noticed Violet still had her hand tightly clasped to mine. I looked up at her and smiled.

"Just for a few minutes more," She begged. "I just need a little more time."

"Fine. Just try and walk a little faster."

Chapter 16

Survival Challenge 1

We had been hiking for several hours and finally stopped to take a break. We lost visual contact with the other teams soon after we left the camp. They're out there though. Everyone seems very anxious about staying ahead but no one is completely certain how far we are from the testing facility and we can't risk burning through our supplies too quickly. From the distance we drove, it felt like to me that it could take two days to get back to the facility. Maybe three.

I fished around my backpack and found a can of fruit cocktail. I was hungry enough to eat everything I had, but I knew we needed to conserve. Just in case.

Violet had been very quiet. She was sitting against a tree with her knees tucked into her chest and muttering under her breath to herself. It's been disturbing watching her lose her cool, but I understand. I guess it was to be expected. The brave front she put up before is just crashing down on her. Maybe she was hoping for some last minute miracle to save her from this. I think we all were, but there was no miracle and here we are in the forest with our survival on the line.

The others on my team seemed to be okay with the situation and were adjusting to the situation. I heard them chatting about fishing and hunting for food, if the need arose. I hadn't really thought about that myself, but hearing them talk about it made sense. We weren't sure how long we'd be out there and the food that was given would barely last a day much less two. I wondered where the other teams were. I hadn't heard anyone for some time yet. They had to be out there. We all started from the same place. Maybe there were some teams so determined to reach the goal first, they were sprinting back. Maybe they would make it, or maybe they'd tire out and fall behind. There's no way to tell. I'm just trying to focus on my journey and my team.

I wish I had seen Mark before we left. I wanted to know how he was doing. We only spoke that one time and I wasn't sure if he was doing so well then. Why was I focusing on other people when I should have been focusing on me? I couldn't help it. I heard the others finishing up their snacks.

We journeyed even deeper into the forest and it's even less clear where we're headed. I'd been checking my compass and it appeared we were on track, but again, we hadn't seen anyone else out there. Not even any sign of anyone else. What if we're closer than I realized and everyone had made it back to the facility already? What if we're last? Thoughts like that sent chills through my spine. Maybe we could just stay out there. We managed to catch some fish and we got a fire going. It's clear this team had the survival skills. We could just stay out there in the forest and live off the land for the rest of our lives. Seems kind of screwed up when that appears to be a more appealing idea than returning to society. I was kind of optimistic until the challenge began. If only we had seen someone else out there I think I would have felt better.

I went for a walk to clear my mind and much to my relief I finally discovered another team nearby. It was Curtis's team. I saw them through the brush and it looked as though they were doing as well as my team was. They had a fire going and they were cooking what looked to have been a raccoon over the open flame. I stepped out and they were on guard at first but when Curtis noticed me, he calmed them down. It was just so great to see anyone, but to see Curtis was even better. I didn't know him well, but I could tell if he wanted to be first to the facility, he would be. To know he was no further along than our team was a great relief.

"How's your team going?" He asked as we sat by the fire.

"They're good. We caught some fish for dinner. We'll be getting an early start tomorrow."

"Shouldn't you be sleeping then?"

"Yes, but who can sleep."

"Right?"

"How about you? Shouldn't you and your guys be sleeping?"

"Perhaps, but me team and I have been talking and we think we have a better plan to win this thing."

"Really?"

"We can't take any chances with this."

"So what's your big plan?"

"I don't really think I should tell you. I'm not even a hundred percent about it."

"Now you're just getting me more curious," I then remembered that Ethan was on his team and I looked around but couldn't see him anywhere. "Where's Ethan?"

"Lazarus? He's not allowed this close to the fire. He's over there." Curtis pointed toward the darkness beyond the glow of their camp and as my eyes adjusted I could make out a lone figure slumped against the trunk of a tree.

"Is that really called for?"

"Mr. Privilege over there is going to get a free ticket out of this and you know it."

"Probably, but why torture him now?"

"Just to let him know a little misery. Give him a little taste of what it's like to be one of the little people his family tramples over on a daily basis."

"Isn't that a little petty?"

"Yes. It is, but we voted on it."

"Fine. I guess I should be getting back to my camp. I'll see you around?"

"I hope so."

"Okay. Good night." I then got up and headed back to my camp.

As I walked into the darkness and I felt only the memory of the warm fire, I heard a voice whisper to me. I turned and saw Ethan skulking toward me.

"Jenna?"

"Ethan. Are you all right?"

"Cold and hungry, but otherwise fine."

"Hungry? You haven't eaten?"

"They looted my bag and took all the food that was in it and as far as dinner, they just toss me the bones of whatever they've been eating."

"Are you going to be all right?"

"I'll survive. I figure I can hunt for something while they sleep."

"Are you sure that's wise?"

"No, but you do what you gotta do, right?"

"I suppose."

"I'm just glad to see you. You're doing okay?"

"Yeah. My team has gotten a strong start. I think it'll be good."

"Great. I really hope you make it."

"Thanks. I hope you do too." Ethan then let out a nervous laugh. "Doubtful."

"Why do you say that?"

"You know what Curtis's big plan is?"

"He told you?"

"I overheard. He's going to hunt."

"Hunt what?"

"People. He figures if they're the only team left, they have to win."

"What are you saying?"

"He's going to kill to win! They've been talking about it since we left the camp. They had this all figured out days ago and do you think they're going to spare me? I'm dead. I am a dead man."

"I think you may have misunderstood."

"You think so? You don't think the pressure to win this wouldn't be enough to drive anyone to kill if they thought that was the only way they could survive?"

"I don't know."

"I'm just telling you so that you know. Keep your eyes open and be on guard. Curtis likes you, but I don't think he would think twice about killing you if it meant saving his own hide. I have to go." Ethan then bolted back toward his camp, trying to be as quiet as possible. I then saw the fire from Curtis's camp go out.

I found my way back to my team and I slid into my sleeping bag. I tried to get some sleep, but what Ethan told me was keeping me up. I knew the tests can push people to do things they would never normally do, but it's hard to believe anyone could be driven that far. At least, I would hope it would be.

Chapter 17

Survival Challenge 2

Our first morning in the woods and it was not pleasant. Terry Nelson appointed himself the time keeper for our team and went around waking everyone up just a few minutes before dawn. We made our way down to the nearby stream and attempted to catch some fish for breakfast. I have never been a good fisher and it didn't help me any that I was only half awake. It was quite a sight to see.

A few kids put together some rather hasty fishing poles while others fashioned some small spears and they just stood over the water throwing their ridiculous sticks into the water. They caught a few fish but after they were cleaned and cooked, they weren't much to fill an ant's stomach. We then began to forge around the forest and we managed to find a bunch of fruit bearing bushes. After determining that they weren't poisonous, we gorged ourselves. I squirreled a bagful away for later and as soon as the sun was fully up over the horizon, we were on our way again.

More marching through this endless forest and not a single clue to the presence of anyone else. I guess the teams spread out pretty far from each other. There weren't even any signs of anyone's old camps. I was getting nervous again. Since the tests began I've tried to act like failing wasn't possible, but there in the forest with so many against me, that idea seemed a little naive.

Violet calmed down a bit. She's accepted her reality and she's doing everything she can to be an asset to our journey. We never stopped to designate responsibilities but everyone just seemed to choose their roles.

Terry was our time keeper. Abigail Mckenna was our food gatherer. She scouted around and found anything that could be used as food. Jerry Price found himself in charge of our water supply and Violet had become quite skilled at setting up camp. She was the only one of us who knew how to start a fire with only two sticks or stones. I asked her how she found out about how to do that and she told me she had been a Girl Scout for six years. I couldn't really see it. I had been a scout for only a few months before I realized it wasn't for me. All the girls were a little too cheerful and energetic for me. It got annoying fast, but I could hardly believe a girl like Violet would be able to put up with it for six years.

"I didn't mind it at first. It was only after I left the scouts that I came to embrace the 'dark side'.

"We tried to hold to a schedule of walking for three hours and then stopping to rest. Someone had suggested it because they said it looked better if we returned in better health than the others, even if we only came in second. No one talked about coming in third. No one dared.

We were about to pack up our second camp and continue on our way. By the looks of how far we had come and how much further we had to go, I didn't see us getting back to the testing facility in any less than three days, even if we walked all night. I wasn't happy about being stuck in the wild for so long, but it made me feel a little more secure that everyone else was going to be trapped out here for that long as well.

Break number two for the day. It was time for lunch and supplies were slim. I only had the last bit of food in my back pack and the others were cooking up what was left of our fish from the morning. I was not thrilled with fish for lunch, but I was so hungry I couldn't think of saying no. I could smell the fish cooking. It reminded me of one year when we went fishing over summer vacation. Dad and the boys caught so many fish; it's all we had to eat for a whole week. It took a month to get the stink out of our clothes when we got back home. One night, Brian bet Bradley ten bucks if he would eat a fish head and much to all of our horror, he did it. Eyes and all. It was so much simpler back then.

Time is funny. It goes by so fast but when we look back, it seems so long and far away. Like a distant star you see in the sky every night.

After lunch, we tried to rest but I was too anxious to sit still; so once more, I opted to go exploring and I'm so glad I did. Not only did I see another team nearby, but Mark was with them! They were just packing up to resume their travels but I had enough time to catch Mark's attention and we finally talked. It was good to see him again. It felt like I hadn't seen him in weeks. He looked a little thinner than usual, but that was typical of the tests. They usually cost you about five or ten pounds. He seemed rather confident about the challenge. I guess one of his teammates was acting as a scout and they knew that among their group, they were in the lead. My heart eased at that news. I had been so worried about him, but it looked like he was doing okay. He kissed me before they left and promised he would see me at the finish line. I wished him luck and saw him disappear into the trees ahead.

I made my way back to camp just as everyone was getting ready to leave. I saw Violet packing my things for me.

"About time. Where'd you go running off to?"

"Just a little walk. I found another team nearby."

"Another team?" Violet asked with urgency.

"Relax. Not part of our group. It was Mark."

"Oh. The boyfriend."

"It was just good to see him again. I didn't get a chance to wish him luck before we started this."

"You should be worrying less about him and more about us. Jerry was checking things up the trail and he found the remains of a camp."

"Whose group?"

"We don't know but we just have to assume they're in our group and they are ahead of us. We're now going for five hours and we rest for a half hour."

"Five hours? We're not machines!"

"We have a lot of ground to cover. Come on!" Violet said as she slid my pack back to me.

We'd been walking for five hours and the sun had gone down and we made our way by only the faint light of a small torch Violet made. We finally stopped when we came to what looked to be an old summer camp that seemed to have been forgotten. Much of the grounds were grown over, but there were a couple of cabins still standing and they even had beds in them.

It was a fight, but it was finally decided that we were going to stop for the night. Not soon enough for me. My legs were on fire and I had to walk another mile, I was sure my feet would explode. We all got ourselves settled and then Abigail went out looking for food. For as dark as it was, I wasn't too optimistic, which was too bad because my stomach was giving me almost as much pain as my legs were.

I walked into one of the cabins and it was dark but I could see by the light of the moon and I could see enough to get around. There was a small bed near one of the windows so I dropped my pack onto it, claiming it as my own. I sat down and it felt so good. It was so good I didn't even care I was alone in an old wooden shack that was probably full of spiders and other little creepy crawlers. I just stretched out on the mattress and smiled. I was so happy I wasn't going to have to sleep on the ground.

I tried to stay awake long enough for Abigail to return with food, but my fatigue beat out my hunger and I fell asleep without dinner. It felt so good to sleep on a mattress again, even if it was a hard, lumpy thing. I tried to enjoy as much of it as I could and I savored every moment.

The morning came too early for my taste. I woke up and I saw the sky outside the window. It was turning a light purple as the sun began to slowly rise. I got up and tried to get my bearings. It seemed I was the first one up. I packed my bag and checked on everyone else. They were all where they were supposed to be, except Abigail. It looked like she didn't come back from her hunting expedition. Everyone was still asleep and I thought maybe it would be good if I could find something for them to eat when they woke up. I headed out into the forest and since I had no weapons to hunt with, I started looking for anything that was growing on the trees. I found a few berries and fruits but then I saw the

Holy Grail. Down a slight hill there were the remains of what appeared to have been an orchard. Most of the trees were dead, but there was one that was alive and well and bearing the finest looking apples I had ever seen. They were big and round and red as blood. I bolted for the tree and I came barreling at it with all my force. I lunged forward and hit the tree trunk like a freight train. The tree shook and thankfully almost every apple on the tree fell down to the ground. I fell to my knees and grabbed up as many as I could. My hands were trembling and my stomach lurched. I couldn't wait. I took one of the apples and took a big bite out of it. It was so sweet and juicy, I nearly blacked out. I gobbled up the rest of it down to its core and tossed it away. I grabbed another apple and took a few more bites until I felt I was properly fed. My arms stopped shaking and I gathered up the rest of the apples, excited to share them with the others. As I was leaving the secret spot, I noticed something in the tall grass. I thought it was another apple by its red color but when I got closer I saw that it wasn't an apple, but an arm. It was Abigail's and it was covered in blood.

I ran back to camp and woke everyone up. After I told them what I had found, they insisted on proof so I took them back to where I had found Abigail. It looked like she had her skull cracked open with a nearby rock and left to rot. I looked around for footprints but there were none to be found. As everyone looked around for more clues, I stopped and remembered what Ethan had told me. I tried to push it away as too crazy to be true, but I turned back to Abigail and I saw the fear that had been present in her dead eyes. It wasn't a four legged animal that killed her.

"We have to go!" I said.

"We can't just leave. Abigail was killed." Jerry said.

"Whoever did this could still be around. We have to keep moving."

"She needs to be put to rest."

"You want to bury her? Out here?"

"We can mark the grave and tell them where her body is when we get back. I just don't think we should just leave her out here to rot."

I looked back at her corpse. I'll never forget the look on her face; in a mask of shock and fear.

"Violet? Help me dig the grave. The rest of you bring her body over here." I said. Violet and I got on our knees and started digging in the dirt as quickly as we could. There was no talking. There was nothing to say. Jerry and the others dragged Abigail's body to the makeshift hole we had dug up and we gently laid her to rest. We covered up the grave and stood over it as we all whispered our prayers. We stayed there with our hands clasped together for another twenty minutes until time could no longer be ignored. We broke away, gathered up our things and soon we were back on the trails.

Part 3

Chapter 18

Chain of Command

As they pushed through the woods, Jenna kept her eyes peeled for any odd sounds. She had only been afraid of mosquitoes or roaming animals, but after burying Abigail she realized there was a greater threat.

As they marched through the woods, all she could think about was what Ethan had told her. She couldn't believe it at first. Curtis didn't seem like the kind of person to do anything so horrific, but the more she thought about it, the more it made sense. In fact, for a moment she was almost jealous she hadn't thought of it first. She started to slow down when she noticed the rest of her team stop and begin to set up camp.

"What are you doing?"

"Setting up camp. What does it look like?" Jerry said as he began clearing the area of loose leaves.

"What are we going to do about food?" Violet asked.

"That was Abigail's job."

"We all saw what she did. We can fish as well as she could." Jenna stood still as they all just went about their chores as if nothing had happened.

"Are you people insane? Abigail was murdered!"

"What do you expect us to do about that, Jenna?" Jerry asked.

"We have to keep moving. I think if we can make the main highway, we'll be okay."

"Maybe it was just an accident. Who would kill just to win this?"

"Are you kidding me? Who wouldn't? I didn't say anything before because I barely believed it myself, but I spoke to Ethan Lazarus and he told me that his team was planning on killing everyone else to make sure they're first. They're out here with us and anyone could be a target."

"That's insane. You really think they could take out all the other teams?"

"They got Abigail. Who's to say they can't get us? I think the safest thing to do is to get out of these woods. We're sitting ducks here."

"I haven't seen anyone out here for hours. I think we're pretty much alone out here."

"I can't believe you are ignoring this like it's nothing."

"I'm not going to panic. If it'll make you feel better, we can get back on the road after we've eaten. I think I saw a stream a few yards back. I'll see what I can find." Jerry then pushed forward through the brush surrounding the campsite, but as he stepped over a large log, a cord leap up out of the dirt around his leg and it pulled at his leg so hard, it broke. Jenna heard his bone snap and he crumpled to the ground, howling in pain. She then heard another snap behind her and the other members of her team were being taken down before her eyes. Violet let out a shrill scream and ran off into the woods. Jenna tried to stop her, but she felt something under her feet. She leapt up just before the trap caught her and she fell to the ground hard. Everything grew quiet and then she heard a footstep nearby. Jenna rolled away under some bushes and as quietly as she could, she buried herself with leaves and dirt. She saw a boot come into view. It was Curtis. Soon others emerged from the surrounding woods. Jenna's heart began to pound. She could hear Curtis whispering to his friends and once he was done, they broke off and went to Jenna's teammates who were still incapacitated. Curtis circled around the area as if in search of something. She then heard Jerry whimpering to someone. It sounded like a conversation but she couldn't hear the other side of it and then a shot rang out and the conversation was over. Jenna was trembling.

A few more shots rang out. Tears were running down Jenna's cheeks. She tried to choke back her breath but it was difficult. She pulled the dead leaves covering her closer and started to pray for a miracle. Curtis and his friends converged in the middle of the camp. There were only six sets of legs. Someone was missing and Jenna was pretty sure she knew who it was. She wondered what they had done with Ethan.

Jenna watched intently, waiting for them to leave but they just stood together in the middle of the area. They began to break apart, but they still weren't leaving. Curtis walked right up to where Jenna was hiding and her pulse leapt. She could hear her heart pounding in her ears. She carefully looked up and through the thin branches of the bush; she saw Curtis's eyes staring down at her. She wanted to scream but there was nothing in her. Curtis knelt down and looked around as if he didn't want anyone to know he had found something.

"I know Ethan told you what we were planning and I know it seems scary, but I told you there's a place for you with us, Jenna. Just come out and join us. I can only control these guys so much. If they find you they might kill you and if you aren't with us that's the only way this is going to end," Jenna wrapped her arms around herself to keep from shaking any more than she already was. "Please, Jenna. I like you. I don't want to hurt you." He looked down and her eyes met his through the dark brambles. Her pulse began to slow. His eyes were so deep and gentle. It almost made her forget how he and his friends had just killed her entire team. He slowly slid his hand along the ground toward Jenna and turned it over, as if offering it to her; offering her a chance to live. Jenna didn't know what to do. Her survival instincts urged her to take his hand and offer. It wasn't how she wanted to win, but they would win and be able to live. It would only take the sacrifice of everyone else trying to live. She was ashamed of the part of her that wanted to take his hand. She curled up under the bush in resistance. Curtis looked annoyed, but understanding. A shot rang out and took all the attention. The other members of Curtis's team went running. Curtis looked back over at Jenna.

"There'll always be a place for you on my team. Just come find me before it's too late." Curtis then leapt to his feet and raced into the words with the rest of his team.

Jenna waited, trembling under that bush for almost two hours until she finally slid out. She looked around and everything was quiet again as if nothing had ever occurred. She took a few steps and she saw Jerry's body on the ground. The dirt beneath him was growing dark red with his blood. Panic took control and she gathered up all the supplies she could and was about to leave, but she didn't know where to go. She walked back slowly and leaned up against a tree. She pressed her back to it and slid down to the ground and she broke down, at last, sobbing into her arms.

Chapter 19

On Your Own

Jenna managed to pull herself together and got back on her way. She was at a disadvantage without her team, but she was determined to get back to the testing facility. She found the trail they had been following originally and continued on. She was determined to get to the main highway. She just felt she would be safer there. In the woods, there were a million places for someone to hide and the traps that Curtis and his team had set were surprisingly complex.

As Jenna made her way through the woods, she wondered how Curtis was able to get his hands on any guns. She remembered that the testing facility monitored any firearms that were brought into it and she just assumed they would have taken them away before sending Curtis away for the survival challenge, but it would seem that assumption had been wrong.

Jenna would stop if she heard even the slightest noise. Whenever a branch shook or the leaves blew, she would jump out of her skin. She tried to be aware of anyone near her, but it seemed Curtis and his team were too good to be detected.

As Jenna turned around a slight bend, she heard soft sobbing from the bottom of a nearby ravine. She looked down and while it was difficult to see, Jenna could make out some dark hair.

"Violet?" Jenna asked. The sobbing stopped and Violet stepped out to the open, looking up at Jenna.

"You're not dead!" She exclaimed with excitement.

"How did you get all the way out here?" Jenna asked.

"I don't know. I just ran and I didn't stop. What was all that?"

"It's what I was saying! Curtis's team is taking out all the other teams."

"What are we going to do?"

"We're going to get to the testing facility and finish this. He has weapons and quite a bit of experience by the looks of it, but that doesn't change the fact that we can still win."

Jenna helped Violet climb back up to the trail above and they continued on together. Jenna divided up the supplies she had with Violet and after a few hours of hiking, Violet seemed to calm down.

Jenna still couldn't help but wonder what Curtis had done to Ethan. Had they killed him already? Was it too late for him? It nagged at her but when a column of black smoke rose up through the trees, Jenna's focus was stolen.

"What's that?" Jenna asked.

"Nothing good. We better just stay on the trail." Violet said.

"What if someone needs help?"

"I'm sure whoever it is can handle it themselves."

"Just go on ahead. I'll catch up." Jenna said as she headed toward the smoke. Violet grabbed Jenna's arm and pulled her back.

"Are you insane? It could be a trap or maybe it's too late to help! We're so close to the highway. Like you said, once we get there, it'll be a straight shot back to the testing facility and we're safe and alive."

"Just go. I'll catch up. I promise."

"Fine, but I'm not coming back if you go missing."

"That's okay. I get it. Just go." Violet turned away and continued down along the trail while Jenna walked off the path toward the smoke.

Jenna pushed through a thick bank of trees and came out the other side to find a camp that had been trashed. Bodies were strewn along the ground and there was blood in the dirt and splashed against the surrounding trees.

Jenna saw the small fire in the middle of the camp and that was where the smoke was coming from. She found a bottle of water on the ground and used it to put out the flames. She looked down into the fire pit and saw what was burning. It was a shirt, but she recognized it. It looked like something that Mark owned. Her thoughts finally came to Mark and she could hardly believe he hadn't come up for her before. She wondered if he was all right as well. He was so close to her team, it wasn't a far cry to believe that Curtis had found them as well. Jenna looked around once more and it was clear she was too late to be of any help. She gathered up anything useful and left.

As Jenna made her way back to the trail, she began to feel as though someone was watching her. She stopped and looked around but it was quiet. A breeze blew by and the limbs of the trees above swayed easily at its force. She returned to her pace and for a while felt safe but then the feeling returned. She spun around and she heard footsteps running. Her pulse rose. There was someone near. She tried to pretend she didn't know. She continued walking. When she heard the footsteps again, she quickened her pace and whoever was following kept up with her. Before she knew it, Jenna was in a full run, praying she'd make it back to the trail, but then something hit her from behind and she fell to the ground. She turned over onto her back and her attacker leapt up quickly.

"Mark?" She asked.

"Jenna!" Mark said.

"What are you doing?"

"I was hiding! I don't know what's going on. Some guys with guns came out of nowhere and they killed my team! Just like that!"

"They didn't find you?"

"No. I was getting fire wood. Oh my God. They're dead! They're all dead!"

"Calm down! They got my team too."

"You? They attacked you?" Mark said with a bit of anger in his voice.

"It's fine. I got away. Violet and I are trying to get to the main highway. I think we'll be safer there."

"No place is safe. You saw what they did to my team! They're animals!"

"Think of it like this; while they're out here killing, we can make it to the testing facility first and pass." Mark looked at Jenna intently as he thought about what she had said. He looked back at what remained of his camp and then turned back to Jenna.

"Fine. At least if we die, we die together." He said. Jenna let out a gentle laugh and smirked at Mark as he approached.

"That's the spirit."

Chapter 20

CHAPTER 53

Split

Jenna and Mark were trudging through the brush as they tried to catch up with Violet. Mark took the lead while Jenna held back. The weight of the past few hours began to push down on her. When the challenge began she thought it was going to be bad enough, but she had no idea how to process what was happening. She had never seen a dead body before and while the blood was horrific, the one thing she couldn't get out of her mind was their eyes. The frozen fear in their eyes. It was like they were staring back at her very soul and they haunted her. She tried to push the images from her mind, but they wouldn't leave and they only became more vivid. Her hands were beginning to tremble and she was having trouble staying on the path. She felt a warm breeze passing over her and then there was a sound and she leapt and dove for cover with lightning speed. Her whole body was shaking and Mark ran to her.

"What? What is it?"

"I heard something!" She said. Mark peered out for anything un-usual, but there was nothing.

"It was just the wind." Jenna looked around and he was right. There was nothing. She got back up and a feeling of embarrassment came over her. It just seemed that every strange sound or unexpected movement in the corner of her eye could be a threat. She turned away from Mark just as she felt a tear slip from her eye.

"I'm sorry." She said, forcing her voice from breaking.

"It's okay. I'm jumping at shadows too. They could be anywhere out there."

"Is that seriously supposed to calm me down?"

"Let's just keep moving. The sooner we get out of here, the better."

They continued on their way and after some time Jenna was able to relax and push away the fear and focus on the goal at hand. She forced herself to see what was happening as no change to her expectations of herself. She intended to survive from the beginning and there was no reason for that to change. Whatever Curtis and his team were doing was not going to keep Jenna from seeing her family again.

They soon found themselves back on the trail and that helped put Jenna to ease. The only thing that did trouble her was the fact that they had not seen any sign of Violet and she didn't think it was possible that she could have gotten so far from them in such a short amount of time. There were no fresh footprints and there didn't seem to be any sign that anyone had been through the area recently. Jenna felt a cold spark in the pit of her stomach.

"Are you all right?" Mark asked.

"I don't know. We should have caught up with Violet by now."

"She probably just hauled ass out of here like we should be doing."

"I just don't think she could have gotten so far ahead of us."

"Who is she anyway?"

"Me and Aggy met her on the bus to the testing facility. She was difficult but she won us over."

"Are really that invested in her?" Jenna looked back at Mark. She knew what he meant and it horrified her that he could have even seriously considered such a terrible thought.

"I don't leave my friends behind; whether I've known them for days or years. Besides, she isn't equipped to handle this. She's probably curled up in a ball somewhere."

"I don't think we have the time to search right now. We are at risk every second we're out here."

"I get that. Just give me a little time. We can't just abandon her. We can just set up camp here for tonight."

"Camp? You want to stay in this spot?"

"We have to keep rested. Besides, it doesn't look like anyone has been here in a long time. Just go and find something to eat. I'll meet you back at this tree in fifteen minutes." Jenna said. Mark fought back the urge to argue with her, but he knew it was pointless. He checked his watch and with a warning glare he turned away and disappeared into the brush.

Jenna walked off the path and tried to find any sign of a human presence but there was nothing. She started up an incline toward a cluster of dead trees and then she heard something. It was faint but distinct. She kept pushing forward until she could accurately identify the sound. It was crying. Someone was lightly sobbing and it was getting closer and closer. Jenna reached the cluster of old trees. They were hard and gray as fog. The dirt was dry and dead. The sobbing was loud enough to hear constantly. Jenna followed the sound to a broken stump jutting out of the dead soil. She noticed the old trunk was hollow and she peered inside and saw Violet curled up, holding her legs to her body tightly.

"Violet?" Jenna asked. Violet looked up and the glimmer of recognition lit up her face.

"Jenna!" Violet cried as she crawled forward. Jenna noticed a trail of blood on the ground and then she saw Violet's leg was bleeding.

"What happened?"

"I don't know. I was making my way and then they came out of nowhere."

"Who?"

"I don't know! Curtis' team I guess. They were fast and I panicked. I just ran as fast as I could." Violet crawled out of the tree trunk and attempted to stand up, but she fell to her knee instantly. Jenna then could see the wound on Violet's leg was deeper than it looked.

"What happened to your leg?"

"I hardly noticed when it happened. One of them tried to stab me. I thought I got away but after I caught my breath I saw that I was bleeding." Jenna forced Violet down and pulled up her pant leg. The wound was much deeper than she thought. She touched the skin around the wound and Violet let out a sharp yelp.

"Infection is already setting in." Jenna put down her bag and pulled out the small first aid kit inside. There wasn't much to use but she made the best of the little she had. Jenna instructed Violet to keep pressure on the wound. It had been bleeding for too long as it was. Jenna cleaned it as best she could and applied some anti-bacterial gel before wrapping it. Fortunately, there was just enough gauze to cover it tightly. Jenna looked around and found some reeds and was able to string them together so that she could apply a rough tourniquet.

"That'll stop the bleeding for now, but we have to get you some real medical treatment fast."

"It hurts."

"It'll get better in a few minutes, but we have to get you to a doctor soon."

"I don't want to die out here, Jenna. I know what I've been saying but now that this is happening,"

"I know, Violet. I get it. We're just going to rest and eat here for the night and tomorrow we start again."

"No! Jenna, we have to keep moving. Curtis is out here! He is out here now!"

"Marching any further without rest or food is just going to make us easier targets. The brush is heavy here. We can keep our cover for a few hours."

"It won't be enough!"

"It's going to have to be. Now come on." Jenna then helped Violet back up on her feet and led her back down the hill.

Chapter 21

Crawling Through the Night

Jenna and Mark were hunched in the dark. They had found an area especially thick with brush to establish camp. They had neglected to build a fire as they were worried it would attract some unwanted attention. Jenna looked over and saw that Violet was resting. She seemed fine, but Jenna could see the dressing of the wound was already drenched with more blood.

"We're going to need more supplies." Jenna whispered.

"How are we going to find any?"

"The camps Curtis has already hit. Maybe he left their supplies behind."

"Or we could just get up and get back on the road. This isn't about winning the challenge anymore, Jenna. It's about surviving."

"That is what this challenge has been all about from the start, Mark. The dynamics have changed a bit, but we're still in this to live."

"You really think Curtis is out here? Maybe he and his team are already back at the facility. Maybe we've already lost."

"He wants to make sure he wins this thing. He won't leave until everyone else is dead. I know it."

"How can you be so sure?"

"I don't really care if I'm right or not, Mark. I'm just trying to get through this and I don't want to lose any more friends. Just promise me you're in this with me. Please." Jenna said. Mark could barely see her face in the darkness, but he could see her eyes. He could see the strength in them as easily as he could see the fear. He thought if he could push a little more, she would come around to his thinking, but he thought about what she had been saying and he wasn't sure if he was ready to take the chance. Death was waiting for them. It was unavoidable and it didn't matter if it happened in the woods or at the facility. There was really no reason to have any hope, but he preferred to be without hope with Jenna.

"Fine. We'll do this your way."

"Thank you." Mark smiled and leaned back against the brush. Jenna reached for him and pulled him back. He then realized the noise he was making and they were trying to remain as quiet as possible. He mouthed 'sorry' to her and they settled back, still on guard.

"How are we going to sleep?"

"Violet seems to be doing all right. As for us, I'm not sure I can sleep even if I tried."

"You need to rest."

"I'll be fine. The stress will keep me strong."

"I'm not moving on this, Jen. You need to sleep. I'll keep watch first."

"Fine. If you anything happens,"

"Just sleep." Jenna gave him a weak smile and got down on the ground and made something of a nest out of the dirt and twigs. She moved slowly and made as little noise as she could manage. Once she was done, she curled up, closed her eyes and sleep came faster than she thought it would.

It felt as though she had only been out for a few seconds before she was awoken by the sound of footsteps. She looked around. Violet was still resting but Mark was missing. The footsteps were close but sounded like they were heading away from the camp. Jenna wanted to see who it was, but it was too risky to give away her position. She crawled over to Violet and gently jostled her awake.

"What?" Violet asked. Her voice was weak and broken.

"Someone is near the camp," Jenna whispered. Violet's eyes widened but Jenna clapped her hand to her mouth to prevent her from saying anything. "I'm going to go around and see who it is. Don't move from this spot. Understand?" Violet gently nodded her head. Jenna then got up on her knees and carefully stalked away through a small trail that they had cleared earlier. It weaved around the area and when she was far enough away, she looked up through the tall grass. She saw figures wandering around. It was too dark to tell who they were, but it was clear that Mark was not among them. Jenna started to get anxious. It had to be Curtis and his team. Had they come here by accident? It seemed their location was too far and particular for it to be a coincidence. They were there for a purpose. Jenna was becoming increasingly worried. She hadn't heard anything, but she had been sleeping so deeply. She had to find Mark. She felt her foot hit a rock in the dirt. It was large. She picked it up and flung it with all her strength. Not only did she hear it land, the intruders did as well. They reacted quickly and soon were headed to where the rock had landed. She waited a few moments and when she thought they were far enough away, she raced back to camp in hopes of finding something that would inform on what had happened to Mark.

Jenna returned and indicated to Violet to remain quiet. She started to search around, but there wasn't much to find. It was too dark. Jenna kept searching around with her hands until she felt something that made her heart sink. She had found a spot on the ground that was warm and wet. It felt like just a small spot at first but there was a bigger spot nearby. She looked at her hand and as she feared, it was blood. Tears began to form in her eyes. She looked down further and as her eyes adjusted, she could see a trail of blood leading away.

Jenna followed the blood trail and it led her into the brush. She pushed on as carefully as she could until she finally came to a clear spot and there, in the dirt, was Mark in a puddle of his own blood. Jenna couldn't control herself as she let out a painful cry. She ran to him. His body was still warm, but there was no life left. His body was limp. Jenna knelt over him, quietly weeping.

"It didn't have to be like this." Curtis said. Jenna spun around and saw him standing before her with a bloody knife in his hand.

"Why are you doing this?"

"That's a fairly stupid question, don't you think? I'm doing this to win. To live."

"You killed Mark!"

"Was that his name? Okay. I'm sorry, but I try to keep a certain distance from my victims. Getting to know them can make it difficult."

"So now what? You're going to kill me?"

"No! No, Jenna! When I told you there was a place for you on my team, I meant it. I don't want to hurt you. I didn't want to hurt anyone."

"Yet here we are."

"What I have done, I did out of necessity. I mean, come on! Our lives are at stake here! I don't know about you, but I want to make sure I make it through these tests."

"You didn't have to kill anyone. We can all get out of this alive!"

"Not everyone. By my calculations, at the end of this survival challenge, roughly thirty-six percent of these kids are going to get a one-way ticket to the death camp. Not counting the others who would move onto the rest of the tests and still fail. I'm doing most of these kids a favor. No anxious waiting. No painful farewells to their families. A quick, clean honorable death."

"And who are you to decide who should die? How do you believe you get to make that choice?"

"Law of the jungle, babe. Survival of the fittest."

"You think you're any better than the people who put us through these tests?"

"I don't care about being better than them or anyone else. All I care about is getting out of here alive so I can live my life. I thought that was what you wanted too."

"Mark was a part of my life! You killed him!"

"I'm sorry for that, but there's really only one place free on my team, and as I have said, it's yours. Join us. You can be free of all of this!"

"You've killed. You've killed so many innocent people."

"But I won't get charged. My dad is an attorney and he did some research into this and it turns out, we are immune from the law, for the most part. If I would be charged, a case could be made that I was driven to these actions by extraordinary stress. He could have the case thrown out just like that; the perfect crime. I'm offering you a way out of this Jenna. All you have to do is say yes."

"Is that all?"

"Well, and take care of your friend." Curtis said as he tossed the knife to Jenna.

"Violet?"

"She's dead weight anyway. Just put her out of her misery and we can get back to our lives tomorrow." Jenna stood up and picked up the knife. Mark's blood was dripping off the blade.

"What's to keep me from gutting you right here and now?"

"The fact that you're surrounded by the rest of my team and one wrong move and you join Mark over there."

"What a friend."

"I'm sorry, but I can only be so generous. Just do it, Jenna. It'll be much easier for you. Trust me." Jenna looked at the knife in her hand and then over to Mark's lifeless body. The tears were forcing their way out, but the anger in her soul boiled away whatever sadness she had been feeling. It was like a tornado in her mind. She looked back to Curtis.

"No." Jenna threw the blade back down to the ground at Curtis' feet.

"Think about what you're doing, Jenna. If you're not with us, you're against us and I can't help you when that happens." Jenna turned away from Curtis and went back to Mark. She looked down at his face. The color was leaving his skin, but he looked so peaceful.

"I'm sorry." She whispered.

"Sorry for what?" Curtis asked. Jenna then reached into her pocket and pulled out a lighter that had also been packed in with her supplies. She quickly several small fires in the dry grass which soon grew out of control. There were screams in the darkness as Curtis' team tried to escape the flames. Jenna leapt up and raced past Curtis, knocking him down as she did. She looked back and the fire was growing larger by the second. The screams and panicked cries of Curtis and his team echoed in the night.

Jenna returned to the camp and pulled Violet up to her feet.

"Jenna! What's going on? Where's Mark? Is that a fire!?"

"Just run!" Jenna barked as she pulled Violet along.

"I can't! My leg!" Violet cried. Jenna took her arm.

"I'm sorry, but you have to. Now run!"

Jenna and Violet ran as fast and as far as they could. Violet's wound started bleeding again and they stopped for a moment so Jenna could look at it.

"Does it hurt?" Jenna asked.

"Yes!" Violet said through a storm of pain. Jenna grabbed some nearby plant leaves and made a makeshift bandage out of them. She wrapped them over Violet's wound and hoped at least they wouldn't make anything worse.

"That should hold until you get back to the facility."

"I can't tell. Is the light I'm seeing the sun rising or the fire getting out of control?" Violet asked. Jenna turned and saw that it was actually both. She could see the sun rising up over the horizon, but the bright aura of the raging fire was lighting up the area almost just as well.

"Don't worry about it. We have some breathing room now."

"What are you talking about? What's going on? Where's Mark?" Violet asked. Jenna looked up at her and tried to say the words, but her throat closed up and she just looked away. "Oh," Violet said. There were no details but it was clear what had happened. "What do we do now?" Jenna stood up, wiped the tears from her eyes and took a deep breath.

"We win this thing."

Chapter 22

Morning Rises

The sun was up and while Jenna couldn't see the light of the fire she had set. She could only see the smoke rising up into the sky. She felt a pang of guilt about causing the fire, but there was no other way. If she hadn't done anything they would have killed her just as they had killed Mark.

Jenna allowed Violet to rest for a few minutes more than she wanted. Her wound was still bleeding, but it had slowed. Jenna kept a look out for Curtis and his team, but it seemed they had lost them. The fire turned out to be a better cover than Jenna had expected it to be.

"How far are we from the road?" Violet asked. Jenna hadn't even thought about that in all the excitement. "I mean, going by the smoke, it looks like we're actually getting further from it."

"Maybe. We had to get out of there."

"But we have to get back on the path. If we don't,"

"Look! I know! I wasn't exactly thinking straight at the moment, okay?" Jenna snapped. Violet slid back into the brush.

"I'm sorry."

"No. I'm sorry. It's just been stressful."

"I'm sorry about Mark."

"Thanks, but we both knew this was a possibility. I guess for all our preparing, we're never really ready when it happens."

"Are you sure we weren't followed?"

"I don't think we were. I haven't heard anyone nearby."

"Maybe they decided to forget about us and went on back to the facility. I mean, if they took out the other groups, they don't need to kill us to win."

"No, but it looked to me like they've acquired a taste for killing. We have to assume they will be willing to take us out just because they want to."

"This is so messed up."

"That is the understatement of the year."

"I just want to get back to the road and back to the facility. I don't even care if we come in second place. I will gladly face another phase of tests if I can survive this."

"Don't worry. We're going to make it. Can you walk?" Jenna asked. Violet took a deep breath and attempted to get to her feet. She stood up to her full height and seemed to be carrying her weight on both legs. She took a step and with a wince of pain, she fell to her knee. Jenna hurried to her, but she waved her off.

"I'm fine. I can make it." Violet said as she got back up. Jenna looked down at the makeshift dressing on Violet's wound and it was clear it was not doing the job. Blood was dripping down into her shoe and it looked more infected than before.

"It looks bad, Violet. I'm not going to lie."

"I don't care. We get to the facility, they can fix it. Let's just go."

Jenna and Violet found their path again and using the smoke from the fire as a guide, they found their way back to the main road. Jenna knew they were headed in the right direction because she could hear the crackle of the fire getting louder. They passed a thicket of dead grass and she could see the fire. It had burned off a lot of dead land and there was more to go. Thankfully there was no sign of Curtis or his henchmen. When she realized Mark's body might still be in the middle of the blaze, her heart seized up a bit in her chest. It had been so long, if his body were there, it was probably burned and charred beyond recognition. She thought of Mark's mother. She was going to be destroyed and it will only make it worse that she wouldn't have anything of Mark's to hold on to.

"Wait here." Jenna said as she found a dark space to hide Violet.

"Where are you going?"

"Wait here." Jenna then headed toward the fire. She could hear the snapping and crackle of the dead weeds and wood burning. The heat was getting intense and she felt sweat all over her body. She stopped short of the flames and tried to see if Mark's body was still there. Through the amber waves, she could see a dark figure laying on the ground. It was Mark. It didn't look like him, but it was him. Jenna closed her eyes, said a prayer and bolted forward with all her strength. She held her arms over her head in an attempt to protect her from the flames. She got past the wall of fire and she ran to Mark's corpse and saw that his skin was charred and burned away. The fire had passed by the area and seemed to stay in the surrounding brush. There was blood dried on his flesh and it stunk unlike anything she had ever seen. She reached for his head and miraculously, the necklace Mark wore around his neck every day had not been damaged. There was no time for final good byes or last words. There was no time to remember and wish him peace. She snapped the necklace off of him and bolted back out of the flames.

When she came out of the inferno, she tumbled across the dirt. She got up and dead leaves and dirt clung to her sweaty flesh. She returned to Violet who got up as she approached.

"What the Hell was that? Are you insane?"

"I just had to get something." Jenna said as she held the necklace close to her heart.

"You're crazy, you know that?"

"Only the sane are crazy anymore."

Jenna and Violet continued on their way. It was clear they had fallen far behind and there was no way to tell how many other teams in their group were in the race. Jenna was assuming Curtis had killed everyone else, but she was hoping that wasn't the case. She looked over to Violet and it seemed that she had gotten used to the pain as she was keeping a fair pace.

They came up over a large hill and when they reached the peak, they say what looked to have once been some kind of farm. There was a barn and a farmhouse which were both barely standing anymore. Jenna saw a torn piece of fabric on the ground and she assumed that it was a part of a tent.

"It looks like someone set up camp here." Jenna said.

"And it looks like Curtis got here and took care of that." Violet added.

"Let's just check to see if they left any supplies behind. We need everything we can get."

Jenna and Violet headed down and searched around. Jenna took the farm house while Violet explored around the barn. As she got close to the main door, she could hear breathing. She pulled the door open and peeked in. It was dark, but the breathing was louder. It was close. Violet walked in and even with the light streaming in through the broken roof, it was nearly impossible to see. She followed the sound of the breathing and when she checked inside a makeshift stall, she saw Ethan Lazarus tied up. It looked like he had been there for some time. He looked up at her and let out a faint cry.

"Please! Help me!"

"What happened?"

"Curtis. He and the rest of my team tied me up in here. Please let me go!"

"You're Ethan Lazarus. The son of the Senator."

"Yes." He said with a guilty tone.

"Why wouldn't Curtis just kill you like all the others?"

"He said it would be too easy. He wants me to fail the test. He wants me coming in last. Said he'd have them send a search party for me after it was too late. He's setting me up to die! Please! Let me go!" Violet looked down at the broken boy before her and she was torn. She was one of the many outraged and suspicious that every member of the Lazarus family managed to pass the tests with no problem. She believed they were using their influence to subvert the tests to protect their own while millions of innocents were left to die. It was one point that she could agree with Curtis. She thought quickly and realized that if Jenna knew he was here, she would want to free him. Violet noticed a white piece of fabric nearby. It looked like it had been keeping him quiet for a while until he had managed to get it off. Violet picked it up and her calm, cool demeanor began to fill Ethan with dread. He tried to beg her to stop, but his voice was weak and he was so tired. He felt tears coming down his cheek and he was shaking his head, protesting what Violet was about to do. She knelt down and tied his gag back on, tight. She looked him in the eye.

"I'm sorry, I am, but your family has to learn that they are not above the law. Particularly the ones they are responsible for." She then stood up, walked out of the barn and shut the door. Ethan could hear Violet outside talking to someone else. He recognized Jenna's voice. He tried to cry out, but it was no use. He tried to make some kind of noise, but he was just too weak. He could barely move. The voices then faded away and he fell silent, accepting his fate.

"Did you find anything?" Jenna asked.

"No. Just some rats in the barn."

Chapter 23

The Highway

Jenna and Violet were pushing forward as best they could. They stayed close to heavily wooded areas in order to preserve as much cover as possible. There had been no sign of Curtis but Jenna wasn't ready to accept that he was gone. Violet was still struggling to keep up, but Jenna had found some fresh medical supplies at the previous camps and was able to make a more secure dressing for her wound. It still hurt and it was clearly infected, but she could stand on it.

As they emerged from a cluster of bushes, they could see the highway a few yards ahead. Violet grabbed Jenna and hopped up and down in celebration, holding back the pain the action brought her.

"We made it." Jenna said with great relief. The highway was a direct route back to the testing facility. It was still a lengthy hike, but the goal was within sight. Jenna could hardly believe they were finally so close. Her joy was dampened a bit as she realized all that was lost. So many innocent lives were taken and even though his reasons were understandable, Curtis was nothing more than a murderer and as long as they didn't know where he was, they were at risk. Violet hurried toward the road, but Jenna grabbed her.

"What? There's the road home! Well, sort of."

"I know, but Curtis could still be out here."

"Maybe he's not going to kill us. I mean, it looks like he got everyone else. He doesn't need to kill us."

"We don't know for sure. Even with all the killings, he may still only be coming in second. If he gets to the facility before us,"

"Stop." Violet said sharply.

"We see the road. That's enough. Keep to the brush for now and stay quiet."

They continued on parallel to the road and for about an hour it was deathly quiet. There wasn't even any breeze or birds singing. It was like a death field.

"Did you see Ethan?" Jenna asked.

"What? Why would you ask that?"

"Because when Curtis and his team surrounded us, I didn't see Ethan."

"Oh. I don't know. Maybe Curtis killed him first."

"Maybe."

"Why do you even care?"

"I know he's the guy everyone wants to see lose, but I guess I felt bad for him. It's hard enough going through this, but going through it with everyone wanting you to fail must be a nightmare."

"It would serve his family right. They pass the tests every damn year. This is the first time someone from their family could actually fail. Maybe if that happens, they'll repeal this whole thing. His death could save millions."

"I don't know if I feel right forcing that much responsibility on anyone."

"It might as well be him. It was his family that started this."

"I know that, but it wasn't his idea."

"Are you actually defending Ethan Lazarus?"

"I've talked to him. I think I'm just about the only one who has since he came here. He's not a terrible person."

"It's not about him being terrible or not. It's about what his family has done to everyone."

"So he has to pay the price for what his family did years ago?"

"It's not fair, but yes." Jenna shook her head to what Violet had said. She recalled Ethan's face. It was always so sad and lonely. She figured he at least had the courage to come. There had been a few years when the subject from the Lazarus family would go 'missing' just before the tests would begin. That caused such an uproar; a law was passed soon after that banned all international travel within three months of someone's sixteenth birthday. The Lazarus' tried to get it thrown out, but there was too much demand from the public and it became law. After that, they were forced to participate. It was hard to see why they were so resistant since they proved to be invincible since they were offered up for the tests.

Jenna and Violet continued on in silence. Violet looked over and it felt like they had been walking for ages but they had only progressed a few miles. Her leg was starting to hurt again and she could feel blood seeping from her bandages. She stopped for a moment and saw a crimson splotch forming over the bandage. Jenna turned to her and noticed the same thing.

"I've got more first-aid stuff. I can redress that."

"No."

"It's bleeding."

"We are too close now. I'm not going to slow down just for a new band aid."

"If you don't, you might just lose that leg and amputees aren't known to pass the tests." Jenna said. Violet thought for a second and realized she was right.

"Fine." Violet said and she walked over to a nearby rock and began to unravel the dressing. Jenna knelt down and took out some gauze, tape and a small tube of anti-bacterial gel. There wasn't much left, but it would be enough.

Jenna had Violet's wound cleaned and covered up and it looked like she would be good until they got to the testing facility. It all felt like it was coming to a long desired end. Jenna didn't care if they came in second and had to endure a final phase of testing. She just wanted it over.

"What's that?" Violet asked. Jenna twisted her head around and her heart dropped. There was something on the ground behind a large growth of reeds. She couldn't tell what it was exactly, but it looked like it had a distinctly human looking arm.

"Wait here." Jenna said as she crept toward whatever it was. She thought she knew what was waiting for her and it was making her sick, but she was getting used to the feeling she got just before she found a dead body.

As she approached, she discovered that it was indeed a corpse, but as she turned it over, she clapped her hand to her mouth. It was Curtis. Her mind short circuited as she looked down on his body. It looked like he had been stabbed many repeatedly in his chest. Blood was trickling down from his mouth. She stepped back and ran to Violet.

"Come on." Jenna said with urgency.

"What is it? What's going on?" Violet asked. Jenna took her hand and pulled her along.

"Just come on! Run if you can!" Jenna and Violet picked up their pace, but just like that, someone leapt out of nowhere. Jenna and Violet stumbled back.

"Not another step." It was a boy Jenna recognized from Curtis' team. He was tall and had an athletic build. He was smiling, but it was a sick kind of smile.

"Who are you?" Jenna asked.

"I'm Barrett."

"You were on Curtis' team."

"I was."

"You killed him?"

"Had to be done."

"Why?"

"It turns out when he was talking about how his dad would get us off, he really only meant himself. We didn't have any promise of protection and we all decided he had to go."

"Now his murder will just be added to the others."

"No. We all thought it out. He killed all those other testers and we killed him out of self-defense."

"And you think they'll believe you?"

"No one to say otherwise. No one but you two." Barrett then produced a knife from behind his back. There was still blood on the blade dripping down to his hand. She then heard rustling coming from all around and it was clear they were once more surrounded.

"What if we promise not to say anything?" Violet asked. Barrett smiled at her with a curious look in his eyes.

"And you really expect us to believe you?"

"Please! We can all still make it and pass the test! It doesn't have to be like this!" Barrett relaxed his posture and paced around slowly. His other team mates appeared at last and they seemed to be waiting for him to signal them. Jenna only assumed they were all armed as well. Barrett finally stopped and his eyes found Violet. He held the knife to her and then flipped it over in his hand, offering the bloody handle to her. She looked at it and then back at him, confused.

"You want to live? Prove you won't tell. Kill her," He said, indicating to Jenna. "If you want to run with us, you need to take a share of the guilt." Violet took the knife and she was trembling. Jenna looked at her, unsure of what was happening. Violet then turned to Jenna with tears streaming down her face.

"I'm sorry." She said and then lunged forward. Jenna leapt away, half expecting her move. The others started to yell, urging Violet to kill Jenna. Violet wasn't quick enough and Jenna was able to break away from the others and she bolted away into the brush.

As Jenna ran away, she could hear Barrett barking orders and the others acknowledging them. Jenna hadn't been totally sure Violet was going to turn on her, but after everything that had happened, it wasn't a total surprise. Violet wanted an end to it all and as she was already badly injured, she probably didn't see any choice.

Jenna back tracked as far as she could manage until she couldn't hear the others searching for her anymore. She finally returned to the dilapidated farm they had found the day before. She realized it was only a matter of time before Violet would lead them there, so Jenna went about searching for anything that could be used as a weapon or a good hiding place. She approached the old barn and pushed the door open and then she saw someone sprawled out on the ground. She ran over and saw that it was Ethan, tied up rather well. She knelt down and pressed her hand to his face. He woke up and his eyes expanded and he began to laugh hysterically under the gag that was wrapped over his mouth. She pulled it free.

"You came back! Oh, thank God! She sent you back!"

"She?" Jenna asked.

"That dark haired girl; She did send you back here to save me, didn't she?"

"No, I'm sorry. I was actually here looking for a place to hide."

"Why? I thought you were on your way to the facility."

"We were, but they ambushed us."

"Curtis." Ethan said with contempt.

"No. He's dead."

"What?"

"Barrett killed him and is planning to claim self-defense after getting rid of any witnesses."

"That's not good. Curtis was a little unhinged but Barrett is flat out nuts. You have to untie me! Please!" Ethan begged. Jenna loosened his ties and he leapt up with his regained freedom.

"Oh God! Thank you! Thank you so much!" He sang.

"Thank me after we get out of this alive."

Chapter 24

Rescue

Ethan and Jenna were hiding in the darkest corner of the old barn. Jenna offered up what few provisions she had left and Ethan gobbled them up in record time. Ethan was in a terrible state. His face was sallow and scarred and he couldn't stop trembling. There were deep and dark lines under his eyes which were both terribly bloodshot. He just looked as though he had been put through some stuff. Jenna could see she hadn't been the only one fighting for their life.

"How'd they treat you?" Jenna asked.

"Like a prince. How do you think?"

"I was just asking."

"Sorry. I'm just not used to being treated nicely."

"It was that bad?"

"It wasn't easy. After they got bored of just insulting me, they started to get physical. It was just light torment at first until they dog piled on me one night and just beat on me."

"You don't look that bad."

"I curled up into a ball. I think they were pissed I protected myself because it just got worse from there. They took my supplies and wouldn't let me eat. When Curtis got his bright idea to take out the other teams, they talked about killing me first, but then he thought it would be worse for me if they just tied me up somewhere so that I would fail the tests. Send a message."

"You don't seem affected by this."

"I knew everyone wanted me dead from day one. None of any of this has been a surprise; except for you saving me. Why'd you do that?"

"While I understand why they did what they did, I can't say that I agree. The test isn't your fault and you're at risk the same as us. You deserve as much a chance to survive as anyone else." Jenna said. Ethan looked back at her with his mouth wide open and a tear forming in the corner of his eye.

"Wow," He said with a catch in his throat. "I don't know if you mean all of that, but it sure is good to hear."

The sound of something stalking through the tall grass outside broke the moment. Jenna pulled Ethan toward her and the slid further into the darkness. She knew any hiding place was going to be discovered inevitably. It was only a matter of time. She could hear someone talking outside. She didn't recognize a couple of voices, but then she heard Violet. She couldn't make out what they were saying, but she knew it was Violet. Their footsteps got closer to the barn and Jenna could feel her heart pounding in her chest. The only way out was the front gate and there was no way of leaving through there without catching hunters' attention. Jenna then noticed Ethan's short, panicked breaths. She looked in his eyes and there was nothing but pure fear.

"Stay here." Jenna whispered. Ethan nodded as she got up and skulked over toward an old workbench nearby. There was a shovel leaning up against the all. She took it and held it tight in both hands. She slipped toward the front of the barn. Ethan tried to beg her to return, but he didn't know how to communicate the message non-verbally.

As Jenna reached the front, the doors began to move and one of Barrett's teammates crept in. Before he could see a thing, Jenna was on top of him as she drove the shovel down onto his head. The sound it made was dull and hard and he fell to the ground in a heap. Ethan ran over to Jenna instantly.

"Is he dead?" Ethan asked. Jenna saw that the intruder was still breathing, but it was clear he was going to be out for a long time.

"Just stunned." She said.

"Now what? They're going to come looking for him!"

"Then we won't be here when they come. I'm going to open the door and when I do, I want you to run like Hell. Just go straight as far and as fast as you can."

"But,"

"You heard me!"

"Yes." Ethan said. Jenna walked over and took a look outside. The coast seemed to be clear. She pulled the door open a bit more and looked at Ethan.

"Now!" She barked. Ethan broke forward and charged through into the tall grass and Jenna was close behind.

Jenna and Ethan put as much distance between them and the barn as they could. They wandered through the woods until Ethan finally collapsed in a heap behind a pile of rocks. The sky was growing dim but Jenna kept an eye out for any activity.

"Where are we?" Ethan asked between breaths.

"I don't know."

"Is there anyone out there?"

"I don't know."

"We're going to die, aren't we?"

"I don't know, but I'm losing confidence." Ethan finally sat up. His face was shiny from the sweat that coated his skin. His eyes looked even darker.

"What exactly is your plan?"

"Go for as long as possible without being killed. How does that work for you?"

"I mean, what are we doing? While I don't know where we are, I do know we are a lot further from the testing facility than ever! If we don't get back soon, we are going to fail."

"I don't know! Okay? I wasn't really prepared to deal with someone going nuts and killing everyone."

"For all we know, Barrett and his followers are back at the testing facility filling out their release forms."

"Fine. You're right. We need to get back but we also need to be sure it's safe."

"How do we do that?"

"We just do it. I haven't seen any activity out there for the last two hours. I'm willing to risk it if you are." Ethan then tried to get up, but his legs gave out and he fell back down onto his back.

"Maybe in another hour."

Jenna sat down next to Ethan and leaned against one of the nearby rocks. As she rested, she began to realize how tired she really was. It was as though every muscle in her body ignited at once. She looked down at Ethan and his eyes were shut and his breathing looked like it was slowing down. She nudged his head with her foot and his eyes popped open.

"Don't fall asleep."

"I haven't slept in almost three days. Please!"

"I'm sorry, but we only have time to rest for a little bit because when we get back up, we're making one last push to the testing facility. We are going to get back there and face whatever waiting for us there."

"If we get there alive."

"I'm starting to think if Barrett is even slightly smart, he and his grunts gave up on us and went back."

"So we get back and then what?"

"With any luck, we'll at least come in second in our group."

"You think that's lucky? We could have won and gotten out of the tests!"

"We could come in last and fail. Coming in second at least gives us a shot at passing."

"This isn't fair!" Ethan barked. "I should have been with the first group. It wasn't supposed to happen like this. No Lazarus in history has ever failed."

"And you haven't failed yet!" Jenna said as she took Ethan by the collar of his shirt. Their eyes locked and while she saw his raw, unfiltered fear in his eyes, he could see the fiery determination in hers. She released him and he fell back down to the ground.

"You really believe all that?"

"I really have no choice. When you're at the end of the universe, you either believe you can be saved, or you die and I haven't gone through everything I've gone through just to die. Have you?" She asked. Ethan leaned up onto his elbows and for the first time since she had met him, he smiled.

"Not a chance."

Chapter 25

Life and Death

Jenna and Ethan said a quiet prayer before setting out to return to the testing facility. She tried to sound confident for Ethan's benefit, but she knew as well as he did that the threat of Barrett was all too real. She took comfort that she still had not seen or heard any activity in the area and the further they traveled the more confident she was that he and his followers had left. She then began to worry what they would be returning to.

Everything was a blur and she wasn't even sure how much time had passed since the survival challenge began. It felt to her like it had been weeks. She couldn't remember the last time she was able to stop for even a second and allow her brain to stop. She was becoming convinced even if she survived the tests, the stress would end up killing her.

The sky was growing black above them but what little of the terrain she could see was looking familiar to her. Her heart was pounding in her chest. She thought back to the first time she had ever ridden a roller coaster. She remembered waiting in that line feeling her stomach hop and her heart skip as she saw the coaster roar across the track. She knew in her brain there was no real danger, but in her heart the danger was real. She recalled her father taking her hand and squeezing. She looked up at him and he smiled at her.

"It only looks worse than it really is," He said as he knelt down to meet her eyes. "Our minds play tricks and when we're scared, they make everything scarier to us."

"Why?"

"Because there's a part of everyone that wants to run away when things get hard, but you have the power to be brave and get past the fear. It's like a test your brain puts to you to see how worthy you are. If you can pass, there's no limit to what you can do." His words echoed in her mind for years after that moment and whenever Jenna felt any kind of fear, she remembered that day and his words.

They began to break through new territory and Jenna was pleased with their progress. She glanced over and saw Ethan keeping pace with her quite well. While he was keeping up, he did look as though if he stopped for even a brief moment, he would collapse. She was thinking it was the first time he ever had to really work for anything.

"How much further?" He asked.

"Just keep going! Harder to hit a moving target!" Jenna's heart started to race. She felt they were close. She knew it couldn't be much longer and as they came upon the rise, she saw the lights of the testing facility glowing in the distance. She could see the gates and most importantly, she could see people walking the perimeter. She let out a loud cry and she began to push herself even harder. Her legs were on fire and it felt as though the muscles in her thighs were going to burst through her flesh. She heard Ethan close behind. Her vision started to grow dark. Her brain was on fire. She felt her feet finally hit the asphalt. She tried to pump her legs harder, trying to go faster. Her legs were shooting with pain. She saw the entrance of the testing facility. It was so close she thought for a moment it was an illusion, but as she heard the voices of other people growing louder, she knew it was real. She had made it and when she realized that, she stopped and her legs gave out almost instantly. She tried to keep her eyes open, but they shut against her will and the sound of panicked voices surrounding her filled her ears. She couldn't pick up what they were saying as she finally gave in to her fatigue.

It felt like it has been days until the light returned to her eyes. Her vision was blurry and she could only see shapeless blobs in white. Her vision began to return and she saw that she was in a hospital room. There were tubes stuck in her arms and her legs were bandaged up.

Panic took her over but as she attempted to get out of the bed, she discovered that her legs weren't as cooperative as she thought they would be. She could feel, but they just weren't strong enough to move.

"Help!" She called out. The door flew open and three nurses came running in and started tending to the machines that she was hooked up to. She was absolutely confused. She tried to ask what was going on, but no one seemed to even notice she was in the room.

"Enough!" An authoritative voice called out. Jenna saw an older woman walk through the door into the room. She had short, dark red hair and was wearing a neatly pressed white lab coat over a rather drab gray suit. The nurses finished what they were doing and filed out as quickly as they could. The older woman looked over at Jenna and smiled.

"Look who's finally up."

"Who are you? Where am I?"

"I'm Dr. Miller. As for where you are, this is the medical ward of this testing facility. You were found collapsed outside the main entrance. We've been very concerned about you and Mr. Lazarus."

"Things got a little out of control out there."

"You don't have to tell me. We know all about Barrett and everything he did to pass this survival challenge."

"You do? Did he confess?"

"No. We reviewed the footage."

"What footage? What are you talking about?"

"The test was monitored at all times."

"Wait. They saw everything that was happening? They saw it all and did nothing?" Jenna's head was becoming warm which was normal when she was on the verge of losing her temper.

"It is not the place of the Testing Committee to interfere with the tests in any way. There was nothing that could be done."

"Innocent people were killed! I don't see how nothing could be done!"

"I don't know what to tell you. It is a harsh reality, but it's just the way it is. I'm sorry." Jenna felt too weak to argue anymore. The weight of the previous days was falling down upon her so quickly.

"What about Barrett? What's going to happen to him?"

"I know you don't want to hear this, but he and his group have been passed. While the actions of Barrett and his group cannot be condoned, the rules of the test have enabled them to evade charges."

"They killed those kids! They killed Mark! Just because it was in the name of the tests they walk?"

"I'm sorry, but yes."

"What about me? Did I fail?"

"No. You and Mr. Lazarus made it, just barely, into the second tier. While you did not earn an automatic pass, you both will go on to the next phase of the test."

"After everything we went through?"

"I'm sorry, but the point of these tests is to weed out the weak from the strong and the rules must be adhered to."

"So why am I here?"

"Because when you came back to us, you were in pretty bad shape. Nothing serious, but we just need to keep you rested for a couple days. After that, you may resume the tests."

"Yay." Jenna said with little enthusiasm. Dr. Miller then walked up to Jenna and smiled.

"It was impressive how you survived. I'm not really at liberty to say officially, but coming in the way you did pretty much assures that you will pass these tests."

"Really?"

"I know it may seem hard to believe now, but I had to face my tests as well. As you can see, I made it, but only barely. There was one girl in my group who just amazed everyone. Skilled and smart. I've seen your results up until now. She didn't do half as well as you."

"Thanks."

"Just get some rest. The sooner you finish these tests, the sooner you can get to the rest of your life."

Jenna finally settled into her rest. There was so much on her troubled mind, but rest was all she could handle. She drifted blissfully into her slumber and swam in the deepest depths of her dreams. She saw a world past the tests. She saw her family and her friends. She could even see college and all the amazing things she would be able to do. She felt her life blooming before her and all she had to do was pass one more test.

She was pulled from her fantasies by a sharp finger poking at her arm. She opened her eyes and saw Ethan standing over her bed.

"Did I wake you?" He asked. He was wearing a robe over his hospital gown and was holding himself up on a pair of crutches.

"Yes, but it's okay. What's going on?"

"I couldn't sleep until I knew you were okay. These doctors don't tell you much."

"Where did they put you?"

"In the room next door actually."

"They let you out of your bed?"

"No, but it's late and the nursing staff at night don't really care what we do. I just wanted a chance to thank you."

"For what?"

"What do you mean 'for what'? You saved my life. If it weren't for you, I'd still be out there. I don't know how you did it."

"Sometimes you just have to push past the fear."

"I mean, why did you save me? I'm the grandson of the man who started these tests. I don't think there's a single person here who wouldn't have gladly hung me out to dry. You could have just left me to rot."

"That's not how I do it. You're not to blame for what your family has done. Besides, honestly? If I let you die and I passed, I'm sure your family would do everything in their power to ruin my life."

"You're probably right. My father can be very vindictive."

"I also did it because it was the right thing to do." Jenna said with a smile.

"I won't forget it. Thank you."

"You're welcome. Now get back to your room and let me sleep. These tests aren't over yet."

Chapter 26

CHAPTER 59

Road to Recovery

After the first night in the medical ward, Jenna felt her strength returning to her. She was adequately hydrated and the pain in her legs was easing away. She was able to stand under her own power and the headaches she had been experiencing were gone. She felt as though she could conquer the world, but the doctors insisted she take one more day before resuming the test.

As the physical tests had concluded and all information about the strength and ability of all subjects had been recorded. The next phase of the test was to gauge mental ability and intelligence. The following tests were to take the form of a series of standardized tests. Jenna felt a bit of relief in that. She wasn't ready to get back into any intense physical training again. She was glad that all she had to do to prepare for the next tests was simply open books.

Several textbooks were sent to her room so that she could get a jump on her studies. The subjects of all the books varied and ranged from simple arithmetic to advanced world history and everything in between. A letter came with the books and advised that the upcoming tests would encompass each and every subject. It was daunting, but Jenna dove in.

She was in deep concentration as she read through her books. Much of the material was familiar. It seemed the tests would be at the level she was at in school, which made her a bit more confident. A familiar voice broke her concentration.

"Hi." Violet said. Jenna looked up and as her eyes fell upon Violet, her anger rose up.

"Violet? What are you doing here? I thought you passed. Along with Barrett."

"He sold me out. He said that the whole thing was my idea and cut a deal for him and the rest of his group."

"Wow. Who would think a psychopath couldn't be trusted?"

"I'm sorry, Jenna," Violet began, but as she took a step forward, Jenna threw her hand up, halting her.

"Not another step. You turned on me out there. You were actually going to kill me."

"I was desperate. You don't understand."

"The Hell I don't!" Jenna barked. "We are all under the gun here! All of us! You were on my team! I trusted you!"

"I didn't think I was going to make it. I was scared."

"Again. So is everyone else. I think that's the one great thing about the tests. It's the equalizer. We all have the same amount of risk on the table, which means there's no reason to turn on each other. We all risk the same thing. Our lives."

"I know there's really nothing I can say to make this better, but I am sorry."

"Fine," Jenna said as she returned to her books. "You're sorry. Got it. Good bye." Jenna could feel Violet's eyes on her; waiting for something to be said, but Jenna had nothing more to say. She realized they hadn't known each other for long and they hadn't really been such good friends, but her betrayal was stinging all the same. It wasn't as though she had told someone something about her behind her back or had done any other thing anyone in the world would consider a direct betrayal. She had directly threatened her life and that was something not many could forgive, and Jenna would not be ashamed to say she was among those. The sound of footsteps walking away down the hall caught Jenna's ear and she looked up. Violet was gone and while she felt smiling would be an appropriate reaction, she only felt sad in her heart. She had never liked turning cold on anyone, but after what Violet had done, she saw no other option.

The day drew on and Jenna had worked her way through nearly half of her text books. Her eyes began to ache and she leaned back against her pillow, thinking the time for a break had come. She stared up at the ceiling and closed her eyes and envisioned her corneas relaxing at long last. All the facts and figures danced in her brain. Then smoky shadows of the past ordeal began to crop up. She saw Mark's body on the ground. It was so clear in her imagination. Every detail was there and it was like she was staring down at his lifeless body all over again. Her eyes popped open and she bolted up from her all too brief rest. Her thoughts were a dizzying swirl and she wasn't sure how she could keep any facts straight in her head while she was still reeling from her moment of survival.

"You okay?" Ethan asked. Jenna looked up and saw Ethan stroll in.

"No crutches?"

"Don't need them. How are you feeling?"

"Physically, better."

"What about non-physically?"

"I'm not sure. I've been studying for the test tomorrow, but all I can think about is the past few days."

"I know. I'm having the same problem. How do they expect us to just get over all of that?"

"I don't know, but we're going to have to. They aren't going to change the rules for us. Not even you." Jenna said with a smirk.

"Don't think I haven't thought about it, but you're right. Maybe if we could study together that would help."

"Together?"

"Sure. I think it might help me if there was someone who could kind of keep me focused. I crack those books open and five minutes later I'm face down on my pillow."

"I don't know how much help I can be."

"It would mostly be moral support. Please?"

"Fine," Jenna said with a hesitant smile. "I guess it would be nice to have someone else in the room."

"I'll get the books."

Chapter 27

The Returning Hero

The next morning, Jenna and Ethan were released from their medical care and deemed fit to continue their test. Jenna was actually relieved to be up and walking again. When she returned to her dorm building, she noticed there were a lot fewer girls and it was a lot quieter. She opened the door to her room and there was a sense of comfort as she looked upon her bed, untouched and waiting for her. She then looked to the other side of the room and as she expected, all of Violet's things were gone. They had told her Violet had been moved to another room on another level. While there wasn't much that could be done, the people in charge at least agreed sharing a room with someone who tried to kill her was unacceptable.

Jenna flopped down on to her bed and she welcomed the expected creaking of the springs of the mattress. She could hear the sink dripping in the bathroom and the unmistakable aroma of cheap perfume and cheap weed still haunted the air. It felt to her like almost a lifetime since she had seen those walls and she was surprised by how much she missed it.

After a few more minutes of reacquainting herself with her room, she sat down at her desk and returned to her studying. She was told the first series of tests were to begin after noon that day so she only had a few hours left to prepare. She opened up the last book she was studying from and tried to pick up where she had left off. It was difficult to concentrate. Her mind was still a swirl of thoughts and emotions. She tried to push away the nightmares she had lived through if only long enough to get through the test. She was so close and she couldn't bear failing after enduring so much. She blocked away all her stray thoughts, but then she thought once more about Mark. The image of him on the ground, lifeless, kept flashing across her mind. The concept of him being gone was still so hard for her to grasp. She was planning on forgiving him after the tests were complete. She knew, in her heart, what happened at the party was just a stupid mistake. She and Mark had something deeper and she didn't want to throw it away and she was sure he didn't want to either. She could see it all.

After their test results came in, they would meet and share the good news that they both passed and that was when Jenna would tell him that she forgave him and they could be together again. She had even thought of finally giving him what he's been wanting for so long because she had come to want it too. She felt the time to take the relationship to the next level had come and she was ready to be with him physically. It wasn't as though she hadn't thought about it before, but lately, the urge to be with him like that was growing stronger and more urgent. It wasn't that she was afraid she would lose him. She just felt she wanted to be that close.

The end of the test was going to be the beginning of a new life for them both. She wanted to share that with him, but it seemed everything had changed and she wasn't sure what she was going to do. She looked down at her book and noticed tiny drops on the page and she reached up to her face and realized she was crying. She shut the book and leaned back in her chair and took a deep breath. Everyone had been telling her how important it was to get past the pain, but she couldn't do that anymore. He was gone and it felt like it was finally really hitting her.

The tears didn't stop and soon she felt her stomach seize up. She finally allowed herself the grief and she cried for almost a solid hour. She screamed and prayed and did anything and everything she could to express her pain. She leapt up onto her mattress and started punching it. She thought of the tests and Barrett and Curtis and everything and with all of that rage, she punched away. She hit her mattress over and over with growing force. Eventually, she managed to break through the sheets and through the mattress itself. Her hand slid through and she could feel the springs scratching against her flesh. After a few moments, she stopped and she noticed the deep scratches that covered her hands.

Jenna ran to the bathroom and ran her hands under the water in the sink. She wiped away the blood and tended to the scratches with the first aid kit that was still in the medicine cabinet.

Once she was done and her hands were well bandaged, she returned to her desk and sat down. She resolved to pass the test because she knew that was what Mark would want. He wanted her to survive and she would; for herself and for him.

Chapter 28

Finals

Jenna emerged from her room and saw that she had fifteen minutes until the final test was to begin. She let out a deep breath and started down the hall. She saw others stepping out from their dorms. They funneled through quietly and it felt like a death march. No glances or passing smiles. Jenna looked around and saw only dead faces with tear stained eyes. Some of the girls were trembling as they prodded themselves on.

When Jenna finally stepped outside, she was somewhat relieved to see the sky and it was even more reassuring to see so many other kids bustling around the campus. It almost felt normal. For just the briefest of moments, she actually was able to forget about the test. It was just a normal day, but that relief was gone all too quickly and her stress fell back upon her shoulders like a lead weight.

As she walked across the campus to the building her group was supposed to meet in, her stomach started to jump. A sharp pain grew deep inside of her guts and she wanted to turn and run back to her dorm room. She just wanted it to be over. She looked around hoping to find Ethan's face among the crowd, but there was no sign of him. She was even hoping to see Violet. Any familiar face would be a blessing. She thought about Aggy and how if she were there she'd be able to make it better, but she was alone; more alone than she had ever been in her life.

She was directed upon entry to a large meeting room off of the lobby. It looked like a classroom from a college movie. There were long rows of seats that were stacked over each other like a stadium and they all seemed to curve so as to force everyone's eyes to the front of the room where there was a lone desk.

Many of the seats were already taken but Jenna spotted a free seat at the end of one of the rows. She sat down at it as quickly as she could. She kept thinking to herself that the sooner it began, the sooner it would be over. She sat quietly as more people filed in and soon every seat was taken and the room went quiet. The doors shut and it was like everyone could feel everyone else's pulses shoot through the roof.

There was a door near the desk at the front of the room and it opened up. A man stepped out. He didn't look familiar to Jenna. He was dressed in a nicely fitted black suit and held a briefcase in his hand. He walked over to his desk and set the case down on it. He looked up and scanned the room carefully.

"Good afternoon," He said. There was no response. "I understand what you all must be feeling right now, believe it or not, and I am sorry how troubled you all must be. I wish I could assure you all that this will be easy and you will pass, but the reality is there will be a number of you who will fail. The sooner you accept that reality, the easier it will be for you in the future."

He opened the briefcase and took out a thick stack of papers. As he set them upon the desk, he looked back up at the kids. He smiled and when Jenna saw it, a chill ran down her back.

"This isn't the test. These are just some forms you need to fill out before you take the test," He then began to distribute the forms. Jenna took hers and she scanned it quickly. It looked like some kind of con-tract. "This is a consent form that states you agree to accept the results of the test, no matter the outcome. I will admit that in the past it was not unheard of for families to sue when the results of their test were not what they hoped for. I'm sure it's been said before, but once more, these tests are designed to test your strength on every level. They are not biased or stacked against anyone. The results are verified three times and are genuine. Please keep that in mind as you continue on from this point."

After reading through the forms carefully, Jenna signed them and soon she saw others signing as well. It took some time for them all to be collected, but once they were, the man stacked them neatly and put them back into his briefcase.

Everyone was then instructed to separate into their groups. Jenna was told her group would be convening on the third floor. She passed on the elevators and decided rather to take the stairs. It would give her some few precious moments of peace, she thought. She trudged up the stairs as slowly as she could manage but as she reached the landing on level two, she accepted that there was no point in putting off the inevitable.

Jenna made it to the third floor and she saw the room where she was intended to go. She walked in and it looked like a classroom proper. There were six rows of desks, seven desks per row. There was no one else there yet, so Jenna thought she was the first. She took a seat in the middle of one of the rows. She wasn't sure what difference it would make if she sat in the front or in the back.

"Oh!" A voice called from behind. Jenna turned and saw a woman racing in. She was also in a conservative suit with her red hair done up in a tight bun. "You're early. I think the rest of your group is outside in the hall. I guess they're enjoying these last few moments before the shit hits the fan." She was carrying two large cases in her hands. She set them upon the desk at the front of the room. Jenna's heart skipped.

"Are those the tests?" Jenna asked.

"Yes," The woman said as she slapped her hand on one of the cases. "I'm Rita Harrison and I will administer your test today." She said as she walked over to Jenna; offering her hand.

"Jenna Holdren." Jenna said with a forced smile.

"Good to meet you," Rita looked back at Jenna with a look of fascination. "I can only imagine what's going through your mind right now. I remember when I was taking my test. My stomach was in a knot three days before. How are you holding up?"

"Still standing."

"That you are. You look like you'll do well."

"How can you tell?"

"I've been doing this a long time. I can't qualify this with anything scientific, but I've just developed a kind sense about who will pass and who will fail. For what it's worth, you've got 'pass' written all over you."

"Thanks." Jenna said. The remaining kids in Jenna's group began to come in and they took their seats quickly and quietly. Jenna turned for a moment and she saw Violet sitting down at one of the desks at the very back. Their eyes locked for a second but then Jenna turned away.

Once everyone was seated, Rita shut the door and took her place in the front of the room. She clapped her hands together and smiled.

"Good afternoon, everyone. My name is Rita Harrison and I will be administering your test today. This portion of the examination will take about four hours to complete. You will be permitted two bathroom breaks. After this test you will have a one hour break and then return for the second portion; which you will have another four hours to complete. When the test is complete, you may return to your dorm rooms. Test results will be posted on Friday morning. Good luck to you all." Rita then turned to her desk and opened one of her cases. There was a large stack of thick booklets inside and she grabbed an armful. She began to pass them out. She set a booklet on Jenna's desk and Jenna looked back at her.

"Is this the test?" She asked.

"All forty pages. My advice would be not to rush. Use the four hours."

After the test books were distributed, Rita then passed out pencils and informed them if they needed more, they had only to ask. Jenna looked down at her test book and laid her hand upon it. It was much larger than she thought it would be. She slid her fingers along the spine of the book. After so long of picturing the moment, to have the actual test sitting in front of her was almost beyond comprehension. Her entire life, or death, sat before her. There were a few spouts of crying coming from all around the room. The boy sitting next to Jenna seemed to be keeping it inside, but he was shaking as he clutched his desk and tears were pouring down his cheek.

"All right," Rita said as she sat at her desk. "You may begin." Everyone opened up their books at the same time and they buried their heads down. Jenna flipped through the pages to the first question. She stared at the page and for a moment, it looked like all the words were blurring in her vision. She tried to read the first question, but as she read it to herself, the meaning became tangled. She then slammed her fists against her forehead. She looked around, afraid her tantrum was being noticed, but everyone was focused on their own tests. Jenna looked back down at the page and it was normal and she could read the words clearly. She set her pencil to the paper and filled in the first question.

The questions started out easy, she felt. She almost felt foolish for having spent so much time studying. She was able to get through twenty pages of the test with confidence in her answers, but she noticed they did begin to become more difficult. She looked up and was shocked to have seen over two hours had passed. She pushed through the remainder of the test and toward the end; the questions were challenging her beyond what she thought she could do. She could feel sweat forming along her forehead. At one point, she found herself reading the same question over and over again without realizing it.

When Jenna finally got to the last question, she almost came to tears. Her hand was trembling. She answered it and with a heave of relief, she closed the book. She leaned back in her chair and saw she had finished only ten minutes early. She looked back down at the book and doubt began to creep through her mind. Certain questions came back to her mind and she was starting to doubt her answers. All the possibilities were rushing back to her. She reopened the book and scanned through as many pages as she could manage. It was blur of words and answer bubbles.

"Time." Rita announced. Everyone set their pencils down and shut their books. Everyone got up and hurried out of the room. Jenna just kept staring at the book on her desk. Rita came up to her and took it away.

"I answered them all." Jenna said.

"Most kids do. I think four hours is a little more than is needed. How do you think you did?"

"I don't know. I thought I was doing okay at first, but it got so hard. I can't even remember most of my answers."

"Don't worry. I'm sure you did fine. Go and relax. Get something to eat. This isn't over yet."

Chapter 29

Accounts Due

As Jenna looked down at the lunch on her tray, she wondered if anyone in charge cared that a cheese sandwich with tomato soup was hardly a fitting final meal. She was curious who came up with that day's menu and what the other options were available. She felt since it was the day of the final test they would have served something a little more impressive. She thought they would have at least had a sundae bar or something fun. She obsessed over the food, hoping to keep any thoughts about the test away from her conscious mind.

She sat down and noted how quiet it was. Everyone was shambling around like zombies. She saw a few kids trying to eat, but before they could take a bite, they broke out in tears. Jenna set down her sandwich and chose to eat her soup first. She wasn't totally sure if she'd be able to keep anything solid down anyway.

As Jenna slid the spoon into her mouth, she saw Violet approaching. Her upset stomach no longer bothered her as rage began to replace any anxiety she had been feeling. By her trajectory, Jenna knew where Violet was going.

"Hi," Violet said in a small voice as she stood before Jenna. "I know you hate me and I don't blame you, but I was just wondering if I could just sit here. You don't have to talk. I just don't think I could stand to sit alone."

"There are other tables. Ask someone else."

"I would except everyone knows what happened out there and they don't like me very much anymore either."

"Yet you come to the person you actually tried to kill. Interesting logic."

"Look, I'm sorry. I know saying that is nothing in light of what I did, but I don't know what else I can say. I was scared."

"You were the one saying you actually wanted to fail the test. You said you didn't care."

"That was before it was so real. I got scared and I made a desperate and stupid choice."

"Especially since you got sold out."

"And I'm paying for it."

"You're paying for it? We could have gotten through the survival challenge and maybe even placed first. We would have passed and been back home by now!"

"I know!" Violet whined. "I'm,"

"No!" Jenna barked as she cut Violet off. "I don't think I could stand to hear you say that word again."

"You're the closest thing to a friend I have here anymore. May I just sit with you?" Jenna leaned back in her chair and thought about the request. She looked around the room and everyone was staring at them. She looked back up at Violet and saw the tears streaking down her cheeks. She was alone; as alone as anyone could ever be and there were so many times that Jenna felt the same way when she first arrived. Even with Aggy along, she felt alone and vulnerable and it was the worst feeling she had ever felt.

"You don't speak a word."

"Yes! Thank you." Violet said as she took her seat. Jenna glared at her for a moment longer and then went back to eating her lunch.

After lunch, everyone went back to their testing rooms. It was a quiet and solemn march for everyone. Jenna and her group filed back into their room and took their seats with no ceremony or noise. Rita was sitting at her desk and was smiling, which kind of annoyed Jenna. There was no malice behind it; it just felt like it was inappropriate. There was no joy to be had in that room and to act as if there were, was a crime.

Rita stood and came around to the front of her desk. Her smile glared over the room and Jenna could sense she wasn't the only one annoyed with it.

"Before I distribute the second half of this test, I just wanted to let you know, on behalf of myself and the United States Government, how proud of you we all are. This isn't an easy thing to do and it is gratifying to see so many of you showing such strength and courage. I remember the day of my final tests. I don't think I have ever been so scared in my life. I realize the reality is that some of you will not pass. I'm sure that's a reality you've come to accept as well, which makes you all the more brave in my opinion. As we move into this final stage of the test, I would like to advise you all to not give up. It may seem ridiculous to you now, but it has been known to happen that some people break under the pressure and actually forfeit the test; which at this point would lead to an automatic fail. I know it seems hard and hopeless to you, but it is far better to see this through to the end than to just quit. Keep strong." Rita then proceeded to hand out the test booklets.

The new booklets were a little thinner than the first ones, which Jenna thought was good. She opened it up and scanned the first page. The questions seemed normal. She then flipped through the rest of the booklet, hoping to spot any trouble ahead. There were much fewer math sections than in the first one, but there were many more essay questions. Jenna hated those the most because it was hard to concentrate enough to string a coherent thought together in her head much less write it down. She flipped back to the front of the booklet and then Rita signaled for them to begin.

Jenna leaned over her test and focused everything on it. The questions didn't seem to get any harder, but they were still exceptionally challenging. They depth of knowledge dipped a little further than her textbooks had equipped her for. She found herself guessing more than she was comfortable with.

The room was quiet as they took the test. It seemed the maddening terror had finally settled into a simple, persistent fear. All that could be heard was the sound of pencils rubbing against paper. Jenna kept answering the questions and flipping over page after page. She wasn't even paying attention to how far she was getting. She just focused what she was doing at that moment. Time blurred in her head. It wasn't even a consideration. She just wanted to answer the questions and get out.

When Jenna flipped over to the last page, she was startled. She looked up and saw that she had only ten minutes left until the test was over. She scanned the page and thankfully she found the final questions to be rather easy. She answered them all and just as she shut the booklet, the time ticked over and it was over. Some kids who had not finished threw their pencils to the floor in frustration. Rita stood up once more and harnessed the room's attention.

"The time is up. Please pass the booklets forward, whether they are completed or not. I would assure you all though, that a finished test does not mean you have passed any more than an incomplete test means you have failed. Whatever answers you have left will be taken into account in the final tally. The results will be processed and you will be notified no later than Friday morning. Your families will be notified to come pick you up after the test results are final, but they will not reveal the exact results until they arrive here. Until then, try and relax and enjoy your time. There will be special events throughout the campus to entertain you and the library will be open all day and night for your convenience."

Jenna raised her hand as a nagging question troubled her.

"How will we get our results?" A light went on in Rita's eyes and she went into her desk and pulled out a small box.

"I'm glad you reminded me," She said. She opened the box and took out a small black device. It looked like a small phone. She held it up for everyone to see. "This little device is wired to the main data banks and your test results will be sent directly to it. Keep it with you at all times." She said. She then proceeded to hand out the devices to everyone and as they took it, they were dismissed."

Jenna walked with the crowd out of the building. All the while, she heard murmurs from all around lamenting answers they should have given or crying over how they were sure that they had failed. Jenna just wanted to get to her room and be alone. She saw a few new flyers being put up advertising some of the special functions that were supposed to distract everyone from the fact they may not have long to live. She doubted some pointless concert by a local band would alleviate any-one's stress.

Jenna finally got to her dorm and rushed in, slamming the door behind her. She dove onto the bed and as soon as she pushed her face against the pillow, she began to cry. It felt like years of sorrow was pouring out of her in one terrible torrent. Her stomach was seizing up but she didn't want to move. She didn't want to eat or drink. She didn't even want to listen to any music. Her only solace was lying on her bed, curled up and sobbing like a newborn babe. Waiting for the rest of her life to be decided.

Chapter 30

Waiting is the Hardest Part

Jenna had fallen asleep and as she woke, she saw light pour in from the window. It was morning but that brought her no comfort. All she had to look forward to was a day of waiting to find out if she had passed or failed. Just the thought of waiting for that news all day made her stomach ache all over again.

She got up and realized she was still in her clothes. She thought that she should shower and change, but as she took her first step to the bathroom, she wondered why to even bother. While the test results were not in, it still felt like the end of the world to her. She was staring at a wall of fire and all there was to do was wait for it to come and swallow her up whole. She fell back onto the bed, feeling hopeless once more. She thought of going out to get something to eat, but she knew everyone out there would just tell her how she had to be positive and to be strong and have faith in your strength and those words, she knew, would feel like sandpaper along an open wound. She didn't want any encouragement and she didn't want any inspirational quotes. She wanted things to be normal, as they were before the tests. She wanted to be home and secure that there was a future ahead of her. She knew there was no promise of that and therefore, there was no reason to go out.

Jenna fell stretched out on her bed and stared up at the ceiling as she forced herself to sleep. She closed her eyes and let her mind wander in hopes she could just fall asleep again; but the more she tried to do it, the more anxious her thoughts became. After an hour of trying, she sat up in frustration, threw her pillow across the room and then stormed into the bathroom and had a shower.

Jenna walked out to the quad outside of her dorm building and it seemed everyone shared her concern. There was no laughter or high spirits. Everyone was shambling along like zombies. It appeared the staff was doing everything they could to help, but it wasn't enough. There were fliers and signs for all kinds of shows and events throughout the day, but it didn't seem anyone cared. Jenna went on to the cafeteria. As upset as she was, her stomach was beginning to require attention.

She walked into the cafeteria and there were more dispirited kids inside. The aroma of waffles and cinnamon permeated the air. Jenna saw that they were offering an honest to God brunch buffet with everything from eggs to sushi. However upset she was, she couldn't take her eyes off the spread. She then decided the only thing worse than being depressed was being depressed and hungry, so she went on to fix that problem.

After she ate, Jenna went back to her room and hoped to be able to sleep some more, but it wasn't working. She then went down to the library. She reasoned that it would be quiet and reading always helped her in times of stress. When she got there, it was empty except for the librarian. She nodded hello and went on to find something to read. She scanned the shelves and just grabbed books. She didn't even look at them; she just needed something to distract her.

Jenna took a seat at one of the tables and set the books beside her. She had gathered a collection of novels and research books and even a few magazines. She set the first book in front of her and started to read. She read the first page nearly twenty times in a row until she realized her brain wasn't letting the information in. Once she got to the bottom of the page, her fears would creep in and everything she had read blurred in her mind. The words became nonsense and it was like she was reading something in another language. After two hours of this, she began to develop a headache and went back to her room to lie down.

Jenna spent the rest of the day desperately trying to occupy her mind but everything resulted in a headache. By about five in the evening, she relegated herself to her room. The day was nearly over and she still hadn't gotten her results. She wasn't sure if it was a good sign or a bad one. She was trying once more to sleep, hoping she would wake up beyond the test and past all the worry, but he was disturbed by a knock on her door.

"What?" She barked as she opened her door.

"Hi." Ethan said.

"Ethan. Hi. What are you doing here?"

"I came by because I wanted to thank you."

"For what?"

"What do you think? You saved my life."

"I thought you already thanked me for that."

"Only with words, but I've been trying to find a way to really say it, and I think I've found it. I need you to come with me."

"What?"

"Come with me. Please." Jenna did not want to leave, but her curiosity was pleasantly taking up most of her thoughts. She hoped whatever he was going to show her would help her to avoid worrying for a little bit more.

Ethan took Jenna back to the medical building. She tried to ask where he was taking her, but he was insistent that it be a surprise. They walked through the doors and none of the staff stopped them as they proceeded into the restricted areas.

"Uh," Jenna began.

"Don't worry," Ethan said. "I've cleared us both. We can go any-where. Come on."

They took the elevator up to the fourth level, which required the use of a key. Jenna's curiosity was growing. She wasn't sure if she should be excited or scared. Maybe Ethan was going to take her to have her brain swapped out or to be part of some insane experiment that would have her dismissed from the test.

They came upon a hall that looked like a real hospital and at the end of the hall was a closed door. Next to the door was a window with blinds which were shut. Ethan took Jenna to the door and then stopped as he turned to face her.

"I need you to stand right here." He said as he positioned her in front of the window.

"What is this?"

"You'll see. Just wait here." He said as he went into the room and shut the door behind him. After a few minutes, the blinds began to move. They opened and then she saw a bed inside the room. There was someone in the bed. It was hard to tell who it was. They were asleep with tubes coming out all over the place. They also had casts on their arms and legs. Jenna stepped closer and she could see the person's face. Her legs began to shake.

"Mark?" She uttered. She ran into the room and Ethan caught her.

"Easy. Easy."

"It's Mark! He's alive!"

"Yes. I know he doesn't look so great now, but he's alive."

"Can I talk to him?"

"He's in a medically induced coma, for his own good; but the doctors are assured that he will make it through."

"I don't understand this. How? I saw him dead out there!"

"It was close, but they managed to get to him just in time. I know it's horrible that they allowed it to happen, but at least they saved him."

"Please don't expect me to be grateful to them for that. They only did it because if he did die, they would be facing legal action."

"You're probably right, but the important thing is he's going to live."

"They're letting you show this to me?"

"I managed to talk to my dad and he was able to arrange this for you. Right now only family members are allowed access to Mark, but I made your case and after some friendly pressure from the family, the ESA agreed."

"Blackmail?"

"Whatever works. I don't ask questions. The point is Mark's alive." Jenna walked over to the bed and took Mark's one good hand. She looked upon his broken and damaged body.

"He looks so peaceful." She said.

"Again, it's just a coma. He will wake up in a few days." Jenna then realized something and she was panicked again.

"But the test! He won't,"

"Automatic pass. After what he's been through, it was the least that could be done. Now after you pass, you two can be together again."

"How do you even know that's what I wanted?"

"I saw the two of you together. I'm not blind. I've instructed the doctors to notify you as well as his mother when he wakes up," A loud signal went off and Jenna and Ethan were surprised by it. They soon realized it was coming from Ethan's pocket. He produced the small device he had been given after his test. "Results are in." He said as he clicked on the small black machine. The screen lit up and he stared down at it. His eyes grew wide as he studied whatever it was he was seeing. He shut it off and held it to his chest. His face looked pained at first. He then looked Jenna in her eye and smiled. "I passed!" He exclaimed. Jenna leapt up and hugged him. She was happy for his good news, but all the while she was still worried about what she would hear. "Oh my God," Ethan said breathlessly. "I passed. I really passed."

"It's great, Ethan."

"Check yours. Maybe you got your results." Jenna took her device out, but there was no news.

"Nothing yet."

"I'm sorry."

"It's fine. It will come."

"I should go tell my dad the good news. I guess you and Mark can hang out for a bit, right?"

"Thanks." Ethan then ran out of the room. Jenna turned to Mark. She leaned over him and kissed him gently on his forehead. She just stared at him as she carefully traced her fingers through his hair.

Ethan brought Jenna back to her dorm room and as they came to her door, she was actually smiling.

"Thank you, Ethan. I know it couldn't have been easy to wrangle that favor."

"Don't worry about it. Seeing you smile is worth it."

"Good night. I guess I'll see you tomorrow."

"On the bus home, yes. I'm you'll pass."

"Thanks."

"Good night." Ethan said as he walked back down the hall. Jenna went into her room and went straight to her bed. She rested her head on the pillow and rejoiced that all her plans she had for her and Mark had not been destroyed after all. He would be fine and they could be together again. Her eyes were growing heavy the more she thought about it. Her peace was disturbed by the sound of her device signaling her results were in. She bolted up right and grabbed the device. She flipped it on and the words were on the screen. She had prepared herself for so long to see them, but it was a totally different thing to see them as a reality. She set the device down and simply fell back down on the pillow. It seemed all the worrying and waiting had exhausted her. At least, she thought, she knew at last.

Chapter 31
The Results Are In

The day had come at last: The final day. The main facility had been closed and all the dorms were empty. The kids were being instructed to go to the parking lot where their families would be waiting to either take them home or tell them good-bye. The buses were lined up and ready to take the failing groups on to the next phase. There was a reception area opposite that where families would come to claim their children. As Jenna approached, it looked like Heaven and Hell in the same place.

It wasn't hard to tell who was going where. The failing kids were gathered together and most of them were crying, as were their families who had just heard the news. Jenna's hands were getting sweaty as she waited for her family to come. She sat down on a small bench and waited. She jumped whenever she heard one of the buses rev up. They sounded like monsters roaring with rage.

Jenna saw Violet appear out of the crowd. Their eyes locked and she approached.

"Hi." Violet said.

"Hi." Jenna responded. Her voice was empty and soulless.

"I passed," Violet said with a little bounce.

"Great."

"I know you don't care and I'm probably wasting my breath, but once more, I'm sorry."

"I know. You're sorry and that's fine. You will have to live with what you did for the rest of your life. That's as much punishment as I can give you."

"If I could do it again,"

"Don't! Don't play that game with me. I don't care what you would do if you had another chance. I only care about what you DID do. That's what matters. That's what lasts. Good intentions aren't worth a whole lot if you don't live up to them."

"Good bye." Violet said sheepishly.

"Good bye."

It felt like hours were going by. The crowds were dwindling. There were only two buses left. Jenna checked her watch and was growing anxious. She saw one of the counselors walking by.

"Excuse me?" Jenna asked.

"Yes?"

"Do you know where I can find Ethan Lazarus is? I haven't seen him all day."

"Lazarus? He was picked up by his father last night."

"Last night?"

"Yes. I hate it when the government plays favorites too, but what can you do?"

Jenna sat back down, a bit disappointed. She had wanted to see him one last time before they departed. Despite everything, he had become rather endearing to her. She also wanted to thank him again for letting her know about Mark. She was happy to know that Mark would wake up and have the rest of his life to look forward to.

At last, Jenna saw her parents' car drive up. Her parents got out and her Brian and Bradley leapt out of the back seat. They all were running to her and they slammed into her with one great big hug. Her mother was crying and laughing at the same time.

"My baby! My baby!" She cried as she held Jenna close. Everyone was talking at once, patting her on the back and telling her how proud they all are. They were swarming in around her. She finally pulled back and stepped away.

"Stop!" She barked. Tears were starting to form in the corner of her eyes. They all looked at her in disbelief.

"Jenna? Baby? What is it? Wait. Don't. Whatever it is, you can tell us on the ride home." Her mother said.

"I'm not going home, Mom."

"What?" Her father asked. Jenna took out her test results and held them up for her family to see.

"I failed!" She said. "I failed the test."

"No," Her mother said. "No. No. NO! You passed! You had to! No! You passed!"

"I failed. I'm not here to be taken home. I'm here to say good-bye. That bus over there is for me."

"There has to be some mistake, Jenna." Her father offered.

"The results were verified, Dad. I failed and before I go, I want you all to know how much I love you," She turned to her brothers and narrowed her eyes. "You two have been pains in my ass for all my life, pretty much, but you have also been a couple of the best friends I've ever had. You watched over me when you could and I want you to know that I noticed. We've fought, but I never doubted that we loved each other." She said. Their only response was to start crying as they grabbed her into a tight hug.

"We can smuggle you out. No one will notice." Brian whispered. Jenna stepped back and smiled.

"If only it were that easy. I'm sorry," Jenna then turned to her mother, who was still crying uncontrollably. She reached out to her and as her hand got close; her mother snatched it and held it tightly in hers. "I'm sorry, Mom."

"No. Don't apologize. This isn't your fault. It's theirs. This has to be a mistake. They screwed up the scores or something. We're going to fight this," She said. "We'll take this to the highest court in the land. We'll get you a make-up test. We'll,"

"Mom! Stop," Jenna said, interrupting her mother. "You know as well as I do that no one has ever successfully challenged the results of the test. There's nothing that can be done."

"I don't care! We'll sell the house! We'll,"

"No, Mom. I don't want this to ruin your lives too. I've had months to prepare myself for this outcome and I am prepared. I was upset, to say the least, when I saw the results but I think I've accepted it. These are the rules and this is how it works. I love you and I want to know that you will all go on to live your lives after this. You remember what you told me when Gramma died? You told me she would always be with me as long as I remembered her."

"You're too young, baby. You're too young."

"It's not about being too young or old enough. Life can make sense and it can be random in equal parts. There's no way to know. I couldn't have asked for a better mother. You were always there when I needed you and sometimes when I didn't know I needed you. You made all the little pains go away and helped to ease the big ones. I love you." Jenna's mother couldn't speak through her tears, but threw her arms around her, holding her so tight she had to struggle to breathe.

Jenna then looked to her father who was clearly struggling to keep the tears back. He had his hand over his mouth as if he were holding it shut to keep from screaming. Jenna leaned in close to him and nudged his arm.

"Dad, what can I say? You always had to play bad cop, but even when you did I knew you loved us. I think it's because of you I'm so hard on myself. You wouldn't let us get away with anything and that has made me tougher on myself and I need to thank you for that. It isn't easy, but I know it's the better path. I love you and I am so sorry." Jenna said as she hugged him.

"Stop saying that," He whispered to her. "Your mother is right. This is not your fault. Don't think for a second that you didn't do everything you could. You gave it your best and for whatever reason, it didn't work out, but not because you didn't give it your all."

"I guess my all wasn't enough."

"It's not unheard of for mistakes to be made. I read an article that said nearly five percent of all test results have turned out to be wrong. We can fight this."

"Dad,"

"Look, you don't have any say in this. I have friends. I'm going to make some calls and we're going to figure this out. We have time. There have been a few cases in which test results were overturned."

"Too few to think it could happen now. Please, Dad, just don't waste your time."

"Nothing I can do to save the life of one of my children could ever be a waste of time. We're going to get you out of this. I promise you." Jenna just smiled at her father's pledge. They were scared and so was she. If there was a way they could rescue her, she would be all for it, but the odds of that happening were too great to even seriously consider.

With one last round of hugs and kisses, Jenna bid a final farewell to her family and gathered her things. She headed over toward the buses and she saw there was only one left. She walked over to it and the counselor standing by the door looked at her with tired, yet sympathetic eyes.

"Your results?" She asked. Jenna handed over the device and the counselor inspected it. "All right. You're clear. Take a seat on the bus. We should arrive to the camp before sundown. I am sorry."

"Thank you." Jenna said. She walked up onto the bus and she looked upon the other passengers. It was somber and heartbreaking as she looked upon their faces and saw their tear stained cheeks. Jenna found an empty seat at the back of the bus and she nestled in and shut her eyes. After a few more minutes, the door was closed and the bus revved to life. It shook slightly as it started up, but soon it became steady as it made it to the main road leading out of the facility. Jenna looked out the window and she saw her family still standing in the middle of the parking lot, waving at the bus as it left. She tried to smile, but it was too much of an effort. She pressed her head against the window and closed her eyes and just felt the steady vibration of the bus as it drove away.

END PHASE I

Thanks for reading this first installment of my new 'Tested' series. I am humbled and grateful for the time we have shared and I hope you enjoyed this book. Please read on for a preview of Phase II of Tested.

Chapter 1

The motion of the bus was smooth and almost comforting after a while. Jenna had fallen asleep at last, despite the many outbursts of crying from the other kids. It wasn't as though she really blamed them. They were being taken to the place where they would live until the day they'd be killed. There was no other reaction to have.

Their crying had eased back and Jenna came to the conclusion that everyone had gone past the point of tears. Crying was a function of fear and there was no more reason to be afraid. They knew what was waiting for them and there was no point in resisting or fighting it. Acceptance seemed to have settled in among them all, but that didn't mean they weren't still sad.

There was no one on the bus that Jenna recognized. There were a few she might have seen on the campus of the testing facility, but no one she had ever spoken to. She knew that none of them were from her group. She was among strangers, but that seemed to be a fact that brought her some comfort. There was no one there to coach her about looking on the bright side or explaining how they knew how she felt. During her time at the testing facility she had come to realize that sympathy could sometimes be a bad thing.

The sky was growing dark and Jenna was wondering when they were finally going to stop. The bus then came to a halt, as if in answer to her curiosity. No one made any moves to get off the bus. The longer they stayed on it, the further they were from death. The bus door opened and a man in a well-tailored suit came on board.

"Good evening, everyone," He said. "My name is Brad Dennison. I'm the director of this facility and I'd like to welcome you here to this resort. I am aware of the circumstances, and for that I am sorry, but I want to assure you all that my staff and I will be tireless in our efforts to make this time of your life the most comfortable and enjoyable you've ever experienced," His words did not rouse anyone and he knew that would be the case. "Your bags will be taken to your rooms for you. Take your time in adjusting. You can register at the front desk just beyond those doors," Brad said. Jenna glanced out the window and as dark as it was, she could tell they were parked in front of what looked like a rather high end hotel. "Whenever you are ready. There's no rush." He said and then got off the bus. Slowly some of the kids got up and went on into the hotel. Jenna took a breath and decided there was no point in putting off the inevitable. She got up and walked off the bus and proceeded into the hotel.

It was warm when she walked in and if felt as though she had walked onto a movie set. The light was dim and the floor was made of a smooth, white marble. Soft music was playing over the loudspeakers. Jenna walked up to the front desk where she was greeted by a bright young man with dark hair and sparkling green eyes.

"Welcome to The Hollow. What is the name?"

"Jenna. Jenna Holdren."

"Right," He said as he typed her name into the computer. He looked back at her and flashed that smile again.

"Right here. I understand why you are here and I am,"

"Please don't say you're sorry. I've been hearing that enough."

"Right. Then you in room two fifty three. Here's the key," He said as he slid a card key to her. "There is a full itinerary of activities for you to enjoy. All amenities will be free of charge, including room service and our spa services."

"Spa?"

"Yes." He said as he pointed toward a large sign that indicated there was a spa adjacent to the lobby.

"Well, it sounds great. If you don't mind me asking, is this a real hotel?"

"Of course. The management of The Hollow volunteers the services to the ESA every year. It's their way of doing what they can to ease your burden. They appreciate the sacrifice you're making. That is why all services are free. You aren't even expected to tip. There are even some services we provide that are 'off book'."

"Oh, okay. Well, I guess I'll just settle into my room."

"Wonderful idea. My name is Andrew, by the way. If you need anything, just ask for me."

"Thanks. I will." Jenna then headed for the elevators. Jenna approached the door to her room and with a trembling hand she jammed the key card into the door slot. It opened easily and she walked in and was hit by the unmistakable aroma of a hotel room. The air was so fresh and cool. The bed was made and the remote to the TV was sitting on the night table. She then went to the bathroom and it was sparkling clean. It was a far cry from her bathroom at her dorm and she realized she didn't have to share it with anyone. There was a full complement of luxurious soaps and lotions sitting next to the sink. She smiled a bit. It may have been the place she would die, she thought, but she was definitely going in style.

Dear Reader

I want to thank you for reading the first part of my new series, 'Tested'. I hope you enjoyed it so far. I really enjoyed writing the character of Jenna Holdren. She's strong and knows her mind but still has a little vulnerability. She may have failed but she's not taking it lying down. Let me know if you want to know more. Find me on Facebook at WWW.Facebook.com/darrensloanwriter and let your voice be heard.

Sincerely,

D.S.

www.ingramcontent.com/pod-product-compliance
Lightning Source LLC
Chambersburg PA
CBHW060859140726
47996CB00001B/38